About the Author

Vanessa Streete was born in North London in 1975. She grew up in a terraced house with her parents and elder sister, who sadly passed away in 2013 at the age of forty-two. Money was short, but love wasn't and they enjoyed a happy life with Nan just up the road and friends in every street, before moving out of London to Essex in the late 1980s. Vanessa wasn't keen on school, and at the earliest opportunity was out in the world, but she was always writing and scribbling. She never settled for long though, being a social butterfly. She was a bouncer for several years and enjoyed the life, then came a career in Education within Attendance, then venue & events management. Her close friends and family would call her inspirational, if not a little out of the box, someone who knows what she wants and how to get it. Others would say she is creative with a real zest for life, is a loyal to a fault and a trusted reliable friend who also happens to be a social networking genius, and of course there are those who would simply shrug. She has worked hard for what she has and enjoys life to the full. She is a devoted wife, married to her absolute soulmate. They have one son who is adored and together with two dogs, a crazy Heinz 57 who was rescued from a bin somewhere in Spain and the family beast, they all reside in the Essex countryside.

Like China

Vanessa Streete

Like China

Olympia Publishers
London

www.olympiapublishers.com
OLYMPIA PAPERBACK EDITION

A CIP catalogue record for this title is
available from the British Library.

ISBN: 978-1-78830-026-1

First Published in 2018

Olympia Publishers
60 Cannon Street
London
EC4N 6NP

Printed in Great Britain

Dedication

To my Mum and Dad
What would I do without your love?

For Paul, who makes it all make sense.

Prayers are said in whispers,
Hopes in hushed voices,
Fear with painful gasps,
And dreams in a tone of laughter...
How then should the heart speak?
(Vanessa (Burke) Streete, 7th December 2001)

Acknowledgments

Olympia Publishers, my insane parents, my husband, our crazy son and all the fab people in my life who said that I could do this.

PROLOGUE

January 1992

The brakes seemed to screech out as the barrier closed in on the still-speeding car. Somewhere in Andrew's mind, it registered that other vehicles were then spinning away from them across the carriages of the motorway and he wondered fleetingly what had happened, then it dawned on him. With a sharp intake of breath Louise grabbed for her husband, her beautifully manicured fingers searching for the feel of his skin. A prayer that she would see her children again left her lips but in the back of her mind a voice yelled that it was never going to be. Her heels dug into the carpet of the passenger side floor with such force that she felt one snap under the pressure. The scream that hovered finally escaped her lips. It was a high-pitched noise that filled the car. It was fear. The knowledge of what was going on. Only seconds later the air inside the car filled with the sound of crumpling metal and smashing glass as the car spun some more, continuing along the central reservation before it finally flipped over, two, maybe three times. Other drivers were now out of their vehicles on the hard shoulder and on the carriageway itself; hazard lights flashing the dreaded warning that more souls may be lost.

They were looking on in absolute horror as the remains of the almost brand new BMW now came to an abrupt and very final stop. A deathly silence fell all around. Even the cars coming the opposite way had slowed to a stop to take in the scene. The road was covered in glass and debris, the reservation was dented and battered but had served its purpose. The car, however, or at least what was left of it, had not. It was a mess; not even the airbags had activated. It must have occurred to one, if not all of the onlookers, that no one could survive such a crash, but all the same they began to move towards the mangled metal in almost respectful silence, not even the sound of breath was evident on the roadside.

Blood ran across the cream-coloured leather of the seats, seeping into the creases; it was absorbed like water into a bone-dry sponge. Louise could feel nothing at all, although even in the haze of her mind she was somehow aware of the state her body was in. She looked down at herself and saw the blood on her black woollen suit. Something was protruding from her chest but she could feel nothing but the fear. Her breath was nothing but a gargle and then the blood came up in splattered bubbles. It ran from her lips and down her chin. She tried to move her hand up to wipe it away but nothing happened. She didn't realise that her arm simply wasn't there any more. She tried to move her head then to look at Andrew. It was a good thing that she couldn't. He was still in the driver's seat but the entire thing had been forced backwards and then forwards again by the impact. He had been almost folded in half as the seat had buckled and then sprung back into his original position again after cracking against the steering wheel. Even his seat belt was still on. He could have been asleep but for the blood over him and the contorted way in which his mouth was set. It was as if a cry had been let out before his last breath.

'Andy?' her voice was nothing but a croak. 'Andy, please!' It rose to fever pitch as the realisation that she couldn't hear him breathing hit her. 'Andy!'

He was dead.

Chapter One

October 1991

Andrew Dobson was a very distinguished, and very good-looking man in his late forties with proud, yet rugged features. He had a full head of thick mid-brown hair and tanned skin from good rich living and hours on the golf course. His big, gentle emerald green eyes took in all around him, and then his gaze settled upon his elder brother Patrick, whilst he sat rolling the ash from his Cuban cigar into the cut glass dish before him on the large oak desk. He made swirling patterns in the ash thoughtfully as he waited for a response to his earlier question.

Patrick stood and took in a long draw on his cigarette. He blew out the smoke silently as he watched his brother's every move with the same green eyes, eyes that hypnotised those who gazed into them. He could tell that Andrew was agitated and with the wrong words from him, would definitely explode and that would be loud and not very pretty. So he waited a few more seconds, still staring at his baby brother. 'I *know* what they're doing. Jimmy said this'd happen!'

Finally Andrew spoke firmly, and again before Patrick had spoken to give his opinion. 'He was right! Jammy Irish bastard! I don't care how much damage they cause. I don't care what they threaten! I don't care what they fucking offer! We ain't selling a fuckin' thing!' His words were forced out of his mouth as he stood up. He looked as if he were about to do battle with his brother, but Patrick didn't falter, didn't flinch. He was, as always in total agreement with his brother when it came to matters of business. 'They can cause all the grief they want. I don't care!' he finished firmly, spinning and walking towards the plate glass window that overlooked the car park and the bleak wet city beyond it.

'Then maybe we should do the same as them? There's nothin' like a bit of bad press to keep unwanted heads down nice and low,' Patrick finally said, drawing the words out slowly, his tone secretive. Andrew turned his head slightly, raising an eyebrow at his brother's suggestion.

'And what happened to going straight? Is *that* your idea of nice and legal, eh?' He almost laughed at the very thought that such a thing may have lasted the two years it already had.

'Desperate times, brother, mean desperate measures!' Patrick's voice took on the all-too-familiar tone of the man he had been in his youth, the man he was nowadays only when provoked and Andrew couldn't decide whether to smile or shudder at the thought.

They'd been kings, the best there was, and now they were ageing. Well, but ageing and both knew that this was a fight that they couldn't win alone. There were new clubs and bars springing up all over the place, sure, but one group of companies, one crew, one man was giving their little empire a real run for its money. The Oxley Corporation. He was a fucking twat, both had thought rightly, but he knew how to steal business and how to make what was a hot spot into a no-go zone in a heartbeat. The reputation of this group preceded itself with the drugs, and the mindless violence, and that was without the damage and the rest of the aggro that followed.

'I'll give Jim a call!' Andrew almost whispered with a slight smile. Oh yeah, this was just like old times, he thought. All they needed was a dodgy mortgage paper and some old codger's bank details and they'd be back to square one. 'He'll get Michael to deal with it.'

Patrick breathed. 'Yeah!'

Andrew let out a snort. 'He was out with the boy last night. And what a state he came home in! God almighty! Give him a shot and he'll take the bloody bottle!' Andrew semi-smiled as he spoke of his son, James and his boy-about-town antics.

'Michael was drunk?' Patrick sounded very, very surprised.

'No, no way! He poured James into the house at about three this morning. And there's no way I'm gonna argue with him.'

Andrew laughed. 'True. He's a boy, ain't he! Trust him with my life, though,' Patrick added. 'This should be fun.' He gave his brother a long stare. Andrew almost smiled, understanding his brother's meaning of the word *fun*.

They had been talking about the third partner in their tier of their little business empire, as they liked to call it. Jim Elliott and his only child, Michael, but Michael was no longer a child, and he was the image of his father, Romany-looking, very dark, cool, calm and dangerous, and at twenty-two, already even more of a man than Jim himself had been, if ever that were possible. He now took Jim's place when anything to do with the business came up in London, but thus far, he hadn't been needed. Jim now was far too busy with his little hotel in Ireland and had long since gone back to run the place that he had always dreamed of owning with his wife Evelyn.

Both Pat and Andrew had laughed at the thought of the powerful, rough and ready Irishman James Elliott running a bed and breakfast in the hills of Ireland. That was, of course, until they had taken time out to go over and see the house for themselves. It was an old country manor house, owned once by some lord or other, that in truth none of them had ever heard of, even Jim. Jim and Eve had seen its potential back then, years before, and now after four years of restoration and thousands upon thousands of pounds, it was well and truly open for business. Over four floors, it had twelve suites, another sixty double rooms and the most amazing facilities, all set within well over a hundred and fifty acres of the most beautiful countryside either Pat or Andrew remembered seeing in all their lives. What a fantastic way to spend the proceeds of what had been such a tedious beginning for the renowned Jim Elliott.

First there had been the debt collecting; collecting for some of the roughest, hardest people in the whole of the United Kingdom, and then, years later, the partnership with the Dobson brothers. Good luck to 'em, Andrew thought. He had to be honest with himself, if no one else. It was at times like these that he envied Jim. He wished sometimes that he could just take Louise and the babies off and away from it all and never look back, but then the rush got him, and wild horses couldn't have dragged him away from his precious London Town. There were some heavy times ahead and silently both men hoped that Andrew's only son James, and Jim's lad Michael would be able to take over where they would eventually leave off. The Dobson brothers were the names, and of course, the hard cash behind the clubs and pubs, and more recently the new wine bars, but were those two young men ready to be the muscle and the brains that would be needed for this fight? Sure, they'd both had their share of dealing with the rowdies and both were very wide receivers, especially Michael. Now, that young man could really handle himself. But this was going to be different to anything they had come up against before. They'd be playing with the big boys, and these bog boys played rough, very rough indeed.

Andrew's thoughts went then to his only daughter, Elizabeth. He wondered what role she would play in their little venture when she was old enough. She already wasn't the kind of girl to let James have all the fun, that was for sure, and on many occasions in the past she had bested even himself with her quick tongue, and he was definitely no one's idea of a fool. She was something of a think tank, the smooth that inevitably followed the rough. But there was something else about her that was evident even at the tender age of thirteen. She had the same look as her mother, features like china and she could cool you from boiling with just a glance. Oh yes, she would definitely have men on their knees when she was older. Much older, he thought firmly.

Pat bought him back to the present by placing his large hand on Andrew's shoulder, squeezing warmly, a mannerism they had both taken from their own father, who when he was nice was really nice and when he wasn't, was usually kicking ten bells out of one or both of them. 'We ain't down. We ain't even started. Relax. It'll be a piece of piss, Andy,' Patrick said softly. Andrew let out a silent sigh. He had a really bad feeling about this one and wondered fleetingly if Pat felt it too. 'Come on, I'm hungry. Let's get out of 'ere, ey?' and Patrick put out his cigarette.

'Yeah. Okay.' Andrew attempted a smile.

November 1991

James sat down silently at the opposite end of the large dining table to his father and the two men locked eyes like bulls locking horns. The apology for being late for dinner was evident in James's expression and Andrew gave him a slow nod of his head, his eyes flitting quickly towards where his wife now sat, patiently waiting for the silent conversation between father and son to end. Andrew knew exactly where James had been; the freshly brushed hair and the excessive usage of aftershave gave his game away to his worldly-wise father. The dirty little bastard, Andrew thought to himself with a sly smile.

'Sorry Mum!' James said as if butter wouldn't melt in his mouth, looking over at her and then at his sister, Elizabeth, who had also been watching father and son with interest. He was about to go on but his mother held up a small tanned hand with perfectly manicured nails on the tips of tapered fingers and he stopped himself.

'I don't think I actually want to know where you've been,' Louise purred. James had the decency to avert his gaze from his mother and instead he looked at his sister and the two smiled at one another warmly. That woman didn't miss a trick.

Louise relaxed in her seat again as she looked at her husband. He was such an incredible man, a powerful man. If only the world outside the sanctity of their four walls knew just what a real gentle, loving pussycat he could really be, really was. He denied her nothing and gave her everything. There was no comparison to the love they had and the family they were together. This man was never stuck in traffic or too busy at the office to be the man that he was when he walked through the door. Sure, the business was a big part of his life, but without his family, what good was the business and all the money it bought with it? Her eyes then went back to James. He was so much like his father had been at that age that it was almost creepy that these two were not brothers, twins born years apart. He had the same sturdy build as his father; broad shoulders, strong arms and a tight waist. His hair was thick, mid-brown with a slight wave to it, their skin tone was exact and those eyes, they could consume you in a second. She was aware of what a rogue he was when it came to girls already in his lifetime and if he was anything like his father had been. She paused in mid-thought as the memories came to mind. Fleetingly she remembered how Andrew had been in his youth and she blushed slightly at the memories. He'd wooed her until she had almost surrendered to him, she could see the past like snapshots in her mind's eye. She would be on the verge of letting go, desperate for him to touch her, but then she'd hear her mother's warning words, they'd be ringing in her head when she was about to give herself to him. *"He'll do the deed then he'll have it away on his toes"*.

Mrs. Carpenter never got the satisfaction of finding out if she would have been right about that. She died of breast cancer, a bitter middle-aged woman too scared of her own body to have done anything about the growth inside her, finally the size of an orange, shaped like a cauliflower, and Andrew had been there for Louise at that time, and not once did he ever take advantage of the situation. He'd persisted for almost two years and then he'd got down on bended knee and asked Louise to marry him. He had been infatuated with her, intrigued by her will power. He'd never been turned down before and the fact that he knew that she was untouched by human hand only added fuel to his heart. The rest was history.

He often said, in the warmth of her that she was all that he knew she would be as a lover as well as a wife and mother and his friend, his best friend. She knew what he said was the truth, knew he felt that way; she could see it in his eyes when he looked down at her. There was trust and honesty there, an unshakeable faith that neither could ever put into words. And when he'd come up with the idea of buying the hothouse with Pat and Jim she'd trusted him. She let him re-mortgage their little house, sell the car and beg and borrow, even with a new baby on the way, because he'd had that sincere expression on his face when he'd promised her that it would work, that everything would be just great.

Now years later there they sat at that beautiful table in that enormous house surrounded by each other and beautiful, expensive things and she was glad that they'd taken the chance.

She watched Beth take a sip of water from the fine crystal glass by her place mat. She moved so effortlessly, so gracefully. She had Louise's skin tone and her lips were full and set in a natural sensual pout. She had the Dobson eyes, emerald green orbs surrounded by thick lashes and perfect eyebrows. And she had their height. She was five feet six inches tall and still growing, an inch taller than her mother was and only a few inches shorter than her father and brother who both measured in at exactly six feet. She was going to be buxom. Not fat, but buxom and Louise often wondered what type of a man would take her on. He would have to be something very special to even get a look in if either of those two had anything to do with it, she thought almost pityingly. James was already throwing his weight around whenever his friends made comments about her, his precious baby sister, regardless of whether they were nice or nasty. Yes, whoever he was, he would have to be as resilient as she was. Yet she was so delicate in her manner. It was something that surprised most people, bearing in mind that she grew up with James and his rabble of friends. He had never bullied her or taunted her. That would never have been allowed in their home, coupled with the fact that it just wasn't in James's nature to be anything but courteous and pleasant to women, especially those to whom he was immediately related. She was resilient because he *had* let her play as an equal. He'd taught her how to ride his BMX bike even though she would have been in an expensive pretty pink dress, play fight and taught her how to throw a mean fist. She played football and God alone only knew what else; she cringed at the thought of what else.

Her thoughts were interrupted as she focused on Andrew again. He and James had finally finished eyeing each other and talking in manly one-liners. He smiled at her and something stirred deep within her, somewhere lower than her stomach. She always got the urge to ask him if they could have more children when he looked at her like that. But she knew that he would make all the right noises, say all the right things but then quietly back away. It was the only thing she ever knew him to back away from. It was sad really because she knew that he wanted more too and the only thing which had stopped him from saying yes in the past was the memories of Pat and his wife Judy's misfortunes and heartache.

Her sister-in-law, Judy, had been pregnant with twins just after Elizabeth was born. Pat had been ecstatic. He was like a giddy schoolboy. They'd tried for years before Judy had fallen, but then something had gone wrong. She miscarried at five and a half months. It had nearly killed her and for a long time everyone thought that the grief as well as the fact that she could have no more would finish her. But Judy bounced back one day and never looked back. She wouldn't hear of talk of adoption and so instead lavished all her love and affection on her husband. They were a little unit all of their own in a way and it seemed to suit them both.

'Mum? You want potatoes?' Beth asked and absently Louise took the serving dish from her, unaware of how long she'd been daydreaming.

'Thank you, baby,' she smiled. 'You back out tonight?' she asked then, looking directly across at her husband.

'Yeah, we've got some stuff to finish up at the club and Peter's coming over with the spec on that place in Bath. It looks good so far.' He saw Louise curl her lip slightly. She was thinking of something to say, but decided against it. She hated Peter. He was supposed to be their accountant but she was aware of his duties outside of the norm, even though Andrew very rarely discussed anything but the money with her. It suited them, the odd set-up they had when it came to the business. She didn't want to know and legally, if she didn't know it could only be for the best, but Peter knew that she was more attentive than even Andrew realised sometimes. He also knew that without her okay, the money quite simply wasn't spent at Andrew's end and Peter was being too nice to her at the moment. There was something funny about this deal in Bath. It seemed to her to be too much of a good thing but for some reason she held her peace on it and smiled across at him instead.

Chapter Two

January 1992

Elizabeth saw Patrick standing in the rain as she walked out of the school main entrance door. He was leaning up against the closed driver side door of his car. His expression was drawn and he looked very grey. She could feel her heart pounding in her chest. Where was the smile that always greeted her when they got her from school early? It was usually for an outing or a surprise, or just sometimes that one of them was bored and needed entertaining. It didn't happen all the time, but enough for her not to have been concerned at being summoned out of class. The last time had been about four months before, and had ended up in a trip to Silverstone courtesy of one of the breweries. That had a been such a great laugh. They were all there, mixing with the rich and the famous alike, and Beth was even spotted on television. Her English teacher even mentioned it the next week, when she'd produced prefect homework.

He had been there for a while, she knew; he was wet through to the skin and rainwater was running down his face and into his eyes and mouth. She couldn't decide what was wrong with him until she was almost directly in front of him. He was crying. Tears fell from his sorrow-filled eyes soundlessly. Something in Beth's insides began to scream at her and she looked around her from under the hood of her coat. She saw the school receptionist looking gravely out of the window in their direction, and then she looked back at Pat, who to that moment hadn't said a thing.

'Oh Bethy,' he said finally. His voice was broken and flat and it sounded doubly strange because in all her life she had never heard her

Uncle Pat sound anything but bold and strong and firm. She was drawn close to him then, his arms squeezing her. It was then, at that moment, that she knew inside what he was going to say to her next; why else he was there crying in the cold rain of the early afternoon? They were silent in the car on the way out of the school grounds. Nothing seemed to sink into her mind and everything around her, even the brightly coloured umbrellas on the streets, was black to her eyes.

James stood dumbfounded in the outer cubicle inside the Royal Hospital, holding Elizabeth's hand so tightly that the blood was stuck in her fingertips, making them ache. He couldn't think of anything to say to her or anyone else. All he could see in his mind was his mum and dad and all he could hear were their voices like ghosts already in his memory. The past few hours' events flashed before him. He'd been having such a good day; the wine bar was full of young women in their business suits, all of them trying so hard to look more executive-like than their purses would allow. He'd spoken to his mum on the mobile; she'd asked him to book a table at the Italian round the corner from the house. They'd agreed to buy the little club in Bath and were on their way home. He'd heard his dad in the background on the mobile. He was in an excellent mood and they were all laughing, but no more than an hour later he'd received another call. It was from Frank. The police were at the club looking for him and he got the impression from Frank that he should get there as soon as possible.

Beth felt her pulse pounding in her face and neck and then the wave of nausea that was threatening to sweep over her arrived and she gulped down the bile. It made her eyes water and her throat sting and she coughed, feeling it in her nostrils like an acid. Pat, still ashen-faced, walking back into the cubicle towards them made them both focus. He looked so much like their dad and Beth held back the urge to cling to him. He went to speak but nothing would come out so he closed his mouth again. He looked like a fish out of water, which was exactly what he felt like at that moment. He had absolutely no control over the goings-on around him and all he wanted to do was scream. Pale-faced James looked briefly down into Beth's eyes as they waited for the doctor before them to speak. Fleetingly Beth felt an odd and frustrated anger well up inside her; she wanted to slap him. He wasn't moving fast enough for such an emergency. He seemed not to have a care in the world and then he spoke, his South African accent soothing in the silence between them.

'We're ready for you now.' He opened the dividing swing door for them and ushered them inside the room he had just come from. 'I'm so very sorry that it has taken so long.' His movements were gentle now, softer towards them. Beth heard Pat move from his standpoint and felt James's grip tighten until she took his hand in her opposite hand and pulled his fingers away from her flesh. They trooped in, not a word and hardly a breath between them. There was a strange smell in the room and Beth wondered if it was the smell of death. She had often heard it said in the past but then she realised that it was some sort of cleaning fluid, disinfectant maybe. They watched in utter bewilderment as the sheet was pulled from Andrew's face. This was done by a male nurse with seemingly no features; he was just two eyes, a nose and a mouth, completely nondescript to them. Neither of them knew what to expect but both were outwardly surprised somehow to find that Andrew was stark white and that his lips were almost the colour of bluebells. They didn't know what they were expecting, but that wasn't it. Beth pulled her eyes away from him and looked at Pat for something, anything. He was devoid of expression because unbeknown to her he had already been into this room, through the door behind the tables and had already identified his brother and sister-in-law. He had been asked to do it with so much compassion and feeling that his faith in the National Health Service had been restored to the former glory. The doctor had also asked him to agree to let the children see their parents and after asking the inevitable question of whether they were badly injured, had dared to look for himself. They'd looked odd without a flicker of movement on either of their faces; they just looked like they were asleep. He had seen more than a couple of bodies in his time but nothing got him, not even the death of his own mother, like the pain that got him at seeing two such lovely lives wasted, gone and never to return. It was something that had never entered his mind.

He'd always imagined that they'd all retire, grow old and keel over on the golf course or on some cruise ship somewhere in the Med. Not die like that, in a car accident without doing so many of the things they'd said they'd wanted to do. Neither of them had even made it to the hospital.

Andrew hadn't even made it out of the car and somewhere in the back of his mind he wondered if Louise had just given up despite her children. Andrew was her life. They'd almost breathed as one. The sound of Beth's scream bought all thoughts back to the present. It was a howl, a deep-pitted screech that came from the soul as she stood in the stark whiteness staring down at her mother. Her hands were at her sides now with her fists clenched so hard that her nails dug into her palms and her feet were firmly on the floor beneath her even though in reality she felt as if she had risen from it. James was at a loss and until that point he hadn't dared move, let alone speak. Suddenly he was close to her, pulling her to him and they embraced, desperate for the feeling of comfort that both so urgently needed. As they stood there another body joined them. Pat huddled up to them, his strong arms taking them both in like a security blanket. 'Oh, Uncle Pat,' James gasped. He looked up and saw that Pat too was crying. 'Me mum and dad, Uncle Pat!' He sounded so young then, so young and vulnerable.

'It's okay, son,' Pat said, sounding far surer than he felt at that moment. He grabbed at Beth's shoulder then, easing both young people away from his body. 'Come on'. He looked across at the doctor who still stood quietly to the side of them. 'Can we go now?' he asked and the man nodded at him, the empathy evident on his face to anyone who could be bothered to look further than the green outfit.

There was utter silence as the four of them sat at the large breakfast table in Pat and Judy's immaculate new kitchen. Judy was desperate for something to do. She didn't handle a crisis very well. She got the urge to wash up and stood up quietly from her seat, a cigarette still burning between her slim fingers. Three other pairs of red-rimmed eyes looked up at her in unison and although she was aware of them, she couldn't meet their gazes. Beth's attention turned to James as he too lit another cigarette. The ashtray was full of filter ends and ash and for a few seconds that held her stare. It was vacant, something that made James's heart break even more than it already was. It was a strange feeling that was inside him; sadness mixed with anger. Anger at the world, his parents and the bastard who had run them off the road; they hadn't even stopped apparently.

Then preservation of the living kicked in and he reached across and took Beth's hand in his. It was cold even though her face was flushed from pent up emotion. Their touch was short lived and broken by the sound of a car on the gravel driveway outside the window. Seconds later the doorbell rang out in the quiet of the house; it was the police. They had said they would call in when Pat had seen them at the hospital. There were personal effects to be signed for but they knew that the family had been in no state to talk to them then. They didn't stay long at the house either. They knew who the Dobsons were and that even at such a time as this, they were not really welcome. But their presence jolted the entire family out of the deathly silence that had up until their arrival surrounded them.

Judy closed the front door and walked slowly back into the kitchen, her stance defeated and tired. James was sat back at the table with the phone in his hand. 'Who's he calling?' she asked Pat, her tone surprisingly normal.

'Michael. Better from us than on the news, 'ey!' His usual cool tone was back and she was glad. Mentally, as she stood there in the kitchen doorway she made a list of people she should call herself and Eve and Jim were first on the list.

'Where's Beth?' There was a long pause between them and Pat motioned with his head that she was in the toilet. 'Should I check on 'er?' she added.

'No, love, leave her. There can't be much more to come up.' Pat almost sighed. Poor Beth. She was so proud. He'd seen her flinch then gulp it back as Judy had left the room. He hadn't bothered to ask her if she was all right when she'd passed him on her way out of the kitchen. Of course she wasn't. Her parents had just died. He and James had just sat there, what could they do? This one was right out of their hands!

February 1992

It was a very cold and very wet day, fitting the mood of those gathered in the grey expanse of morbid marble and cheap concrete. The wind was biting and the clouds above the large congregation blackened with the passing moments as they filed out of the church and into the graveyard. The noise of the traffic on the main road was a distant din, although it was all that could be heard except for the low droning tone of the vicar now before them.

Elizabeth stood silently with James close by her side as the vicar began to speak. Pat and Judy were close by them, Pat's hand resting around Judy's waist ready to catch her if she fell again. She was trying not to cry and the sounds that came from her lips were like small hiccups and gasps. Elizabeth was trying desperately not to start crying again either, her eyes were red-rimmed from it, as were James's and her entire body ached from the fatigue of the act. She slid her hand into his grasp and for a second or two she tried to remember where she had put her gloves. James squeezed it gently, warming her cold fingers as he stood numbly at his sister's side. He was unsure of how he should be feeling, other than devastated and completely protective of Elizabeth at that point, so he stood with his head held high, though his stance looked as if he had a rod attached to his back and that was all that was holding him up. He was so tired and if he were completely honest, terrified of the future and what it would hold for them. All he knew was that he was to be the man of their house and it was a heavy burden for someone just into their twenties, especially as he had a thirteen-year old sister to look after too. Being in the business was one thing, but this, this was completely different and he couldn't help asking himself if he was up to the task. But those were the thoughts he had alone at night; they were not the thoughts he should be having at the gravesides of his beloved parents.

Pat obviously sensed his uneasy feelings and reached out, putting a strong hand on his shoulder and squeezing it affectionately. Judy then glanced glazed-eyed at Elizabeth and James in turn. They looked so much like Andrew and Louise in their own little ways; they had Louise's china-like complexion and features, almost chiselled into perfection. They had her long eyelashes but Andrew's mid-brown hair, the curly wave more evident in Elizabeth whose hair settled just above her waist. They had the Dobson eyes too, of that there was no mistake, huge emerald green orbs. She felt painful pride as she studied them through tear-filled eyes.

She wondered again, as she had so many times in the past, what her own children would have looked like; would they have had the same features that were so evidently Dobson? Then she pushed those thoughts from her mind, she was sad enough today without thinking of the past as well. James and Beth were coping so well with the day so far. Far better than she was anyway, she was almost ashamed of herself for all the tears but then she thought about how much Andrew and Louise had meant to her, how much she had loved them, loved their lives and all the pain and heartache was somehow justified. Her thoughts turned to her husband. He was such a proud man, such a strong man in comparison to others she had met in her lifetime. But even so, it hadn't been more than three hours since she had held him in her arms as he'd cried for the loss of his brother and his wife, two such wonderful people.

Elizabeth scanned the sea of people around her; she recognised maybe half of them, but they all appeared genuinely saddened at having to be there, and she knew that she would never forget how it all felt just at that moment. There was so much emotion surrounding her. The scent of the wreaths and flowers was something that she knew she would never forget either, it was beautiful and yet made her feel sick with the scents.

Louise had loved fresh cut flowers, and Andrew had loved giving them to her; in fact Beth couldn't think of anything that her mother had liked, that her father had not given her. He had worshipped her; he had loved her from a very tender age, and loved her right up until the day they had died. Elizabeth imagined without question that he would have gone on loving her, had they not been cut so short on time. They had both doted on Beth and James too. The two of them had been spoiled almost rotten with both love and affection, but Andrew in his wisdom had always reminded them of how it was before the business had taken off and become the success it was now; how the house was mortgaged up to twice its worth and just how much hard work had gone into making it what it had become. It was something that they all carried with them, their beginnings, but Beth could only just remember those days; she would have been no more than five years old. She could remember the little mid-terrace house that was always full of people. Aunt Judy with her endless cups of tea, Uncle Pat always coming up with new ideas and ventures and the constant stream of people always coming and going. Eve and Jim always came to mind whenever she thought of the past. Jim was a lovely man; his sheer size used to frighten her, but his eyes were always so warm and friendly. Evelyn was great too; she was a cuddly woman and she always smelled nice. Beth recalled her soft southern Irish accent. She remembered when she'd cooed over her, saying how much she wished she'd tried for a little girl.

Suddenly she thought of Michael and she squeezed again at James's fingers. He was needed there and somehow she knew that he was there, even though as she looked up at the faces again she couldn't see him. He always made her smile, made her feel good inside and she needed that now, as she knew that James did too and she found herself saying a prayer, asking for him to be there when she looked up again. Then her thoughts were off again and she could hear her mother's voice clearly in her head. She could smell her perfume and as she closed her eyes for a couple of seconds she could see her as plain as she had in any day in the past. She could see her father in her mind's eye. His wicked grin, the one that made his nose wrinkle, the one he gave their mother when he was late home or as he lit a cigar in the lounge, something that they all knew that Louise hated. She'd been so house-proud, something that was so insignificant now.

Two beautiful dark oak coffins were lowered into the ground before the congregation and it bought Beth back to the present. She took one look at the beauty of the craftsmanship and that was when something inside her snapped. She let out a low, lonely groan at first and then the tears came again, thicker and faster than they had yet.

'No. Please!' She reached out a cold hand to the wood before her eyes, not quite touching it. 'I want them back!' she sobbed and James was undone; tears welled up and fell down his cheeks in a constant stream. 'Please get them back.' The sound of her grief followed by the sight of James pulling her to his chest left no eye dry. It was more moving, more emotional than anything the vicar had said in the fifteen minutes they had stood out in the cold weather; in fact, even he stopped speaking to observe the two young people before him. There were no words; not even from the good book or God himself that could have stemmed the sadness and the grief that ran through these two young people and not another word was said until the coffins were in place above the gaping holes in the cold dark ground. There was absolute silence then as Andrew and Louise were lowered the rest of the way into the ground and Beth pulled away from James with a breaking heart to see them finally laid to rest.

'Let us pray,' the vicar said finally in a strong tone and all eyes focused on the ground. 'Our father, who art in heaven ...' he began, but Beth couldn't settle her gaze and she couldn't concentrate on his voice either. Her eyes were stinging and she wanted to scream again. She looked across the congregation again, watching bowed heads, then her emerald green eyes met a pair of the darkest brown, surrounded by thick lashes and strong brow. She felt herself warm inside for a second or two. Theirs were the only two pairs of eyes looking anywhere but at the cold dark earth at their feet. He looked like a dark angel. His stance was strong and proud and he seemed to tower above those around him at well over six feet. He filled out his rich woollen overcoat with broad shoulders and a full chest, and for his almost frightening size he seemed warm and comforting to her. The fringe of his thick dark brown hair was blown into his eyes by the wind but he didn't falter, his eyes never left hers. His saddened, understanding expression changed slightly into almost a smile after a moment or two. His features were then warm and seemed to calm her from the inside out. She stared and was in two minds whether or not to return the gesture when she realised that she already was. It wasn't a grin, she didn't have one of those in her, hadn't had for weeks, but it was a greeting, a welcoming gesture. She nudged at James's arm gently and directed him with her eyes to where Michael stood.

'Michael!' James's voice was almost a whisper but both Pat and Judy heard and looked across to where the two now stared. They needed the past then. Needed to be reminded of better times when everything was new and fresh and the world was just beginning for them.

From open car doors people watched as Beth and James stood hand in hand beside the sea of flowers, and it was a sea. Not one inch of bare ground was left uncovered. The two watched silently as the holes were filled, and as a mark of respect the grave hands laid the headstones lightly down on the earth ready to be put in firmly once all mourners were gone from sight. James turned on his heel, his eyes settling on Michael as he walked up to them. Beth turned too, but looked further on to observe Eve and Judy's embrace; it was heartfelt. Jim and Pat's greeting to one another was warm too and then they embraced like brothers, their own grief shared. She realised then, that for all they were her mum and dad they had been in Pat, Judy, Eve and Jim's lives for much longer. Every son or daughter expects to bury a parent at some time, but to bury a younger brother, parents so young, it all seemed like such an awful waste. She looked up at Michael then, hearing his voice as he spoke to James about the service and almost smiled at him again. Without a word to her he reached out and touched her cheek with warm fingers. The three hugged close together then and it was like the joining of forces unexplainable. They needed him and he was there for them, with them.

'You better now?' he asked James, his accent thick with emotion.

'Yeah. I'm okay now,' James replied, rubbing his hands together for something to do at an obviously awkward moment for him and Beth got the feeling that she'd missed something. Was that where James had gone that morning, to Michael's?

Pat and Judy had insisted on inviting everyone back to their house rather than one of the clubs or to what was now James and Beth's house. Judy had thought it too much for Beth to handle even with Mrs. P, their daily lady, but she understood completely Beth's need to do something for her parents, because everything else seemed to be done already, what with solicitors and accountants and staff bending over backwards to help. So it was agreed, and the two had worked through the emotion in preparation for the day. The house was, as with everything about the Dobsons, magnificent. It was a large red brick detached mock-Georgian affair with a sweeping driveway and detached garages to the side that showed the width of the plot width off to perfection. The interior was tastefully decorated and the furniture was the finest, most fashionable around. It was like a show house and people walked around inside like they were in an old country house, and unable or not allowed to touch anything.

For the number of people there it was strangely quiet; not silent, just quiet and Beth actually wished that people would stop talking in whispered, hushed tones. Andrew and Louise had been loud and outrageous, garish almost and she knew in her heart that they would have been pleased with a party in their honour, not all this creeping about. But she wasn't in the mood to make a fuss and so she decided to slope off, almost completely unnoticed. She stood alone out in the conservatory, smoking the cigarette that she had taken from James's packet only moments previously. She stared out into the garden, watching the rain as it made patterns on the glass before her eyes. The door from the main house opened behind her but she didn't look round; she presumed it was James come to join her for a quiet smoke, but it wasn't. It was Michael.

'Do you want to be alone?' he asked, looking across the room and she spun about in surprise. He looked into her eyes and then at the cigarette that burned away between her fingers.

'No,' she sighed. She had wanted to be, if she were honest, but not then, she always felt a strange kind of peace and safety when Michael was near. 'I thought you were James. Where is he?' She fought to keep her voice light, keep the conversation going in case she cried again.

'With Pat and my dah.' He said it simply, and meant it innocently, but she felt it deeply and the tears began to fall from her eyes as the word, "dah", echoed in her head. She'd never be able to say that word again, never be able to call down the stairs for him or drag him out of the study. She'd never be able to argue with him about what time he'd collect her from a friend's house or the cinema again. She'd never be able to talk to him again, hold one of their little conversations, but most of all, she'd never be able to breathe in the sweet smell of him, feel that safe again and it was suddenly mortifying.

She didn't feel as if she was crying. The tears fell out as if her whole head was filled with them and was now just overflowing. She shoved the cigarette butt into a nearby plant pot, and grief-stricken, she looked across and up into Michael's eyes again. He took a couple of bold steps towards her and suddenly she was in his arms. 'I'm sorry,' she managed. 'I—I—They're gone.'

Michael let out a sigh, wrapping strong arms even further around her. 'It's okay!' he breathed. He let her cling to him, the tears now coming in shudders that wracked her entire body. He was grateful too that she had buried her head so deeply into his chest, she didn't see the tears that fell silently down his own cheeks. He had loved her parents too and her open emotion today had moved him like nothing he had ever felt before. He understood her pain better than he could ever have expressed in words. He knew how she was feeling. James had cried and cried for days on his shoulder and explained his emptiness to his friend. He was then well on his way in to a semi-drunken state, and Michael guessed rightly that it was the only way to be on a day like today. He'd left him with Pat and his own father, quietly, as they had continued to drink somewhat steadily in the kitchen and gone in search of Beth. He'd seen her walk through the crowds of people in the house and stop to talk. She accepted their sympathy almost like the perfect hostess accepts gratitude but he knew that she was desperate to be out of there, could see it in her body language and he had had held back on the urge to drag her free from them. He wanted to yell at them, *"She doesn't want to talk. She wants to be on her own. She just buried her parents for God's sake! Leave her alone"*. But most all he wanted to make sure that she was holding up okay. He knew that she was a strong little creature. She always had been; growing up with him and James could make you nothing else. But he was as worried about her as the others were, and he had been since his brief conversation with Judy after his mother had had her say on the phone a couple of days before the funeral.

They had been over from Ireland for two days already and were staying at Michael's house in Enfield. They'd agreed, and thought it best, to leave well enough alone at such a time and it had been hard for him not to go to his friends immediately in their time of need, but he knew that they had to do those days alone together with no intervention. It had been less than twenty-four hours before James had called him and asked him to go there. He'd dropped everything and within half an hour was sitting in the lounge with James crying his heart out beside him; it had been gut-wrenching.

The day was almost over and Michael watched from the sidelines as his mum helped Judy straighten the house up a little so that the morning wouldn't be such a big task for the cleaner. He'd offered to help but got the impression that they were glad of the distraction. James was already upstairs in one of the spare rooms, sound asleep and from what he could gather from Beth it was the first real sleep he would have had in weeks.

'You want another?' Pat asked, taking hold of the empty glass Michael was holding so intently. He looked into Pat's eyes and saw the sadness there and the two stood for a long moment just staring at each other.

'No thanks, Pat. I'm driving,' he said quietly and Pat nodded at him. Michael, always the old head on young shoulders, he thought.

'Have you two seen Bethy?' Judy sounded worried and looked somewhat stressed as she appeared in the doorway.

'She's in there,' Michael said, pointing with his head towards the conservatory. 'She's sleeping. Leave her for now!' His tone was almost demanding and he startled himself at such a statement.

'It's cold out there!' Judy said in a half whisper.

'She's got the comforter over her!' Michael added, 'She's fine, Judy, honest.' His tone was gentle again then and he met Pat's stare head on. Pat had watched Michael all afternoon. One second he was holding James up, the next he was at Beth's side. It was a strange sight to see, all that power dissolving into love and concern for his friends, his family. He was so much like his dad, and Pat had found himself remembering things that were deep in the memory of his past. The things those three used to get up to. It was a wonder to him, looking back as an adult, that they all made it as far as they did in life.

March 1992

Beth tried to stem her tears as she heard the door open. She felt movement above her in the darkness of her bedroom. She knew that it was James who now sat by the bed comforting her and not her mum, as she had hoped and prayed it would be. The smell of his aftershave was familiar and it came as close to comforting her as his touch did then. Six weeks had passed now and still she thought that she might wake up and find that nightmare of the past weeks had been just that, a nightmare. But in the darkness of her room, with tears sticking her lovely long hair to her china-like features there was no mistaking that this was no nightmare and that it was very real, very real indeed.

'Oh, Babe!' she heard James breathe as he cradled her in his arms and wiped the tears from her face with warm palms that seemed to cool the burning of her cheeks. 'Please don't cry. Please don't cry. I want to make all the pain go away, like she did when she used to kiss you when you fell down, but I can't'.

Beth breathed deeply. 'I want them back,' she said, gasping for breath. 'James, please. Get them back!' she begged, and he too let the tears that welled up in his eyes fall like rain. 'Promise you won't leave me too.'

He was undone. 'Never, baby. Never in a million years!' he managed. 'You're my baby. Nothin' and no one's ever gonna hurt you while I'm 'ere. I promise.' They clung to each other for a long time. Neither of them wanting to be the first to pull away and finally, in unison they parted and looked at each other with red-rimmed emerald green eyes. So much was said then without a word passing their lips. They had become one suddenly; a team, inseparable and that knowledge alone seemed to warm them both inside.

'We'll be okay,' he said softly. 'And I swear I won't leave you, Babe. You're my life. It's you and me!'

No more than a week later, Elizabeth and James sat in the plush reception area of the offices of Willis, Allan and Partners, Solicitors, and they were greeted warmly by Mr. Willis, a tall thin man in his early forties with a firm face, and he settled them down in front of the desk in his neat office; a large suite with windows overlooking the city from ten floors up in the red marble-fronted building. They talked amicably for a while as coffee was served by a young girl only a few years older than Beth was, and then with that done, he settled back in his own chair and paused before speaking.

'Your father,' he announced, glancing down at the open file in front of him, 'has made this as simple as I have ever seen before.' He paused and looked at them both in turn. 'The will, such as it is, is quite simple. You two get almost everything barring a few bequests for other family members and close friends. There is a document here,' he continued, turning through the pages so neatly bound together with ribbon, 'Signed by him. It is to be read to you both in the event of his and your mother's death.' He paused for a few seconds, scanning the piece of paper. 'I, Andrew Dobson, being of sound mind hereby bequeath all holdings, moneys, positions etcetera to my son, James Andrew Dobson and daughter Elizabeth Louise Dobson in equal shares. The property in Finchley is to be sold—' He heard them both gasp and looked up at them from the papers, holding up his hand to bid them let him continue. 'The proceeds of this sale are to be added to the remaining moneys. There is a property in Islington, currently occupied by tenants—' He paused again, then explained. 'The tenants are aware of the terms of the lease. They have been notified that they have a maximum of three months to gain alternative accommodation. Their costs will be settled through this office.'

'Jesus!' James whispered. He was a little taken aback by what was going on but he noticed that Elizabeth just sat quietly, staring intently at the odd-looking man before her.

'I've spoken to the Pearsons at length, they seem quite amicable,' Mr. Willis said with a warm smile. He was confident that their father's wishes would be carried out to the letter for their best interests and with this in mind he went on. He was coming to the end of the document and he pulled his glasses from his face before going on any further. He looked directly at James and began to speak again.

'You will be ward to young Elizabeth here, being over eighteen now, along with whoever you see fit. I presume that that will be your father's brother and his wife. They appear within the documentation along with Mr., Mrs. and Master Elliott?' James nodded at him with a bewildered expression on his face and Beth took his hand, giving it a little squeeze. Mr. Willis gave them another smile and then read briefly through the remainder. 'The shares in the business will be split between you both. Your father had the controlling share, but obviously that changes now. Patrick now has that. Elizabeth, you are entitled to these at eighteen or, I'm afraid, unless your uncle decides otherwise; but I'm sure you'll sort that out between yourselves.' He didn't want to get into the middle of that one if it ever came to pass, that was for sure. He'd been dealing with the Dobsons since they'd started their business and was aware of their capabilities. 'Until then, James, you are responsible for them, again, with your uncle's guidance. Separate life policies cover funds for your father's brother and again, the Elliotts. These funds are just over five hundred and fifty thousand pounds.'

'Bloody hell!' Elizabeth finally said, her voice harsher than even she had expected it to be.

'Quite.' He smiled. 'Other policies have been transferred automatically into your names and mature over the next ten years.'

'Pensions!' James said finding his tongue and Mr. Willis nodded at him.

'The breakdown of funds is as follows. Policies as discussed totalling eight hundred and seventy thousand pounds. Present market value of Rosebay House, four hundred and twenty thousand pounds with a mortgage remaining of eighty thousand pounds. Greenview Park Square, three hundred and fifty-nine thousand pounds, owned outright. The family business is a going concern. James, I believe you are aware of the figures. Your salary will now be amended to the same as your late father's. Elizabeth, you will now automatically receive a monthly sum of one thousand pounds until you are eighteen. You will then receive a monthly income of two thousand or salary well above that figure, depending upon your decision as to whether or not you wish to be a silent or operative partner in the business.' He finished speaking and James smiled at him. 'Funds in account, bank accounts and so forth to date are just over one hundred thousand pounds. So all in all, you have no financial problems for the foreseeable future!'

'But I can stay with James!' Beth said.

He nodded at her question. 'He is your ward, Elizabeth!'

James breathed out. 'That means I'm the boss!' he said, giving her a little tap on the knee. He was ecstatic. Completely ecstatic. Fuck the money. As long as he and Beth were together the world could just fuck off as far as he was concerned.

'Oh James!' she breathed, the relief evident in the tone of her voice. The money was irrelevant to her. They had always known that that wouldn't be a problem. Their main, no, their only concern had been staying together.

'Yes. Your parents have been very careful in that respect. They were very thorough and there was never any other motive for their employing my services in a personal respect. If you were not of age, James, you both would automatically have been warded to your uncle and aunt. And if for any unforeseeable reason that were not possible—' he hesitated.

'Eve and Jim!' James whispered in interruption and Mr. Willis nodded at him before going on. 'My fees for this service have been paid. There are some documents to sign, but that doesn't have to be done right now. You can do that at a later date. I'm sure you will have questions for me at our next meeting, shall we say a week from today?'

It wasn't a dismissal, but both knew then that the meeting was over and stood up to leave.

Back at the house, James stared at the papers Mr. Willis had given him as they'd left. They could stay together and they would stay together. '*Thank God,*' he said, over and over in his mind. He stared for ages at the figures so neatly typed on the page now before him. The characters swam and merged together because he focused so hard. They were absolutely loaded and he couldn't help but notice the feeling that the financial security gave him at that time, now that the relief of their main concern was there. It was never an issue, he knew, but it was the extent that had shocked him and the house and everything. He'd never had his dad marked up as an idiot, but neither had he ever given much thought to his plans for the future. Christ. This was incredible. Andrew had thought of everything. Nothing was in question. There wouldn't be any long drawn out nightmares and bickering about who got what. It was all there in black and white for all to see.

Beth walked into the kitchen and stared across the dark wood expanse at him. He looked different, calmer than he had in a long time.

'Couldn't you sleep?' he asked. Of course she couldn't. If she didn't and couldn't sleep at night, why would she be able to do so at four in the afternoon?

She shook her head. 'I'm okay,' she sighed, planting herself down next to him. 'Is all that real?' she asked, staring at the pages.

'Yeah.' There was a laugh in his tone and he fingered the corner of one of the pages. 'Its real all right.'

Chapter Three

April 1992

James was becoming increasingly worried about Beth. To anyone who didn't know her she looked fine and behaved as if she was holding up really well, considering the situation. But he knew that she was sleeping probably less than he was lately, and that that wasn't much. She was eating next to nothing too and the toll on her body was beginning to show, with dark circles around her eyes and the shine from her hair had all but gone. She had her good days, but the bad still outnumbered them. He saw her off to school, the best place for her in his humble opinion. It wasn't that he didn't want her there in the house with him. Far from it; he loved her company, she was at an amusing age to him. As a young child she'd been all questions, and now as she reached her teens she was all answers. It was that he knew that she was upsetting herself, sitting and staring at the walls in the house. They'd tried Pat and Judy's but that wasn't much better. Pat was being strong for all of them but even he broke down every now and then and it was the inconsistency that was the killer in their house. So school, surrounded by friends, was definitely the best place for her.

She needed the normality of life and being away from it for so long would only make going back even harder than it had been after just a few weeks. He didn't want to worry Pat and Judy with any more either. He wasn't actually sure of how much more they could take just then; they'd been so good. And besides, if he was going to make a stand about him and Beth living together without other people butting in he was going to have to deal with this himself. But he didn't have the first clue of where to start or what to say to her. He dialled the number and waited for the receiver to be picked up at the other end of the line.

'Mike. It's me. No, mate, I'm fine. It's the baby.' He had taken to calling her that because she answered to it, everyone knew her as that and, well, it felt like home to him. 'Have you got some time? I need to talk to you. Nah, it's nothing like that. I just need to talk, you know?' He visibly relaxed as he heard Michael almost laugh at his question. James knew the answer. Michael would drop everything for his friend, but again he was concerned about taking the piss and pushing people too far. They spoke briefly some more and then James replaced the receiver and sat at the table, wondering what he was going to say to Michael when he arrived. It didn't matter, he knew that Mike would sit and listen and comfort and then when that was done, would come up with an excellent solution. He always did and James loved him for it and wasn't ashamed or embarrassed to say it. He was the best friend a bloke could have and James was honoured to call him his friend.

The following Friday evening Beth sat down on the counter top in Michael's kitchen. She watched him in silence as he made her a cup of tea. He was such a methodical person and for his size, he moved with real grace and ease. It was such a stark contrast between his and her brother's haphazard way of doing things. She was a funny thing, he thought, feeling her eyes on him. There were two chairs and two stools in the room but she had to sit in the middle of it all, on the counter. It looked to him as if she were in an observation tower and always in the centre of where the action was. She could almost hear him thinking as he busied himself. He had that placid expression on his strong features that he only got when things got heavy and he was hiding his true feelings.

Fleetingly she wondered what she had done wrong. She wracked her brains. No, nothing that Michael was going to have a pop at her for doing and then she smiled to herself, the corners of her mouth turning upward slightly. He never had a pop at her except for when she swore and that was only for her massacring of the English language, not for the act itself. He always said that it wasn't his place, but she saw him as more of a family member than friend and therefore she figured that it was okay for him to help in her upbringing.

'What's funny?' he asked, noticing the slight smile.

'Nothing!' she said and they were quiet again for a while.

'You know, you're the first young lady I've had in here for, oh, um—' He thought for a couple of seconds.

'About a week?' Beth interrupted, her tone sounding sceptical. He had to laugh at her. She was so worldly in some ways and yet so innocent in so many others.

'Y'know, I think you're right!' he replied, a laugh in his tone.

He finished making the drinks and she followed him into the lounge. It was warmer than the kitchen because the heating hadn't been on long and they settled down into two well-padded chairs opposite one another. 'You look really young in your uniform,' he laughed, observing her from head to toe as she re-adjusted her skirt.

'I am really young!' Her tone was flat and for a second or two he felt that she was making a statement but as she smiled at him, the thought left his head.

'I presume you want one?' He offered her a cigarette and she took it from him with a nod. As she lit it and inhaled the smoke he watched her. 'Not too young for a cigarette though, ey?' No, she was no child. She was a woman in a child's body, yes, but definitely no child and the moment felt right suddenly to open the conversation, the reason that she was there for the night. 'I think we need to talk. Person to person.' She looked into his eyes and saw the intensity there.

'Man to man? What about?' She was leaning forward.

'You!' He paused for a few seconds. 'Why you're not sleeping or eating properly. And why you've not come talk to me before now. Why I've had to ask you here.' His tone was neutral and didn't change pitch but his face was expressive.

'I'm okay!' she managed.

'You don't look it!' His observation was true, if not a little harsh. She didn't look sick, far from it. But she looked tired, ashen and as if she was about to burst in to tears all the time. Her features were pinched and the almost-smile that had been ever present on her lips was gone.

There was a silence between them and they just smoked until Beth leaned forward in her seat again and began to speak. Her voice was low and almost distant and Michael listened intently without interruption.

'I miss them every day. It's like I can't breathe sometimes because it hurts so much. Everything I look at in the house reminds me of them. Stuff still even smells of them. It's such a sick feeling, like it's all a big joke. Like they're going to walk through the door and laugh with me at how funny it was that I believed that they were dead. And then it hits me that they are dead and it is true and I'm right back where I was again. The strangest things remind me of them. Music, food. Christ, even my homework. I feel so alone, Michael. I'm scared and I can't tell James how I feel. He's being so brave but I hear him cry at night. I watch him, he's trying to be the man and that must be tough. Do you think he needs to hear my problems?' She looked into his eyes, he'd moved towards her and was now on the floor in front of the chair where she sat and she saw the tears in his eyes.

'Yes. Yes, I do. He needs to hear yours and you need to hear his. And yes, he is the man now, and you're the woman now and it means being old all of a sudden. Older than you feel now, than you felt last month. You two have each other now and you have to trust each other. But to trust you have to know that person from the outside in.' He leaned back on his haunches before he went on. 'I'll tell you some things about me, shall I, Elizabeth? Things that'll let you know me better than you do now, maybe better than James does.'

She nodded at him, feeling the tears in her eyes disappear and fade back into her head. 'Nothing filthy though, please. I have a very high opinion of you. And I'm impressionable.' She laughed then.

'No, nothing like that! Deeper stuff, you know? Like, the best feeling I ever had. It was suddenly knowing for sure what a friend I have in your brother. He'd always been my friend, but lads are different from girls. We rarely bare our souls.'

She looked at him. 'How?' she was intrigued.

'A couple of years ago I had a girlfriend, you remember?'

Beth nodded then spoke. 'Sophie.' She almost spat it out. She wasn't sure why, it was just the way that girl's name was spoken in the house.

'Yes. Well,' he said, his own tone clipped. 'At the time she was nice. And I thought that maybe she was the one, but then something happened and it all went a bit off the rails, you know? James, for all he was only a kid himself was there for me; to hold my hand, if you like.' He laughed at his own terminology. 'I cried, I cried a lot! After I'd finished being angry with her.' He looked deep into her eyes; she was so attentive. 'Men cry, you know that, but they rarely cry in front of other people. When you've cried with someone it gets to you both, you never forget it. I've cried, James's cried and you've cried and we know each other better for it, don't we?' He stubbed out his cigarette butt. 'And I knew that no matter what I did, what I said, how I played it, James'd be there for me, and respect my decision. We stopped being buddies then and became friends.' Beth liked his voice, despite the content.

'What's the saddest?' She was inspired by him and loved to hear him talk. His voice was so soft and gentle to her ears, it relaxed her. Everything he said was good, even when it was bad. Everything he said was said for a reason, be it to advise, teach, guide or inspire. And he did inspire her.

'The saddest?' He thought then about whether or not to tell her. She'd find out one day, he wouldn't gain anything from lying to her. 'The saddest I've ever felt was when you cried in the rain!' he said finally and as he carried on he looked away from her, as if he was watching in his mind's eye. 'It got me right here in the heart.' He touched his own chest with a broad open hand. 'All I wanted to do was hold you like James did, comfort you like he was, and when we were at the house and you cried on me, I cried too. I was gutted for you, truly gutted. I'd have done anything at that moment to make your tears stop. Make the pain go away.' He took her by the hand and gave her a little squeeze as he looked back at her. 'I promised myself that I'd always be there for you, to cry on, yell at, hit or just be with and I meant to tell you before but the time wasn't right. The time is right now, Elizabeth, and I'm telling you that I'm here for you! Always! Just like I am for James. You're not alone, could never be alone. I won't allow it. If you have a problem, or you just want to sit, I'm here. Always, I promise. I am your friend.'

His speech moved her to tears and one fell from her eye. He wiped it away with his finger before it had reached her cheek and he smiled into her eyes. 'Never not talk to me, Elizabeth, never think that I'll judge you or think less of you no matter what you do. And I know that your brother, for all he's a prize pain in the arse, I know he feels the same way too, and so do you. It's one thing to be his sister, but you two have to be friends too. It's not the gap you have to deal with, it's the closeness.' His tone was sincere and intense and she was reminded again of what a friend she had in him and just how much she loved her brother. It raised her spirits.

'Did you cry because you loved her?' she asked suddenly.

He looked away from her and then he spoke. 'I thought I did, but it wasn't love. I know what love is now and that wasn't it. It was lust maybe or what they call young love, which is very different from love as an adult.'

He didn't go on. Didn't tell her the whole truth. It had been love, or at least what Michael had thought love was, but Sophie hadn't cared. She'd been screwing around because he was *never there* and she didn't bother to hide it in the end. Michael had lost that famous temper of his with the last poor bastard she'd been fucking. He'd received a six month suspended sentence for good old actual bodily harm. The sentence had been suspended because of the circumstances. Michael had come home from a few days away on business. He'd come home to patch things up with her and found them in his own bed. He'd seen him, picked him up and thrown him, stark naked, down the stairs. He'd broken his arm, not from the fall, but from Michael's grip. He'd quite literally snapped him like a dry twig. He decided to lighten the subject and he lowered his head as if about to tell her a great secret. 'I really cried because the silly little cow scratched up my new car.'

He scoffed out a laugh as he remembered that. It had been a parting shot from dearest Sophie.

'She keyed your car?' Beth had to laugh then. If he was anything like James about his car, and she had never thought that of Michael, he would have been in tears, floods of tears.

She was sound asleep, lying on her front with her hair fanned out around her on the pillows. He watched her from his leaning position at the doorway for a long while. Her breathing was soft and light and he found himself keeping pace with her in the darkness. He felt good inside. They'd talked a lot that evening. He'd fed her with one of his specialities, spicy Chinese food, followed by ice cream. And when she'd nodded off next to him on the sofa during the late night thriller he'd taken her up to the spare room where she'd practically fallen straight back to sleep in the double bed. He closed the door after a long while and walked back down into the lounge. The television was still on and by its light he dialled James's number. 'James? Yes. No, she's asleep. I'll drop her off in the morning. You just get yourself some sleep too, do you hear?' He listened as James talked on the other end of the line. 'She's worried about you too, my friend. I think that maybe you two need to talk to each other a bit more. You have to understand her too; she's so fragile for all she's tough, she's like china.' He paused again as James spoke on the other end of the line. 'Aye, I'll see you in the morning, we'll talk more then.'

Late April 1992

James knew what it was that he needed that night and with Beth safely tucked up at Michael's house for the second time in as many weeks he had every intention of getting it, quite literally in fact. Dressed in his favourite suit and shirt he knew that he looked good and he checked himself in the reflection of the glass doors as he walked into the club. 'Evenin', lads.' He was on top form and he felt better already than he had in weeks.

'You're looking rather dapper, young Jimmy. You all right?' Frank's tone was jovial and he tapped James's shoulder lightly as he passed him in reception. It was good to see him smiling again. James in a bad mood was bad, but James as he had been lately, that was unbearable. That kind of pain could eat you up inside if you let it, Frank thought and he was glad, truly glad that James was dealing with it.

'Yeah, cheers, mate. I ain't bad, ain't bad at all!' He went straight to the bar and ordered a bottle of beer, his eyes never leaving the blanket of women than seemed to be all around him.

He leaned over her, pushing her forward across the bonnet of the car. Her bottom was exposed to him and he ran his hands across the warmth of her skin. She groaned, enjoying being touched by such expert hands. She was wet and receptive to his caress and it was only seconds before she felt her first stirrings of orgasm. James didn't want her to talk to; this was not the beginning of a wonderful relationship by any stretch of the imagination. This situation was simple. He'd asked, she'd said yes and there they were.

Women fell over themselves for him and he enjoyed it, but he was still waiting for the one that turned him down, the one that didn't cater to his every desire just because she thought he would show her the high life. And there was no high life really, if he was honest. There was work, which was hard and tiring, although the pay was obviously very good. There was his baby sister and she was priority over even the business at that time. Then there was the sex and that was his release from the stresses that he was under, his escape from the world and the pain that it poured over him at that time in his life. With both hands firmly on her hips James entered her and she let out a loud groan of pleasure. 'Fuck me,' she purred, over and over again. He took her to the edge, thrusting deeper and deeper until she was begging him to let her come. He grabbed her hands and held them behind her back, holding them with a firm grip. He didn't need her intervention when it came to her orgasm. She'd have one when he was ready and not before. He loved the power he had over these women, loved the fact that they loved him and was never less than surprised at how he could affect them, make them do pretty much anything that he wanted them to. What a gift to be blessed with, he thought. He recognised his own excitement as it took him over and then with just a few light strokes from between her legs he felt her come around him, her pulsing bringing him to his own release. Minutes later it was all over and James pulled himself from her warmth. He kissed her neck and hair but there was nothing more to it. This one wouldn't ask for his number or press him as to when she would see him again. There was an unspoken conversation as they re-adjusted their clothes in the dim light of the sports centre car park.

'I'll drop you home!' he said finally.

'Thank you.' Her voice was light, friendly and fleetingly he thought of asking her for her number. After all, she was rather tasty. She put light fingers on his arm and smiled up into his eyes warmly.

'Maybe we can do this again some time,' was all she said, both outside and inside the car, other than give him directions back to her house.

May 1992

A car horn sounded and Beth looked around the car park by the small parade of shops on the opposite side of the road to the school. She saw James's BMW and smiled, although in the setting sun she couldn't actually see his face from behind the glass. She approached the passenger door, opened it and got in. ''Ello, Bab.' His tone was jolly and she sensed mischief. She kissed him on the cheek, feeling the light brown stubble from the day. 'And did we have a good day? Learn lots of really useful things at that amazing place of learning?' he continued and she pouted with a little shrug of her shoulders.

'Are you taking the piss?'

He looked hurt. 'No.' He laughed the word out. 'And stop swearing!'

Settling in, she replied, 'Well, in that case, it was average. What about you?'

He nodded sagely at her, trying to be interested in school. 'Interesting, actually, Babe, very interesting.' He leaned into the back of the car and pulled a mid-length peachy coloured dress and strappy shoes from the back seat.

'What on earth—' she began.

''Ere, put these on!' he smiled.

'Why?' She took the items from him, wondering how he had known just what to pick for her to wear on such a nice evening.

'Coz you and me are going for a drink and I don't think even you'd get in to the pub wearing your uniform,' he said, a matter-of-fact tone to his voice and she laughed then. He was always doing little things that made her smile lately. He was trying so very desperately to be both her father and her mother, as well as the best brother a girl of fourteen could hope for and she warmed inside at the thought that he was doing such a fantastic job of it.

Once settled in a quiet corner of the pub James lit two cigarettes and passed one to her. She accepted it without a word and for a while they just sat smoking as they watched the world go by outside on the opposite side of the bay window. Beth noticed how many people, not just women, but men too, looked at her brother and she concentrated on him for a long moment. He was very good looking. A right *jack the lad* expression on his face all the time now that the smile was back. His hair was cut quite short for the summer, almost shaved at the back and was held in place with the minimum of wax. His eyes sparkled like her own when he removed the sunglasses that she was beginning to think were surgically attached to his face, and they too were framed with long lashes and neat eyebrows. He was getting broader, too, she thought, looking at his tight white T-shirt. That was all that hard work at the gym. His tanned arm muscles seemed to explode from beneath the material.

He brought her back to the present with a sniff. 'I've bin to see the house,' he said casually.

'Oh.' She was a little unsure of how she should reply to a statement like that. They had a buyer for theirs but nothing else had been said about it until then.

'It's not bad, quite nice,' he said a bit more enthusiastically.

Beth let out a billow of smoke in a vain attempt to blow a smoke ring and James had to laugh at her efforts. 'You'll learn,' he smiled. There was another pause and then he went on, 'I thought maybe you'd like to go and see it.' His voice was neutral but Beth of all people knew when he was hiding something and she looked into the mirror of her own eyes.

'Do you think we should go?' she asked innocently and her question reminded him of just now young she still was.

'Yeah. I do, Babe,' he said, his expression making his eyebrows rise and the lines on his forehead show up against his tan.

'When do you want to go then?'

She was expecting him to suggest the weekend and she was surprised when he replied. 'Now?' He focused on grinding out his cigarette into the cheap round blue glass ashtray on the wooden table between them, rather than look at her at that moment but he could hear her reaction. Beth swallowed a large gulp of the Coke she'd been sipping and then extinguished her own cigarette in the same manner that James had.

'Come on, then,' she half sighed and he waited until she had stood up before moving himself.

They pulled off the high road into a large mews square of four-storey Georgian houses flanking a well-kept central communal green on all four sides. There wasn't one unkempt house among the fifty or so and Beth found herself staring open-mouthed at the sheer beauty of the place, and the cars that were parked at angles to the properties seemed as though they were clean. Even from inside the car with the windows closed shut, the air conditioning on and the stereo playing quietly in the background she could hear that it was a tranquil place. 'I bet Mum picked this one,' she heard herself saying as they pulled up in one of the three empty spaces outside the end of terrace row.

'I reckon she did, Babe,' James replied quietly, understanding completely the feeling that he knew was running through his little sister at that moment.

It had got him in the same way once he had made up his mind to go and look at it. He hadn't actually made up his mind, if he was totally honest with himself. He had been going out that morning after he'd dropped Beth at school but he'd forgotten some papers and had gone back to the house just as the postman was making his rounds. He'd recognised the packaging of the solicitor from under the man's arm as he signed for it and he'd known what it was. After about three-quarters of an hour spent staring at the package he'd opened it. There was a set of keys and the full details of the property along with the address. It seemed to leap out at him and just as Mrs. P was on her way in through the door he'd made up his mind and was off.

They both sat silently in the car for a while longer before James broke it with the sound of his door clicking open. 'Come on,' he said lightly and she nodded at him, following his lead in getting out of the car and walking up the four stone steps to the large pale green front door. With bated breath Beth followed him into the house and it was only when she saw just how beautifully kept it was that she let out a strange sigh-like sound. The hallway and stairwell were a pale peachy colour with white gloss spindles and paintwork. A pale sandy coloured carpet ran throughout the entire house, except where there were varnished wooden floors and the doors leading to the ground floor rooms were enormous. 'Do you wanna start at the top?' James asked and Beth nodded at him, letting him lead her up two broad flights of stairs in silence. There were two large double bedrooms on the second floor, one to the back and one to the front and a massive bathroom between them with corner bath, a separate shower cubicle and bidet in white porcelain. There were large windows to both the front and back on the landing and Beth looked out over the extensive gardens below and then out over the green at the front. She opened the cupboard that backed up to the stairwell and had to laugh.

'You could hold a party in here!' she said, looking back over her shoulder at James who was watching her every move. The first floor was identical to the second except for the cupboard and even though the sun was on its way down Beth couldn't get over how bright it seemed. 'It's beautiful,' she kept saying as they wandered from room to room, taking in the ornate coving and original carved skirtings. The lounge was to the front on the ground floor; it was spacious and it felt comfortable to be in, with its grand fireplace on the far wall and crisp white paintwork complemented by pale pastel walls. There was a large study to the back of the house which still had some of the original book shelves on the side wall from when it would have been a library. A reasonably sized cloakroom was tucked discreetly behind it and there were double doors leading from the hallway out onto a veranda, which in turn led down stone steps to the patio, which was also accessible from the basement and led into the landscaped garden.

They walked down another flight of stairs at the back of the hallway and down into the kitchen diner, which spanned the entire basement area. There was a door and large window to the front dining area that stared out to a small set of stone steps that led from the street above; these were decorated with potted plants and obviously hadn't been used as access for years. A fireplace took up most of the far wall in the dining area; the remainder of the wall was treated exposed brick. The shades of colour warmed the room as with the lounge above, giving it an almost rustic feel. The kitchen was pale washed wood that complemented the dark wood flooring and again, pastel shades on the walls and Beth couldn't decide whether it was a modern or country style kitchen, it just seemed to fit with the rest of the house. She let her eyes take in all around her; the plate rack, and the built-in oven, the butler sink, the discreet dishwasher and washing machine. It was all so perfect. Even larger French doors led out onto the patio and James unbolted them as he lit two cigarettes and they stepped outside into the warm evening fading sun.

'How do you feel?' he asked quietly.

Beth took a long moment to answer him and she looked around the garden.

'Do you think we should do it?' she didn't sound displeased.

'Yeah, Babe, I do. I really do,' he said honestly and she gave his arm a little squeeze.

'Then we'll do it,' she half whispered. 'If you think it's the right thing to do for us, we'll do it.'

Chapter Four

Late May 1992

Pat looked across the desk at James, then at Michael. He was waiting
for some kind of reaction to what he'd just said but none came so he
went on. 'It's the fact that we've heard nothing that bothers me though,
boys. There's respect for the dead, and this ain't it, so keep your eyes
peeled, okay? We've worn black too much lately and I for one think I
look crap in it! Makes me look ill, and it upsets Judy.' He pulled a
pained face.

'Sure, Pat, we understand!' Michael said finally. Pat looked at
him. He hadn't actually told Michael just how glad he was that he'd
decided to stay permanently, but both men knew it. It was one thing to
be there some of the time, and another entirely to change your life and
be there all the time without even being asked. He'd always said that
he imagined to others that running a business like theirs was like
having children. It can't be done at half cock, and both Andrew and
Jim had agreed with him.

'I ain't heard a thing, Uncle Pat. Not so much as a little whisper,'
James said as he lit another cigarette. 'I dunno if its good news or bad
news though, that's for sure.'

The other two men then looked at him. 'Bad news, young James.
I get the feeling that it's bad news,' Michael answered for both himself
and Pat. Neither could shake the feeling of foreboding that was all
around them. Oxley's crew were being far too quiet, as were some of
their other usual irritations.

Pat looked out of the window again, away from the boys as they
continued to talk about business and the club takings from the last

week. He looked fleetingly with annoyance at the newspaper on his desk, the headline *Double Vodka and Rape* seemed to leap out at him; the word 'rape' was in the Coca-Cola font. A play on words with little taste. Someone was very sick, very sick indeed. The club in question on the front page was owned by one of their competitors, and someone had kindly tipped off the press about how it was not a safe place to drink in, and people, the council and the do-gooders, were calling for its closure, or at least a change in management. Quite clever really; very sick, but clever and Pat couldn't help but think that these events were all connected. The Oxley Corporation were being very quiet, and in Pat's book, that meant that they were all over this and the other recent events. He closed his eyes. How long would it be before they and theirs were back in the firing line, he wondered.

June 1992

James took one last look around the house. He felt odd inside; it looked strange without their furniture and their belongings. But it wasn't a bad feeling. It was the end of something old and yet the beginning of something new and exciting. This was a good move, he thought with a forceful nod of his head. There were memories in every corner here and it would be easier to start again somewhere else. He and Beth could go on with their lives without welling up every time that walked in to a room or looked at an item of furniture or ornament.

Michael stood on the driveway having seen off the removal men. There hadn't been much need for them really. There were only a few bits of furniture from the house going to the new one. It was mostly bedroom, loft and garage boxes. All the furniture from this house had been sold off, and new purchased. Greenview Park was to be their house, their new home and it was to be filled with their furniture and belongings and just a few reminders of the past. He was dressed like something straight from Hollywood, an un-tucked, short sleeved Sherman shirt, beige mid-length shorts and brown brogues. He slid his sunglasses onto his face and smiled at her, the gesture lighting up his entire face.

'You got the keys?' she asked.

'I have!' There was a jingle from the palm of his hand.

'Okay, we're right behind you!' she added, looking pensive.

'Take your time. I'll see you in a bit,' he grinned. Beth watched him get in to his car and drive away and then she turned and walked back into the house to find James.

'You okay?' she asked, finding him in the lounge and he turned and half smiled at her, showing perfect white teeth from between sensual, pouted lips. She had suddenly grown up in so many ways, it was like she knew all his innermost secrets and fears and was easing his pain as well as her own when she smiled at him with those pretty china-like features.

'Yeah,' he sighed, taking her by the hand. 'Are you ready?' and she nodded at him.

'As I'll ever be' she replied. 'Michael's gone on ahead and the removal men had to get diesel or something,' she continued and the sting of tears got her in the throat, making her cough a little. James pulled her to him and encircled her in strong arms and she snuggled into the safety of his chest.

'Don't cry, Babe,' he said, smoothing her hair. 'This ain't the end. It's the beginning.'

She nodded. 'I know,' she said with a sniff, pulling away from him slightly and wiping her eyes with the back of her hand. 'Come on. Let's get a move on, aye?'

Beth placed a *welcome to your new home* card on the kitchen counter for the new owners, who she'd never met, and probably would never meet, and with that they walked out of the house and into the early afternoon sunshine. They moved towards the car; it was parked on the driveway in the same spot James had always used since he had started driving, under the shade of the big fir and without a backward glance they got in and closed the doors with gentle thuds. James started the engine and they pulled off the drive, past the *SOLD* sign that was nailed to the wall, and away from their past.

July 1992

Mrs. Papworth looked around the house leisurely, making the odd comment now and then as she did so. 'It's not as big, for all its floors, is it?' she said leading the way back down to the kitchen. 'But still big enough for the two of you, hey?' she added.

'Your hours won't go down, Mrs. P,' James said with a winning grin as they reached the kitchen. 'They'll probably go up, if that's okay with you. I ain't much of a cook and Aunty Judy said she'd help but I—we—' He stopped himself as she looked up into his eyes.

'I know, son,' she said, gently patting him on the hand. She was, she had to admit, more than impressed with how well the two youngsters were coping on their own. She had thought they would fall flat on their faces when she was informed that they would be moving out of the family's house and living alone together. She had been under the impression that they would stay with Pat and Judy, at least until Elizabeth had finished school but it was evident that they had no intention of doing that. They were too much like their parents had been. Determined, strong willed and she was pleased for them. 'It'll take me no longer to get here, so that's not a problem,' she mused as she busied herself making a pot of tea. Everything was where it should have been in the pale whitewashed wood kitchen. Just like their parents' house had been; everything had its place and nothing ever seemed to be out of place. 'And don't you worry about cooking. I'll do a couple of good meals a week and the rest you can split between Bethy, Judy and takeaways. And it wouldn't hurt for you to learn a bit from me. It's not like you work nine to five and won't have the time now, is it?' she added. James had to smile at her, she was so motherly and it was nice to know that she would be around. Everything seemed to run smoothly when she was about, like it had when she'd worked for his mum and dad. He'd felt bad about asking her to cut her hours down earlier in the year and during the move but it hadn't seemed worth having her there almost every day as she had been in the past. Before the sale came through, he and Beth didn't make any mess at all, then when it did come it was too messy to attempt a clear-up, what with the packing. It had been a personal time for him and Elizabeth. And Judy had kept up a supply of food not prepared in the microwave or in less than ten minutes on the hob. But just before the move he and Beth had talked and they had decided that they not only missed her housekeeping skills, but her company too and so, here she was not only back to three days a week, but more likely five, or at least until they really found their feet.

'I could stay late for Bethy some evenings when you're not in.' She always pronounced Beth's name with an 'f' rather than 'th' and James watched her mouth as she spoke. Pouring two cups of tea out she added, 'Give you a bit of time to be twenny, ey?' She laughed at her own suggestive tone.

'Cheers, Mrs. P' He smiled then and she stared at him for a long moment.

'Oh, you look like your dad when you do that,' she said wistfully as James ran his fingers through his mid brown hair and it was then that James knew that he and Beth had made another good decision. It didn't hurt when she chatted about the good old days and said things like just how much he looked like his father, in fact he quite liked it. Their mum and dad would never, ever be forgotten in their house and it was something that they still needed constantly to be reassured was okay. It was okay to feel good and laugh; they were young. But it was also okay to cry and feel sad sometimes because they had lost something as precious as their parents and of course it was going to hurt like hell; hurt like hell for a long time to come.

When Mrs. P had gone, James found himself thinking of the past, back to his childhood and it occurred to him that she had been there for those years too, that she had loved and lived with them and that she probably missed them in her own way too. He smiled then, he felt good. Not as good as he had in the past, before all of this, but good all the same.

Chapter Five

Late July 1992

The summer holidays felt strange to Elizabeth. She had been dreading feeling sad, like she had on her birthday, and that had been absolutely horrific for her. She'd woken up in tears, and gone to bed in tears and no matter what anyone said or did that day or what they bought her she couldn't shake the lonely feeling, the desolation and the desperation to have just another hour with her mum and dad. She'd just wanted to hug them both once more, smell the scent of them that had comforted her through her childhood, hear their voices once more and tell them that she loved them just once more. She and her Mum had always spent so much of the holidays together doing all manner of different things. Every day in her memory had been filled with excitement and love, genuine love, and she was pleasantly surprised when it occurred to her one bright morning that she didn't feel sad at all, she felt warm when she thought of her instead. She realised that her life was still full of excitement and love and it came at her from every direction, from friends and family alike, and that was when she really tried, made the effort to get through it.

It was a hot summer and she looked almost Mediterranean, with a deep tan that she'd started off courtesy of one of James's many girlfriends, one of his squeezes, who worked in the beauty salon on the high road. She was a rather too pretty to be anything but thick as shit kind of girl called Katherine, with a K, not a C. But thick or not, pretentious and orange or not, Beth liked her and was glad that they were still friendly even though James had long since given her the old ta-ta. He was seemingly getting through an average of a girl a week but none of them seemed to let his short-lived relationship track record bother them; far from it. It appeared to Beth that the more he went through, the more were just queuing up waiting for their turn. One evening over dinner she questioned him on it.

'What do you do to all those girls?' Her tone was as innocent as the question itself but James, being James, took it the wrong way. He looked at her for a long time, an amused smile on his face, hiding the inner fear of what would come next. They were at the sex questions stage. He was the parent for this one, and she the child.

'Why you asking?' he said, his hand to his mouth which was still full of food.

'I'm just interested.' She was casual, pushing food around her plate with her fork so that she didn't have to focus on those alert green eyes.

'Well, I shag 'em,' he replied. There was no point in lying to her. He was aware of the fact that she knew that already. He was, in fact, stalling. He didn't want to have to explain himself to his little sister, explain the male need within him, but for all the stalling, he looked at her face and knew that he'd have to, if not then, sometime soon.

'I know that!' she laughed. 'What I mean is, why is there always a line of them? What do you *do* to them?' she finished.

He was right. *Shit. Where was Michael when he needed him? He always knew what to say when she asked questions like that.* 'Oh, that!' He was the one sounding awkward then as he finished this mouthful. 'Sorry, can't say. Trade secret!' he shoved in another forkful.

'Will it happen to me?' she asked.

He coughed. 'Not by me it won't, no!'

She laughed then. 'No. For God's sake, James, you know what I mean!' He looked at her for a long moment. Her eyes shone with her innocence and he reached out and touched her hand with his.

'I hope so, Babe. I really do.' He wouldn't go on and there was no point in pressing him so she took what he said and filed it in her head with the intention of asking Michael. He always told her the truth or just said that he wasn't going to answer her.

On the days she was alone and not out with friends from school she was either with James, Pat and Judy – albeit more Judy than Pat – with Michael or with Mrs. Papworth, first name Johanna, who was teaching her the fine art of being a housekeeper, something she took to very well. She wasn't at all surprised that Beth could handle a wok and oven chips. She'd never shied away from helping her mum in the kitchen when she was younger and Mrs. P could recall more than a few occasions when she'd arrived for work and found the whole kitchen trashed and covered in flour from their baking efforts. But she took pride in teaching her how to cook full roast dinners and cakes without making a mess and secretly, how to make sloe gin with the sloes they had discovered grew in abundance at the bottom of the large, well-stocked garden. When she wasn't being entertained, Beth entertained herself with books and going out for long rides on her bike, a gift from Pat and Judy for her birthday. But no matter how far or where she went or what route she took she always found herself at the cemetery and by the end of the second week of the holidays, if she was going out on the bike she took her books or magazines out with her. She would sit for hours in the sunshine by their graves, reading and watching the world go by.

Pat watched Michael and James arrive. They walked across the car park and on passing under the window, Michael looked up and directly at Pat. He was sure Michael was psychic. He did that kind of thing all the time and it creeped him out a bit. It was like Michael just knew everything, and what you were thinking too, and for all he was really still just a kid, he was very, very clued up, and clever too, very clever.

They nodded at one another and then Pat moved away, settling back down at his desk. They entered the office after a minute or two, and immediately looked at Peter, the company accountant. He was pale faced and sat uncomfortably on one of the sofas. 'Sit down' Pat's tone was hard, it was that way for effect. He had to talk himself into being this man, playing this role. He hated firing people. They always ended up coming back and biting you in the arse. He looked at the pathetic effort on the sofa. Let him bite, fuck him. 'Peter. This meeting will be brief,' he began. 'You're fired.' There was absolute silence and James felt the laugh in his throat rise. Had Pat dragged them in just for that? He was losing it big time.

'You can't—' Peter began.

'Oh, but we can!' Michael said, his voice even harder than Pat's had been only moments before. 'You'll get six months' pay and a reference, if you want one. But that's it. No *unfair dismissal* bollocks. And no kickbacks—' Pat breathed. 'You've had the rest already.' His tone was thick with innuendo. He'd spotted Peter's game not long after the funeral. The finances had been left up to Peter and Andrew. Peter had been skimming for so long that Andrew simply hadn't noticed. It had taken a fresh look and new eyes to see it and there it was. More than two grand a month, cash. Peter's only saving grace in Pat's eyes was that he wasn't greedy. He was a thief, but not greedy; he could have taken much more.

'James, son, get the door,' Pat said, his tone now rather gentle.

'Sure.' He stood up and pulled on the handle. They watched as Peter stood up, deflated but resigned.

'Can I get my things?' he asked. Michael pointed at a storage box on the floor by the door and Peter nodded. He picked it up and without turning back, left the office and the club for good.

'Thanks!' Pat said in almost a whisper as Michael passed him on the way out.

'It's okay, Pat,' he replied and an entire conversation took place as they stood there, one that James wasn't privy to. He wasn't annoyed about it either, and that was the strange thing; he had secrets, conversations and dealing with Michael too and it occurred to him that Michael didn't tell him that he was aware of the day's agenda because Pat had talked with him about it in private. When Michael was told something in confidence, it stayed that way. It was how it was and it was how they liked it. It was just another reason Michael was Michael, all honour and brawn.

August 1992

Beth had been in bed for about two hours but she couldn't sleep. She couldn't hear the people downstairs in the kitchen but she was aware that there were people down there. She looked at the clock, it was just past midnight and then with a sigh she climbed from the bed, pulled on a pair of cotton trousers and top and padded silently down two flights of stairs and into the kitchen. James and Michael sat with Jason and another young man around the dining table smoking and drinking and laughing. She couldn't remember his name, although she knew that she knew him. James and Michael had so many friends. She watched them, unnoticed, for what felt like a long time from the stairs and then Michael looked up at her with large brown eyes. He focused on her immediately, as if he had been aware of her since she had first arrived and he smiled at her warmly. 'Ah! It's the baby!' he said gently and three other pairs of eyes focused on her.

'Did we wake you up, Babe?' James asked motioning with his hand for her to join them at the table and she walked across the room and settled herself next to him.

'No. I just couldn't sleep. Am I disturbing you?'

They all looked at each other. Was it okay for her to be in there with them?

'God no!' Michael exclaimed before any of the others could say either yes or no. She wasn't, she knew, but it was out of courtesy that she asked. It always paid to be polite, something her mother had taught her.

'How do?' Jason smiled and she shrugged.

'Good, you?' She sounded so much older than she was that it was quite startling.

'Yeah, Good thanks'. His reply was light. He liked Beth. Most of their mates had little brothers and sisters and they were usually really annoying, but Beth was really cool, like one of the lads, you just had to watch what you said to her, not in front of her.

'You've met Darren, ain't you, Babe?' James enquired and Beth smiled across at Darren as he pulled off his glasses and looked at her with small blue eyes. 'Yeah. You all right?' She smiled at him.

'Yes mate, I'm all right.' There was a pause.

'What you lot doing?' She was fiddling with the carton of cigarettes in front of her on the table. She had just then noticed that the edge of the lid had been ripped off.

They had obviously been having a smoke and fleetingly she glanced at the ashtray. It had un-smoked cigarette butts and scrunched up Rizla papers in it. She looked up and found that Michael was watching her every move and it was as if he could almost hear her thoughts. Without a word he passed her the joint he had been holding. It had gone out and with the other hand he passed her a plastic clipper lighter.

'Mike!' James exclaimed, his tone shocked but holding amusement.

'Oh, what?' he replied, waving his hand up to brush off James's comment.

'Don't give 'er that!'

Michael smiled. 'Why ever not?' He was stoned, his face flushed, his eyes glazed slightly. James's outburst was amusing to him, he wanted to hear the answer to this one.

'Coz it's a joint and she's a minor!' James replied as both Darren and Jason began to laugh at the ongoing conversation.

'Oh, so she can smoke cigarettes, drink alcohol, stay up all night long with a bunch of puff smoking, half cut men but not smoke a bit of a joint herself?' He laughed then, tilting his head down in question and James raised his eyebrows. 'I know! Let's send her out into the world without all this experience and let her find out about it all with a load of Fiesta-driving one-strokes—'

James was pondering the logic of it. If they let her do these things she wouldn't go off the rails with her pals, but if they let her do these things—He stopped. He couldn't justify why she shouldn't. He was beaten.

'Well?' Michael went on waiting for James's retort but it was too late. Not that he was going to say anything, he had the defeated expression on his face then and besides, Beth was lighting the thing and she inhaled a little of the smoke like someone who had done it before and James pursed his lips at Michael.

'I'd say it's not her first time doing that,' Jason smiled as he watched her.

'A real pro!' Darren agreed, his eyes glazed from the smoke he had been inhaling that night.

'Mind, it's strong,' Michael warned her, aware that James was scowling at him. He'd obviously let Beth smoke it before tonight and it niggled him a bit.

He let her do pretty much what she wanted but Michael always seemed to be one step ahead. It didn't bother him that much, but he sometimes got to feeling that maybe his mum and dad were up there somewhere looking down on them, and what would they see? He closed his eyes. They'd see their son and their daughter and their friend. They were happy, well, as happy as they could be. He hoped that they'd smile. 'Well, I'd say it's a bit fucking late now!' He was laughing now, as were the others.

All of their friends knew how well James was doing with Beth. It couldn't be easy for him to bring up his baby sister almost entirely on his own no matter how much financial security they had. No, they didn't envy James on that score and instead they all felt a strange kind of pride towards their friend. She was such a nice girl, which was something that surprised everyone because James could be such a complete pain in the arse and she was so funny with her quick wit. And on top of that, Jason mused as he watched her take another lug of the joint, she was going to be an absolute stunner when she was a little older. Rich, good-looking and clued up, the only downer was going to be getting past James and Michael. Now that he couldn't wait to see.

A few days later Beth opened the front door to find Michael standing at it. He looked more than a little pissed off. He was dressed in a suit, but it was obvious that he hadn't been home since the previous day. 'Your phone's off!' he said, following her inside.

'E-mail's on, it's charging,' she replied over her shoulder. She caught the waft of cigarettes and perfume and turned to look at him. 'Did she not have a shower?'

Michael scowled at her. 'Is he up yet?' was the response. Obviously not in the mood for small-talk.

'Don't be daft. It's not even eight yet. You want a drink? I'll get him up for you.'

He stopped and breathed. 'Yeah, thanks.' He was calmer then and he managed a smile for her, realising that she was just trying to be nice. She had no idea of what was going on around her and that alone made him feel bad. He for one was sure that she was more mature and capable of handling this crap than some of the others actually in the middle of it all.

Beth disappeared up the stairs as Michael made his way down into the kitchen. Minutes later she went back down. 'Give him five!' she smiled.

'Grand. Tea?' He busied himself at the countertop.

'Michael, is there a problem?' she asked then.

'Nope!' he lied.

'So why do I feel like there is?'

He still didn't look at her. 'PMT?' he suggested. He'd go with the embarrassment. That'd make her back down.

'Bollocks!' was the reply he got. He was saved from having to give a response as James came down the stairs.

'What do you want, you ugly bastard?' was his greeting. He was smiling, then he caught the look on his friend's face and stopped.

'You know that thing we were talking about?' Michael said, keeping his tone light. James nodded, looking suddenly more awake than he had a few minutes before. 'Well, it happened!' he finished.

Beth watched James's face. Was it a good thing or a bad thing? He didn't flinch in front of her. He just looked at her. 'Go and get my phone for me, Babe?' he asked her.

She huffed. 'Funny handshakes, secret handshakes, boy conversations—' She half sighed then. She knew that he just wanted her out of the room for a few minutes and there was no argument from her. He waited until she'd gone before looking back at Michael.

'How much damage?' he asked then. Michael shrugged 'Rough guess, I'd say about ten, maybe twelve—' and he waited a few seconds for James to respond.

'Fuck me!' was all James could manage.

'They did, James,' Michael breathed.

'Anyone hurt?' James asked suddenly then.

'No. Everyone was gone.' Michael's answer pleased James. He hated dealing with injured bystanders; they were like thrush, very irritable cunts, cunts that didn't go away no matter how much money you spent on them or threw at them.

'What about the old bill?' James lit a cigarette.

'We said it was just one of those Friday night things. Unless we part with the tapes there's nothing they can do. And we like it that way!' Michael was still very calm. After all, there was nothing they could do, the damage was, literally, already done.

James breathed and focused. 'Did you tell Pat yet?'

Michael scoffed at him then, and pulled an indignant expression. 'No, I thought I'd leave that part up to you!' There was almost a smile there, too.

'Oh thanks, yeah, cheers!' James raised a cup in cheers to him.

'Hey, he's your uncle!'

Both hands went up in mock-surrender. 'Don't I know it!' James said flatly.

September 1992

Beth pulled at her hair irritably and let out several huffs and puffs of anger. She was late for school and wasn't in the mood for her hair to do its own thing. James looked across the kitchen to where she stood in front of the mirror. He was dressed for work in a suit and his expression showed concern at the way she tugged at that amazing hair. 'God damn it!' She stamped her foot in frustration. 'I don't need this today!'

He watched a while longer. 'What you tryin' to do?' he asked then and Beth spun around to face him.

'A simple friggin' ponytail,' she snapped. It wasn't going to work. It never did when she wanted it to. It only ever looked great when she was practising in the mirror, exactly the same as her make-up. 'Maybe I'll get it cut off!' she whinged.

'Bollocks you will! Come 'ere!' he sighed in mock anger. 'And don't swear. It makes you look ugly.'

'Sorry!' Beth did as he said and he turned her bodily around by her shoulders so that her back was to him as he stood up.

'Brush,' he said holding out his hand and she passed it to him, handle first. She felt him run it through with swift strokes and snatching the band from her wrist he secured her hair in a neat ponytail at the nape of her neck. 'There!' he said twirling her tresses in his fingers. 'Can we go now?'

Beth moved away from him and checked it in the mirror. It wasn't half bad, not a stray hair in sight. She looked back at him, giving him a little smile of appreciation. It was strange, the things they missed. But what was stranger was just how much they did do between them.

James waited until Beth disappeared into the crowds of uniforms filing through the gates before pulling out onto the snail's pace stream of traffic leading back into the town centre. He turned the radio down and dialled in a pre-saved number on his phone. 'I'm on me way now!' was all he said into the receiver before clearing the call and pulling off down a side turning. James pulled up in the Hothouse car park and got out of the car. By the time he'd walked across to the doors Michael had come down from the office and was waiting for him. James noticed how tired Michael looked that morning and before business was discussed he made the usual comments. 'Do candles, wicks and burning them at both ends ring any bells with you, boy?' he said suggestively.

'Kettle and black?' Michael retorted with a smile.

'Yeah, yeah, whatever,' James said with a wave of his hand. 'What's up?'

Michael sighed. 'Suppliers. Again!' Michael now sounded bored with the topic of conversation, but it was actually irritation. He was tired and pissed off and it wasn't even nine o'clock.

'For fuck's sake! Can't the friggin' muppet just quit it!' James exploded. Following Michael inside, he was all swinging arms and hand gestures. 'He's got stamina, I'll give the man that.'

'Okay, Mike, what's the rub?' James breathed.

Michael picked up a wad of papers and invoices from the bar and flicked through them. 'Out of date beer and lager. The pump stuff seemed okay until we tried it. The labels and packing are wrong. We've got soda, Coke and lemonade but Christ knows which it which. If it wasn't costing us money it'd be funny.' He raised his eyebrows at James who was standing there, looking too calm. His face was devoid of expression and he was staring into the distance, at the dance floor with no particular focus.

'I remember when me Dad first brought me in 'ere. It was a fuckin' right old state.' He looked at Michael who nodded, also remembering the past for a brief moment and then he looked back across the dance floor. 'We can't fail, Mike. No matter what happens, we can't do it!'

Michael agreed with a nod. 'So, what do you want to do?' he asked, but there was no way that he needed to really. He could read James like a book, blank faced or not. This was war again but so long as things stayed as petty as having the barrels switched and the packaging changed on drinks, and not having the places ransacked, so be it.

Chapter Six

October 1992

The front door opened reasonably quietly but someone or something leaned on it and it crashed to the wall, sending the knocker and the letterbox clattering to a standstill. Beth sat up in her bed, her heart pounding in her chest from the shock of the noise. She listened and after a few seconds she heard voices. It was James. He was obviously drunk because his speech was slurred and his tone had risen. Getting out of bed she pulled on her earlier discarded tracksuit bottoms and went to the door. From the landing she looked down the stairs. He was there, clinging to Michael's shoulder and there was no question, he was absolutely plastered. 'Good night?' she asked getting Michael's attention and James raised his head and tried to focus on her but it was no good. He had no will to help himself at that point. 'You frightened the shit out of me!'

'Sorry, it was him. Grand night, can't you tell?' He tried to keep his voice light but she knew that tone, it was an apology even thought they were both aware that it wasn't Michael who should be apologising. James didn't need goading into drinking so much, or indeed anything else.

'Just drink?' She reached the bottom step.

'Yes. But rather too much I think, eh?'

James raised his head and tried to focus. 'Stop talking about me!' James almost gargled and both had to suppress their amusement.

'Come on, chuckle, let's get you to bed,' Beth purred.

'I love you,' he slurred. 'Bethy. I really love you.'

She took an arm. 'I love you too, James. Come on now, up to bed.' Beth took some of his weight on her arm and together she and Michael got him to the landing. It was some struggle because his legs kept buckling beneath his body. But Beth noticed how much of his weight Michael took and it occurred to her that the only reason James wasn't over his shoulder was that he was worried for his clothes and the fact that James would probably throw up on them. 'Did he puke yet?' It was said as if he always got into this state but they both knew that this was a rarity.

'Not yet, but he did eat so I guess we'll just wait.' Michael looked up at the next flight of stairs, they seemed to loom before them.

'Spare room?' Beth suggested, also daunted by the thought of getting him up another flight of stairs.

'Excellent idea.' Michael's tone was strained. He was tired and obviously concerned about his friend. He shouldn't have let him get into that state. But who was he to tell a grown man to stop, that maybe he'd had enough, especially in his own club.

'He smells like the barrel,' Beth observed as James breathed on her in heavy huffs.

'Ah now, that's because I think he drank it.' Michael laughed then. They had to see the funny side of it; if they didn't they would probably have dropped him on the floor and walked away from him.

Once on the bed they pulled his shirt and trousers from his body, change and keys scattering into the corners of the room. 'I'll get a bowl,' Beth said.

'Don't bother, just get a bath towel. His aim'll be shite.' Michael had a point. James couldn't even stand, alone let alone throw up into the confines of a bowl so she went into the bathroom and came back into the room with a large towel. She laid it beside where Michael had got him on to his side. He was sound asleep and for the state he was in, Beth noticed that he looked remarkably peaceful.

'Come on,' Michael touched her lightly on the arm and she looked up at him. 'You can make me a very large, very strong coffee.'

December 1992

Not a thing had changed since the last time Beth had been to the cemetery two weeks before. There were no more headstones near her parents' graves and it even felt as if the same flowers were there too. It was strange to observe people's habits in such a way. Always the same graves were kept tidy and always the same ones looked untouched and unloved. She settled herself down on her haunches in front of the two thick slabs of shaped marble and placed the two single yellow roses that she had bought on her way there from school in front of them. The stones had recently been washed and she was pleased by it in a small way. They were, after all, paying to have it done and she thought that Mum and Dad would appreciate the gesture. It was her way of saying that even though she didn't go all the time, she was always thinking of them and always would. She reached out and touched the engraved words, first on her father's gravestone and then her mother's.

Andrew Dobson
Loving husband, father, brother and friend.
Tragically taken from us without a word of goodbye
Died January 29th 1992
Aged 49 years.

Louise Dobson
The most wonderful mother and friend the world knew
Always now with her beloved husband Andrew
Died January 29th 1992
Aged 46 years.

'I miss you,' she said out loud. 'I feel bad though, coz it doesn't hurt so much any more. James said you'd understand. He's being *so* great. *So* strong for us, but you know that, don't you?' she went on looking up at the sky above her. 'He still can't come here. He hasn't said it, but I know. You understand that, too, don't you?' She was silent with her thoughts again for a long while. She felt people walking by her, she could hear them slow down in their step as they read the stones over her shoulder and could almost feel the pity they gave out to her but she didn't mind it. 'I should go soon,' she sighed. 'I haven't told James where I am and he worries about me.' She laughed then, thinking about how much like their father James was becoming despite his youth.

Walking out of the cemetery towards the bus stop Beth pulled her overcoat closed around her uniform and hitched her bag further up on her shoulder. She hesitated. Leaning up against an expensive-looking dark coloured, sleek saloon wrapped up in a large full-length navy blue overcoat was Michael. He had his head down and he smiled at her from beneath dark lashes and a day's growth of dark stubble. 'You want to go for a ride with me, little girl?' he asked as she approached and she laughed at his suggestive low tone and deep facial expression.

'Pervert!' she said leaning forwards and planting a light kiss on his cheek in greeting. Her nose was cold upon his cheek and he instinctively placed a warm finger on it 'What are you doing here?' she asked then.

'I was just driving down the road and I saw some strange girl coming out of the cemetery and I thought to myself, now I bet her brother doesn't know where she is. I'd better stop and give her a lift home!' That was a lie. He had seen her outside the school, he was going to offer her a lift home, seeing as he was in the area, but had seen that she walked in the opposite direction from home. He followed her on foot until the florist's and on seeing her enter it, had gone back for the car. He knew where she was off to and something inside him felt sad suddenly.

He'd sat in the car park watching her for maybe an hour and it was only when he saw her walking towards the gates that he got out.

'Where were you going?' she asked then.

'To your house actually. I've just been to Pat's and he's not there so I thought I'd stop in on you two before I go to the airport. I'm going back to Mum and Dad's for a few days.'

Beth looked a little sad. 'James isn't in. He'll be at the club by now, won't he!' she said glancing at her watch.

'Grand. I'll take you there then!' he said firmly, opening the passenger door for her.

'Home's fine, Michael.' Her tone was blunt.

'Elizabeth—' he began.

'Michael!' she interrupted. 'Haven't we had this conversation?'

Michael smiled at her little statement of independence. 'Okay, okay,' he said. He recognised the tone of her voice. She didn't need babysitting and he knew it. He just didn't much like the idea of her spending so much time on her own. 'Sorry,' he said and he meant it. She wasn't fourteen in his or anyone else's eyes. She didn't look it or indeed, sound it and fleetingly he wondered if she would one day look back and regret missing these most wondrous years of teenage discovery.

New Year 1993

'Three; two; one; Happy New Year!' was the cheer that went up in the wine bar and then there were kisses and hugs from every direction as the music blared out of the speakers. Beth looked up into James's eyes and gave him a little smile. It hadn't been as bad as they had both secretly thought it would be; maybe they *were* really just getting used to being on their own. 'Happy New Year, Babe,' he mouthed to her. Screeching above the noise around them would have been pointless. He wrapped his arms around her and gave her a bear hug and then he took her about the waist and lifted her off the floor, settling her across his shoulder like a fireman would.

'No James! You'll drop me!' she shrieked into his ear and she felt him shake his head against her hip at her fears. She had no faith in him at all, he thought. 'Take me over there.' She was laughing now and although he didn't see what direction she was pointing in he began to move across the bar. 'Happy New Year, Uncle Pat' she said and he planted a kiss on her cheek.

'Happy New Year, darlin' he smiled, giving her cheek a light pinch. She felt another pair of hands on her and was dragged from James's body. Michael heaved her up on to his shoulder and supported her with one arm. He carried her around the bar and she felt infinitely safer on his shoulder than she had on James's. He kept pausing so that she could kiss and hug everyone who danced and wandered past them in the crowds, and it was crowded.

The capacity for Baileys was two hundred and it was packed to the rafters with friends and family. It had truly been a great night. James and Beth had been determined that it would be; the only thing they both thought was how much they missed their mum and dad.

'There's your mum. Take me there,' Beth said and Michael spun around, giving his mother a warm smile. 'Eve, Eve. Happy New Year.'

'And to you, Elizabeth, and to you.' She laughed at the pair of them and watched then as they made their way away from her.

'You want to get down now?' Michael asked and he put Beth down on unsteady feet.

January 1993

'You bastards!' James's voice rang out as the all-too-familiar strip tease music began and a rather large, half-naked black woman wobbled towards him from between parting male bodies on the dance floor.

'Don't you go blaming us. It was your sister's idea!' Michael managed between gasps of laughter. 'I just booked her!'

James grinned. 'Her allowance is so fucking cancelled!' he screamed with laughter as the woman gyrated in front of him, reaching out for him and when he was finally cornered she touched him. Her fingers were gentle and expert, she pulled at his shirt and unbuttoned it with one hand.

'Just you relax, honey,' she cooed. 'You're gonna love every inch of me, I promise.' With that, she pulled at her own items, flimsy cheap chiffon articles held together with poppers. Michael could hardly bear to watch as she rubbed her more-than-ample breasts in his friend's face. Now Michael liked them big but this, this was gross. No wonder Beth had begged him not to ask questions, just asked him to book it. It was priceless. He reached over the bar and grabbed at the camera he'd seen one of the waitresses put behind it earlier. He began then to behave like David Bailey and moved around his friend, practically pushing other men out of the way.

'Go on there, James, give us a big old smile!'

James was now seated on a chair that had appeared from nowhere and she squatted above him, baby oil in hand. 'Just relax,' she whispered. 'This isn't going to be *too* filthy.'

James was still grinning. 'She is so fucking grounded when I get home!' and he laughed, wiping baby oil from his face and hands with a bar towel. 'What's she like, ey?' he continued but Michael couldn't answer. He was still laughing and his stomach ached from the act.

Chapter Seven

March 1993

Beth followed James into the house. It was cold outside and the warmth of the central heating hit them both like a warm fuzzy wall. She stopped in her tracks for a second or two. Something was different inside the house. There was an air that she couldn't quite find a place in her mind for.

'I am so hungry!' she said finally, changing the subject in her head after looking around her. Nothing seemed or looked different.

'Me, too. Busy day, Babe, very busy day!'

She turned to look at him. 'You said you hadn't done anything when I asked you in the car!'

James looked sheepish. 'Yeah! Its hard work doing nothing, y'know!' he replied, stalling. She looked harder at him, her eyes almost merging with his. He was lying to her, she could see and smell it. What was going on?

'Is Mrs. P still here?' Beth asked, the smell of a casserole wafting up the stairs.

'Dunno,' he shrugged casually, pulling off his jacket and draping it over the banister. Beth did the same, and as she did she noticed a set of keys on the stairs. She looked up at James as he leaned against the hallway wall, crossing his arms. He knew she'd seen them.

'But someone's—home!' It was a statement. Her facial expressions changed several times in those few seconds. 'He's here!' she gasped, her eyes bright.

'Better go and have a look, ay?' he smiled, and before he could say any more Beth was off up the stairs, taking two at a time.

She bounded up to the second floor and as she got there the spare room door opened and Michael appeared at it. 'It would appear we're house sharing!' he smiled, putting down the clothes he had in his hand.

'You said yes!' she laughed as he picked her up off the floor and gave her a big hug.

'Now, how could I turn down such an offer? James called me at the weekend, I flew in last night got my stuff together and here I am.'

She was thrilled. Really thrilled. She was almost crying. 'What about the house?' she said suddenly. 'Going to rent it out, some time?'

He smiled his reply as he thought just how much she sounded like him. Thinking of more than what was right in front of her. It would hold her in good stead in the future, he was sure of it and he knew then that coming to live with them was the right move. He'd pondered it in the weeks since they'd first mentioned it to him, weighing up the pros and cons of such a set up. How it would be, what people would say. He'd already heard whispers that he and James were gay lovers. But those comments had come from jealous people, who didn't understand just how deep their relationships ran. It was after an evening at his parents' home spent thinking of the amount of time he did spend with them, all the laughter they shared and how much he missed them when he made that short journey back to his empty house just a few miles away that he decided to accept.

May 1993

Mrs. P put her key in the lock and she and Judy walked through the front door after meeting on the street outside just as Michael, followed closely by James, chased Beth up from the basement in a haze of screams and laughter. Both men were soaking wet and Mrs. P put her hand to her mouth to stem the gawking as she saw the plastic water rifle in Michael's hand. None of the three noticed the two women stood at the door for a second or two and then abruptly they stopped in their tracks as if of one mind. Beth, pausing on the second stair up to the first floor looked at Michael. He smiled at her, seizing the opportunity of the moment and without a word he sprayed her, soaking her face, neck and top. 'No!' she shrieked as the water splattered the painted walls and carpet and then for a second or two all that could be heard were heavy breaths as the three focused again on the front door.

'What in God's name?' Mrs. P began but it was too late. Before she'd got any further in speech or movement James's multi-coloured rifle appeared from nowhere and her face was soaked. 'Why you little shh—' she began and then she stopped, laughter getting the better of her.

'Don't even think about it!' Judy said, pointing her finger out in front of her, her tone clipped as James aimed at her. He smiled then, lowering his rifle. He glanced at Michael as Judy went to speak and he fired, getting her in the side of the head with freezing cold water as she tried to get out of his way.

'Enough!' Mrs. P yelled, holding up her hand. 'That's it. Playtime over!'

Down stairs they stood in the dining area, drying themselves on warm towels from the tumble dryer. Mrs. P busied herself boiling the kettle, in preparation of the long day ahead of her, and Judy sat, still not sure of whether to laugh at their antics or not. There was always something going on in their house and it always reminded her of the Madness song, *Our House*. 'Never a dull moment, ey, Judy?' Mrs. P called over her shoulder.

'No, Jo, I dunno how you put up with 'em,' she replied.

'Coz she loves us, don't ya, Mrs. P' James said, making his way across the expanse of room towards her.

'I'm afraid it is, son,' she smiled, touching his face with a warm hand.

July 1993

Having run out of sensible things to do with a bored fifteen-year-old during the seemingly endless days of the school holidays, when there were no friends around Michael decided to take it upon himself to teach Beth how to drive. She'd learn soon enough, he'd thought, justifying his actions and he'd rather it was properly. Repairing the damage to a sloppy driving manner would cost a fortune in professional driving lessons. He'd slipped Steve, the chef at the Hothouse, fifty pounds to let Beth drive around the car park in his little car, a burgundy Fiesta that had really seen better days. Steve hadn't accepted the money, but with a grin had passed her the keys. 'Y'd know Jimmy will go off bang, don't ya?' he'd laughed.

'Only if someone tells him,' had been Michael's light, but subtle statement reply.

Beth had been behind the wheel for less than half an hour, and Michael had to admit that she was really rather good, an obvious natural, albeit somewhat nervous. He'd slowly let off the hand brake and Beth had held the car steady on its biting point for the third or fourth time. 'Now take your foot off the clutch really lightly and ease down on the accelerator,' he said. Beth followed his instructions to the letter.

'This is easy, Michael!' she laughed as the car began to move around the empty car park in the early afternoon sunshine.

'That's it. Now, change up to third,' he instructed.

'Oops.' She laughed as the car gave a little shudder when she put it into fifth and not third the first time around.

'The gearbox is small. Tight, like a—' he began and she glanced at him in question with raised eyebrows.

'Tight like a what?' she asked, already half knowing what he was going to say.

'Forget it, no matter. What I mean is that you don't have to reach for the gears; it'll go in naturally, all on its own, it just needs a gentle talking to.' He gave her a sideways glance as he spoke.

He always found her embarrassment slightly amusing, and yet it always startled him, bearing in mind that she was now living in a house with two of London's hottest male commodities and surrounded on all sides by rude, hard men who swore and talked about women and sex like it was making a cup of tea. Not a day went by, he mused, that someone didn't suggest or say something inappropriate in front of her. It was never at her, obviously; who would be that stupid? But all the same, her innocence in that area was very endearing to him.

'Oh, okay.' She spoke with some scepticism but upon trying again she got it exactly right. She grasped changing gear and they drove around and around in large circles as the sun went down.

'Now. Reverse,' he smiled and Beth got the impression from his tone that he was expecting it to be a tough lesson.

'We can stop?' she suggested in the half-light, not wanting to press him but he shook his head. He had absolute faith in her ability.

'Oh no Elizabeth, it's not you, it's me. I wonder if I'm good enough for this one,' he laughed.

''Course you are, you're good at everything, Michael,' she replied with a wave of her hand in his direction. 'I've known you all my life and I've never known you to fuck up yet.' She gave him a big grin.

'Language,' he laughed and then she gave him her cute, apologetic look.

By five o'clock she would have been ready for the roads if she were allowed. They'd chatted and laughed the hours away as Beth had gone around and around the huge car park, in and out of spaces, backwards and forwards, and both were relaxed and very pleased with her efforts. Michael told her to park the car back in its original spot, but she lost her nerve reversing it back into the space between two other cars and he agreed that perhaps it was a little optimistic for the first day. But all in all, Michael was pleased with her progress and impressed with his own instruction. She was calm, confident and above all else, she hadn't hit anything!

'Now' he said, his voice taking on the tone he only used when very serious, which wasn't too often at all really. 'You have to promise that you won't drive unless I'm with you.' He pointed his finger lightly in her direction and she nodded solemnly at him.

'I promise!' she said taking off her seat belt.

'I'm serious now, Elizabeth. No showing off to your friends when you're out, do you hear? It's dangerous and it's not clever to show off, you know?' He paused, a smile crossing his dark features. 'And for the sake of God in heaven, don't tell Pat!'

'Okay!' she smiled and Michael shook his head at her.

'He'll have me hanging by dusk,' he said, shaking his head in mock fear.

August 1993

The sun beat down hot and hard on the vast expanse of rolling open fields and the difference in temperature with the air conditioning on inside the car was quite breathtaking, as was the view. Getting out of the car, James walked around and opened the boot. He'd said nothing since they'd pulled off the A12, which was maybe eight miles back, in what Beth thought was the opposite direction to that which they were now pointing.

'What we doing?' Beth asked after getting out and taking in more of the view of golden fields and a small village far into the distance. 'And where are we?' she added.

'Suffolk' he said, popping his head up above the boot to look at her.

'Really? Thank you!' she replied sarcastically.

'Oh, um about ten miles out of Ipswich,' he said, being a little more exact, but not too much.

'And what are we doing here?' she asked again, a little more impatiently this time. 'Is there a body in the boot?' she laughed then. James looked over at her across the car. 'Ah ha?' he smiled wickedly then, putting something into the back of his jeans as he closed the boot down again. 'That's the fun bit! But no, no bodies today.'

Beth looked away. 'Fun bit?' she asked, shaking her head at him then. She both loved and hated it when he was being mysterious. She had to admit that it was very rare for him to not please her but the waiting and the guessing at times like this got the better of her typically patient nature.

'I'm besting the Mick!' he smiled with a determined nod of his head.

'You're what?' Beth looked really confused.

'I'm besting the Mick!' he said again.

'Why, how?' she toyed with her hair as it settled on her shoulder.

'Coz I was gonna teach you to drive,' he said, his voice tight.

'Oh.'

She sounded a bit awkward and then he grinned at her, showing off his immaculate, straight white teeth. 'So, I had to think of something even better to teach you,' and he raised a finger.

'And have you?' she asked feeling brighter suddenly, seeing that his grin was going to stay.

'Yeah. I have' he grinned again, pulling a small silver handgun from the back of his trousers.

'Jesus Christ, James!' she exclaimed with a gasp of real shock. 'Is it real?' she leaned in to touch it.

'Yep. It was Dad's.' He smiled then, a little sadly and she looked into his eyes as they leaned on the bonnet of the car in the mid-morning sunshine.

They were lost in distant memories of years gone by and Beth could just imagine her dad tutoring a young James on how to use a handgun. It would have been so typically Dad, teaching James something like that, as to him, she mused, it would have been like teaching him to change a tyre. 'Did he teach you how to use it, then?' she asked, breaking the peaceful silence.

'Yeah, he did. And to drive and—' he paused for a few seconds. 'He taught me almost everything I know. Now its my turn to pass all this *useful* information on to you.' He laughed then; it was a sound that warmed her whenever she heard it, it was so natural and reminded her of their childhood when that was the only sound that could be heard in their house. They were quiet for a while again, deep in their own thoughts and far away, back in the past as they watched the beauty of the place they now stood in.

'Useful?' she said thoughtfully.

'Yeah, if our lives've shown us anything, it's that you never know, Babe.'

She studied him. 'Is it easy?' she asked finally, reaching out and touching it lightly with her fingertips.

He passed it to her handle first. It was light and she instinctively grasped at it around the trigger. 'It ain't loaded yet,' he said, watching her point it out in front of her. 'And as for being easy, I reckon we should find out, don't you?' His tone was almost excited and she had to react in the same way.

'Absolutely!'

Beth ran her left hand over her forehead to wipe away a bead of sweat that threatened to run down into her eyes. Being out on such a day was nice, but in the middle of the field with no shade at all was something else entirely.

'Now, remember the kick back!' James said leaning back on the bonnet of the car crossing his arms across his bare chest.

'It's not that. It's the bloody noise,' Beth said. 'Are you sure that no one can hear us?' she looked very nervous.

'You're standing here in jeans and ya bra and you're asking that? Will you chill out, Babe, I promise there ain't a soul for about five miles,' he said pushing his sunglasses up a little.

'Okay, if you're sure?' She was sceptical. She took aim and pulled the trigger, supporting the little silver handgun with both hands. The crack didn't seem as loud as the last couple and she wondered fleetingly if she was just getting used to the noise.

'Top girl' he exclaimed as the can she had been aiming at jumped into the air from its perch on a milk crate about twenty-five feet away from where they stood.

'I got it,' she laughed, turning her head to look at him, remembering to keep the gun pointed away from him this time.

'Yep. Now do it again,' he said, still grinning at her. He was thrilled, really thrilled. This was fun.

September 1993

Beth walked into the club through the open kitchen door. She was greeted with warm smiles from the small group of kitchen staff, who were preparing themselves for another busy Friday night of feeding people so that they could stay and drink more. It was an odd sight to see in the kitchen of a popular nightclub; a young girl in her school uniform complete with tote bag, white socks and flat shoes – well, as flat as Beth was going to wear. 'Where's my brother?' she asked, as Steve looked up from the stainless steel counter at her. He usually went off the wall when non-essential people were in his kitchen, management or not, especially on a Friday but on seeing her he smiled, a rarity in itself. He had never raised so much as an eyebrow at her, let alone his voice, and he'd known her since she was knee high to a grasshopper.

'He's in the bar, my lovely. Did you eat yet? I've got some lamb here with a rather nice sauce.' He held up the pan he'd been stirring intently to show her. 'I'll do you some with spinach mash, yeah?' He was tempting her, and she surrendered to him with a warm smile. It did all smell rather good.

'Are you sure it's not too much bother?' she asked then, and he shook his head at her. It wasn't, she knew, but she asked anyway.

He was such a nice bloke, she thought. A bit aggressive and shouty with people, sure, but he never had been with her. She was Elizabeth, James's baby sister, Pat's niece, Michael's ward and on top of that she would one day join the business. But she had a sneaking suspicion that it was none of that that made him nicer to her than anyone else. It was that she wasn't and had never been even remotely intimidated by him, even though she knew all about where he'd learned his culinary skills, in the kick. She knew that he respected her coolness, especially when everyone else about him panicked when he lost his little red-faced temper. She'd seen bigger men than him go off at an angle, as her dad used to say, and indeed do.

'You go on in, I'll have it brought out.'

'Cheers, Steve, you are a darling.' She sounded really cheerful and he grinned at her, the gesture making his hard features soften and it was at moments like that that she realised that he was actually quite a young man, maybe early thirties, no more. It was his ever-present frown that aged him so much and she gave him another smile over her shoulder as she left. Steve liked Beth, always had, but he liked her more for the way she'd bounced back from the death of her parents, and all the crazy shite that was thrown her way. He liked the way she took no shit from anyone, especially him, and he liked the way she was always like a breath of fresh air, in what was, and could be a very tiring, tedious job.

She wandered into the main bar through the swing door leading from the kitchens and made her way across to where James sat smoking a cigarette. He was looking at some papers and Giles, the bar manager, looked decidedly wary. It was obvious that James had already taken a chunk out of him for something or other, probably the takings again. Figures without breasts attached were definitely *not* James's strong point and on more than one occasion in the past Beth had looked over the takings with him at home. She was always able to make the books tally and it was often said, even by their new accountant, that she would probably end up doing just that in years to come and put him out of a job.

James's entire face lit up when he saw her and he held out his hand to her, taking her fingers in his own as she kissed him on the cheek and put her bag down on the floor beside them. 'Did you have a nice day, Babe?' He was gentle now.

'Yeah. You?' She tilted her head to the side at him as she spoke, making it plain that she knew that he had been having a go at Giles.

'I've had better. You hungry?' He changed the subject none too subtly.

'Yeah, Steve's doing me some dinner.' She said it as if he offered his culinary services and free food to everyone who dared to enter his kitchen.

'Fuck me! You're touched, ain't ya? I just got bawled out coz I went for the fridge. I won't be doing that again, I can tell you!'

She giggled then. 'What? he's a honey,' she smiled, giving him the hint of a cheeky grin. 'You working tonight?' She then changed the subject again, and lighting a cigarette he nodded at her.

'Yeah, someone's got to run this fucking place!' His tone rose and he looked at Giles. The comment wasn't lost on him and he edged off his seat beside them. 'Are you still 'ere?' James snapped then, looking directly at him. 'Go away! I'm talking with my sister!'

Giles didn't need telling twice; James had hardly finished his sentence and he was off across the bar and away up the stairs towards the office. 'When you gonna quit school and come and work with me, ey?' He was smiling again and she shook her head at him.

'Turn it in,' she laughed, coining his phrase. 'If I did leave school you'd have a pink one!'

James looked at her. 'True, Babe, true.'

'You here all night?' she asked.

'Yeah, why?' He saw that she looked disappointed and he flicked through his mental diary; had he forgotten something?

'Oh, I just fancied going out, that's all,' she sighed.

James looked long and hard at her, then he smiled. 'I got a plan!' he said, his eyes sparkling and that much was obvious from the expression on his face.

'Go on?' she said, leaning in.

'Eat whatever God in there provides for you–' he waved a hand towards the kitchen doors. 'We'll nip home, you can change then we'll come back 'ere'. Beth looked at him as if he'd just grown another head. Sure, she'd been in the club before, but had never been his idea. 'Fancy it, a night out on the tiles with your brother?' He was mentally preening himself for this suggestion.

'Do I!' she beamed. 'That'd be great!' and he was grateful for the pleasure on her face. It was hard for her, he knew, because it was hard for him too, juggling, always juggling.

October 1993

Eve took Judy by the arm and led her through into the formal residents' lounge, chatting casually as they walked. It was evident to them that the men were talking about business, and it had never really interested either of them to get too involved with all of that. They were interested in it, yes, of course, but it really was a man's trade and they both considered themselves far too feminine to meddle in the daily issues. 'Never too early for a gin and tonic, ey?' Judy laughed at Eve's suggestion. 'Beth, you coming with us?' she added.

'No, thank you, I'll stay here!' she said taking James's hand firmly in her own. Neither woman argued with her, and none of the four men did either. She wanted to be with the action, and that was definitely not in the bar with those two women; it was with her brother, Michael, her uncle and Jim.

The five walked around the outside of the hotel again, and Beth noticed just how clean and tidy it all was; even the stores by the main kitchen door were spotless. Like father, like son, she thought, glancing at Michael as he and James chatted between themselves. Jim led them through the main reception hall again with a wave of his arms; he was always gesturing boldly. He was, after all, a very bold man. 'The pool's done now, too,' he smiled.

'We'll be off then,' James laughed, pretending to make a move towards the doors leading down to the basement.

'We'll take a look at the land,' Jim smiled. 'I just bought another ten acres from the local farmer.' His face didn't change but Pat caught the tone in his voice and shook his head.

'Good price?' he mused and Jim shrugged. Some habits didn't die, no matter how wealthy you got.

Michael and James led the way down the stone steps and outside into the courtyard. 'It's going to rain,' Michael said in a matter-of-fact tone, raising his face to the sky.

'Best take the motor. It's too far to walk when you're wet through,' Jim said, sounding even more like someone's father than he usually did.

'Can I drive?' Beth asked simply and James gave her a light shove on the arm and Michael shot her a warning look.

Jim looked at Pat and then down to where Elizabeth now stood and shook his head. 'And where exactly did you learn to drive, young lady?' he asked, his tone light. He was fantastic at extracting information from her when he spoke like that, but there was really no need to ask. The look that Michael received from Pat was enough and Jim stifled a laugh.

'She was bored!' he said defensively. 'I couldn't think of anything better to do with her,' he added, the men almost laughing at his tone.

'So to top that you'll teach her to fire a gun, I suppose?' Pat said, sounding angry, but even he had to laugh when he saw the way that James looked down at his little sister; all that was missing was the casual whisper. 'You better not 'ave,' he said, pointing his finger.

James shrugged casually, a slight smile on his features. 'Knowledge is only any good when it's passed on,' he said as if reciting words from a book of famous quotes.

'Useful, I think was how you put it before.' Beth smiled at him.

'Yes, Babe, I believe it was.'

'Hang on a bit! So I've got you teaching her how to drive cars,' he said looking over at Michael, 'and you giving her hit man lessons,' he finished, looking back at James. 'God almighty. Whatever next?' It wasn't really a question. He didn't really want to know. She was going to grow up into one funny and strangely educated young woman, of that there was no doubt.

'Relax, Uncle Pat.' She smiled warmly up at him and he let out a long sigh.

'Are you any good?' Jim asked, passing her the keys. He knew that Patrick wasn't really pissed off, but he thought he'd better break the ice just in case.

'She's not too bad actually, even if I do say so myself, Dah.' Michael smiled, touching his chest with a broad hand.

'Her aim ain't too bad either,' James added with a smile.

'My aim's better than yours is, thank you very much, James,' she laughed, a scoff in her tone. 'Was that four two or five two? I can't remember now! It's all a bit hazy,' and there was a real gaggle of laughter then from all of them.

'We'll see,' Jim said, sounding distant. 'Tomorrow, we'll see, and today, you can drive.' He threw her the keys and she made a dash for the four-wheel drive. 'And you,' he said, looking into his son's eyes, 'Mind what you teach that young lady.' They kept eye contact for a while and then Michael nodded at his father's request. There was an unspoken conversation. Warning for the wise. There was a chemistry there that Jim could smell at fifty paces and it almost bothered him.

Chapter Eight

December 1993

'So?' Lucy dragged out the two letters and sat with bated breath waiting for Beth to continue. She looked almost agitated by Beth's obvious reluctance to spill the beans, as it were.

'We kissed.' She sounded unsure of herself.

'And?' Lucy was on the edge of her seat in anticipation.

'That was it,' Beth added with a shrug.

She then looked indignantly at Beth. 'What do you mean, that was it? Did he kiss you, did you kiss him? Was it any good?'

Beth thought for a few seconds. What was Lucy rattling on about? It was a kiss, just a kiss. There was nothing spectacular about it, in fact the only thought she had was that it felt rather wet. She had also wondered why guys always seemed so eager to shove their tongues in. That wasn't how she'd seen James kiss women, or Michael for that matter. Whenever she'd seen them, the girl, or rather the woman always seemed to want them to carry on, not pull away and wipe their mouths as she had, and Lucy's relentless pressure on Beth to get into it with whoever was popular at the time was a little irritating.

The conversation was cut short by the sound of James's footfalls on the hallway floor above them. Both girls sat silently as they waited for him to continue down into the kitchen. He could sense the air around them. He had interrupted something, probably heavy and probably instigated by Lucy. He liked her well enough but something inside him told him that one day she would have a hand in the corruption of his little sister and that pissed him off. She was wayward, in his opinion. Her parents were never about, and always at work, so she just appeared at their house regularly and hung about. She had a bit of a reputation already, or so he'd heard. And he didn't much like what he'd heard.

'Ladies.' He sounded mischievous himself and watched as two pairs of eyes followed him into the kitchen area. He took a glass from the cupboard and poured water into it, half expecting them to continue their conversation with him pretending not to be at all interested, but they didn't, and the silence continued.

'You busy tonight?' Beth asked him, finally breaking the tension with her light tone of voice.

'Why, what's up, Babe?'

'We fancied going to see a film, can you drop us off?'

James looked at them both in turn. Had she just asked him to do that so he would think that they were at the cinema? No, Beth wouldn't do that to him, she wasn't that conniving. His eyes flickered to Lucy who was giving him her "butter wouldn't melt" expression and suddenly he felt annoyed. The expression now on his face spoke volumes to Beth and it was as if she could actually hear his thoughts. 'Why don't you come too? If you're not doing anything,' she suggested.

He found himself nodding at her and then he smiled. 'Yeah, go on then, Babe, I ain't bin to the flicks for yonks.'

This appeared to please Lucy immensely. She mooned over James a lot, and though flattered, it creeped him out, because of her tender age, coupled with the fact that she was his baby sister's best mate.

January 1994

Beth woke with a start. She was being shaken gently by the shoulders. She opened her eyes, brushing her hair away from her face. 'What?' she croaked, focusing on Michael as he loomed above her in the darkness.

'Look!' he said in a half whisper, though his tone was excited. She was still trying to decide what the time was. It was bright, but not light outside, and something in the back of her mind, a memory, called out in her head.

'Snow!' she shrieked, leaping from the bed and dashing to the window. He leaned his arm on the frame and his head on his arm as he stood next to her. 'How long's it been going on?' she asked. It was deep, really deep.

'I woke about an hour ago. It's been coming down thick and fast since.' He was excited, he liked the snow too.

'Is it really deep?' She sounded so excited, and she did a little jig on the spot.

'Well, I don't know. D'you want to find out?' he asked.

'Now?' She was still hopping about and looking out of the huge window.

'Sure. Get dressed, we'll go and play in the square. It's almost six. People should of course be up at this time on a Sunday.' They laughed together then; of course they should!

'James, get James,' she said excitedly.

Michael stopped smiling. 'He's not in yet,' he replied with a shrug.

'His loss' Beth added, not really bothered and before Michael was even out of the door she was pulling open the wardrobe door and pulling out trousers and a jumper.

February 1994

If there was one thing that could warm James's blood when he was feeling down, it was a woman. And as of late it was *any* woman, provided that she was available and unattached, but he had to be honest, even that didn't much matter to him these days. He stood at the bar sipping cool beer straight from the bottle and let his eyes take in the wonderful sights before him. There was every colour and creed, every imaginable outfit from the sublime to the ridiculous and he loved every one of them. His attention went across the bar to Michael who was, as always, surrounded by young hopefuls himself and James smiled to himself.

Michael was a funny bloke. He'd have them tripping over themselves, had the pick of the crop and yet he was almost uninterested in them. He'd pick one if he was in the mood and that would be about it; usually at the end of an evening, have his fun and never even think about her again. Well, he thought with a shrug, if that was how Michael wanted it, that was how Michael was going to have it. It was a case of each to his own and after the crap Mike had been through in the past, James couldn't really blame him for not wanting to get even close to heavy. He was like him in that way. He wanted sex and he had sex. There was no romance and no heartache involved, not for them anyway.

His attention was drawn then from the crowds and across to the other end of the bar. He watched with interest as two men showed the telltale signs of beginning a fight. Michael watched James's eyes and followed his gaze. He too watched with interest as the men did the shoving thing. They'd obviously passed the verbal abuse stage, which was odd. He didn't usually miss things so close to him and fleetingly he got the impression that it was staged. His attention went back to James and the two looked at each other for a long moment. Did James get the same impression? He thought, maybe so.

There was a shrug of shoulders and then, in unison they made their way across to where the action was about to be.

'Okay lads. The party's over!' Michael's voice bought the two men and the other club goers near them to an abrupt halt. They both stared up at him, his size alone telling them both who he was. 'Do you want to do this in here or outside?' he asked as he watched one of the two before him debate with himself whether or not to carry on regardless of Michael's presence. 'It's entirely up to you!' He waited, stood firmly on the spot, his hand clasped together at his front.

James appeared next to him then, also looking rather menacing and it looked as though the other two had thought better of it. 'It's okay,' the smaller of them said, raising his hands in a gesture of surrender. The other was neither here nor there with who Michael and James were, and went for the bottle on the bar beside where he stood. There was an intake of breath from surrounding people but he couldn't have said with any certainty that he even touched it. The next thing he knew, he was on his back on the floor and everyone seemed to have stepped back, away from him. Michael didn't look like he'd even moved. The smaller looked up into Michael's eyes. The question was there. Was he going to try his luck too? Absently he shook his head and Michael nodded, pleased with his choice.

'Maybe next time Mr. Oxley would like to come in person,' Michael said.

'Yeah, we'll accommodate him,' James added, watching as the other man got back up onto his feet. 'Oh yeah, and the door's that way.' He pointed behind them. Four large doormen now stood ready to make sure they made it that far without a change of heart and they watched as the two moved through the crowds, and then with them gone, both relaxed. Was this how it was going to be now? Were they going to have to do this every night of the week? Was Oxleys plan now to just grind them down and burn them out?

'Did you want to go over there, make a statement?' Michael asked above the din of the music.

James looked away from him and across the bar. Was this place really worth all the aggro? he wondered. He felt Michael's hand rest on his shoulder. He knew what James was thinking and as James looked back at him, he was slowly nodding his head. 'No, mate, we'll leave it, for now.'

March 1994

Beth took charge of the trolley. James was far too irresponsible to push it around a busy supermarket on a Friday evening, what with all the commuters in their nice suits bustling up and down the aisles stocking up on wine and nibbles for the weekend.

With a slight rise to her head Beth strolled off ahead of them as they lingered by the magazines and papers. They didn't want to read anything, it was just that there was a rather "tasty bit of stuff" as James put it, also flicking through glossy pages. Beth had seen her, she was desperate to be noticed; then she'd seen the expression on her brother's face, he'd noticed and she surrendered gracefully, resigning herself to having to shop alone and only find them when it was time to go to the checkout.

'Wait for me!' Michael's voice called after her and she paused in mid-step. 'Just leave him, he'll catch up,' he finished with a smile as he reached her.

'Sorry? I thought you were right with him' she purred, her tone sarcastic.

'Well, you thought wrong then, didn't you, little one? Not all of us men are completely distracted from the job in hand by a pair of tits, you know,' he laughed as she put some more fruit and veg in the trolley,

'Can't say that I do know, no, Michael!' She was smiling as she spoke but he caught the undertone.

She was feeling a bit left out lately. All he and James seemed to be doing was working, and when they weren't working they were playing, and lately they were playing hard. He made a mental note as they stood there in the toiletries section to make more of an effort with her. Spend more time with her again, and also to make sure that James did too.

They walked slowly down the aisles, Michael leaning on the trolley as they went. They chatted casually as items were taken from the shelves.

'So are tits important, then?' Beth asked as she picked out a loaf of bread.

'Tits?' Michael pondered her question for a second or two. She was asking a lot of questions like this lately and he had to make sure that he gave the right answer. He didn't want her to think that sex was the only thing on his and James's minds. 'Now that depends. If you like someone, then no, they're not. But if it's just fun you're having then you have a mental picture of what you want at that time, for inspiration, you know?'

Beth chose a deodorant and then went on to shampoo. 'So, if you like them, it doesn't matter, and if you don't and you're just trying to get your leg over, it does? That doesn't make sense. What about all this *never looking at the fireplace when stoking the fire* crap?'

Michael chuckled at her question then. She had a point. It didn't make sense. 'Ah, that's it exactly. It's crap, well, most of the time.' He shrugged. 'Take me, for example. I look, sure, in fact, I'm probably the world's worst, but that's about as far as it goes nine times out of ten. If it's not love at first sight, then I'm a bit more choosy about the attributes she does have, if you know what I mean!' He looked at a middle-aged woman who was paused next to them. She stared at him, obviously having heard most of their conversation. He lingered and then turned back to look at Beth. 'When there's nothing there between two people you either walk away, or find consolation in tits or arse or—' He stopped and Beth urged him on with her eyes. This was getting rather informative. The woman walked away with a wiggle and Michael raised his eyebrows.

'Any consolation there?' Beth asked.

'Age old knowledge?' Michael laughed.

Mrs. P was still there when they arrived back at the house. She'd been waiting for them to get back and had the kettle boiling by the time they reached the kitchen, each of them laden with white plastic shopping bags. 'Good day?' she beamed, beginning to help unpack from the bags and onto the counter top.

'Not bad, thanks,' Michael smiled.

'And you, young man?' she looked at James.

'Yeah, it was okay,' James added with a shrug.

'And what about you, my love?' she asked, smiling across at Beth.

'Interesting,' Beth mused.

'And how was school?' she asked Beth directly, it being obvious that Beth wasn't referring to school with her "Interesting" comment.

'Average, and way too much homework.'

James tuned in then, sort of semi-aware that he may have missed something. 'Do you need a hand, Babe?' he asked, spinning cans up into the air and catching them simultaneously in both hands.

'With business studies?' She sounded sceptical.

'Ah, no. I do biology and history. See Mike, he's the stockbroker.' There was a laugh on his lips as he spoke.

'Stockbroker?' Beth questioned.

'Yes. I have hidden talents, young Elizabeth, talents beyond your comprehension,' Michael replied, his tone suggestive.

'Mike, don't start with all that again, she'll get all embarrassed!' James laughed, still spinning cans in the centre of the room.

'Not in front of me, she'll not.' Michael smiled, giving Beth a wink. She was unmoved. 'She's too much woman for all that crap'. Beth pursed her lips at them.

'That's all well and good, but what about business studies?' she was still untouched by his words, and his tone.

'Yes, I can help.' He sounded serious again then. Michael was a real dark horse, was there anything he couldn't do? He was old beyond his years and knowledgeable about the whole world. There was little, Beth mused, that he couldn't tackle.

'After dinner though, ey!' Mrs. P added, quite firmly as she slipped on her coat and prepared to leave the house. 'There's a casserole in the oven. Mash's warming in there too. It'll be ready at eight.' She glanced at the clock.

'Cheers, Missus P.' James leant and kissed her cheek. 'Do you wanna lift home?'

She smiled. 'Pah, no. You just eat and I'll see you all in the morning. I'll be 'ere about nine.'

'Thanks, Mrs. P,' Beth called after her. 'Have a nice evening.'

May 1994

Getting into the car Beth looked across at Michael. He looked at her briefly, and then past her, and out of the closed window at the crowd of youths she had just been standing with while she waited for him to collect her outside the school gate. 'They're sixth formers!' she said settling back in her seat and he nodded absently at her.

'They're quite special,' he replied with a "tut" on his lips. She laughed then. He was so protective of her. 'What were they saying, anyway?'

She looked down at the bag on her lap. Suddenly the clasp upon it had become really interesting. 'Nothing! Why?' Her tone was defensive.

'Because you didn't look very happy about it, whatever it was.' He lit a cigarette and instantly she leaned over and took it from his lips.

'They were just sodding around and stuff,' she said between lugs before handing it back to him.

'Stuff?' he asked, suggesting with his silence that she elaborate. 'I'll not get out and kick them into touch, Elizabeth. Well, unless you want me to, that is. I'm just interested, that's all?'

She looked over at him. 'They were talking about sex if you must know, you know, who has and who hasn't. They think I'm weird because I haven't,' she said. He could tell from her tone that she was telling the truth but he thought he'd better ask, just in case.

'And have really you not, like really?' he asked anyway.

'What?' She knew full well what.

'Had sex?' He was crisp about it and she felt her cheeks flush even though there was nothing to be ashamed of, especially not in front of Michael.

'No, I have not!' She was indignant.

'Are you sure now?' he laughed, taking the cigarette back from her.

'Um yes, I'd like to think it would be something I would remember, Michael,' she said then, aware that he was teasing her.

'Right answer.' His tone was light and she found herself smiling with him.

He nodded at her then and after a long stare he spoke again. 'There's nothing worse than a first time quickie that you don't really want to have, up against a wall in the dark somewhere, praying that you're not caught. Things like that should be completely forgettable, but they're not, things like that stay with you forever.' He looked back at her as the car pulled almost silently away from the kerb. 'The first time should be like every time. Wanted, respected and enjoyed.' He finished with a brief nod of his head in her direction, before he looked in the rear view mirror, committing each lad to his memory. Should any of them appear at one of the clubs or bars he'd recognise them and they'd have a wee little chat about life, love and the universe.

Chapter Nine

July 1994

Judy knew that there was something on Beth's mind that Saturday morning. She immediately suggested that the two of them go shopping. It was something she knew that Beth and Louise had always done when she had been a child, and she knew that Beth found it easy to talk openly as they walked through shops and between market stalls. They would wander around for an hour or two, then go and have a coffee or sometimes something a little stronger and maybe something to eat in a nice restaurant and then go and buy whatever they had decided upon.

Today was no different and the two of them settled down at a table by the window in their favourite coffee bar. Judy opened a fresh pack of cigarettes, discarded the wrapper on the table, took one and then offered the pack to Beth. 'Do you want to talk?' she asked, blowing out the cigarette smoke from her lungs loudly. She wanted to help. Beth rarely let her into herself and she was almost grateful for the confidence that she was about to receive. 'Yeah?' She paused in mid-sentence.

'Can I ask you something a bit weird?' Beth said finally and Judy smiled at her.

Judy looked softly at her. 'You know you can, honey,' she said in her singsong, motherly voice, her facial expression urging Beth to continue. She was, however, a little worried about the content. What could it be that she couldn't tell James and Michael?

'It's a bit embarrassing really. I can't ask James about this one. I don't think he'd understand and Michael—' She paused, a blush on her cheeks. 'I can't ask him.'

Judy looked intrigued and leaned on the table with both elbows. 'Go on,' she urged and Beth took another lug of her cigarette.

'I keep getting thrush,' she said bluntly, her voice low. 'It's really bad sometimes. I've tried that cream and the other thing, but they don't work.'

Judy relaxed inwardly. She was dreading it being about men or something and she was no expert; she'd only known Patrick in her life but this, this was her area. This she could deal with and she brushed her fringe to the side of her face with a perfectly manicured hand. 'How often?' she asked and Beth thought for a few seconds before answering.

'Twice, three times a month. Why?' She looked concerned but there was no need.

'Tights?' Judy said finally. Beth looked a little confused so she went on. 'I bet it's tights. You wear them and your knickers?' she asked and Beth nodded. 'You're getting too hot down there, lovely, now you're a woman and all,' she finished and Beth let out a breath. 'We'll get you some stockings and some looser undies, that should do the trick.' She was sure in her tone.

'Stockings,' Beth laughed cautiously. 'Sexy!'

'Yeah, you know, nice ones, maybe hold-ups or something, something pretty!' Judy said with a warm smile. 'We'll go lingerie shopping in that little shop up by the church when we've had this, ey? And if there's nothing in there we'll pop into Marks and Sparks.'

Beth smiled at her then. For all she was a bit of a dolly, she loved her aunt. She was always smiling and happy and full of energy to the extent that James had once commented that she looked like she was on speed. But all the joking aside, Beth had known that she of all people would be able to help her with this little problem. But it was at times like these that she really missed her mother. And she guessed that Judy knew this. It was hard being constantly surrounded and yet so alone.

August 1994

'Where do *you* fancy?' James said finally, chucking the last of the brochures onto the dining table between himself and his sister. 'Don't you worry about Mike and me, we'll find entertainment wherever we end up! Where do you wanna go?' Beth looked up at him from the sea of glossy, sun-drenched photos and right back into his eyes.

'Oh, no. You decide,' she replied, not wanting to be the one to make such a choice. There was a long pause.

'Okay, what did we say? Heat, peace and quiet.'

'And tits,' a voice said from the stairs. They both looked up and Michael walked down towards them. 'James said he wanted tits!' Michael was smiling.

'He's right. You did,' Beth said with a nod and a point of her index finger in James's direction.

'Okay, and tits,' James laughed.

'So what about Greece? Greece is meant to be grand,' Michael suggested, picking up the top glossy brochure and flicking through the pages of pools and sandy beaches.

'What, for tits?' James asked.

'No, I meant generally. It's hot. If we go to a decent hotel it'll be peaceful and if we go to a really decent hotel, James'll find his tits!' Michael added, replacing the brochure. He liked the idea of a break in the sun, he thought they could all do with it.

Late October 1994

Her head swam as she tried to focus on the front door and the key in her hand. It was late, she knew that even in this state, and yet she hoped that James and Michael were in bed or even better, still out. She'd had such an excellent time with Lucy and the girls. They'd been to a pub in the City then Brown's, a club she didn't own and it was nice not to be recognised by every door and barman, or so she thought. It was also a result because they hadn't been asked for identification, and she was now a little worse for wear. Alcohol didn't usually affect her like this and although she wouldn't admit it, she was regretting drinking so much in such a short period of time, especially the shots. When she burped she could taste them and this was not good.

She opened the door. The lights were off in the hallway but as she looked towards the lounge she noted that the television was still on. She headed quietly for the stairs, hoping that she hadn't been spotted but that would have been too lucky.

'Don't even think about it!' James's voice rang out in the silence, making her spin toward the lounge doorway. 'Where the 'ell have you been?' It wasn't really a question and as Beth walked into the lounge she saw him sitting on the sofa still fully dressed, his face like thunder.

'Out with the girls,' she said, trying to sound sober and casual all at once, perhaps a little too much and it was an epic failure on her part.

'It's three o'clock in the fucking morning!' he snapped jumping to his feet. 'It's only because I *know* where you've been, Babe, that I ain't called the old bill.' He'd called her Babe, he wasn't really angry, she thought fleetingly. 'Dave saw you and Lucy in Brown's.' He looked down into her eyes, noting the fact that she was definitely drunk. 'And I ain't happy!' he finished.

'I told you that I was going out,' she said defiantly despite her swaying, and that was when he snapped. 'Not into a fucking club, Elizabeth,' he yelled. She'd been too hopeful, he'd called her Elizabeth, he was angry. 'Not at your age with that slapper in tow, and definitely not without me knowing where you are.'

Beth winced. 'Don't you yell at me, James,' she said, suddenly feeling very sober and he paused, hearing footsteps coming up the stairs from the kitchen. It was Michael, he was walking deliberately loudly to let them know that he was on his way up to them, he appeared at the door, also fully dressed and he and James locked eyes.

Beth couldn't help getting the feeling that the two men held an entire conversation without actually saying a word to each other. 'She's pissed!' James announced with a wave of his hand in her direction, and Michael looked her up and down. She was growing up so fast, too fast. She looked much older than her sixteen years and he knew that it wasn't the drinking, or the fact that she'd just walked in at three am that James objected to, it was the fact that she was looking so attractive and both men were concerned for her wellbeing.

'And she's home,' Michael said calmly, his tone soft. He was always the clear thinker and she was grateful to him, even though she could tell from the expression on his face that he was about as impressed with her as James was right then.

James grabbed his carton of cigarettes, pulled one from it and lit it in one continuous motion. 'We were worried,' he said to her finally, his voice softer, and Beth looked down at her feet. She should have phoned and let them know where she was going. It wasn't like they were going to tell her that she couldn't go. They had never said that to her, ever.

She felt ashamed suddenly, realising that both of them had been waiting up for her. 'I'd have come and got you,' James said, frowning at her. She looked in to his eyes and he saw the apology there. 'From now on, Babe, you call. Day or night, wherever or whatever you're up to. I need to know where you are. All right?'

'All right!' she said quietly, and she reached out and touched his arm lightly in apology.

'Go on now, Elizabeth,' Michael said, taking his hands from his pockets and motioning for her to leave the room. She did. She was tired now and all she could think about was her bed. She hadn't noticed that both men were overly anxious and that perhaps it wasn't about her being out on the town.

Once they were sure that she was in her room they walked slowly back down into the kitchen where Dave sat waiting patiently. He looked anxiously around the expanse, and then up at them and waited until they had both settled back at the dining table before he spoke again. 'D'you want me to call a glazier?' he asked, looking over James's shoulder at the hole in the French doors past the kitchen area. 'They can be 'ere within a half-hour.'

James nodded at him, aware that Michael was waiting for him to explode again. James's eyes still had the telltale signs of the fear and panic that had rushed through him when he'd come home that night, finding glass all over the kitchen floor and every door in the place closed tight. And it was because of the break-in that James had scoured London, looking for his sister.

His first heart-wrenching thought had been that she'd been taken. He'd yelled and yelled as he rushed up the stairs, opening and slamming doors as he went. He grabbed at his mobile, ruthlessly dialling Michael's number and swearing into the silence as he waited for a connection. He'd been almost hysterical when they'd spoken and it seemed like years before Michael had arrived home at the house. They systematically searched it from top to bottom again, aware then that Beth was not in, but safe in a club with Lucy and their pals. They checked the study and computer; it was untouched. The bedrooms and drawers were so too. Nothing was out of place, not a thing. It was the fact that nothing had been taken and nothing had been disturbed other than the internal doors that bothered both James and Michael. Someone was showing strength. Showing that they could be got at and neither man liked it, neither man liked it at all.

Dave had had everyone he could think of on the phone. Every pub and club was checked. He'd eventually found her about thirty minutes into the search, and sent his younger brother Eddie to keep an eye on her until she left the club with her friends. Eddie was under strict orders not to let her out of his sight under any circumstances, and he'd followed his elder brother's request to the letter until she'd stepped out of the taxi and made her way up the steps and through the front door. He'd then called Dave on the mobile and told him that she was on her way into the house above them. He was still outside. He would be there until James or Michael told him he could go, and not a second before. He realised immediately that this was serious, and not just James being funny about his little sister being out and about.

He'd heard the rumblings around town about the Oxley Corporation, as had everyone else. Knew their nasty reputation for taking things too far and for a minute or two he'd actually thought about just tipping her over his shoulder and carrying her out and home, but thought better of it, so instead he had made the call, followed her and watched her and now she was home and safe, a job well done.

Chapter Ten

Early November 1994

Michael let the workmen out with a cash *thank you* of about fifty pounds each, and leaned against the closed door. He closed his eyes and opened them again, slowly, his face up to the ceiling. He watched as the little red sensor flashed in the corner of the coving above him as he moved his hand up from his side to his hair line, and then his eyes went to the new key pad, so neatly placed next to the light switches and he hoped that the three thousand pounds they'd just spent on the new alarm system was worth the money. It all seemed very technical, designed to make you feel safe inside your own home, but he knew from bitter experience that there was nothing you could do if someone really wanted to get into the house. He also hoped that Beth would never have to use one of the four panic buttons that had just been fitted about the house and with that he pushed himself from the wall and turned towards the lounge door.

He sat down with her on the sofa in the lounge, something that was very rare indeed. It had become a place to escape to from other people, not to join them. Somewhere to go to be alone, rather than the study to play games on the computer, or their bedrooms and today it had been the quietest place to be, what with three alarm fitters crawling all over the house all day.

But this evening they were both there, suddenly alone in the house and he felt that it was the right time to broach the subject that he and James had skirted around for the week following her last night out on the town. James had agreed that maybe Michael was the one who should talk to her, seeing as he'd already broached the subject with her on a couple of occasions. This had also been confirmed by Mrs. P, who had been half listening to their conversation as she'd gone about her business.

'Are they gone now?' she asked, looking up as he moved the cushions around from behind him.

'Yes. Noisy bastards, weren't they?'

She looked annoyed. 'Yes, and unnecessary!' she said flatly.

Michael looked away. 'No. Not unnecessary, Elizabeth,' he said, his voice almost harsh. Beth looked into his eyes as he turned back to her. She would have asked more, dug deeper but she knew that there was no point. She'd done that already, that morning and all she'd got from either of them were blank shrugs and the odd grunt about house insurance policies and upgrading security.

She pushed the thoughts of not being let in on the bigger picture from her mind and focused on the present. Knowing him, and that fatherly look, as well as she did, Beth smiled and studied him some more. This was going to be an intense one, she knew it. 'Did you two draw straws?' she asked and he smiled then, the serious expression disappearing from his dark rugged features.

'Is it that obvious?' he breathed.

'Yeah, so what's up?' she asked and he sighed.

'Nothing's up, I just thought you and me could have a little chat, you know.' He leaned back some more on the sofa, letting the padding of the cushions surround his broad frame as he ran his hands over his face.

'No, I don't know, but you have that look on your face like you're going to tell me,' she said, again flatly.

'I've, I mean, we've noticed that the babe isn't a babe any more. It's more of a full-on babe and it's a bit worrying.'

Beth suddenly cracked up laughing at his comment, covering her mouth with closed hands. He smiled sarcastically, quickly, nodding his head slightly as he did so.

'Am I the babe?' she managed.

'Yes, we're worried, Elizabeth. You're not a child any more. You're a very good-looking young woman with attributes and things, you know.' He made a hand gesture in her general direction and Beth looked away from him, aware that she was blushing at his comment.

'Shut up, Michael!'

He was serious. 'No, listen to me please. We're, no, I'm worried for you. There's a lot you don't know about out there. Maybe we should just let you get on with it. But we care and so we can't,' he added.

'This sounds more like a James conversation!' she observed correctly, and Michael had the decency to look away. They both knew what a slag he was; he was proud of the fact, almost.

'We talked about it and agreed that one of us should talk to you. Presuming that you need talking to?' He raised his eyebrows in question and the urge to laugh got her again but she held back. This must be hard for him in a way. Theoretically she was nothing to do with him but whenever anything really technical came up, it was Michael who did the talking; the hitting they generally left to James.

'Yes, I'd say it's a bit late for sex education!'

Michael looked a little taken aback by her comment and she laughed then, realising what it was that he must have thought at what she had just said. 'No, no, I mean. Aren't I a bit old for this talk?'

It was his turn to laugh then. Every word she spoke was the wrong one, and it made him laugh. 'I know you don't need the birds and bees talk, woman!' he smiled.

'Good. Besides, isn't James better versed than you for that one? Shouldn't I learn from a master?' She was staring right at him and he looked back at her for a long moment.

'Ah.' He paused for a few seconds, judging the situation. 'It's the quiet ones you have to watch, Elizabeth. We're the sly ones that come up and take you from behind.' His tone was suggestive and he watched as she blushed again.

'Thank you, now I'm embarrassed!' She laughed her reply and he shook his head at her. That hadn't been the idea or his intention.

'Just be careful, you're an attractive young lady and we don't want you getting into anything you can't get out of! Okay? I know you've been getting a bit of pressure from your friends and—'

She stopped him in mid-sentence. 'Michael! Really, I'm fine. Not so much as a sniff as yet, thanks to you two and I'll probably die a virgin if you have anything to do with it!'

He smiled again. 'That's not quite the plan, but it'll do for now.' he laughed then.

'Yeah, well, it's working out that way. But thanks for the concern.'

February 1995

James appeared on the stairs. He looked as if he'd just risen from his bed, but neither Michael nor Beth were interested in him. In his arms, clutched to his chest was a wad of post, and that's what had their attention. 'It's here!' he announced, 'And we also know that there'll be a ton more at the club and bars!' He sounded really pleased with himself.

'Come on, man!' Michael laughed, watching as James walked deliberately slowly, reading out their names from the envelopes as he went. 'M. J. Elliott. James Dobson, J.D., Michael. Michael, Jimmy, James.' He paused. 'Elizabeth Dobson? Beth Dobson? Miss E. Dobson?' He dumped all the post on the counter.

'Did I get more than two?' she asked, sounding really excited. This was a rarity.

'You got four,' Michael said, flicking through the pile and separating them.

'What about you?' she asked him.

'Seven, eight.' He went through the last few. 'Nine. I got nine,' he announced cheerfully.

'I'm the winner!' James laughed, holding up a large wad of envelopes.

Chapter Eleven

March 1995

Debt collection was an art form. You were either good at it or you weren't, and Michael was good at it, very good indeed. The presence he had was the key, according to his favourite regular employer, who would always use Michael as an example of what made a good collector. Michael didn't need to elaborate on what would happen if payment wasn't made or goods returned; it was simply plain to see on his face. There would be judgement and Michael would win hands down. He was grateful for that presence at times. He hated getting aggressive with people who were already down on their luck. It almost upset him, because he had a conscience. He understood the need to thrive, the need to better yourself, and as he stood watching goods being loaded into a van to cover the costs of an unpaid cash loan he actually felt sad.

The man who sat in the little office had had such big plans. Steven Hamilton had had dreams of making it big in computers and now Michael was watching his dreams fade with every box that passed him from the storeroom. 'It's over,' he whispered. 'Without the gear, I'll never pay him back. Fuck it! What am I gonna tell her?' Michael looked down at him. All this was going on around him and all he could think about was what his wife was going to say. 'That's the baby idea gone. Fuck it!' He rubbed his hands over his pale face. He looked tired out and more than a bit stressed. There was something in his tone that caught Michael's heart. Something in the tone that wasn't a sympathy ploy. Something in the tone that made Michael look at the paperwork again. He read a few lines on the sheet so neatly typed.

'You owe six thousand,' he said, the statement making Steven look up at him. He hadn't even realised he'd been talking aloud. 'How much can you make this little thing work for?' he asked then. The other thought for a few seconds, his face confused.

'What's there! It's not money that's missing, mate. It's time!' There was silence between them for a while longer.

'Good little business, computers,' Michael observed.

'Could have bin. Shops only bin open three months,' he sighed. Defeated and close to tears.

One of the two men loading the good into the van parked outside the shop front walked past him for another box and Michael stopped him in mid-step with his arm. 'Stop. Put it back!' he said quietly. They stared at each other as Michael's words registered. He wasn't sure of what to say. You just didn't argue with Michael Elliott. It wasn't done. Steven too looked up and that was when Michael looked back down at him.

'Six grand's not a lot to fold over, is it!' he breathed. He really felt for the man in front of him, really wanted to help. 'I'll have the money back when you get on your feet,' he said.

The man lugging boxes went to open his mouth and Michael snapped his head towards him. 'I'll clear this one. Unload the van!' he stated.

'But—' he went to speak. Michael stared at him.

'Don't you stand there and "but" me. Just do it!' he snapped, making both men jump. He looked back at Steven. There were more tears in his eyes. He opened his mouth to speak, but nothing came out.

'No time scale. I'll get something written up and sent to you. Just make it work and have your babies,' he said, and with that, he was gone from the shop.

April 1995

Beth stomped down the stairs into the kitchen, helped herself to coffee without offering James a refill and then sat down abruptly on one of the stools at the counter. James looked up at her from his paper at the dining table and on seeing the stressed look on her face, got up from his seat and took up a stool next to her.

'What's up, misery chops?' he said, giving her leg a light slap. 'Credit card been cancelled?' He was trying to make her smile, he hated to see her with a strop on, it didn't suit her no matter how few and far between the strops were.

'No. I've got it again!' she said flatly.

Michael walked down the stairs behind them and busied himself making a coffee after nodding his good mornings at them both. 'Got what?' James asked ignorantly.

Beth gave him an indignant sideways look, as if she thought she should know. 'My bloody period!' she snapped.

James smiled despite her mood and realising what she had just said, Beth almost laughed with him.

'Now that was funny!' James said, pointing his finger out at her.

Michael hadn't been listening to their conversation, he was looking out over the garden, a cigarette in hand, but on hearing that he looked over at them from his standpoint. 'You've got it again?' He sounded surprised but was far more aware of the significance than James obviously was. Beth nodded at him. 'But you only just had one!' He moved towards her. James gave him a strange sideways look.

'How d'you know?' he said, his tone sounding slightly more than bothered, and Michael shook his head. James never ceased to amaze him, and he would never learn. Michael was just that kind of man, he noticed everything that went on around him, in the house and out of it and he had noticed the erratic nature of Beth's cycle. 'That's every two weeks almost,' he said, lighting himself the second cigarette of the day. James took one from the open carton and lit one himself.

He was a little uneasy about this discussion and the fact that Michael was yet again a step ahead of him. 'Is it bad?' James asked. He was truly concerned but had never been any good with *women's things* mainly because he was so tactless and also, if he was honest, because he got a bit embarrassed. It was yet another reminder that she wasn't a little girl any more and it made him realise that the next issue would be men. Men like him, not the little boys he and Michael had been shielding her from so far.

'Not really, it's just there, you know?' Beth replied. Both men looked at each other and then at her, their expressions amused. As if they would know how a period felt, to them it was just a girl's excuse not to have sex, or at least that was how James viewed it. Michael very rarely commented on the subject.

'Sounds like you need to go on the pill,' Michael said simply.

James's head snapped up. 'Yeah, bollocks!' James snapped.

'Would that work?' Beth defused the situation between the two men before her, she knew that it probably would but supposed that she had to ask.

'Yes. It'll make you regular,' he said, sounding more like Doctor Peterson than Doctor Peterson usually did.

'Really?' Beth's voice was enthusiastic and Michael nodded at her.

'Mike. Shut up, you sound like a Tampax ad. Idiot!'

Michael ignored James. 'Yes!' Michael's voice was final and then he looked back at James, who was still deciding whether or not he preferred her bleeding to being on the pill. What if she— He stopped himself. It didn't bear thinking about and besides, who would dare go near her? Everyone she knew was aware that he, Pat and Michael would kill anyone who so much as looked at her in the wrong way. Yes her virtue was safe.

'Call the doctor's. Let's get you sorted out,' James said, surrendering to her pleading look. 'You can drive me. You need the road practice. If you wanna pass on your birthday you'd better sort out your road positioning, it's shit.' There wasn't actually anything wrong with her driving, in fact it was perfect. James was just being picky. He got like that instead of angry.

'She'll be fine,' he said in answer to Michael's unspoken question of whether or not Beth should be driving on a Saturday morning in the middle of London. It was a discussion they'd had before. 'If she can go on the pill, she can drive a friggin' BM.'

Michael looked at James for a long minute and then he smiled to himself. He was only too aware of what had just been going on in James's head. The same thoughts had crossed his, but what could they do; it was natural. She was growing up and one day, probably quite soon if she continued to look and smell as good as she did lately, she would become a woman. He just hoped that whoever he was, he was worthy of her and the treasure that he would take from her.

Chapter Twelve

May 1995

Beth watched Lucy as she watched Michael going about his business in the kitchen. His moves were precise and even though Beth couldn't see the sandwich he was making from her position, she knew that the bread would be even and cut exactly in half with nothing poking out of the edges. He was such a perfectionist and the thought came to mind that if he was so precise about a sandwich, what must he be like in bed? She felt her cheeks redden at the thought. The thought that had entered her head on more than a few occasions lately. Her attention fell back on Lucy. Her blue orb-like eyes were boring into Michael's back, taking in every detail of him. Beth watched her friend's cheeks redden as Michael turned and caught her staring at him. Beth rolled her eyes to the ceiling, catching Lucy's eye as she did so.

'Did you want one?' Michael asked, holding up the plate of sandwiches filled with the left-over roast beef from the previous evening. Both shook their heads at him and he shrugged before turning and making his way back up the stairs.

'He's so friggin' sexy. Sexy hot, dirty!' Lucy half whispered in Beth's direction once Michael had gone.

'Really?' Beth said bluntly, bored at her friend's constant chatter about men, especially Michael. Lucy nudged her gently with a thin elbow and gave her a sweet smile. Beth returned the gesture, but her mind was off again. Lucy was definitely not backwards in coming forwards and that fact always got to Beth. She never ceased to amaze with her statements of lust and Beth felt almost sorry for poor Michael sometimes. She hadn't felt sorry for James though, when Lucy had decided that she loved him not so long before. He loved all the attention that Lucy lavished on him. He was a tart of the first order, but Michael, Michael was always courteous and friendly and Lucy always launched herself at him, embarrassing him and he would leave the room looking rather agitated. 'Don't you think he's gorgeous?' Lucy said, looking into Beth's eyes, bringing her back in to the conversation. Beth looked away from her again with a laugh on her lips, but the laugh was a disguise. Of course she thought Michael was gorgeous, everyone did but she was not about to tell anyone, especially not Lucy. She had a sneaking suspicion that it wasn't what her friend wanted to hear. 'No. Of course you don't!' Lucy continued without letting Beth speak. 'He's more like a brother to you, isn't he? And aren't you the lucky little sister!' The innuendo was there.

'Yes!' Beth said, keeping her tone neutral. She was aware that Michael had stopped walking and was now standing at the top of the stairs. Somewhere in her mind it registered that he hadn't gone any further than the hallway above them. 'The only thing I don't like is that he's got ears like an elephant and he's so vain! He'd take a compliment from anywhere!' She raised her voice very slightly and waited for him to cross the hallway and go up another flight of stairs, which he did almost silently except for the creak of the floorboard at the very top of the staircase.

'She's gone!' Beth called loudly up the stairs after seeing Lucy to the door about an hour later. 'You can come down now, it's safe.' She listened for a few seconds and then he padded down two flights of steps towards her. He had a smile on his face and she shook her head at him. 'I get the impression that our Lucy wants a bit of you!' she said with a wave of her finger in his direction.

'That's nice!' His tone was almost pinched.

'So you're not interested, then?'

Michael gave her the strangest look then spoke. 'Um, no!'

Beth laughed. 'What, a bit young for you, is she?'

Michael looked indignant. 'Good God, no, woman! I get the impression that she'd eat me alive.'

Beth had to agree. 'Probably,' she smirked and she pulled a funny face at him, poking her tongue out. He paused in front of her at the bottom of the stairs and then grabbed her suddenly around the waist. He began to tickle her sides, making her yell out. 'Yeah, Elephant ears, huh?' he laughed. 'Thought I'd forgotten that, didn't you!' He tickled her some more.

'Stop it, Michael!' she yelled. 'It's true. You love hearing about how great she thinks you are. About all the things she'd like to do to you, how hot you are, your drawling Irish sex. It's almost twisted!'

He paused. 'Why, don't you think I'm gorgeous then? Don't you want me Elizabeth, like your little Lucy does?' He almost screeched above her laughter.

Beth slid to her knees on the carpet, trying to escape him. 'No. You're as big a tart as James is!' she laughed. 'Now get off me!'

'Never!' he laughed. 'And I'll give you tart—' he began. He landed on his knees, straddling her. His grip upon her was pulling her close on the floor and then, bang! Their lips were almost touching, he could feel her breath upon his face, almost taste her perfume. He let go of her and jumped back onto his haunches, snapping his eyes shut suddenly. When he opened them again a second or two later they instantly met with hers.

There was always something about eye contact between them, a spark, a suggestion of something more, but never up until that second had it ever occurred to him that it might be sexual. Seconds later, he pulled her back to her feet. They were both breathing hard and suddenly the laughter was gone from them and the hallway filled with another emotion. Michael wasn't sure which one of them it emanated from but he felt like someone had just that moment punched him in the side of the head. It was sexual! It was hot and even he, the cool, calm Michael Elliott felt the stirring of something deep inside. He was suddenly unsure of himself, and aware of his flustering. He was still staring into her eyes, watching as her pupils dilated. He was speechless, all he could do was breathe, and that was suddenly a chore.

Beth stood stock-still, the feeling within her was making her heart pound inside her chest. She swam in his eyes, her thoughts unclear suddenly. She wanted to say something, but her mind was blank and her voice gone. A car horn sounded outside and the moment was past and with a mumble about having to make a call, he left her there, staring after him.

Later on that evening he sat watching her as she prepared dinner. He would have offered to help but something inside told him that it wasn't a good idea. He'd spent the past four hours almost gobsmacked that he could have felt such a thing for her. Good God, he'd almost touched her, kissed her. And from that moment to this, it was all he could think of. She looked so alive, so vibrant, suddenly so womanly. He closed his eyes, trying desperately to put her from his mind but when he opened them again there she was, looking over at him.

'I said, are you all right, Michael?' she said, her voice sounding concerned.

'I'm fine!' he snapped, getting to his feet. He made his way to the stairs, his hand hovering at the banister. Perhaps it would be best if he went back up to his room for a while, or even better, out.

'Have I upset you? Was it about this afternoon?' She wasn't looking up from the pan on the hob which now boiled as the tomatoes heated up with the onions as she spoke. He paused in mid-step and snapped his head to where she was. He studied her profile; nice, but she was biting at her lip, a sure sign that she was unhappy. That little insignificant gesture made him feel bad. He turned and walked over to stand beside her.

'No, no, you haven't. And no, it wasn't.'

She pressed him. 'Then what's up? You've been weird all afternoon,' she persisted. He sighed as he leaned on the counter next to her. She turned to face him then and their eyes met again.

'It's nothing, really,' he smiled and she nodded at him. It was never worth pressing him for the truth if he didn't want to give it.

'How long'll dinner be?' he asked, changing the subject.

'Whenever James gets back, unless you're hungry now. I can leave his?'

He hesitated. He wanted to get out of the room, but he really wanted to stay. His head was running at about a thousand miles an hour and he was lost inside. 'Yeah, go on then. We'll eat now.' His tone was light but Beth noticed that he checked his watch more than once. He was going out later, and she heard a little voice inside her head tell her that he would be going to see a woman. The thought irritated more than she cared to think and subconsciously she scowled.

As they ate in relative silence she found herself watching him. His jaw-line and the dark stubble from the day showing upon it, his breadth and the way his shirt tightened about his arm as he moved his fork up to his mouth. And then she watched his mouth and his lips as he spoke to her and she found herself in a different place to where they were. She wondered how those lips would feel against hers. They'd always felt nice against her head and cheek and he always smelled so good, his scent would linger in the air long after he was parted from her. She thought back in her mind to her first memories of him. Even as a small child she'd always thought of him as safe, a safe haven. When she thought she would fall from her bike, she always remembered Michael being there with her, holding the seat of it, telling her that he wouldn't let her fall. She remembered one occasion, when she was maybe five or six, she'd followed them to the play area out past the back of their little house. She'd seen them from afar, James, Michael and a couple of others. They were playing on their bikes. She ran towards them, calling James's name. She got as far as the swings and she stumbled. Before she hit the concrete, she was caught. A firm grip caught her around the waist and she was put back on unsteady feet. She'd looked up and into those warm brown eyes, her heart still pounding in her chest from the thought of the fall. Her mind flitted from memory to memory; all of them seemed to contain Michael and it was at that moment that she realised just how deeply he had affected her life to that point. She was staring blindly at nothing, and only when she seemed to focus again did she realise that he was looking straight back at her, his eyes deep.

'Finished?' he smiled.

She had the decency to blush even though she wasn't sure why she should. Michael was good at many things, could do more than most, but he couldn't read thoughts.

'Yeah.' She sounded far away, and then completely back again, she smiled at him.

Whatever the blonde said to James as they stood at the top bar amused him. He threw his head back and covered his open mouth with his hand. Michael watched them from afar. Watching James at work was always entertaining and tonight was no different. He watched her give him the eye and then move away from him like a snake, slithering through the crowds, catching the odd gaze here and there. She was slight, but had large, well-rounded breasts that she seemed to thrust out before her to stop her from falling over. Her outfit was so *market* that she may as well have left the tags on, but other than that, and in that there was nothing surprising, Michael would have given her one, he thought.

'She was new?' Michael smiled, leaning up against the bar next to where James still stood.

'Oh mate! You won't believe what she said?' James sounded amused.

'Try me!'

'She reckoned that for a drink she'd go down on me!' James's tone rose despite the whisper he tried to maintain and his facial features didn't give anything away.

Michael gave his friend a slow look from the toes upwards. 'Did you buy her one?' he asked casually.

'Fuck off did I!' James laughed.

'Why not?' Michael asked, his tone questioning.

'It was blonde, it's Friday, it's redhead night!' He laughed then and Michael nodded at him knowingly. It was James's way of saying that he wasn't really interested.

'But she'd definitely give out for alcohol?' Michael sounded disinterested but James saw the sparkle in his eye. Michael hadn't had anything worth talking about in almost a month. He must be gagging by now, James knew *he* would be. 'Knock yourself out, mate,' he laughed, giving Michael a hard slap on the shoulder.

It was dark outside as Michael followed her in his usual strolling strut across the car park, admiring her backside.

'Which is yours?' she asked.

'The biggest one,' Michael replied, bleeping the alarm on his car, sending the hazards to a flash.

She got as far as the side of the car, wiggling all the way, and then he grabbed her, spinning her around to face him. He pushed her onto the bonnet in the semi-darkness and slipped his hand up her skirt, running his fingers roughly up her thigh.

'Here?' The question was one of shock, but her tone depicted excitement.

'Right here!' he replied. 'No-one can see.' He was telling the truth. She may have been a bit of a slapper, but he wasn't that much of an arsehole. Not even for a laugh would he give those bastards in the office a show.

He was pleased with the fact that she was wearing no underwear and he found her wet and receptive as he slid his fingers into her. He rubbed at her bud, watching her face as she got closer and closer to orgasm. She laid right back then, as she came, letting him see her. She wanted Michael Elliott to see her, to feel her. The rumours she'd heard were right. He was considerate, even to the quickies in a car park. She'd come across his kind before; nothing to prove, so nothing to rush for. 'Let me get off. Stand back,' she breathed as she struggled to a sitting position on the side of the bonnet and reached out for his waistband. She struggled with his belt, sliding to her knees and then a crouch between the cars in the darkness and took him into her mouth. He groaned, grabbing her hair and pulling her gently to a good pace. She toyed with him, caressing him with her tongue and lips. 'Oh yes—' he breathed as the sensation took hold of him. 'Jesus!' He grabbed at her head again as he came quickly into her mouth in the dark.

June 1995

Beth walked through the front door feeling deflated. She walked down to the kitchen with the handful of birthday cards she'd picked up off the mat and sat down at the counter. She began to open the envelopes and read the greetings within. Money and cheques fell out from almost all of them and she smiled to herself. What else would you give the girl who has everything? Of course, money. It wasn't even ten o'clock and already both James and Michael were gone from the house. She was bored and Mrs. P wasn't due for another hour. She'd seen the boys early that morning; both had given her cards and kisses and then dropped her off at the test centre before going off to an urgent meeting. There were lots of those lately, but today's had irritated her. It was her birthday. She'd just passed her driving test. She wanted to go out and buy a car at the auctions and there was no one there to go with her until after lunch when they promised they'd be back.

Her thoughts were interrupted by the sound of her mobile ringing. She looked at the display. It was James. 'Hi, Babe.' She smiled.

'No, no. You said you were busy, I thought I'd wait till I saw you. Yes, I passed!' She listened to him talking as she put the envelopes in the bin. 'Where's the key? Blimey, where it should be!' she nodded. 'It's got your name on?' she asked. 'Shall I call you back then? Okay, give me five!' She cleared the call and went to the drawer. She rummaged around and found James's spare car key.

Up the stairs, she went and outside onto the street. With a bleep of the alarm the locks flicked and she opened his passenger side door. On the seat there was an envelope. She took a double look at it. It had her name on it, not James's, as he'd just said it would. She picked it up and closed the door again. Leaning on the car she opened the envelope. There was another electronic key inside it. She pushed the button for the sake of something to do and a bleep went off a couple of cars down the row. She moved. Standing in the middle of the street then, she did it again. The hazard lights of a brand new metallic black Vauxhall Calibra flashed in time with the bleep. 'Oh, what a car!' she exclaimed under her breath as she studied it.

There was a noise behind her and she spun. James and Michael were walking across the road towards where she stood. 'We thought you'd like to go to the auctions in it, Babe,' James smiled, pointing his finger at the car. 'Do you like it?' he asked and she nodded.

'Do you want it?' Michael asked then, the smile turning in to a grin. She saw the number-plate. *ELD1*. Her hand just made it to her mouth before the squeal came out and her face flushed red.

'Happy Birthday!' they said in unison.

She didn't know what to do. Which of them to thank first and so, she threw her arms around them both, tears and laughter coming from her all at once.

'You have no idea how hard it was not giving it you last week!' James laughed as she opened the door of her car and got in.

'Can we take it out?' she begged, clutching the leather of the wheel and taking in the detail of the plush interior.

'Yeah. We thought you were driving!' Michael said, sticking his head into the car.

'Where we going?' she squealed.

'After you've got into something a little less casual, lunch!' he smiled.

'There's a table at Antonio's booked for twelve,' James added. 'Birthday without a party or a present, honestly!'

Chapter Thirteen

July 1995

None too quietly was the only description for how Beth came through the front door. It crashed against the wall, her keys rattling with it as they lay still in the lock. She struggled with them, her shoes in her other hand and then, with a flick of her shoeless foot, she pushed the door closed behind her. Michael observed this sight from the top of the stairs, having come down from his room to find out what all the noise was. She was absolutely plastered, her swaying giving it away more than anything else in the darkness. He walked almost silently down towards her, shaking his head as he went.

'Dear oh dear!' he smiled at her in the light of the overhead fitting, which he took pleasure in flicking on as he reached the switch. What a mess, he thought as he took in the sight before him. She squinted in what she thought was a bright light. 'Where *have* you been?' he sounded amused.

'Brown's, then Icon!' she announced with a wave of her hand, leaning on the wall.

'Drink?' he asked.

'I did!' she replied with an assertive nod of her head.

'I would suggest water?' he added then, still smiling at her.

'No, no thanks. I need to sleep!'

He laughed then 'Water. I'll get you lots of water. You go up,' he said, ignoring her last comment.

He entered her room silently, holding a pint of cold water. There she was, sprawled out on the bed in only her underwear, her clothes in a dumped pile on the floor, looking as if she had quite literally stepped out of them. He put the glass down and was about to cover her up when she opened her eyes. She got to her hands and knees; it was a sudden movement and Michael, being an expert on alcohol and people having had too much of it, knew what was about to happen. Without saying a word he almost carried her into the bathroom and landed her over the toilet, on her knees. She crouched, heaving up what smelled like red wine and beer. And if that was the case, no wonder she was sick. He held her hair out of the way for her and soaked a towel in the sink, wiping her head with its coolness. She retched some more, making the strangest sounds Michael had ever heard from her as he flushed the toilet. 'Finished?' he asked gently. She nodded, pulling up, grabbing for the flush handle when it had refilled. He did it for her because she missed the handle completely.

'Thank you.' she groaned.

'Don't be daft now. It makes a nice change for it not to be your brother.' The laugh was back in his tone, easing the embarrassment that she obviously felt as the sober stage came to the forefront. 'What did you drink?' he asked then.

'Wine,' her voice was rough. 'Followed by tequila!' She heard him chuckle to himself as he leaned away and flicked on the extractor. 'Sounded like a great idea at the time!'

He sat back a little. 'Ah! Tequila,' he nodded his head, as if in recognition of how she was feeling at that moment, and he was. 'That stuff should be banned from the world. And oh, what a head you'll have in the morning.' The chuckle was back again.

'Why do we do it, Michael?' she asked as he helped her to her feet.

'We? Don't you involve me in this!' he laughed. 'Come on. To bed with you,' and he scooped her off the floor and into his arms.

August 1995

Before he could be told who Beth was, James was upon him from the short distance across the bar. James grabbed him by the throat and took a couple of steps forward, knocking him off balance as he moved backwards on unsteady feet. 'That's my sister, you ignorant little fuck!' James's voice echoed through the now silent bar as the two men landed on the floor. James kneeling above him, the grip around his neck still firm. 'Did you really just touch 'er?' he said, his voice sounding almost incredulous, and the other man was beside himself. He hadn't meant anything by it. Christ, she was gorgeous, he was sure men touched her all the time.

'James. Leave it, it's okay, really!' Beth's tone was as soft as her skin had been, the man thought and it seemed to ease James's grip upon him. 'Come on. Please, James,' she purred and she let her gaze settle down on him. Her features were warm, but her eyes showed the warning there. She could have him dead within seconds if that was what she wanted. He was and had been right about her, she was special, very special indeed. He just wished then that he'd spoken, or at least tried to chat her up before going for her arse. It was only when he saw James that he realised who she was; he'd seen those vivid green eyes somewhere before, and it was within the face of the owner of the bar he was drinking in. James Dobson, and that made her Elizabeth Dobson. And it was then at that moment that he was grateful for her compassion.

'Someone get him out of 'ere!' James spat, jumping back to his feet with a fit spring in his step.

Within a couple of seconds he was being escorted none-too-gently from the club. James then looked back across at his sister. She looked pinched then and he knew that he'd made a mistake in making such a scene. He was just tired of fending them off all the time. Men saw her as a trophy, something to be claimed, like the prize for a dare and it got him so mad sometimes he could literally kill. He knew full well that he should have done what Michael did in that situation, which was pull the offender to one side and mention, none too politely, that perhaps his attentions would be better paid off elsewhere. It always did the trick and had the desired effect, but James wasn't like Michael. He was on a shorter fuse and always hit first, asked questions after, and on top of that, for all he was a bit of a boy he was not Michael and didn't have quite the effect that Michael did when he stood firm. 'You all right, Babe?' he asked, the apology evident in his tone. She looked him up and down, debating on whether or not to be angry, but she wasn't really, she couldn't be. She knew why he was so protective, they only had each other but she also knew that he'd have to let go one day, let her become the woman he and Michael were so adamant she already was.

October 1995

Michael took the two shoe bags that Beth had been holding from her grasp, adding it to his suit bag as she made her way into the fitting room. He stood by the entrance and looked back around the shop. It was quiet and one of the sales assistants watched him with curious eyes. Their gazes met and she immediately averted hers with a slight blush to her cheeks. 'Did you want the blue ones too?' His attention focused on Beth once more and he noticed a pair of trousers in her size on the rail next to where he stood.

'Yeah, go on then.' she replied. He took them off the rail and stuck them through the gap in the curtain. 'What's all this for anyway?' he asked lightly.

'Just fancied something a bit more, well, a bit older!' she called out. He pulled a face to himself. Older?

Seconds later there was a really heavy sigh. 'What's up?' he added.

'I'm getting fat!' she exclaimed.

'What!' he sounded shocked at the statement. She was far from fat in his eyes. She appeared at the gap in the curtain and Michael took in the sight. She was in a cream blouse and the blue trousers. 'I hate it!' she announced.

'You've changed shape is all,' he smiled. 'You need classics, you're buxom!' He was light about it.

'Buxom?' she gave him a sideways glance.

'Don't move,' he smiled and with that he was gone, off across the shop. She watched him expertly pick things from the display rails. He knew her tastes and what would look good on her and that was why, out of everyone she knew, she loved going shopping with Michael. He came back with a completely different array of clothes. There was a black trouser suit, a snug fitted jacket and 'forties flared trousers, a dark brown dress and fitted jacket and a long charcoal wool dress with a very low neckline, along with a strappy black dress and another suit. 'Nice!' she purred, taking the garments from him.

She came out first in the brown outfit. The shift dress was very becoming and the jacket just set it off. It wasn't too much.

'I like the colour—'

'What is it with you and brown?' she laughed.

'Just like it, that's all. What do you think?' he was asking her opinion.

'I like it,' she said over her shoulder as she went back inside. Next was the wool dress. Michael starred at her as she adjusted her cleavage before him, slipping her hands inside her bra to get her boobs higher. She did a twirl.

'VPL,' he said, pointing, so she waved her hand at him.

'So I won't wear any!' she laughed then.

'Really?' he raised an eyebrow at her comment.

'Really!' she was pretending to try and shock him.

'What about the black?' he changed the subject again.

'Okay!' She was out again within a few seconds, doing up the buttons on the jacket as she walked.

'Wow!' He looked her up and down. 'Now that's nice!'

She smiled at his obvious pleasure at his choices. 'Classic and classy!' She did a little twirl. 'You like it?' She looked really coy all of a sudden, and Michael felt the beginnings of a stirring within him.

'Very much!' He was now looking into her eyes, swimming in the feeling she stirred within him on days like today, when they were together. She blushed, feeling something strange, a tingling up her spine as his eyes bored into her own. 'Which are you having?' it started softly and ended quite harshly as he tried to rectify the tone.

'Which do you think?' She was fumbling with her voice too.

'To hell with it, have all of them, Elizabeth. My treat today, seeing as they were my choices.' He smiled then and his eyes sparkled.

December 1995

The four of them stood back and admired their handiwork. The tree was lovely, decorated with not too much, but just enough. The light on it twinkled gold, something that always reminded Beth of her mum, and she felt sadness for a brief moment. She felt James's hand reach for hers and took it warmly. He felt this time of year deeply too, she knew it. She'd overheard him and Michael only a few days before. He'd expressed himself openly. He missed them like breath itself, he'd said. That statement had bought tears to her eyes as she'd stood silently in the hallway listening to their conversation. She'd listened as he'd told Michael about his last visit to the cemetery, and how he'd cried and cried and cried and how he'd wished that he could have had just another day with them, just another hour or two. There was so much that had been left unsaid, left undone. He was only glad that their last words on each other had been good, warm and loving. Beth hadn't heard the rest, she'd begun to sob quietly and had made her way up to her room to calm down. She'd missed James telling Michael how proud he was of her and how beautiful she was to him and how he wanted, more than anything, for her to find someone who loved her and wanted her and that second best wouldn't do. But that was then and now they stood quietly.

'It's the dogs, mate!' James announced, looking over at Michael and bringing Beth's thoughts back to the present. She watched him nod.

'Grand, just grand!'

James finished a heated telephone conversation and replaced the receiver with a bang. Without saying a word to Beth, who he knew was watching him like a hawk, he called very loudly up the stairwell for Michael and waited none too patiently for him to come down from the study. 'We've gotta pop out, Babe,' he said finally, his tone tight.He was very angry and eyed Michael as he reached the bottom step. 'We'll be at the club, yeah?' he said to her then.

'I'll get my coat!' Michael announced, giving Beth a smile before disappearing back up the stairs again. While he was gone James unclipped his mobile phone from its charger, got a fresh pack of cigarettes from the drawer and pulled on his own coat. She watched his profile, the muscles along his jaw line tightening with every move his body made. 'We won't be long!' he said, trying to sound vaguely normal and she nodded at him, wondering what was going on now. Lately more and more problems were cropping up and as usual, she got the feeling that she was the mushroom. Fed on shit and kept completely in the dark. Michael came back down, his features now dark too.

'A problem shared is a problem halved,' she remarked lightly as she got up from her seat at the dining table. Two pairs of eyes looked at her and she smiled coldly. 'So I'll see you later then?' she added. It was obvious that she wasn't about to be let in on this one. James leaned over and kissed her on the cheek.

'I'll give you a buzz in a bit, yeah,' he promised.

'I promise he will,' Michael added, turning to look at her from the stairs.

'Fine!' she managed and then they were off and she waited for the sound of the front door closing above her before she moved from her seat.

In the car James let go of his pent up emotions and banged hard on the steering wheel as they made their way through the night towards the Hothouse. 'That fucking man and me are gonna fall out. I'll fuckin' kill 'im. I fucking will, just you watch me!'

Michael let him shout. 'I've no doubt' Michael soothed. 'Do you want to tell me what's going on now or just continue to beat the shit out of your new car?' Michael sounded cool and James laughed at his words then. Michael was so smooth, but he, too, was steaming inside. It was just problem after fucking problem and all Pat could say was, "Deal with it". That was all well and good, but how? Short of putting one straight between Oxley's eyes, both were clean out of ideas. 'Every fucking window in the place!' he breathed with frustration.

'What about them?' Michael asked, but he didn't really need to. He presumed, no, he knew that they were no doubt smashed.

'They just drove up, just drove up!' he paused as he focused on the junction ahead and then turning through the traffic, he continued. 'They drove up and got out and cleared every fucking one.'

'Was it definitetly him, James? Are you sure now?'

James looked at him as if he was mad and then he shrugged. Maybe Michael had a point, maybe it wasn't him. Maybe someone had had too many at lunchtime. No. That was wrong. It was Oxley. It had to be.

Chapter Fourteen

January 1996

Michael sat wrapping himself a joint. It had been a long night and he was passed being tired, so the only thing for it was a smoke. After making two cups of tea Beth sat opposite, watching. But she wasn't watching what he was doing; she was actually watching him. He concentrated, his head tilted to one side, his eyes focused on the task in hand. As always, he could feel her eyes upon him. She studied him, his every move. He didn't object, although he often wondered what was actually going on inside her head. He had an idea, sure, but he wanted to know for certain.

'You want some?' he asked finally, lighting the end. A flame appeared and then went straight out again in a cloud of pale hazy smoke. She looked up into his eyes, the blush appearing on her cheeks in the soft light of the room making him smile to himself. 'Go on then.'

She took it from him after he'd had another couple of lugs of it and inhaled the smoke herself. It wasn't as strong as James's were, but Michael didn't want to get stoned. He wanted to feel calm and relaxed enough to sleep. 'Did you check your messages?' she asked as they sat in the haze of the smoke.

'No, not yet. Anything good?' he replied.

'Just your usual harem,' she breathed, a hint of sarcasm in her tone.

He looked at her then, watching her eyes. Her facial expression was calm. She was getting too good at hiding things behind that smile. It was her eyes that gave it all away though. And as he searched, he saw it, the knowledge making him smile to himself.

'There was another message. Didn't make much sense though,' She was smiling with him then.

'Oh?' He wasn't too sure of what to say. They had strange messages left all of the time, usually from women, unaware of Beth's presence in the house. 'Some bloke. Nice voice, well spoken. Said something about an inconvenience. That he was sorry?' she said then and suddenly Michael was all ears, but that was all she had to say. She looked at him, noticed the expression on his face change as she spoke.

He rose from his seat and made his way to the answering machine. 'Let's have a listen,' he breathed. There was silence in the room, and then a voice filled it. A well-spoken male voice. *Just thought I'd ring to apologise for all the inconvenience. Never mind. I'll speak to you again soon, I'm sure.* It was Sean Oxley. He didn't flinch, just pressed the *save* button and sat back down again. 'Michael, what's going on?' Beth asked, but she could already tell from his face that this was a fruitless question.

February 1996

Beth pressed play on the answer phone and listened as it went through its, *You have seven new messages. To play these messages press go,* her pen poised to take the long list of names and numbers for both James and Michael. There were two of the usual ones. The ones sounding desperately unsure of whether or not they should be leaving messages, or even be calling at all, and then there was another one. She sounded very sure of herself and Beth found herself replaying and playing and replaying and playing it, again and then over and over again. Her voice was rich and a mental picture of long legs and big brown eyes came to Beth's mind. The word *Michael* echoed in her head like someone else in the room was actually saying it, and her name, Caroline, made Beth's teeth ache, she could see lip gloss and— she stopped herself, it was nothing to do with her and she was sure that this Caroline was very nice, but again she pressed *rewind* then *go*.

Michael stood a couple of steps down towards the kitchen listening to the message play over and over again. He listened as Beth tutted, paused and then replayed it. He wracked his brains for something to say so as not to make it obvious that he'd been standing there listening to her, but he couldn't speak. He moved down a step and watched her. Her hair was up in a loose bun and he got a perfect side view of her face. She was so beautiful, he thought, standing there. The way she leaned on the edge of the counter top, arching her back. Was she aching? He almost missed the thought himself because he was so taken with her. The thoughts of touching her, feeling her, washed over him like clean cool water and he let out a low quiet sigh, a wanting sigh. Something made Beth turn, a noise, and she saw him, his deep eyes boring into her body and then her eyes. 'Oh, fuck!' she breathed, obviously embarrassed.

'Sorry, I didn't mean to startle you. Didn't know anyone was home,' he lied.

'Michael! How long have you been there? You made me jump.'

There was a long pause, a minute, maybe more. 'Not long'. More lies.

'Ah, good, um—' She was flustered. 'A girl called for you, Caroline. There's her number.' He had moved close to her and they were almost touching as she handed him the small square post-it note.

'Oh yes, Caroline! She's a nun, y'know,' he laughed. It was a gentle soft noise on her ears, one that made her heart race.

'Why don't I believe you?' she smiled, taking a step backwards as he took another forwards.

'I don't know, Elizabeth, why don't you believe me?' His pitch had dropped and he sounded really husky, making her heart thunder in her chest some more. She was saved from responding by the telephone ringing and he leaned right across her to answer it, brushing against her as he picked up the receiver.

March 1996

'Back before twelve, please, mate.' James's voice brooked no argument and Daniel felt suddenly decidedly small for his six feet as they stood in the hallway.

'No problem.' He sounded cocksure and could have kicked himself as the words came tumbling carelessly out of his mouth.

'I know there won't be,' James's tone had dropped and was now like ice. Both men knew that it was nothing to do with James what time Beth got in, she was a big girl now and could make her own choices. James was just stretching and flashing his tail feathers somewhat, and he was enjoying watching this poor young man squirm. He imagined that his dad was looking down at him from heaven and laughing to himself at James's brilliant performance, and it was brilliant!

He'd opened the door still dressed in his suit and he looked like a gangster, a real criminal, a real hard case, something straight out of a movie, and to top it off he had said nothing, not even hello. He'd just stood holding the door ajar looking Daniel up and down slowly, sizing him up. He was grateful somewhere inside that this Daniel was a bit weedy-looking even for his height; he'd had visions of someone that made even Michael look small and then the thought was gone from his mind and all he could think of was his dad. James knew that Andrew had been looking forward to giving any of Beth's young suitors as hard a time as he had had with Louise's father and James intended to make this one count for the memory and sake of his Dad.

The air seemed to lift as she breezed down the stairs towards them, and James controlled his irritation at Daniel's obvious pleasure at seeing her there. She looked so beautiful, so full of life and fun that for a second he wanted to hold her back and keep her there in the house and not let her take the next step towards womanhood just yet. But he knew that nothing was going to stop that progression and that Beth was no fool and wouldn't jump into bed with this idiot. She needed someone far stronger, someone to control her, but at the same time let her have her head and this little prick was definitely not the one.

Michael watched from the second floor-landing window. He couldn't help feeling annoyed as Beth practically skipped down the steps with Daniel towards the waiting car. His saving grace was that it was a shit car. Who, at under forty, drove a Citroen, honestly? He'd heard James laying down the law from the landing and had smiled to himself. He knew what James was doing and he knew why he was doing it. He just hoped that that Daniel idiot had the brain to work it out too and not take James too much to heart. Not that he, or James for that matter, gave a toss if they ever saw him again anyway, but he hoped for Beth's sake. She was priority number one no matter how they felt and for all that, Michael couldn't get his head around how he felt.

One minute he was avoiding her like the plague and the next he was following her around like a lap dog. If anyone had seen him and caught on, they would have laughed. And the problem for him was that it was getting worse. Every night it was the same dream, albeit in different scenarios. He'd kiss her, feel just how warm those lips were on his own, and he'd touch her, caress her, make her come so hard and so much that she'd be screaming his name, begging him not to stop. He'd caress her naked body, feel her warmth on his and he'd imagine the sensation of being inside her, being the one to welcome her to the world of womanhood. He opened his eyes just in time to see the car pull away. He steadied his breathing from its rapid pace and turned to go down stairs. As he reached the hallway he began to clap his hands together, slowly. His face showed admiration for James's performance and James took a very camp bow.

'My friend, that was magnificent!' he said.

'Mate, it was a pleasure,' James replied, grinning like a Cheshire cat.

'Not too much, no?' he asked, his tone as camp as his bow had been.

'No, definitely not too much. But I do wonder what she's going to have to say to you when she gets in tonight?'

James laughed then as he knew Michael had a point. 'Nothing, I ain't gonna be 'ere.' James grinned again. 'I'm off out to play, mate!' He nodded.

'Me too,' Michael smiled. He needed to be out of the house and he knew exactly where to go.

He watched Caroline undress. Her every move was precise and calculated to give him the best, most perfect view of her slight frame. She stood back upright clad in nothing but her shoes, black high-heeled affairs with straps that wrapped round and around her ankles. He pulled at his own clothes then, slowly; this was like doing a dance with her, not having sex. Every move had a place in time. 'I'm glad you called,' she purred as she moved towards him in the bedroom. 'I didn't think you would.'

He studied her. 'Thought wrong then, didn't you?' he breathed. His tone was gentle, but he didn't really want to talk to her, didn't want to hear how pleased she was that he wanted to see her. That made him feel almost guilty about what they were about to do. He just needed to be held, and he needed to hold, and she was always such a willing partner for such things.

Caroline loved the feelings that Michael made sweep through her. He was such a powerful man, but not demanding and she liked that; with him she could be herself and that affected her deep inside. It wasn't love; definitely not, she was a realist. But it was something, maybe it was because they both knew that it was never going to go anywhere that it was so good. He looked down at her, could feel her heart beating beneath him, could smell her perfume and the scent of her surrounded him, but something was missing. Something wasn't as it had been in the past between them. He didn't show it in any way even though it made him falter; in fact he acted and spoke as he always had with her. But inside his head he could hear a voice telling him that he shouldn't be there, that it wasn't right and he knew why it was so. He tried to push those thoughts from his mind as he moved above her, and found himself again drifting into the wakeful dreamy state he was so familiar with as of late.

He arrived home at maybe two am, he wasn't really sure of the exact time, but was aware that it wasn't *really* late. His mind had been filled with so many thoughts as he'd driven back, and the time wasn't one of them. He looked up as he got out of the car and saw that Beth's light was off. Someone was up though, because he noticed that there was soft light coming from the window in the basement. It was then that he thought of why he'd gone to see Caroline in the first place; Beth's date! He wondered then how it had gone and if she was angry about James's performance that evening. He walked in, throwing his keys onto the pile already on the stairs. James's were there, so were Beth's.

The surprise was evident on his face as he walked down into the kitchen. He'd been expecting James and instead found Beth. She was sitting at the table, cup of coffee in one hand, a cigarette in the other. She looked up at him and in her eyes he saw something deep. She was questioning him without saying a word. Was she angry with him too? He actually couldn't tell and usually he could read such things of her so well. There was more silence for seconds that seemed like hours.

'Did James apologise?' he asked quietly.

'You mean, am I pissed at you, too?' she said quite rightly.

He smiled at her, settling himself down opposite her. 'Yes!' He was honest and the air between them warmed.

'I thought it was very sweet, a bit heavy, but very sweet.' She smiled then and something inside him stirred, making him want to reach out across the table and touch her. 'Where've you been then?' she asked then, before he had time to say or do anything. There was another silence, a strange silence and the two just stared at each other for a long while. 'Shagging?' she added finally with a slight tilt of her head to the side as she spoke.

'Something like that, yes,' he replied honestly.

'Caroline?' Beth's voice was clipped.

'What makes you say that?' he asked, taking her cup and sipping her coffee.

'You have an almost satisfied look on your face,' she said bluntly. There was another long pause and then Beth finished the remains of her coffee. 'You want another one?' she asked, standing up and he nodded at her. The coffee was the suggestion but the innuendo was right there.

'Go on then.'

He watched as she switched on the kettle and got him his own mug from the cupboard. Her back view was so natural, there was no pretence there at all and he suddenly found himself aching for her. He wondered what she would do then if he got up and walked over to her, put his arms around her and kissed her. The thought was still clear in his head when she turned and she caught the expression on his face.

'What?' she asked.

'Nothing, sorry,' he said, his tone almost apologetic, the guilt evident. She smiled again then turned and carried on making coffee.

'I forgot to ask, did you have a nice evening? Before Caroline,' she said, sitting back down with him.

He looked at her, almost through her and then nodded. 'Not too bad, as evenings go. And you, Elizabeth, how was your date?' He was changing the subject, he didn't want to discuss Caroline with Elizabeth, it made him feel dirty somehow.

'Okay, we just went for a drink, y'know?' She was vague, to say the least.

'So he showed you a good time, then!' His tone was that of a sceptic and he raised an eyebrow as he spoke.

'No more than I'm sure you were shown,' she replied coolly as she made eye contact with him. He looked away from her, amusement evident, then he looked back at her, that expression of lust on his strong features again.

'I hope not. You hardly know him!' he laughed.

She studied his face. 'Not that it's any of your business anyway,' she added. He didn't reply. He knew her too well sometimes. That was a *fuck you* more than anything and he could almost respect her for it.

April 1996

He only breathed when the door clicked shut behind him. He leaned up against it, almost fearful that someone was going to follow him inside. He was hot then and his face quite flushed. He could feel his heart pounding in his chest and his pulse was thundering in his ears. *Jesus*, he thought as he closed his eyes again. He could still see her, smell her. He looked at his watch. It was still early. He'd go to the bar, no, even better, the club. He needed to find comfort and comfort he would find. He waited for her to leave the house and watched from the window as she got into the back of a taxi. He tried to remember where she'd said she was going, but he couldn't. All he could see in his mind was how good she'd looked. It'd caught him off guard and he went completely to pieces for the first time in his life. She'd breezed out of her room dressed in one of those dresses that stops hearts from pounding. It was all straps and cleavage, hadn't he picked that out? She'd spoken and for the first time, he hadn't heard a thing.

He arrived at the club at maybe eleven and it was heaving, both outside in the queue, as well as in. He made his way through the crowds still queuing to get in and passed through the glass doors leading in to reception. He was greeted with the same light-hearted banter and obvious respect that he always got and tonight it pleased him. He needed the reassurance of being a big man, well respected and well, feared, and not a sad little schoolboy, which was how Beth was making him feel. 'Is the boy here?' he asked Frank as they nodded their greetings at one another.

'No, mate, but the baby's inside, alone! But not for long in that dress, I can tell you. She got so old so quick!' he added, checking people as they walked past to go inside.

Michael caught his tone and Frank caught the look in Michael's eye. It was gone before it was really there, but he was a man, too, and he saw it. It was an expression he was seeing a lot from Michael. He was always there, not two steps behind her, and it wasn't out of duty that he was so close, of that Frank was sure.

'Does she need rescuing?' Michael asked quietly.

Frank stared at him for a long moment, a smile on his lips. 'Where d'you think Paul is, ey?'

Michael smiled. 'You're a good man!' he said more firmly, despite the smile. He tapped Frank's arm.

'More's the pity, Mike, ey?' Frank replied.

Michael began to move away from him and towards the club doors, turning back only once to give Frank another smile, letting him know that he'd heard him. He knew that look, he knew what Frank had been thinking just then, and it bothered him. He should be more guarded with himself, his own self.

He should know better even than to joke about such things, but he was being a little transparent of late, he knew it. He couldn't help it. It was almost a cry for help, he sometimes thought. He needed saving; saving from himself, and saving from Elizabeth.

As he walked down the stairs he scanned the whole place in one sweeping glance. Boom. There she was, at the bar with Paul only feet from her. He wasn't minding her as such, but he was there, which was lucky as she was almost totally surrounded by men. The mood was jovial, she was laughing and sipping a drink. There was no issue there, and still Michael's face set hard. It was jealousy.

Chapter Fifteen

May 1996

Michael drove back to the house very carefully with James in the back of the car. The last thing they needed just then was a tug for speeding. James was leaning on the car rug so as not to get any blood on the interior upholstery. Michael helped him up to the door and then down the stairs into the kitchen. James could have walked with not too much of a problem but he was not good with his own blood. He could deal with everyone else's, but not his own; something that only Michael and a select few other knew about James. It wasn't the pain, as his threshold was actually quite high. It was just seeing it coming from his own body at such a rate, it made him woozy. He sat at the dining table, clutching the large white T-shirt that Michael had given him from the sports bag in the boot of the car, to his thigh. The bleeding had slowed and the blood on the cotton was now turning from red to a dark brown colour as the heat from his hand dried it. Michael looked up at him after ripping his trouser leg up the seam by the front pocket and briefly examining the wound. 'You'll need to get that seen to,' he sighed, peering at the hole in James's leg and the blood now quietly seeping from it before him.

'It's fine!' James protested. But both men knew that it was a lie and that he would need to see a doctor, or a nurse at the least. 'Besides, if I go the Royal, they'll call the old bill and then I'll probably spend the rest of the night in the fuckin' cells,' he said quite rightly and Michael nodded at him.

'What was that nurse's name?' Michael asked then.

James looked blankly at him. 'Jo. Why?'

'You got her number?' he said.

'No.'

'You fucked her! I thought you might have it,' Michael breathed and there was silence.

As they pondered on what to do they heard Beth come through the front door. She walked heavily across the hallway and down the stairs. It was obvious that she knew that someone was in, she was making her own presence known just in case it was James with one of his many Saturday night conquests. It wouldn't have been the first time she'd strolled around the house and caught them in indelicate positions.

'We're decent!' James called up as he saw her edge down the steps. His voice was pinched and Michael looked at the colour of him. He hadn't lost much blood and his cheeks were flushed, not ashen, a good sign.

'Fuck me!' Beth said in half whisper, the shock more evident by the expression on her face than the tone of her voice as she laid eyes on her brother. 'What in the hell have you two been up to now?' She looked at Michael for the explanation, aware that if it had anything to do with James it would more than likely be a massive mouthful of lies.

'He got stabbed.'

He said it so casually that both Beth and James almost found themselves laughing at him. 'Happens all the time,' he added, realising what they found so amusing despite the situation.

'Where?' she asked.

'In the fucking leg!' James replied.

She rolled her eyes, stepping closer. 'Idiot. I meant where. Like at the club or where?' She crouched before him on the floor, looking up at him, the amusement evident in her expression.

'Outside the club,' Michael replied for him. He could tell that James was on the verge of a wonderful story and as usual, thought it best just to tell her the truth. 'He intruded on a prior engagement.' His tone was suggestive enough. There was no need for him to go on. James didn't, hadn't and probably never would care if his choice for the evening had a man in tow already. He'd take on anyone, no matter what the consequence and here and now, being in the kitchen with a hole in his leg was the price he was to pay for his chosen way of life.

'Did you win?' she smiled, making light conversation. If there was one thing she knew, it was never to make James panic when he was bleeding from more than a scratch or bloody nose.

'Yeah. I won.' James half smiled at her, aware of what she was doing. He was grateful to her.

'She gave him her number,' Michael said with a sigh and a shake of his head. Beth got the picture purely from the expression on his face.

'Was she worth it?' she sounded sceptical. Her gaze fell on Michael, who shook his head at her question.

'Too skinny, far too skinny!'

James scoffed then. 'Yeah, for you! Anything too small'd die under your weight,' he said, looking up at him.

'Nice tits though,' Michael added for effect.

'Did you see 'em?' James almost laughed.

'Did I! Actually, as you'll be laid up for a while, d'you mind if I—' He paused, catching Beth's eye.

'Bollocks. She's mine!' James added, sounding pained.

'Hey, I was just asking.'

'You'll need stitches,' Beth said, pretending to ignore their banter as she pulled the T-shirt away from the wound, prodding it a little so that she could get a better look at it. 'Did you clean it yet?'

James looked worried. 'No!' He suddenly sounded as if he was about to panic.

'Michael, can you go and get the box for me? It's in the cupboard,' she began with a point of her finger.

'By the washer. Aye. I know.' He began to cross the room, into the kitchen area. He opened a cupboard and came back to the table with a large white and orange plastic box that looked more like something that would be found in an ambulance. In fact, it was something that had been found in an ambulance, by James actually. It was a full medical kit and Beth unclipped the two hinges and pulled it open on the table next to where she now stood. After washing her hands at the sink she cleaned James's leg carefully and studied it further. 'Knife or glass?' she asked without looking up.

'Knife,' James breathed as she gave the two sides of the gash a squeeze together.

'Her bloke carries, and you want to see her again?' She shook her head at him. 'Well. It's clean, but you'll need a couple of stitches or it won't knit back together properly.'

'Do you really want to touch him without gloves on? There's a long list of places *he's* been and I don't have it on me right now,' Michael smiled.

'Fuck off,' James laughed. Michael was silent for a few moments and he stared at the hole in James's thigh, deep in thought. He then looked up and into Beth's eyes. He tilted his head to one side, raised his eyebrows at her and just for good measure gave her his secret smile. The one that usually got him what he wanted with the ladies.

'Forget it!' she said before he had even opened his mouth to speak. 'If you want it done, lovey, you do it!' And she thrust out a firm finger in his direction.

'Now, you know I can't sew,' he said, gesturing at his chest with large fingers and James looked at the pair of them in turn, his mouth gawking.

'Fuck off! You're a fuckin' loony!' he exclaimed, realising that they were taking about stitching him up themselves.

'We've the stuff to be doing it with, all you have to do is pretend it's the—the Christmas turkey.' Michael kept his tone neutral then but a grin cracked out on to his face as he finished speaking.

'Do I look like a fuckin' turkey?' James said firmly and Michael patted him on the shoulder.

'You do that, yes, unless you think that going to the hospital's a better idea.' He paused. 'I'll just go and call the police now, shall I? Save the wait when we get there!'

There was another pause as Beth pondered the situation; she knew that Michael was right. That was exactly what would happen. All the while Michael looked at her face and he could almost hear her talking herself into it.

'Oh, go on then!' she said with a long-drawn-out breath.

James looked nervously at the pair of them as they both now crouched before him with their noses practically in the hole in his thigh.

'You *can* do this!' Michael breathed. Beth looked into his eyes and he saw her nervousness.

'You're very sure!' her voice was light.

'I'd trust you,' he almost whispered. There was a spark between them that only they felt, and there was a sincerity in his tone that only she heard, but it was like lightning striking inside her. She pulled the short piece of thread through the needle that she had bent into an arc and with her eyes almost closed and a deep breath, she pierced James's skin. He didn't flinch.

June 1996

The crowds were loud and jovial. Michael was the first to appear from the car, dressed in a fitted dinner suit, complete with tie, followed by James, dressed the same way. It suited both well, being dressed up like that, and they looked like movie stars, standing on the edge of the pavement on that busy Dublin street in the warmth of the evening, fiddling with cufflinks and checking their expensive watches for the time. Beth slipped out of the car after them, adjusting the long black evening dress she wore. The material settled very well just on the tips of her evening sandals; it was cut to perfection, with its bustier and chiffon. She did love getting all dressed up, and she was absolutely thrilled at being there just then. How Michel had secured tickets to the premiere of *Lord of the Dance* she would never know, and she didn't really care if she was honest; they were there, outside the Point Theatre, with all its glass, and all the finery, and she was so excited.

'Are we late?' she asked as the car door closed behind her, and the driver moved to get back in to the driver's seat.

'No, we've time for a drink,' Michael smiled. He was excited too, but didn't think it was very cool to show it, especially in front of James, who had not been overly keen on joining them at first. This type of thing was not his scene, but he knew that it was important to Beth, and he knew that a couple of days in Ireland was just the ticket. He also knew that the tickets had been very hard to come by, and therefore probably worth taking a gander at this Flatley bloke's moves.

Michael was actually mentally still preening himself. He was a genius, and he knew that it was an actual fact that it was who you know, not what you know, when he's got the tickets, which had sold out months before. The production manager was a good friend of his father's and had been more than happy to ensure that they received three, and passes, and of course, all for the premiere night in Dublin. He was also pleased, as this had pleased Beth beyond words. She really wanted to be here, and so, here they were. He looked at her; she was magnificent in that dress. A good choice, a very good choice, worth the tag, and the start of a small dispute with James as they'd met in reception at his parents' hotel that it was a bit too "booby", as he'd called it. What was he talking about? She was killer, absolutely beautiful, and by the way she walked ahead of them to the chauffeur-driven car waiting for them, she knew it too.

July 1996

The heat hit them like a wave as they got off the plane. It was hazy heat, the type you can almost touch, the type that surrounds you and consumes you and the type that confirmed that you really were indeed on holiday. Inside the airport wasn't much better. There was no air conditioning and there were far too many people there for it to be anything but clammy, but despite all of this the three of them still wore broad smiles. With their luggage accounted for and collected they made their way outside into the taxi rank.

'Where we going?' James asked looking at Michael.

'The Dassia, Chandris.' He had it all written down, and it always amazed him that James would travel thousands of miles in the hope that one of them would know the final destination, though he had a suspicion that if he were to frisk James, he'd find all the details of where they were going and at least three pre-planned routes on how to get there.

'You can't just wear that!' James half whispered as Beth slipped off her sundress to reveal the wide-backed thong and bikini top she wore beneath.

'Oh, really!' she replied, sitting on the beach towel he'd just laid down for her. He was about to speak again when the top came off too.

'Oh, Babe,' he whinged, aware of the all the male admiration she was already receiving on the beach. Michael, woken from his doze by James's whining tone, turned his head from one side to the other as he lay on his stomach on the other side of her. He tilted his sunglasses down and glanced at her before looking further across to James.

'They're only staring because she's so white,' he laughed, lightening the moment. James had been aware of what would happen now that she was older and far more shapely than even the year before.

'I'm not white!' she exclaimed.

'Okay, pale then,' he smiled.

'This is two weeks' worth of sun beds, I'll have you know, thank you very much, Michael,' she added. He didn't reply. He was having a hard time focusing on her face as they chatted in the heat of the day, let alone stringing together a coherent sentence. She turned over after about half an hour, putting her hands over her face and that was when Michael got up and announced that he was going for a swim. He couldn't deal with her being so close and so naked.

The sun set across the beach, and a kind of peace crept across them as they watched its beauty. This was their third night and all three were just beginning to feel the benefits of the tranquillity. There were no phones here; they weren't looking over their shoulders all the time, watching to see who was behind them. It was truly fabulous and very plush. Beth stared out across the sea from her seat at the drinks table on the edge of the beach. The water was almost still, but for calm waves and the moonlight twinkling upon it. Michael poured the remains of the bottle of wine into his glass and sighed lightly. James put his beer down on the table and settled back in his chair. He was humming a tune, a tune that both Beth and Michael recognised. Absently they too began to hum it.

'Fuck it,' James exclaimed suddenly, and then, as if all of one mind they got up and made a dash straight for the sea. Cheering and laughing as they ran, making the other holidaymakers stare across the sand in bewilderment. Still clothed, except for their shoes, they dived in, laughing and joking in the warmth of the water.

'Night swimming! Honestly!' Beth managed between gasps of laughter.

August 1996

Elizabeth went down into the kitchen, dressed and ready to leave the house. She was like a fresh breeze, a breeze of perfume and hairspray. Michael sat at the dining table swigging tepid coffee. He watched her, taking his time, enjoying that fact that she hadn't noticed him. He watched her put her bag down on the counter and root through it, looking for a pack of cigarettes. She lit one and blew out the smoke with a sigh. He saw the rise and fall of her chest beneath the cotton of her fitted shirt and he let his eyes take in the rest of her.

'Nervous?' he asked loudly after a time and she jumped with fright.

'Fuck me!' she burst out, snapping her head to where the voice had come from. She'd been so wrapped up in thought that she really hadn't seen him sitting there so quietly.

'Obviously! I'll take that as a yes, shall I?' he laughed and she turned and frowned at him. 'What time are you going?'

'The doors open at nine. Lucy'll be here at eight-thirty, so I have an hour,' she said, looking at her watch.

'Oh! I'll be gone by then,' he said giving her a glance from beneath thick lashes. She laughed at his expression. He was the toughest man she'd come across in her life, and she'd met a few of the best. He was also more than a bit of a Romeo when it came to the women, but he'd shied away from Lucy's unwanted advances over the past year with real fever. He didn't mind the banter, she knew that; it was the fact that they both knew that Lucy was quite serious and indeed, quite experienced in matters of the opposite sex that bothered him. 'Will you call me on the mobile?'

'If I don't top myself first, sure!' she said and although he knew she was joking, her tone was decidedly serious.

'You'll do fine!' he said firmly, 'And it's not like you don't already have a career ahead of you, is it?' He lit himself a cigarette and studied the carton rather than look at her.

'No, I know. It's just that I've worked really hard, Michael.'

He nodded at her, understanding exactly what she was saying. It had been the same for him when he'd taken 'A' levels and passed his business degree. It was all very nice to have all those qualifications but what good did they do you when your path was already set as his was? 'I know you have,' he said seriously and it was true. She had studied hard for months. He had every faith in her and he knew that she wouldn't fail, couldn't fail. 'I'll not take excuses for failure,' he laughed lightly, pointing a finger in her direction. He paused, watching her flick through the pile of telephone messages on post-it notes on the counter top by the phone. She read them, screwed some up, and others she stuck back down on the counter again.

'Where's James?' She looked up, lighting another cigarette for herself. Catching the look in Michael's eye she smiled. 'Anyone we know?' she added sarcastically.

'Probably not!' came Michael's reply.

'He is such a slag,' she laughed, shaking her head at the thought of James's continued sexual antics. He was the original walking male hormone. If it was still wet and warm, James'd have it.

'That he is.'

'But then, so are you!' she said, holding up a small yellow note with a scribbled name and number on it in James's bold scribble script.

'Me?' he said indignantly.

'Yes, you! And who is Marie?' she continued, a vision of a busty Spaniard coming to mind as she spoke. 'Another nun?' Her eyebrow was raised.

'A friend!' He was smiling; she was obviously more than that.

'Oh, really?' her tone almost urging him on.

'Yes!' he breathed.

'How friendly?' she laughed, noticing that there were four messages for him from her there within the small pile. 'Come on, tell me!' She was pleading with amusement.

'Reasonably. Not quite on par with your brother, but close enough,' he smiled and she made a suggestive face, raising her eyebrows at his comment.

'Yuck! You two share?'

Michael too pulled a face of disgust. 'Elizabeth.' It was a warning tone.

'That's all you're going to say, isn't it!' she said after a short pause between them. He nodded. She knew him so well, he thought.

October 1996

Beth heard the commotion in the reception area before the doors from the bar swung open and a youngish man with thick blonde hair was literally thrown out and on to the reception carpet, head first.

'Tosser!' he heaved.

'Oh ey, whatever!' Michael spat. He was breathing hard and his face was blank, devoid of any expression. He was working. This wasn't personal and no-one else moved to assist him either. 'I told you once!' He grabbed him up from the floor and the young man struggled. 'And I don't tell people twice.' He glanced at Frank. 'Get the door!' His tone was hard and Frank snapped into action. 'Get on the link, this one's night is over,' he added, then handing him through.

Beth stepped back into the alcove by the back office door and watched as he escorted the man out of the doors, now aided by Frank. Something tingled deep within her as she watched him. He was so powerful, and he excited her way beyond her own comprehension. Her heart was racing as she studied him. His strength was breathtaking and a thousand thoughts bounced through her head, but as to their exact nature, she couldn't be sure.

'He's a boy, ain't he!' Paul laughed with a shake of his head.

'Yeah, but a bit rough!' one of the other doormen replied, his eyes still on Michael through the glass of the doors.

'Rough? You should 'a' seen it. Michael said no, lad disagreed. He thought it was okay to grope the ladies up at the top bar, so Michael escorts him out. Beautiful!' Paul sounded really impressed and in awe of Michael. Most were, if she was honest, and Beth listened to his every word. He was right, it was beautiful, Michael was beautiful, and Michael disliked pervy blokes, he always said that everyone should be able to have a night out without fear.

When Michael came back into the warmth of the reception his gaze instantly settled on her, and she felt her cheeks flush with colour. His features changed, softened and he smiled across at her as she thought of something to say to him. 'People skills, Michael! People skills!' she managed, because she was still trying to sort out the emotions that were stirred by his actions. She'd seen worse, far, far worse than that display, but still she couldn't hide the fact that he intrigued her; not just with his strength, but the fact that he could turn his strength on and off at will.

'That was my people skills for tonight! And what, may I ask, are you doing here?' His tone was thick and he was still trying to steady his breathing.

'I was passing,' she smiled.

'Sorry, you can't come in! It's over twenty-ones tonight and management's *very* strict. The boss is a bit of a slave driver, likes to use her whip!' He tried to keep his voice serious but couldn't and they both laughed then.

'You wish I used a whip!' she smiled. There was a moment between them then, a silent conversation between two bodies. 'Kinky!'

'Is Pat here?' she asked then, breaking the unspoken conversation in half, as if with a knife.

'No, no, just your brother, he's the in-house entertainment tonight,' Michael replied. Beth cringed, she knew that tone, that face. James was drinking.

'Oh dear! Has he stripped yet?' she dared to ask.

'No, not yet.' He looked at his watch. 'But the night is still young, Elizabeth. Are you coming in?'

'Yeah, go on then. I'll let you buy me a drink, but just one, mind!' and she stepped forwards.

'Oh, okay!' Michael laughed putting his hand around her shoulder and leading her into the bar. 'Oh yeah, I have a joke for you,' he smiled.

'Uh, hu?'

'Okay, a group of girls go on holiday. They see a five-storey hotel with a sign that reads *For Women Only*. They haven't booked anywhere to stay so they figure they'll go in. The man on the door explains to them how it works if they want to stay. "We have five floors, you go up floor by floor, and once you find what you're looking for, you can stay there. It's easy to decide, since each floor has signs telling you what's inside". They start going up, and on the first floor the sign reads *All the men here have it short and thin*. The friends just laugh and without hesitation move on to the next floor. The sign on the second floor reads *All the men here have it long and thin*. This wasn't good enough so they move up to the third floor, where the sign read *All the men here have it short and thick*. This still wasn't what they wanted, but there are still two floors to go so they move on to the next floor. On the fourth floor, the sign was perfect. *All the men here have it long and thick*. The women get all excited and are about to go in when they realise that there's one floor left. Wondering what they're missing, they go to the fifth floor, where the sign read *There are no men here! This floor was built only to prove that there is no way to please a woman!* He almost laughed himself and Beth smiled, then the laugh came.

'Where did you find that one?' she asked. 'At least it's vaguely clean.'

He smiled again. 'Stevie boy.'

Beth looked at him. 'What, you two talking now then?' she asked cautiously.

'Hey, hey, it was just a heated discussion!' He held his hand out to her in a gesture of righteousness.

'Pha! Mexican stand-off, more like!' Beth looked into his eyes as she spoke, the look there more gentle than her tone. 'What were you two arguing about, anyway?' she asked lightly.

He looked at her, then shrugged. 'Boy stuff. And we weren't arguing!' was all he said on the subject.

Beth settled into the passenger seat next to Michael and James climbed in to the back, head first. He was on his stomach and out for the count almost immediately. James lay softly snoring on the back seat of his car by the time Michael pulled away from the club. Soundlessly they pulled out onto the deserted roads. It had been a good night considering that Beth was only going to stay for one or two.

'I am so hungry!' Michael said in a half whisper. 'You?' He looked across at her.

'I could eat?' she breathed. 'But I'm not cooking and everything's closed.'

'What about burgers? Kebabs?' He didn't give her time to argue or ponder.

He pulled onto the ring road and sped up towards the city. There was always a van about up there at three am and he was right. They parked and got out, leaving James where he lay on the back seat. 'What d'you fancy?' he asked as they waited to be served. Beth stared at the painted list on the side of the van. There were burgers, sausages, chicken and kebabs on offer. 'What you having?' she asked, wanting inspiration.

'Three burgers and chips!' he replied, rubbing his hands together.

'Yeah, go on then!' she nodded.

'What? The same?' he almost laughed.

'No, crazy big person! Just a burger and small chips.'

Michael looked back towards the car. 'What about sleeping beauty?' he laughed.

'Get him a really greasy kebab with hot soggy salad.'

'You're a cow sometimes, you know that?' Michael said with a shake of his head.

'Yeah, but only sometimes.' There was a drop in her tone and he turned his head, looking down at her as he did so. There was something in it that caught him, made his own voice falter in his throat.

They waited for their food and stood by the roadside, watching the cold world go by. It was strange, Beth thought suddenly. This wasn't the nicest part of town by any stretch of the imagination, in fact it was a bit on the ropey side, but with Michael there with her she hadn't noticed until that point, actually thinking about it. He made her feel safe and secure wherever she was and whatever they were doing. It was a strange thought to have, but a nice one and as she watched another car load of hungry club goers get into the queue she slipped her arm around his and found even more safety in the warmth of him.

November 1996

Pat and Judy's firework parties were almost legendary and everyone wanted to attend. Thousands and thousands were spent on the occasion every year, and no expense was ever spared. People were dressed for the cold outside, but mostly tonight would be inside, with excellent catered food and fine wines, again something Pat and Judy enjoyed. It was a real event on the local social calendar within their circle. Beth, Michael and James pulled up in a cab, each holding the bags and boxes retrieved from the boot of the taxi, each quite excited.

James had been out that afternoon and had spent four hundred pounds on one box. He was like a kid when it came to times like that, and he was so excited about playing with explosives, despite the fact that Pat always had his gardener, Lewis, deal with it to be on the safe side. He was more cautious of late, everyone had noticed it; especially when it came to his family, and especially when it came to anything that could end up going horribly wrong.

'It won't light,' Beth said standing out by the conservatory doors with a sparkler in her hand. 'It's a dud!' she sounded deflated.

'Child!' Michael almost whispered to her as he tried to light it. 'Here, try a plain one,' and he passed her another already lit one.

'But they're really rather crap!' she laughed as the sparks began to spring out before her eyes.

'Stop your whingeing woman!' As he spoke, he managed to get her original sparkler to light. It glowed pink, then burst into glittering life before their eyes. 'There you go now!' He passed it to her, taking the other from her.

'See, pretty!' she smiled.

The sparks made her eyes sparkle. The glow made her face seem even warmer to him. He let out a long sigh, clearing his mind of the thoughts that entered it. Now was not the time or the place to get a hard-on. He looked away from her and across the garden towards the fire. He looked straight at Pat, who was looking right back at him. As the two stared at each other, pretending not to, Michael's mind wandered again and he wondered what Pat would say if he had any idea of Michael's thoughts. They weren't particularly honourable at all, but he could think of worse, that was for sure.

He suddenly focused on Pat, and it occurred to him that the reason Pat was staring was that he did have an idea, that he did know what Michael was thinking. No, he thought then, there was no way Pat would think that. He'd never given him reason to think such things. And besides, it was Michael who was supposed to be the psychic mind reader, not Pat.

Christmas 1996 and New Year 1997

Michael went home to his parents in Ireland three days before Christmas. Beth and James dropped him at Stanstead and with heavy hearts they'd wished him a Merry Christmas and left for the drive back to the City. The days that followed were really strained and the house seemed quite empty without him. It was oddly quiet without his voice, his banter and his music and neither of them could settle. They hadn't faced a Christmas alone together and it was strange; not bad, just strange.

The morning before Christmas Eve James sat in the dining area. He opened the post. There were always masses of it and sometimes he really felt sorry for the postman. He opened every piece, junk as well and put them into neat piles of bills, business, personal and of course, just junk. The phone rang and within two rings he had jumped from his seat and answered it. ''Ello?' he paused. 'Mike! Yes, mate, you missing us already?' He was smiling as he spoke.

Beth walked down into the room and grinned at him. 'Is that Michael?' she mouthed and James nodded at her, his chin and shoulder supporting the receiver as he lit two cigarettes. 'We're all right, mate,' he continued and Beth took the cigarette he was holding out to her and leaned close to him.

'We miss you already!' she said down the receiver. He began to talk to her and James passed the receiver to her.

''Ere, Babe, he wants a word.'

'Michael. Oh, I'm okay. We miss you. How's your mum and dad? Excellent! Yeah, we're okay. I will. Do you want James again? Okay, you too. Bye!'

When James finally got off the telephone he looked remarkably pleased with himself. He was a man with a plan. An hour or so later his mobile telephone rang and he answered it. The conversation was short and Beth took no notice whatsoever. He was being shady, which usually meant that he was on the phone to a woman she wouldn't approve of so she busied herself emptying the dishwasher, which was only a quarter full and that was only with cups, a couple of spoons and an ashtray. He cleared the call and walked up behind her. 'Leave that, Babe.' He sounded odd and she turned and looked up at him.

'Why, you going to do it?' She sounded sceptical. He laughed at such a ridiculous suggestion. James did many things, but filling and emptying the dishwasher was not on the list.

'No way. We are, though, on the four o'clock flight out to Dublin so may I suggest that you go and pack!' He sounded almost regal.

'Oh! I don't believe it!' Beth screamed with delight as his words sank into her head and without another word she was off up the stairs, with him hot on her heels.

Chapter Sixteen

February 1997

The navy-coloured Jaguar pulled up quietly in the car park and the darkly tinted passenger side window came down with a quiet buzz. The chill in the air bit deeply and the two people sat inside shuddered a little as the frosty air whipped at them.

'Is that her?' a crisp, clean voice asked as the window buzzed some of the way back up again. He was well dressed in a suit and coat with his hair cut long. His blue eyes scanned all around him.

'Yeah, pretty little thing, ey?' another voice, more common and gravely than his replied.

'Very, but not so little.' He sounded interested, very interested.

'Pure as snow,' the other laughed. 'Or so they say. Jimmy and the mick won't let anyone near enough, if y'know what I mean.'

Sean Oxley nodded to himself slowly. 'So they say! And where did the baby go? What has arrived in its place?' he almost whispered the words. 'Oh Elizabeth, Elizabeth. Out on your own without the Irish gypsy to protect you from the world, and what of that brother of yours?' he tutted to himself. 'It almost seems as though they want something bad to happen to you, allowing you out alone.'

His companion sat silently, listening. He wasn't moved by anything he said. He'd heard it all before from him. He himself was actually looking forward to some of what had been muttered in hushed tones about Elizabeth Dobson. Nothing they'd done had riled the group up yet, but he'd bet his own mum on them being ready for battle if he was allowed his way. They watched. She was standing in front of her parents' graves. She stood for a long time. Still they watched.

He watched her standing, talking. Talking to the dead, honest to fucking God, were this lot for real?

Nicholas King was a sadist. He got his kicks from inflicting all sorts of pain, and hurting, and making to suffer, those who entered his world. He liked to make people cry, especially women, and especially when he was having sex with them. He shifted in his seat a little as a twinge of excitement went through him. He liked to inflict just enough discomfort to lull them back into a false sense of security, and then he'd go all out on them. The things he'd do to that one, he thought, still looking at her. Fuck her cunt, he'd stick his cock right up in to her arse, right up hard and deep, the sort of thrust that'd make you puke. Oh yeah, he'd make her cry, and puke, and bleed.

He glanced at his employer, who too sat in silence then, just watching her. He was totally focused on her, and her alone. He could see the cogs going around and wondered what his employer had up his sleeve for their next move on the Dobson empire. He hoped it was as, so many other things they'd achieved lately, and as pleasurable.

She stood tall and proud despite the weather and was grateful for the warmth her coat gave. She could remember the funeral as if it were that day again. The sting of tears got her and she sucked in her breath, desperate not to let them fall. She'd cried too much in her lifetime already to cry any more. She thought back over the past years. How their lives had changed, how they'd coped with the world and all it threw at them. And then, as always of late, her thoughts went to Michael. She wondered how it would have been without his presence there with them. How they would have coped without his calm in their storm and more tears came into her eyes then. Not tears of sadness; tears of love, love and affection. 'What do I feel, Mum?' she asked softly. 'It almost hurts when he's not around. I know you see me. Sometimes I hope you close your eyes, but something's missing, and as much as I'm sorry, it's not you. He looks at me sometimes and all I can see in my head is you and Dad. How you two used to look at each other. Is that what I'm feeling? Is it? God, I wish you were here. I really need to talk to someone about this, and I don't think James is really the person to talk to.' She stood for a while longer and then after a few more whispered words, promising to come again soon, she was off down the newly laid path and heading towards the warmth of her waiting car.

'Let's go!' Oxley said with a nod. Both had been transfixed, watching her. And both secretly wondered what she had said to those graves. What words she could have had to say so many years after they were gone from sight. It didn't cross either mind that she may be talking to the dead about the bane of their lives, and if they had known, all the better for their plans and plotting.

March 1997

James could hardly believe his ears. He sat on the edge of the desk, staring at Michael with a gormless expression on his face, and he fidgeted with the lighter he held in his hand.

'Of course, it's only a rumour, James. It's just talk, we don't know for sure that that was said, if indeed anything was really said at all! It could be just bollocks, y'know.' If anyone else had been so casual about what had just been said, about what they were discussing right at that moment James would have gone off the wall, but he knew that she meant as much to Michael as she did to him so instead, he digested Michael's logic.

'Tell me again!' He said, his breath hard through his nostrils.

Michael lit himself a cigarette and then got up off the chair he'd been sitting in, opposite James.

'It's just scare tactics James, and it's working!' he almost snapped.

'Again!' James banged his hand on the desk then as he too rose from his seated position. 'Frank heard a rumour, you know. Oxley isn't stupid enough to make a move like that, is he now? It's scare tactics, James, that's all. Trust me. If there's any truth in it I'll kill the bastard myself!' Michael's own tone was sure and strong but inside, somewhere deep down inside he shuddered. He knew he shouldn't have told him that Oxley was seen watching Elizabeth on more than one occasion, and worse still, King, too, had been seen. Now she wouldn't be let out of James's sight and no one would get any peace. He sighed at the thought, and the thought of King being within feet of Elizabeth.

'Sorry, am I bothering you?' James snarled then, and Michael glared across the room at him and suddenly James felt very small, very small indeed. He rubbed his eyes.

'I'm sorry, Mike. I just—I can't—' He stopped.

Michael's gaze was gentle on him again then. 'I know, my friend, I know. But, as I've said, if it comes, we'll deal with it!'

James huffed again. 'Should we tell the old man?' James said then, referring to Pat. Michael kissed his teeth and tongued the inside of his mouth as he stared then at the floor before him.

'Yes, if he hears this from anyone but us, he'll put the devil himself to shame!' Michael said finally, his tone almost amused. 'And, don't worry yourself!' he ended.

'That's easy for you to say, ain't it?' James's tone rose again.

'Hey, I care too!' Michael's tone was sure and hard.

'Yes, mate. I know you do. Oh, bollocks. Fuck this. Come on, let's go get a drink, ay?' James said suddenly. He didn't want to think about it. It didn't bear thinking about. They'd just have to be careful, more careful with her.

April 1997

The stereo was on low and the sound of U2's *Without You* came from the speakers as Michael lay on the bed in his neat room, on his back. He rested his hands at the back of his head and stared up at the ceiling, watching the light from a reasonably warm day fade away in the dusk. He could hear Beth's music in her room and the echoes of George Michael's *Father Figure* drifted up through the floor. It was obvious that she thought she was alone in the house. She was too courteous to play her music so loud if it was going to disturb anyone else. He could see her in his mind's eye, pottering about at her dressing table.

159

He got up from his position on the bed and turned his stereo right down so that he could hear hers more clearly and then settled back down on the bed. She was always listening to the gush stuff, as James called it, and he thought he heard her singing along as the music went on below him. Something came over him and he found himself thinking about her more again. The feeling that rushed through him wasn't unfamiliar but it made him catch his breath. Something inside him felt incredibly dirty, like he was cheating on someone or something, but he wasn't, was he? She was a lot younger than he was, true, but other than that—

He stopped himself and realised that someone was knocking on the door.

'Come in.' He sat up on the bed as the door opened. She took in the sight of him, making him look down at himself. He was dressed in only a small pair of shorts, having had a shower not half an hour before.

'Oh! Sorry, I didn't realise!' She blushed. How innocent, he thought, checking that he wasn't giving her too much of a view.

'No, no, it's fine. I just had a shower.' That wasn't technically true. 'Have you been in long?' He knew the answer to that question. He'd heard her, listened as she'd gone about her business in the house below him. 'What can I do for you?' He meant to ease her but something in his tone made her redden to burning as she clung to the door with one hand.

'I wanted to borrow a blank tape. Kerry wants a copy of my new CD for the car and I don't have any. I did have, but James took them for that ghastly garage crap!' Michael smiled at her, taking in every feature, every movement, as if someone was going to be asking questions on her once she had gone from the room.

'Of course.' He stood up and moved towards her, grabbing two wrapped black cassettes from the top of the stereo stacking unit.

He noticed that for all her blushing, she didn't move away from him and he wondered if she even realised that she did blush when they were together. 'Thank you.' She was so courteous. Why couldn't she see it, feel it, didn't he ooze it?

'Pleasure,' he replied. She stared at him for a long while, they both had hold of the tapes and it was a while longer before Michael let go.

'Thank you,' she said again. She couldn't think of anything else to say instead. 'I'll see you in a bit, yeah?' she added and he nodded at her as she left the room. Left him standing there, practically with his cock in his hand.

Back in her room Beth sat on the edge of the bed listening to her heart as it thundered in her chest. She was aching again, from the outside in, and it was killing her. Nothing she said or did eased it. No one she spoke to or *played with* seemed to come close to him. She wanted him, she knew she did, but she didn't understand it.

Why was it hurting inside? Why did she almost die every time he was so close? She had visions in her mind of doing things with him, things she'd never even seen before, but she was sure. She could almost feel what his fingers inside her would feel like. And then her thoughts were back on his body. He was so bloody big, he made her feel like an eight, not a sixteen. He didn't have a six-pack, he was broader than that; he was solid and covered in dark hair that ran all the way from his chest to his belly and lower. She opened her eyes, focusing on the LCD on the hi-fi. *Out of your reach, little girl* a voice said inside her head and she signed.

May 1997

There was trouble brewing, James could feel it and he grabbed at the radio that was by the till behind the top bar and called for Michael on it, wishing then that he wore one of the radios the doormen wore, but they were too pretentious for him. 'Frank. No problem, no problem.' He waited for the reply.

'Go for, Frank,' came the response.

'Is Mike wiv you?'

'Yep, hold on,' came the reply. There were a few seconds, then Michael's voice came clearly over the radio.

'James,' he said firmly. 'Anything goin' on down your way?' he asked. There was a pause.

'Not a whisper, which is why I'm thinking that something's about to go down, James.' Michaels' voice was still firm.

'Where are you now?' James asked.

'Still in reception. Why, do you want me to come to you?' Michael asked.

'No, mate. Wait there, I'll come to you. I wanna check the tellies!'

James replaced the radio where he found it and made his way down the stairs and out through the doors and into reception where Michael stood waiting for him. He dwarfed the two doormen, who reminded James of pit bulls. He stared at his friend and still couldn't help feeling apprehensive; he had a really bad feeling. Even Michael, the calmest man he knew in situations like this, seemed to be on edge.

'Ere, you don't think they'll try anything at one of the bars, do you?' James said as they stood by the desk, watching the club from eleven different angles on the monitors. Michael looked into his eyes as he thought and then he shook his head at his friend''s suggestion.

'Go on. There's nothing doing here. Go get a drink or something.' His tone was gentle, overly soft and James double took him before turning to leave.

He waited for James to go back into the club before he moved from his position behind the desk. With a wave of his hand he motioned for Frank to leave his menacing place at the door, leaving the other two to it. He pulled a twenty-pound note from his back trouser pocket and held it out.

'Sorry Mike, don't do the wild thing with ugly Irish bastards like you,' he laughed, unclasping his hand before him. 'Not even for money!'

'Hey now, are you saying you don't find me attractive?' Michael laughed. Then the laugh was gone from his features and Frank instantly stopped smiling too. 'Can you do me a favour?' he asked and Frank nodded. Course he could. Michael was the man, a top bloke.

'Yes, mate!' He sounded really pleased to be asked.

'Go to Baileys. Beth's there tonight. Don't leave there without her. If she wants to go home, you take her. If not, only when we get there do you go. You don't leave her side tonight, Frank, do you hear!' It wasn't a question.

'I'll just get me coat,' Frank said, giving Michael a wink. It was the middle of May and Frank didn't have a coat with him. Michael nodded at him as he moved away from him. He understood Frank completely. Go ready. Go prepared for the worst and go home happy that it didn't happen.

Michael watched him get into the taxi from the doorway. There would be a very large drink in Frank's pay packet that month, regardless of the outcome and it would come straight from Michael's own pocket. When he turned away James was standing at the bar door watching him. He had a strange look on his face and Michael recognised it. It was gratitude. He'd seen it on James's face many times before. He shrugged, looking away again, a slight smile toying with his lips. James watched Michael's back profile then, he was a fucking big lad, he thought. And it was strange that with such size could come such compassion, such love. He wanted to say something then, at that moment but nothing fitting came to mind. He wanted to thank him for taking care of them, him and his sister. Wanted to hug him for all the hugs he'd given in their hours of need. But there was no need for such a gesture. Michael knew.

'Come on, I'll get you that drink,' Michael said, finally turning back around and breaking the silence between them.

It was a refreshing, quiet and very lazy Sunday night in. Michael lay on the floor, his head supported by a cushion from the armchair. Beth lay on her stomach on the sofa, resting her head in the cradle of her arms, looking down at him as they talking in the lamplight. She loved their little talks as much as he did. It was something that James was almost incapable of doing. If he was awake and not in his bed then he was out and about, he couldn't just sit and relax. It wasn't in his nature. Both knew this, and neither were offended when, after the film that they'd rented had finished, he'd made his excuses and left the house.

'What do you want from a man?' Michael asked, draining the remains of the bottle of red they'd opened not half an hour before into his own glass, having filled hers again first. She thought for a few seconds before answering his off-the-cuff question. She presumed it stemmed from the movie they had just finished watching, a girl meets boy sort of movie.

'I want goose bumps, like in the movies. I want *my* fairytale. And I want to feel completely relaxed. I want to be able to talk to him, whoever he is, like I talk to you.'

He looked away from her, his thoughts clear. *I could do that,* he thought, giving her a nod.

'Why do you ask?'

He looked up at her as she spoke, watching her lips move, almost un-hearing, but taking in every word she said.

'It's getting near that time, y'know. You've had them sniffing, but you're not inspired, are you!' It was a statement.

'They're cute. Some are just fucking filth. But no. I'm not inspired!' She smiled. He laughed slightly at her comment, but didn't go to speak. She wasn't finished, he could tell.

'None of them compare to what I have in my life already. They don't really listen, they don't really care. They want me because of who I am and because I'm—' she paused, almost laughing at the fact herself, 'A virgin!' she paused again.

'Does it bother you?' he interrupted then.

'Sometimes it does. It's not such a big deal, I don't think. Sometimes I feel like just getting it done, out the way, y'know?' and she laughed.

'Can't say that I do.' He laughed, too.

'But then I do want to wait for the right bloke. None of them make me ache—and I want to ache,' she finished.

He nodded. 'So you know the ache,' he said quietly, his voice almost a whisper. He already knew that she did. He could see it on her face when he looked at her sometimes, feel it coming from within her like an actual touch.

'We make it sound like a disease!' she smiled.

He nodded, understanding exactly what she meant.

'What about you? You have all these women, but do any of them do more than satisfy a need? Do any of them get under your skin?' She moved and shifted. 'Satisfy a need?'

He was thinking.

'Yeah—' her voice was low. 'Is that how you see it?'

He pondered it as she spoke again. 'Sure. You're a man. Animal instincts and all that, having to blow your load—'

He truly laughed then, and looked up at her 'It's not always like that, Elizabeth.'

'Really?' she was quizzical, and rightly so.

'Yes, really. Sometimes men do things just to please a woman. The act itself is secondary. Sometimes the thought of making someone else happy, pleasing someone else is enough to tip a man over the edge! Enough to keep him going for a long time.' He sat up, leaning on an arm of the sofa.

'Please introduce me,' she laughed. 'All I've seen so far is, suck this, rub that, grind the other!' Both laughed then. It was true, she was surrounded by love, from every angle, not sheltered from any of the banter, which in their profession was either violent or sexual, and sex itself was not something they'd taught her to respect. Not taught her that they all respected, with the right person. And now, here she was, making the cracks in their wall show with just a few simple words. And that fact saddened him. He felt then, just for a moment that he might lose her to this wonder, this ache, this curiosity about which she was so well versed, but never introduced.

Chapter Seventeen

June 1997

Beth pulled into the car park, stopped right up by the exit and got out, locking the car behind her with a bleep of the alarm. She was annoyed. Someone was in her usual space and she didn't recognise the Jaguar, for all that it was very nice. She strolled across the car park towards the entrance to the Hothouse, through the doors and into the reception area just as he was coming out of the main bar. She recognised him immediately. He looked aggressively unforgettable. He had been in to see Pat with another man a few days before and she remembered that he hadn't looked particularly happy then, either. He was about an inch or so taller than she was and almost nondescript except for his eyes; they were hateful and cold. As he made eye contact with her he hesitated, as if he was going to reach out to her and grab her. She shuddered inwardly at his obvious recognition of her, bearing in mind that she definitely hadn't been introduced to him in the past. She'd seen them the other day, but they had not seen her, she was sure of that. In fact, she had felt at the time that Paul had deliberately kept her talking in the back office behind reception as they had left that day, but she had paid it no more attention then. But now, as Paul moved swiftly and suddenly, standing slightly in front of her, protectively, it came back to the forefront of her mind.

Looking past him she noticed both James and Michael standing just inside the bar area, looking out at the scene. They looked angry too, and she got the distinct impression that she had just missed something very big. Right until he was through the doors and out of sight he held her gaze, his features blank and she returned the gesture with fever. Beth could, if she really put her mind to it, change her beautiful features from glowing to the darkest, blankest, in the blink of an eye. Something else she inherited from her father's side of the family. She didn't do it often but when it was done it was with good reason and it was indeed quite a statement of the power within the Dobson family.

'Elizabeth!' Michael snapped as he and James entered the reception area. 'Come here!' His tone brooked no argument and she turned quickly to face him.

'Who was that?' she asked sharply once he was out of sight completely. She was annoyed that Michael was being so aggressive in his tone towards her.

'Nicholas King,' Michael began, his tone now a little softer, as if he was about to apologise for his harshness.

'Did I miss something?' she asked.

Michael was about to speak again when, once again, James interrupted.

'He's a prick! And you're to keep away from him!' James replied with a point of his finger, before Michael could go into any more detail. The two men looked at each other then. Another silent conversation was held. Beth had been right in her perception of the past moments.

She had just missed something, something rather major. In he'd walked, bold as brass. He didn't actually say her name, or make any real reference to her, but both men had been aware of his little mission. It'd worked. They were now aware of how close Elizabeth was to the dangers of what was going on. How close she'd already come, with his references to the cemetery and cars and the clubs and bars she frequented with her friends, being a young lady about town. They were then aware that she was no longer a child and it had hit them both like a bucket of cold water, and fuck the ice, there were shards of glass and razor blades in it.

She was going to have to be told what was going on, how Oxley was going to push them into selling the club, and then probably the rest of the business, to him for her sake. They could do nothing else. He wasn't the sort of man that you could just shoot, or have shot. If he had been, both would have done the deed already. They were going to have to tell Pat about this visit too. That was something else neither really wanted to deal with just then; he'd go off the fucking wall about this one, that was for sure and Beth watched them. She knew when to ask questions and when to keep her opinions to herself and now was one of those times, so she didn't push it any further. She just looked into Michael's eyes and saw something there—was it pain? Fear? She looked away from him for a second or two and when she returned her gaze the look was gone and he was Michael again. The fearless warrior she knew him to be.

Late June 1997

The television was still on, although the sound was muted and the blank screen from the end of the video channel was the only light emanating from the lounge. Michael walked in silently and let his eyes adjust to the dimness. He took a deep in breath and could smell the sweet scent of her perfume; it lingered like the visions of her did, the ones that were locked in his memory, ready to recall at any given moment throughout his days. Looking down at the sofa, his heart lurched in his chest. She was so beautiful. He felt ashamed then, as the thought of her naked before him suddenly entered his mind. She was like a sister to him and it wasn't decent of him to think such things of her.

She lay there, sound asleep on her back, slightly turned towards the edge of the cushions. Her hair was down and she looked so peaceful that he hardly dared to breathe. Her blouse was open slightly and he could just see the lace on the edging of her bra. Her cotton skirt was long and clung to her legs, accentuating their shapeliness. Michael glanced at his watch; it was just gone one o'clock in the morning. He turned off the television and hesitated before moving further towards her. He slid his arms beneath her as he crouched down and rose again with her in his arms. She weighed no more than eleven, eleven and a half stone and he lifted her in his strong arms as though she weighed nothing at all. Her arms instinctively found his neck and she snuggled into the warmth of his shirt-covered chest, stirring only for a second or two as he began to walk across the lounge.

He trod soundlessly up the stairs, pushed the door open with his foot and entered her bedroom, which like the rest of the house was in complete darkness but for the light coming from outside in the street. She opened her eyes slowly as he placed her on the bed and looked up at him sleepily. 'You should have got me up,' she whispered and he brushed her cheek lightly with the back of his hand. 'I'm too heavy for you to carry now.'

He smiled softly at her. 'You looked too peaceful, and you're not too heavy,' he replied, his husky voice low.

'You getting in?' he continued, dragging the quilt away from underneath her.

'Clothes!' she said sleepily, half sitting up. He hesitated for a second or two then watched her undo the button on her skirt. It slipped away from her body with relative ease and inwardly he trembled slightly at the sight of the lace panties that were now revealed.

'Leaving that on?' he asked, referring to her blouse and she nodded, slumping back on to the fat pillows behind her head. Michael pulled the quilt up to her shoulders and leant over her, brushing stray hairs away from her face. 'Sleep well,' he said and she sighed. He left the room as silently as he had entered it and made his way back up to his own room, comfortable now in the knowledge that she had not spent the night downstairs on the sofa.

Once inside his thoughts turned to ones of self-pity. He ached from what felt like his head to his toes, the familiar sensation stirring within him. Still leaning on the closed door, he made his mind up to go back downstairs and with that, crept back into her room where he stood, silently watching her sleep until the dawn hour was upon him and the urge to sleep finally took him over.

Chapter Eighteen

July 1997

Pat always looked so regal when he sat behind the large expensive desk in the Hothouse office dressed in a business suit, but today he was different and Beth couldn't quite pinpoint why, or quite what it was. He looked her up and down as if for the first time. As she sat down in the chair opposite him something inside told her that something bad was going to happen. He re-lit his cigar and leaned forward in his chair, his elbows resting on the desk edge.

'Your dad—' He paused for effect, as well as to think about what he was actually going to say now that she was here in front of him. He watched her watching him and then he looked across at James and Michael, who had quietly settled on the long sofa to the side of desk in the large office.

'What?' she half smiled, feeling the hairs on the nape of her neck stand up on end.

'He always wanted you to become an accountant.' There was a slight laugh in his tone and then it was gone. 'He wanted you to join the business when you were *old enough.*' He emphasised the last two words and paused again, suddenly noticing how much like her mother she looked now she had grown to an age.

They were right, she wasn't a child anymore and for a second or two he felt a great sadness. 'We decided to wait until we thought you were mature enough to take all this on board,' he said, looking at James and Michael again. Obviously one of them, if not both, had been in discussion with him about the situation and it was also evident that he wasn't entirely pleased about it. She looked at Michael fleetingly.

He looked cooler than both other men. It was a Michael idea. Considering Pat never took anyone's advice, especially since Andrew had died, he seemed to listen to Michael. He respected him more than he'd ever say.

'All what?' she said without the laugh in her tone. Pat's eyes bored into hers and she saw the power then, she saw what men saw when they looked at him.

She saw the man that he was, the powerful man that he was. She'd almost forgotten that he was her father's elder brother. Had the same power that he had possessed. She'd forgotten that he'd started this business with her father, fought real fights, bled real blood, until that exact moment.

'Something's come up and it would appear that it's that time now, Beth.' He opened his desk drawer and took out a plain white sealed envelope. 'Your shares!' he said, pushing the envelope towards her. She put her fingers to it and he pulled it quickly away from her again.

'Do you really want in, Beth? Are you sure you're ready to play with the big boys?' he asked.

She looked around at James, then at Michael and then back at Pat and nodded at his question. She was more than aware that this was something serious and that there would be no turning back once the door was opened. 'This is to do with those men the other day, isn't it?' she stated the question, her tone making it quite plain that she was indeed more attentive than any of them had given her credit for.

'Yes. And more,' Pat said, letting out a deep breath as he watched her light another cigarette.

'Then yes, Uncle Pat. I do want in, very much, and perhaps you should go from the top. And relax!' Her accent was perfect and he wondered as he did often where the upper class tone in her voice had come from, bearing in mind that none of them spoke what he would call proper English. He also wondered just when it was that she got so old for her years, and wise. She took the envelope from him and placed her keys and cigarettes on top of it as she replied, settling back in her seat.

'There've been some problems. Well, one problem really, with a bloke called Sean Oxley.' He looked at her for recognition of the name. She nodded her head in recognition and he went on. 'We go way back—' Pat began as he now sat back in his large chair like a library storyteller.

Beth sat silently as Pat told her about him from the very beginning, with help from James and Michael. In Pat's eyes, Sean Oxley, like them had been in the entertainment business back in the early eighties, but he had preferred the strip joints to the nightclubs, and the hustle to the tidy, so their paths hadn't really crossed much until Dobson Elliott Limited purchased the Hothouse. The club purchase had seen them rocket from average to one of the top companies on the club scene within a year and that was when the real problems began. When they'd hit the big time, Oxley had decided that he wanted to buy the club from them then and when they wouldn't sell, took it upon himself to make trouble for them with everyone from common thugs to suppliers. It didn't work. Pat, Andrew and Jim had retaliated with everything they had and for a long while things died down. They didn't expect, and didn't get, any trouble when Andrew and Louise died, and had presumed that it been a mark of respect when he was seen at the funeral.

Sean Oxley, like them, was of the old school and would not have done anything untoward to a family in a state of mourning. That would have been very, very bad business. But time had moved on, and the business carried on along without Andrew, and Sean Oxley had recently raised his head again.

'Why tell me all this now?' she asked out of the blue, stopping Pat in mid-sentence.

'Because we think that you're the one that they want,' Michael interrupted flatly. He looked straight into her eyes and a cold shiver ran down her back. 'They think that you're the vulnerable one.' Both other men breathed out heavily. Trust Michael to say it as it was.

'Don't fucking scare her, Mike!' James said abruptly.

'Let's not lie to her now, either, ey!' He retorted and both James and Pat looked harshly at him with eyes suddenly made of emerald flint.

'Don't start again,' James breathed, rolling his eyes to the ceiling.

'Oh, okay then. But I thought we were going to be completely honest with her,' Michael retorted sarcastically.

'We are!' Pat said flatly.

'Come off it, Pat,' Michael almost laughed. 'She needs to hear all of it. Not the edited *Elizabeth's too young and too innocent for this shit* version. All of it, then maybe our fuck-arsing around about her welfare will sink in, and make some sense. She's not likely to just do what we want because we say so now, is she? She needs to know why and what's out there and what can happen, and what has happened,' he finished, settling his gaze on her, and her alone. She nodded at him, in agreement.

Beth sat for a long moment and listened while they bickered amongst themselves and on hearing Michael's final comment stopped them.

'Want me for what? What are you talking about?' Pat went to speak but she raised her hand to silence him and remarkably it did. 'No, Uncle Pat! Michael, you tell me.' She knew that he wouldn't lie to her, or frill things up if she asked him a direct question, and he rubbed at his eyes as he thought about how to start.

'We heard a whisper that maybe Oxley would—' he paused with a sigh. 'He knows how important you are to all of us. He's going to squeeze us into selling this place through you. It's all he wants and he knows that you're far more important.'

Beth blanched. 'How?' she snapped, angry suddenly that no one had said a word to her before now.

'Maybe scare you. Maybe threaten to hurt you,' he added, aware that she was now quietly steaming. 'He has threatened to hurt you!' he said, correcting himself.

'We didn't wanna upset you—' James began, slipping off his seat to the floor beside her. He paused. Her expression had changed.

'Upset me?' she blasted. 'Are you fucking insane?' She calmed her breathing. 'How long have you known?'

'A while,' Pat said finally, his voice crisp. James stood up again and walked over to the drinks cabinet. He poured them all a whisky as Pat carried on. 'The last time we had a visit, you were mentioned. Before, it was just hearsay.' Beth looked at each of them again in turn.

'What was said?' There was silence. All three men looked at each other, their expressions pinched and she settled the urge to yell that suddenly took her over back into the pit of her stomach. 'What was said?' she said, her tone a pitch lower.

'He said that it would be a shame if something was to happen to you, if you were plucked.' Pat said, almost repeating Oxley's words to the letter and Beth looked a little confused.

'Plucked?' she repeated questioningly.

'Yes,' Michael sighed, settling his steady gaze upon her and the expression on his face said it all.

'Fucking hell! You mean he threatened to—to have me.' She stopped herself from saying the words but they knew that she understood just what had been inferred. 'What, and you lot thought I didn't need to know till now?' she yelled suddenly, standing up from her seat and pulling the velvet band from her hair. It was her gesture of frustration yet incredibly feminine, sexy despite the fact that she was absolutely furious.

'I said she'd flip!' James said waving his empty glass at Michael, who was now almost as angry as Elizabeth was.

'Do you blame her?' he barked. 'We've done nothing to be proud of, in not telling her. We don't shelter her from anything else in life except sex and this is what happens. It's a weak point and everyone knows it!' he exploded and James snapped his mouth shut with shock.

'Michael! That's enough!' Pat said sharply.

'Shelter me? Will you all shut the fuck up?' Beth said, her tone powerful.

Michael watched her. He knew that he was right. His next thought made him feel almost sick inside. Would she go out now and just do it, get it out of the way? Had they just pointed the finger at her and said that it was her virginity that was a problem now, and not the lack of it? She went to the window and looked out over the car park below, and at the haze that seemed to cover it in the evening heat. She took a deep breath and turned back around to where they all stood waiting for her to speak.

'Can we have this again, please,' she sighed, rubbing her eyes. 'With nothing left out to shelter my delicate sensibilities!' Her words were simple but she touched each of them. Pat nodded to himself. They should have told her before, just like Michael had said, but he thought he knew best because he was old and wise. He was wrong. He thought James knew as much, if not more than he did because she was his baby sister, but he was wrong. It was Michael who knew the most about the young woman now standing gazing out of the window before him. It was Michael who had said that enough was enough, that she was ready, and that she should now be brought in on the business and it was Michael who was right about telling her about Oxley. At least she did know now and would be maybe a little more cautious.

'Sit back down, Bethy,' he said calmly and Beth perched on the arm of the sofa next to Michael. 'You're a smart man,' he added, looking at Michael who in turn looked at James.

'You're right, Mike,' James said softly. 'It's time.'

Pat left nothing out and nothing to the imagination. It appeared that there had been a more violent aspect to the problems with Oxley as well as there being more angles to the business than anyone would have imagined and Beth, to her credit, sat and took it all in like an apt pupil in front if a teacher. He told her everything that had ever happened; every bloody, despicable sexual act, every broken bottle, every gun, every nasty move and throughout she sat and listened. For over three hours she sat in the at room with those men and listened. She now officially knew absolutely everything there was to know about the past and she didn't flinch, not once.

'So now you know!' Pat said finally, and she was silent. She had sat almost completely still as he reeled out everything there was to know about the businesses and the trouble that was brewing.

'So what's next?' she said simply, keeping her voice light, and she felt all three other pairs of eyes settle upon her.

'We wait,' Pat said gently and Michael watched her eyes. He had watched as she had grown and this step seemed to him to be the last but one towards her adulthood.

In the days that followed the meeting something happened to Beth, she looked older somehow. Maybe it was the clothes, her hair, her make-up. None of them were sure what it was but there was definitely something. It wasn't bad, just different and even James gave her a double take as she walked down into the kitchen ready to go to the club the following Saturday evening. She was dressed in a mid-length strappy dress with a low back. It was well cut, obviously expensive and it accentuated her full figure. Her tan looked even deeper than usual, in stark contrast with the lilac of the material. Her hair was high on her head, with the occasional wispy curl falling from the style and the evening sandals she wore showed off her perfectly pedicured and painted toes. Michael padded down the stairs following the scent of her perfume like an invisible trail and stopped dead in his tracks at the bottom step. 'Sweet Jesus!' he exclaimed before he could stop himself. Two pairs of green eyes were suddenly upon him and he consciously closed his gawping mouth. 'You look—very nice!' he finished, his tone a little more composed.

'Tell me about it!' James's tone was almost offhand but he understood his friend completely. Where had the baby gone?

'Does that mean you like it then?' Beth asked, breaking into their private thoughts as she did a twirl before them.

'Like I said, Elizabeth, you look very nice.' Michael's tone was pinched and he locked eyes with James. How could he have been so unguarded? He stood there silently, mentally kicking himself.

'Will that Peter prick be there tonight then?' James asked, changing the subject from Beth's appearance to her personal life. He asked Beth directly and she looked at Michael, who was waiting for her response with interest, before answering him.

'Probably, why? Is there a problem with me seeing someone for a drink in the middle of a crowded club?' The air filled with tension as if someone high above them had turned on the taps and let it fall like water.

'Leave her be.' Michael said lightly before James could reply to her question. 'Come on, we're late,' he added. The conversation was over.

Michael watched Beth from beneath those thick lashes. He sipped at the liquid in the glass in his hand, it was making him feel warm inside and he knew that with just another one or two he would be well on his way. And that was exactly what he wanted to be at that moment. He wanted to be blind drunk, actually. He wanted to drown his sorrows in a very deep barrel and sleep the sleep of the dead, for just one night. For just one night he wanted to let his head hit the pillow, and not lie there thinking about her, aching for her. He didn't want to smell her perfume or look into her eyes as they made their way up to separate bedrooms. He didn't want to hear, "Good night", from a distance. He just wanted to be free of her, and the torment she caused him, for just one night.

He watched her. She was beautiful, and he knew that so many others thought so too. He got a refill from the bar and wandered back to his viewpoint. From the balcony he could see almost the entire club. He looked down at the bodies beneath him on the dance floor and searched for her. Panic hit him as he searched again. Then he looked around him; where in the hell was she? He was about to turn and make his way back down stairs when he breathed her in. She was close, he could smell her, feel her and then she spoke and he could hear her.

'I'm going to make a move home, you coming?' Her voice was light, like music, for all she was raising her voice above the beat and the bass. He turned and looked into her eyes. He was glazed and he almost grinned at her. 'Jesus Michael!' she exclaimed, her voice then nothing but a whisper.

'Don't say it, Elizabeth. Please don't say it!' He was gripping the handrail with one hand, swaying his glass in her direction with his finger pointed outwards in the other. 'I'm aware of my state and I don't care! Tonight, I don't care!'

She looked him up and down, trying to recall the last time she may ever have seen his like this, and she couldn't. 'Definitely home time!' she smiled and then he did grin at her.

Beth walked with Michael up the steps and opened the front door for him. It was late and she was tired, but Michael drunk was something rare and it amused her. She laughed as he took off his jacked in the hallway and went to hang it on the banister. He missed it completely and it landed on the floor by the stairs. 'I've got it!' she breathed, picking it up and draping it over her arm. 'Come on.' She held out her hand to him and he stared at it. He wasn't that drunk that he couldn't find his own room! He was in complete control, which was lucky for her because he'd just had a rather excellent view of her cleavage as she'd bent down. If he hadn't been in control, he may have been a little more than tempted to— He stopped there and closed his eyes. *Don't think about it!* A voice inside his head said.

'Shall we have another drink?' he asked, focusing his thoughts on something else.

'Not a very good idea, ey Michael?' She took him by the hand and led him up the stairs. 'This makes a change,' she added as they reached the landing, 'Me, putting you to bed.'

As they made their way up the next flight it occurred to him that perhaps he was a little more the worse for wear than he had thought himself to be. The warmth of her lips on his head was soothing and he breathed her in. She was sitting on the edge of the bed, next to where he lay. She was looking down at him in the street light from the window. He tried not to think of how easy it would be then to flip her onto her back. He closed his mind to the question of what she would feel like, how warm she would be, just how she would be. She was caring for him then. She was safe in her home with him there and not even the feelings that raged through him then could have made her feel like that in her own home, with him there. He was her protector, her Michael.

'D'you want a glass of water?' she asked softly. He stared up at her, feeling very small all of a sudden and shook his head gently. She remembered the two-pint rule. *Two pints of water before bed and you won't wake up with a sore head!*

'No thanks. I'll enjoy the pain in the morning. It'll remind me not to drink so much.'

'Quantity wasn't the problem, was it?' she replied. 'I think *what* you drank may have been a bigger factor.' He was going to speak then, ask how she knew what he'd been drinking but the question was gone from his mind as he watched her move across the room. He looked after her and watched as she opened his bedroom door.

'Good night, Michael. Sleep well.'

August 1997

With her elbows on the dressing table Beth cupped her head in her hands and let out a long sigh. She got the urge to cry. Wanted to, but couldn't. If one of them heard her, what would she say? Her entire body was screaming to be touched, but not by her own hands; it ached to be touched by Michael and the thoughts of the hot steamy sex that only ever happened in the movies bounced around in her mind. She stood up and then settled herself on the edge of the bed, her dressing gown falling open as she pulled on the cord. Her hand slid down her cleavage, down her rounded belly and down to between her legs. She was already wet and she knew exactly what to do. Caressing herself gently, she closed her eyes. She saw him, his broad body making hers hotter and hotter as he pushed against her. She held her breath, making the pounding pulse between her legs shudder through her body. Her breathing was hard, so hard that she wondered just how loud it was in the silence of the room but then she didn't care. The wave that hit her was hot and she lay back, her legs apart, her fingers sliding from her.

As she sat up and adjusted herself there was a knock at her door. She turned white, then red. Had she cried out?

'Can I come in?' a voice called. It was him!

'Yes!' Her own tone was harsh but on seeing him, the harshness left and she looked quite subdued. He closed the door behind him and stood for a while just staring at her. He could almost smell the sex that emanated from her and he breathed in deeply.

'James's gone out!' he announced, still watching her from the doorway. 'Did you want to get something to eat? There's a grand film on the TV tonight—or go out?' He stopped himself. 'That is, if you're not already going out.' He knew damn well that she wasn't. She'd said as much to Lucy on the phone just before going up for a bath not even an hour before.

She looked into his eyes. The ache there was clear to see and for a second or two she got the urge to open her dressing gown, lie back down on the bed and beg him to make the pain stop, make the not knowing leave her, make her understand the emotions that ripped through her.

'The film idea sounds good,' she smiled instead, moving towards the wardrobe. 'Let me just chuck some clothes on. I'll come with you to get food. Do you fancy an Indian?' She opened it, dramatically swinging the huge doors apart.

'No, but I'd eat a curry!' he replied jovially. She glanced at him, and then flicked quickly through the hangers and pulled out a long black cotton dress. Aware that he was still there by the door, she took off her gown between the open doors and gave him a rather nice back and side view of her naked body. He tried really hard not to look at her, to look anywhere but at her, but he was a man, a hot-blooded man and so he took all he could for those few seconds. She slid the dress over her head, wiggled it down her naked body and then turned, taking in a sharp breath. He'd moved and was now just beside her. He leaned towards her and then, just as he was close enough to feel her breath, he bent and picked up her discarded gown.

'You're too much of a woman now, to be doing that, even in front of me.' *Especially in front of me,* he added in his head.

'What? You've seen my arse before. Used to wipe it, apparently.' She was almost laughing, but the fact that she wanted him to see her was blatant. She was going to unwittingly take him as far as any woman had ever taken him before. And although it really did have him up at night, he didn't care.

They'd eaten huge amounts of chicken korma, pilau rice and naan bread with lots of garlic. Had drunk a rather nice bottle of '94 white between them and watched television. And now the film was over but Michael didn't make any move towards the remote control. He watched the credits and it was then that he moved, muting the sound with the remote control. Beth lay asleep, her head in his lap, her hand resting on his leg and it felt good to him. He wasn't aroused; it wasn't that kind of good. It was a peaceful good, a comfortable good, an easy good. It was the sort of good that only came with time and knowledge of a person, with a person. He listened to her breathing below him and instinctively he brushed stray hairs from her face with a gentle touch.

'You always do that' she breathed, still half asleep. Her voice was soft and when she opened her eyes he was staring down at her.

'That's because you've so much hair that it's always in the way,' he smiled.

'It is bed time?' She stretched out a little.

'Yes, it's late,' he breathed and she sat up, aware suddenly that his other hand had been on her hip the whole time. He slid it from her lightly, his touch making her quiver.

'Is James back?'

Michael switched off the television with the remote control. 'Been in and gone out again. I don't think we'll see him till the morning now.' His tone was soft, and the suggestion was there, but she didn't pick up on it. 'Come on,' he added, helping her to her feet once he'd risen himself. 'Time for bed.'

They walked upstairs in darkness, Michael following her. They got to the landing and Beth flicked on the light in her room, but didn't go to enter. Nor did Michael go to move away up the stairs.

'Good night, Michael. Thanks for dinner,' Beth almost whispered and without warning, she tilted her head up and kissed him on the cheek. Instinctively he brushed her shoulder.

'It was a pleasure. Sleep well,' he managed and then she was gone.

Alone in his bed Michael stretched out and nudged the duvet from himself with his feet. He was restless and he turned his head, looking at the clock. It was three am. *Give it another three and you can get up,* he thought. He lay there for another few minutes, his hands covering his face and then he heard a noise. He held his breath, not moving. There it was again. It was a really light tapping and then his door opened. He was so surprised that he sat upright, completely forgetting that he was naked. Beth's head appeared at the door and her focus was immediately upon him even though the pile of duvet blocked her view in the light of the street lamps outside.

'Are you okay?' he asked urgently.

'No! Someone's outside by your car.' She was whispering.

'Just one?' he asked, already leaving the bed.

'I think so,' she managed.

He grabbed his tracksuit bottoms and pulled them on, making his way to the window. When he turned around Beth's mouth was almost completely open. She snapped it shut as she met his gaze. She'd seen him naked before, but not for a long while and it affected her, despite the current situation.

'Stay here!' he demanded brushing past her and out of the room. She heard his footfalls on the stairs and then she became agitated. She hesitated then shot to the window. There was nothing there that she could see. Maybe they'd gone. She left the room and made her way down the stairs.

Just as she got to the front door she saw Michael's back. He was moving silently and fast, but to her eyes it looked like slow motion. Whoever it was by his car landed with a bump, setting the alarm off. The headlights and the hazards flashed as the horn sounded. There was a brief moment when Michael paused, holding whoever it was off the ground by their jacket, his left arm poised as if ready to punch. He stared at the young man, or rather, boy in his grasp. He couldn't have been more than sixteen.

'Get out of here,' he spat, giving him a shake that rattled his entire body. He let go and the boy was off down the road, his fear giving him speed that Beth bet he didn't know he had in him. Michael turned around, his breathing hard. Christ, he was something Beth thought, watching him from the doorway. He was one hard-arsed, hot Irish fucking work of art. She let out a slow breath and then it occurred to her that she hadn't feared for his safety at all. In her eyes he was indestructible.

'Can you get the keys?' His tone was soft and when she was gone from the doorway he looked around the close of terraced houses. Lights that had come on inside surrounding houses flicked off as the alarm stopped sounding, leaving only the lights flashing the warning that their safe little street had been invaded for a short while. Locked inside again, they both sat on the stairs, neither speaking for what seemed to be a very long while. Beth leaned her head on her lap and sighed, watching Michael as he calmed.

'Well, that was fun,' she almost laughed.

'Oh aye, grand!' he chuckled then. There really was never a dull moment for them.

'You're really not scared of anything, are you?' she said lightly.

He made a scoffing sound as he turned his head to face her. 'Some things, yes,' he answered honestly. 'I'm only human, Elizabeth, just a man.'

She hesitated. 'What scares you then?' she asked, and he thought for a second or two.

'Me. I scare me, but only sometimes,' he said finally. 'Now, go on, up to bed. We've a busy day tomorrow,' Michael suggested before the conversation had time to continue or escalate to another whole new level. She'd ask why he scared himself and he wondered if, with being there alone, he would be able to stop himself from telling her the truth. With a ruffle of his hair she was off to bed, but there was to be no sleep for him. Once he was up like that, he was up for the duration.

Sean Oxley was a slim man with fine blonde hair and neat little facial features. He dressed like the man in funds that he was. His nice well-cut pale grey suit and tie were obviously straight out of the tailor's. He didn't look very threatening at all without his minder, Beth thought, sizing him up as she watched him get out of the back of the Jaguar that pulled up below the window. He looked around him with his nose in the air as if he owned the place, and that gesture alone annoyed her enough to make her want to bang on the window and swear at him, but she thought better of it.

'He's here!' she said without emotion and she looked over at Pat, who just nodded slowly at her.

'Is this a good idea?' James asked, sounding awkward. He looked tired and harassed, but both Beth and Michael knew that it wasn't Oxley's presence that had him like that, it was the fact that he'd been out on the tiles all night. Beth sneaked another look at Michael. He looked fine on a couple of hours, but then, that was all he usually got, she thought.

'Yes!' Pat said flatly, as if for the thousandth time.

Oxley walked into the office with a bold step, but everyone already there saw him falter as he suddenly noticed Beth standing by the window. She was dressed in a black suit jacket and pencil skirt. The heels on the black leather shoes she wore accentuated the length of her legs. Her hair was up in a softly pinned bun and with the make-up and discreet diamond stud earrings she looked everything *but* vulnerable. In fact she looked like a young barrister, almost powerful, and for a split second he wondered if indeed it was her. She looked nothing like the person he'd seen in the past, even recently. The look in her eyes was dangerous. But there was no question as their gaze met, hers were that unmistakable emerald green he remembered of her father, and glancing across at James who now stood just to her left he saw that the distinct Dobson features were the same.

'I thought you two should finally meet properly, so she could get the measure of you!' Pat said, getting Oxley's full attention with a cough. 'What with Elizabeth being a partner now,' he said, trying not to sound too sure of himself. 'She's aware of *all* the business details,' he finished.

184

He watched Oxley's smile fade as he eyed Beth again. Pat didn't like the way he was looking at her either; he was thinking one of two things at that moment and Pat didn't like the idea of either and the urge to have Michael throw him out of the window was almost too much to bear.

'Well, well, well.' Oxley smiled; he had readjusted his stance. He was ready then and the slight smile that toyed with his lips was back. He settled himself on one of the leather chairs to the side of the desk and gave everyone in the room a few seconds of his gaze, like royalty. He looked at Pat who was still sitting behind the desk, a deep thoughted expression on his face; then at James, who had now settled himself back on the sofa; then at Beth, who still stood by the window and then he looked up, past her. Michael had been standing silently to the side, just between her and Pat the whole time, and until that moment he really hadn't noticed him. He saw the expression on Michael's face. He was her shadow, and where she went, he was sure to follow these days and that fact annoyed Oxley intensely.

'Truly the jewel in the crown!' he said settling his eyes coolly back onto Beth. His accent was absolutely perfect. Beth looked at him from top to toe and then back up again. She did it slowly and deliberately, wanting him to feel the distaste that emanated feverishly from within her.

'You look very different from what I recall,' he said finally.

'What were you expecting? Something innocent, a child perhaps?' she smiled coldly back at him, the innuendo in her voice making it quite clear that she had been given chapter and verse on him, and that he was obviously at a disadvantage when it came to her. He suddenly got the urge to slap her around the face. Who was she to stand there and talk to him in such a way? But he saw the way the Michael was standing, ready to intervene with that dark expression, taking in every move, every gesture. He looked like a bodyguard. But then again, since the day he had moved into the Dobson household he had taken on that role. The fucking Irish gypsy was annoying at best. Oxley paused, still debating on whether or not to retaliate. He thought better of it. The last thing he needed was a hiding from Michael Elliott or indeed, James Dobson. He was a brave man, but not that brave, no, and he wasn't stupid either. He'd bide his time and wait for the right moment before striking out. He needed the Hothouse.

'Shall we begin?' Pat said finally. He wanted Oxley in then out and he wanted it within the hour.

Chapter Nineteen

Late August 1997

He didn't want to know anything but her name. In fact he didn't really want to know that. All he wanted was to feel the warmth that only a woman could provide. He wanted to drift away with closed eyes and imagine that he was elsewhere, elsewhere with Elizabeth. The feelings of pure lust he had for her now had become almost unbearable, and he had to get the ache out of his system before he did something that he knew he was sure he'd live to regret. He didn't want to take her kicking and screaming; he wanted her to go with him because she felt the same way about him as he did her. He wanted to look into her eyes and not have to look away in case she read him too clearly. He wanted to undress her and touch every inch of her, slowly and sensually. He wanted her more than anything else in the world. More than his money, more than his job or family; almost more, he was sure, than his life itself, and it was killing him a little bit more with every passing day and night that he spent thinking about her, and filling emptiness with meaningless flings with unfulfilling women. What was it she'd called it? Oh yes, satisfying a need.

He looked around at his surroundings as he followed her into the bedroom of the small flat. It was clean and tidy but not particularly comfortable, and fleetingly he wondered whether a hotel room, or the back of his car, would have been a better option. He watched her pull the little cardigan from her small frame and throw it casually on to the chair beside the door which was already overloaded with other discarded items. He found her appealing, sure, but he had to admit to himself that she was far too thin for his liking. He liked to feel his women and he liked the warmth and comfort of a full body.

They eyed each other but didn't speak. She seemed to know instinctively that he was there for nothing but to use her body and she didn't seem to care. She enjoyed sex, especially sex with men as important as Michael Elliott; it thrilled her more than the act itself, the danger of it, the power he had. He pushed up against her and pinned her bodily to the now closed bedroom door. His breathing was erratic and he tried to calm it, and he could feel his erection straining against the fabric of his trousers. She went to kiss his lips but he moved his head down so that she missed, and he began to plant little biting kisses on her neck, all the while pulling at her garments until she was almost completely naked before him. Pushing her onto the bed behind where they now stood, Michael pulled at his own clothes and within seconds it seemed he was inside her, pounding at her receptive mound with all his might. He closed his eyes tight shut and then suddenly he was in a different place, and his pace slowed to that of a man making love and not just fucking. He was savouring every movement and every moment. He was touching her body with the warmth of his; she was warm and soft and he could hear her enjoying him from beneath. But by then, in his mind it wasn't her that he could hear and feel. It was Elizabeth then, and he was so far gone in his little fantasy world that he could almost smell the scent of her, and feel the curves of her body although the woman below him now was, without question, not Elizabeth. She was so much smaller in build and her hair was short and stark blonde. Her eyes were green, but not the vivid green that sparkled like jewels and she didn't have the smile that had captured his heart. He felt her wrap her legs around his back and with a loud groan, clutching at the pillow above her head, he came and he was spent until the next time the urge overtook him and desire got the better of his usual good judgement.

The next evening Michael closed his bedroom door and turned to lean against it. He took a deep breath, still trying to inhale the scent of her but it was gone. The familiar ache was there again and he closed his eyes, imagining that he could still see her standing at the bathroom door in only a towel, as she had been only a few moments before. What had she said when he'd finished the call on his mobile that had interrupted their conversation? *What, more casuals, Michael?* He didn't know what to say to her. It was none of her business what he did, but he was ashamed all the same. She'd given him such a look that he had had to put his hands deep into his pockets to stop himself from reaching out and touching her. He'd stepped backwards away from her space by the bathroom door, their eyes still locked, and then without a word being spoken he'd turned and continued up the stairs to his own room. But in his mind he hadn't moved away from her, he imagined that he'd pulled the towel from her curved body and pulled her back into the bathroom where he'd pulled her to the floor, tugging at his own clothes. He opened his eyes and looked up at the ceiling. He was hard and his breathing was erratic. Pushing himself away from the door with a sigh, he closed his eyes again, willing the torment to stop but it didn't, it just worsened and worsened. She had to stop walking around the house like that! It was killing him. Not to mention that it was beginning to become really unsafe for her to do it, especially after the last time. But what could he say? "Elizabeth, can you stop being so young and attractive please, you've got me walking about with a constant hard-on, and if you're not careful I'm going to give you what you're asking for".

He almost laughed to himself. He'd probably last about ten seconds before he let James, very rightly, beat his head to a pulp. But the way she looked at him sometimes. Did she have the same thoughts about him, herself? He thought that maybe, no! Definitely, that she did. Oh yes, she wanted him all right, he thought with a smile as he opened the wardrobe to pull out a fresh shirt. The question was, what to do about it?

Elizabeth sat in front of the mirror and looked at her reflection. Her hair was high on her head, pinned there to stop it from getting wet while she'd showered and her face was devoid of make-up. She leaned on the dressing table on both elbows and sighed heavily into the glass.

She thought about touching herself and making the feeling of loneliness subside but she changed her mind with a long sigh. She wanted Michael to touch her. She wanted to feel his hands upon her; she wanted to breathe in the scent of him until she went dizzy, wanted him to look at her with those big brown eyes and not look away. She could have wept with the frustration of it. She was nineteen and didn't even need to count on her fingers the heated kisses she'd received and as for touches and caresses, well, she alone had discovered those in her over-protected teens.

She applied her make-up skilfully, but her mind wandered on to thoughts of him and his body and his strength, but most of all the way he looked at her. He never failed lately to catch her with those sparkles from beneath those long dark eyelashes. She hoped that despite the summer heat he would wear a suit. He did look good in a suit; one of the single breasted black ones with a crisp white button-down-collar shirt and no tie. When he dressed like that she always fantasised about pulling it all off again, even though in all honestly, she had absolutely no idea of what to do with a man of almost thirty, unclothed or otherwise.

Dressed in a short black shift dress and strappy sandals, she walked down into the lounge. Both James and Michael sat chatting as they waited for her. She smiled to herself as she eyed Michael when he stood up. Did he know, she wondered as she watched him straighten the collar on his tieless white shirt in the mirror above the fireplace.

'Sure you look grand!' He caught her eye and smiled deeply at her, awaiting the blush that came then and went. Oh, there it was! He liked it, and often wondered if she would do the same as she came. Would her cheeks redden and her pouting lips swell even more than they did without the sexual stimulation? Would she whisper his name into his ear, beg him with her entire body to come inside her as she came? Would she taste as good as she smelled to him, would she like the taste of herself on his lips? He smiled to himself then and took in a deep breath of her scent, letting it pulse around her body like a drug.

'Told you it'd look good!' James added, breaking into his thoughts with a distinct *told you so* tone in his voice. He'd picked it when they'd gone out to get Pat's birthday present. He was getting better at that sort of thing.

'Are they meeting us there?' Beth asked generally, but settling her gaze on Michael. He nodded, still keeping a steady gaze upon her.

'Yes, and we're late,' he added.

'Ready?' James questioned and she nodded at him then, giving him her full attention.

'Yes, and I'm bloody starving!' she added lightly, aware of the strange deep-set look on Michael's face. He made her hot just by looking at her, and she could feel her heartbeat as it slowed back down to a normal rate. James led the way out of the lounge and Michael motioned for Elizabeth to go before him. Chivalry had nothing to do with it. He liked watching her walk. In fact, he just liked to watch her. There was something about her, something so innocent, yet absolutely unbearably sexy about her. Maybe the wiggle, so concentrated yet seemingly so effortless. He didn't know exactly, but whatever it was it had him firmly by the balls and wasn't letting go.

All the way through dinner Michael sat opposite Elizabeth, watching her and observing her body language as she spoke to the waiters and her family members alike. Every now and then she'd catch him looking at her and hold his gaze, then with a slight rise to her chin, turn away and continue eating and talking and drinking. The meal ended on a high note, with Pat paying the bill in a rather blasé manner. They finished their coffee and began to gather their belongings up from the table when James's phone rang.

'Oh 'ere we go!' Pat laughed.

'Leave him be,' Judy's voice called out from across the table.

'James's service centre, can I help you?' Beth laughed and there was an outburst of giggles. With the phone to one ear and his hand to the other James spoke briefly into the receiver, nodding his head at whatever was being said to him on the other end on the line.

'He's like a drug. Just say no!' Michael added, leaning towards James as he spoke.

'It's Jenny,' he beamed, clearing the call and looking at Michael. He smiled at his friend. He got the impression that James wasn't going to rush, or use and abuse this one. He got the feeling that she did to James, what Elizabeth was doing to him. She wasn't playing, just looking for something a little deeper.

Arm in arm, Michael and Beth walked through the streets of the City. It was a hot night and the traffic seemed muffled by the heat. 'That Peter fella called for you earlier,' Michael said, breaking into Beth's thoughts.

She looked briefly up at him and then down at her feet.

'I said you were out. Was that okay?' he asked, stopping in mid-step. Beth nodded casually at his question; she was aware of the fact that Michael knew that she was having a bit of a problem with Peter. He didn't seem to be able to take no for an answer.

'You don't like him much, do you?' she said.

He sighed then with a small shrug. 'Not really no, sorry.' He sounded really apologetic.

'He's a bit pushy.' She sounded awkward, as if waiting for Michael to explode the way James would at such a comment. He didn't.

'In what way?' he asked leaning up against the low wall behind them.

'You know. Pushy,' she said, joining him.

'You mean he wants some!' Michael added with a smile.

'I think he wants the lot!' she said flatly.

'You're not interested, no?'

She winced. she had to be honest; well, about Peter anyway. 'No. I'm not a fucking prize, Michael. And that's how he makes me feel. I feel like I should be made of gold and stood on a black pedestal, have someone's name etched on the plaque at my feet!' Her expression made him laugh out loud, although he knew she was right.

'Well, that's a new way of expressing it,' he breathed, but he understood this situation from both sides of the fence. After all, wasn't some of this problem his making? They had made her so inaccessible that of course every young man in the vicinity was going to try his luck. Maybe they should just let nature take its course, let her get it over with. On the other hand, he didn't even want other men to look at her or talk to her, let alone make love to her. He sighed. His emotions weren't helping the situation so he pushed them aside and went with the big brother approach. 'Do you want me to have a word with the little fucking shite, I mean Peter, put him straight about our expectations maybe?' he asked, his tone lighter than even he had expected it to be, because they both knew that it wasn't really a question. It was Michael's way of telling Beth that he would deal with it, deal with it finally and discreetly.

'Can you?' she asked. 'Nicely though, yeah?'

He didn't answer her, just sat there staring at her, his eyes saying it all. Of course he'd deal with it. He was Michael Elliott. He breathed in and out and glanced at his watch. It was almost midnight.

'You want to go to the club?' he suggested.

'What, now?' she was debating this plan.

'Sure, come on, the night's still young, you're dressed to impress, and I don't know about you, but I could do with another drink!'

There was still a queue when they arrived but they strolled past it and inside, Frank opening the doors for them with a really cheesy grin. He was always so happy to see them. ''Ello... Come for a boogie?' he laughed, wiggling his hips. That man had no rhythm at all, but he was one of the funniest and nicest that Beth had ever met.

'Oh, sure!' Michael laughed with him, as he let Beth pass and go towards the reception desk.

'Hi ya, how are you?' Beth asked Linda, the receptionist.

'Okay, thanks,' she smiled. She was really pleased to be asked. But then, Beth always asked, and not just because she thought she should; she asked because she wanted to, and Linda liked her for that.

'Can I stick this behind there?' Beth asked then, bag in hand.

''Course.' She took Beth's bag with a big smile.

They went in and stood at the bar waiting to get served. It was a busy night and surprisingly, mainly filled with women and not men. 'Nice ratio,' she laughed. 'They obviously knew you'd be in tonight!'

Michael scoffed at this. 'Well, obviously! I'm a very popular man, you know, Elizabeth.' He leaned in to her as they talked to save shouting and lip reading and Beth found herself taking in deep breaths.

'Is that a fact?' She was playing it cool. He nodded at her and then they made eye contact. 'That is a fact!' she corrected herself and he laughed then, the action making his entire face light up from within.

They were on their second drink when Beth spied Peter. He'd seen her too and was making his way across to them. Michael didn't even turn around, he knew who it was just from the expression on Beth's face. She had her professional smile on. 'Can I hurt him?' he asked with a laugh and Beth slapped his arm after placing her drink on the bar.

'Not here, no!' she began. 'Peter!' She let him kiss her cheek and it was obvious that he was disgruntled at the reception she gave him.

'Peter.' Michael said his name in greeting but it made him jump anyway. Beth picked up and took a sip of her drink to hide her amusement. She watched as Michael watched him from beneath a rather excellent glare. He was a good-looking bloke, sure. But he wasn't manly enough, a bit limp-wristed for Michael's liking, and as for being good enough for Elizabeth— That Dan or whatever his name was had been much better, and he'd ended up to be only one step from being as well behaved as a priest.

'We're going off in a bit, you want to come?' Peter asked her.

'No thanks, we've already had a bit of a long one,' Beth replied casually.

'Not yet, you ain't,' he laughed.

Beth looked across at Michael. She thought he'd go absolutely mental at that comment but all he did was raise his eyebrows at her. The comment wasn't lost on Michael though. He stood sizing Peter up. He was such a tosser, with his crappy office job, his dad's BMW and probably his dad's credit card too.

A while later Michael stood next to Peter in the toilet and the two nodded at each other as they did their business. Toilets were always awkward places to have conversations but Peter talked anyway.

'She's a bit, that one!' he said casually. He was showing off to the others in the room that he knew Michael, and Michael was not impressed. 'She plays it so innocent, but I know her game.' He winked at Michael then. They washed their hands for the sake of something to do and as they checked themselves in the mirrors Michael closed in on Peter and began to talk quietly at his reflection.

'I'll tell you what, if you promise not to go near her again—' he paused, 'I'll promise not to have someone rip you a new arsehole,' he said and then he smiled. It was a full-on grin and that, along with the words, were not lost on Peter. He went white and then left the room. Michael knew that he was leaving. He wouldn't even say goodbye to Beth; she'd never see him again.

September 1997

She watched Michael flitting too and fro around the smoke-filled club all night. She hadn't hidden the fact that she liked him. She liked the way he walked, his stride. He had power; it was obvious by the way the club staff behaved towards him. He demanded respect without opening his mouth and he got it without question. There was also that rough and readiness about him that so many men lost when money was no longer an issue for them. Michael had been annoyed by her persistence throughout a very busy Saturday night; he was covering for the duty manager, who'd called in sick at ten to six that evening, and wasn't in the mood for games. He'd watched her watching him, following him with cool blue eyes. She was slim, not particularly tall, with over-exposed breasts and mid-brown hair. She was almost nondescript, but he did have a design on her. He had to have a release from the loneliness that had again crept up on him and he thought back to that morning.

He'd lain alone in his king-sized bed on the second floor of that house acutely aware of the erection that had woken him from such a sweet dream. His hand had instinctively gone to it and he'd rubbed at it, slowly at first and then his pace had quickened to almost violent. His eyes were closed and as always, his mind had filled with visions of Elizabeth. He'd come hard, holding his breath for the fear of crying out when the release hit him in a hot wave. He felt dirty when he did it, but couldn't help himself. It was either that or resort to casual fucks. That seemed to satisfy something within James but that really wasn't him, although he had to be honest, there had been more than one over the past few months, and that's all they were. He definitely didn't look at it as making love by any stretch of the imagination. It was the release that the sex gave him for a short while that his body craved; that he, as a hot-blooded man craved. It was something that wanking himself off couldn't quite aspire to. He could deal with the emotions within him much better without the rage of lust that seemed ever present lately. But for all the justification he gave it, for all he told himself that both were okay, he couldn't help feeling guilty whenever he did anything or said anything. He'd look into her eyes and see the confusion that only the lack of something you don't yet know of brings, and he'd have to hold back from grabbing her and shaking her. He wanted to tell her that she only had to say the word and he would show her everything there was to be shown, and more than gladly teach her everything there was to be taught about love and making it. He wanted to feel her as she came beneath him and hear her calling his name as he did within her, but there was no way on God's good earth that that was ever going to happen, and he knew only too well what would happen if it did. James would kill him! And if there was anything left of him after James had finished, Pat would top the job off. No, the emotions within him would have to stay there within him and his thoughts of ever being the one to take her for the first time would have to be locked away for good some time soon, before he did blow it by slipping up or saying the wrong thing.

Matthew, the Saturday night D.J., announced the end of *what he hoped had been another top night* after one final slow dance and Michael found himself letting out a long sigh of relief. He wondered fleetingly what Elizabeth was doing and looked at his watch; almost a quarter to three. She'd be well home by now; she should have left the wine bar at one, half past at the latest. *I'll call*, he thought, moving towards the locked door that lead up to the main office. Once inside he sat at the desk and flicked on the lamp. He picked up the phone and dialled the seven-digit number. There were two rings before her voice broke onto the line.

'It's me,' he said in a low tone. 'I just thought I'd call. I'll not be back till late. No, I've no idea where he's got to,' He laughed, knowing that Beth understood what he was saying about James and his whereabouts. He just hoped that she didn't realise what he was saying about himself. It was no good, she was too clued up for her own good sometimes, and he heard the tone of her voice change somewhat dramatically from cheerful to sarcastic.

'Four, maybe half past. That's if I come home at all tonight!' he replied, suddenly feeling very irritable. 'No, don't lock up! Just put the alarm on, okay. I may not! Look, I'll see you later on, okay?'

With every conversation, passing comment or look lately she seemed to confirm to him that she had feelings for him that she couldn't put in the surrogate brother box or the friend box or the brother's best friend box. He shouldn't have called her; it was a stupid idea. He should have gone back to the house, locked the door, grabbed her, ripped her clothes from her body and ravished her wherever they stood, but instead he said his goodbyes and hung up. He sat back in the chair and looked out of the mirrored glass; there she was. Now what was her name, he thought? 'Oh yes, Kelly.' He said the last few words out loud before walking from the office.

Being the gentleman that he apparently was, Michael drove Kelly back to her flat in the back end of Finchley. They chatted about nothing in particular along the way and Michael's designs faded. He didn't want this woman tonight, although she did seem very nice; he just wanted to go home. He wanted to get out of his suit, make a cup of tea, smoke a cigarette and just be there, in the house, with her safe asleep in her bed, or even better, down in the kitchen with him. He'd really pondered upon it though. It would be so easy to get this one into bed, but no, it was no good. He'd go home and make all the right noises at her, then just before it got too unbearable, go on up to his room and have yet another wank. Oh yes, being Michael James Elliott was really great and he would quite gladly have swapped lives with anyone else, but for the fear within him that he would never ever see her again. Kelly's voice broke into his thoughts and he pulled up outside a pleasant-looking block of newly built flats.

'You wanna come up?' she asked and he shook his head at her. 'No, I've had a long day. But thanks,' he added, giving her a winning smile and she shrugged casually as she pulled a card from her purse.

'Call me then?' she said lightly, opening the door of the Rover noiselessly.

'Sure!'

'Bye now.' She got out and Michael pulled away without a backwards glance. It was getting light and by the time he parked outside the house everything had a greeny-blue tinge to it that told him that it was not worth going to bed and he sagged. No sleep tonight, he thought.

Without a sound he locked the door and mounted the stairs to the first floor landing. He faltered as he reached the top. She stood in the doorway of her bedroom in rather cute pyjamas and looked him up and down, a strange expression on her face, lit by the lamp on in her room. 'What? Couldn't you stay at hers then? Nice time anyway, I'm sure!' she said, breaking the silence in a sarcastic tone. Michael looked at her and shrugged dismissively, even though everything in him yelled at him to lunge at her and put a stop to this ridiculous charade. He couldn't think of a decent fitting retort and it was obvious that she wasn't about to continue the conversation.

'*Very* nice, thank you!' he said finally, emphasising the word "very", and with that she closed her bedroom door, leaving him standing alone in the hallway. She waited behind the door and listened for him to go up the stairs, but there wasn't a sound and after another pause of a few seconds she flung the door open and they were face to face again.

'What?' her voice was tight. He almost grinned at her but got the distinct impression that he would probably receive a slap around the face for his trouble, so he didn't move. She still had a hold of the door handle and turned to go back into her room again but thought better of it and hesitated.

'Why?' he questioned, his voice in the heated silence keeping her from closing the door again.

'Why what? What are you rattling on about?' She was flustered again.

'Why are you pissed at me?' he demanded, although the laugh was still evident in his tone. She looked him up and down slowly and then into his eyes. He saw the confusion and felt ashamed of himself then for pushing her. He understood her feelings so much better than she did but it wasn't for him to say anything, so he sighed instead.

'Good night, Michael!' she said dismissively and with that she slammed the door behind her again.

The next couple of days were strange. Beth seemed to avoid Michael with fever. She was angry with him, but couldn't quite decide why. James put it down to PMT, but Michael, being Michael, knew better. On Tuesday night, just after James had gone out, Michael mounted the stairs and knocked on Beth's bedroom door. 'Yes!' was the response he got. He took it as an invitation and so he walked in. She was sitting at the dressing table, taking off her make-up. He watched her reflection in the mirror for a long moment. Her skin beneath the foundation was clear and fresh.

'I was wondering how long you were going to ignore me for,' he said, settling casually down on the edge of her bed. It was soft, the whole room was, and it smelled of her; not her perfume, but her.

She continued to look at him from her viewpoint in the mirror. 'Ignore you?' She looked confused suddenly. She was angry with him, but hadn't ignored him. Avoided him, sure, but not ignored.

'Aye, y'know. When one person doesn't speak to another for days even though they share a house. It's called ignoring.'

She looked cross, then hurt, then cross again before she answered him. 'Oh! oh! You know everything, don't you, Michael,' she interrupted, spinning in her seat to face him. She was going to go on but stopped. He was looking into her eyes. There was something there in them that made her stop. There was another silence between them and the reason for her behaviour was clear.

'I didn't sleep with her!' he breathed, his eye still on hers.

'It's nothing to do with me!' She really didn't want to hear about it. He turned away from her for a few seconds, thinking of what to say to her next.

'I know. It's just—' He paused, looking back into her eyes again.

'And I'm sorry I made you uncomfortable.' She sighed, a slight smile appearing on her lips.

'I know.' He stood up. 'And I understand.' That was all he said. Before she could reply he'd left the room, left her wondering just what it was that he thought he understood.

Chapter Twenty

Late September 1997

'It's for you!' Beth said abruptly, holding the telephone receiver out at arm's length to Michael. It was the second call since arriving home. And what with it being one o'clock in the morning, Beth was, with good reason, a little short on patience because both callers had been female and both had been for Michael. He looked up at her, then got up slowly from his seat at the dining table.

'Who?' he asked, already half-knowing. Beth's purely irritated expression said it all. It was obviously a woman.

'It's Kelly!' Her voice sounded impatient and he took the receiver from her grasp. 'Apparently she wants to talk to you!' He had his hand over the receiver. 'Fuck you, more like!' she added in a whisper.

He took the phone. 'Hello?' he sighed, keeping his stance casual as he watched Beth, who was stubbing out a cigarette. 'Yes. We just got in,' he continued. 'Just me and Elizabeth, why?' As he said her name she lit another cigarette. She threw the lighter onto the table with a clatter as she listened to his half of the ongoing conversation. It irritated her so much that she bit on the cigarette butt to stop her teeth from grinding. He was smiling deliberately now and her heart sank down into her stomach.

The conversation ended and he put down the receiver, his gaze settling steadily on hers. She broke the silence before he had the chance. 'You're getting as bad as James lately!' Her voice was now hard and Michael shot her a look that would have had the hardest of men quaking in their shoes, but it didn't affect her even a little in the same way. She didn't flinch. In fact she just glared at him, daring him to go to the edge.

'What are you on about now, woman?' he half spat, half choked. He wasn't about to let his male pride or indeed his temper get the better of him.

'You know! Your dick'll fall off having rotted from some nasty disease!' she snapped.

'And what would you know, my little innocent one, eh?' he snapped back, ignoring his thought of male pride, and going with temper instead. He regretted the words as they came out of his mouth. He watched her eyes, they turned to pieces of flint again as she stood proudly in front of him.

'Not a fucking thing, Michael.' She ground the words out, watching him as he pulled off his tie in frustration and whipped it on to the counter top with a thwack. A strange feeling filled him as he watched her seething there in the middle of the kitchen with every passing second. 'You're such an arsehole sometimes!' she added, and for a long moment he stood staring at her. She'd never said anything like that to him before. She was really pissed off with him this time, and it made him really angry too.

'Let's not do this now!' His voice was raised. He felt uncomfortable with the brewing situation and with a passing glare he turned and walked up the stairs, away from her.

Furious suddenly that he had backed off so easily, Beth followed him up, pulling her long skirt up so that she could take the steps two at a time. 'That's right, you fucking walk away from me, Michael!' she yelled, feeling even angrier than before, and he stopped dead in the dim light of the hallway. 'Go and call your Kelly, your Caroline, your whoever, up in your room.'

He turned to face her, his breathing hard. A thousand thoughts bounced around in his head, but the main was just how much he wanted to kiss her at that moment and he felt his lips part slightly and his tongue moisten them in anticipation of the deed.

"I suppose you're banging her, this fucking Kelly?' she said, the jealousy evident in her tone and he hesitated before her; was that two or three swear words? There was that urge again, but just then it had changed some more. She wasn't hiding the fact that she was madder than hell at him, wasn't pretending to not give a shit. She was there in front of him, absolutely livid because she'd had enough sidelining. What should he do, he couldn't kiss her, could he? No of course he couldn't so instead he went with the angry option.

'God damn it, woman! You are not my keeper, Elizabeth!' He forced out his finger in her direction aggressively. The words came out quickly and standing there, he knew it was a lie. She was his keeper, the keeper of his very soul and at every available moment she seemed to squeeze it. He knew she didn't know for sure how he felt about her. It wasn't *that* obvious that he tore himself away from her so as not to force himself upon her. She had no idea that it was almost unsafe for her to be alone with him sometimes, to the extent of him making an excuse to go out, or hide up on the second floor in the solace of his room. But the running and the hiding never lasted for long because he wanted her. But being the man he was he never said anything and never did anything. He was just good old dependable, reliable Michael and sometimes the urge to do something really outrageous almost got the better of him.

She looked magnificent when she was angry, he thought, eyeing her as he awaited the next bout of verbal abuse. Her suit jacket was gaping and he noted immediately that she had nothing beneath it but her bra. Her skirt had risen with her ascent into the hallway from the kitchen below, and the split on the side just gave a hint of a stocking. Why did she have to wear such underwear? It wasn't like anyone was going to see it, he mused suddenly. He snapped his eyes away from her thigh, aware of the fact that he had already lingered upon her leg for too long. Then he focused on her hair; it had been in such a neat style but it now rested in loose curls around her shoulders and she flicked it impatiently away from her face. His eyes then bored into hers, pools of darkest brown merged with emerald green and the only sound then was their breathing which was heavy and had quickened to a rapid pace.

She was suddenly unsure of what to say to him. These recent pauses and extended silences between them always got the better of her, and instead of thinking of something witty to retort with, she found herself almost drifting away to dream land. She wanted to kiss him, but knew that that was a stupid thought to be having during an argument and she shook her head absently, shaking the thought from her mind. 'I don't want to be your *keeper*!' she said finally.

'So why the interest in my sex life then, eh? What's the problem, Elizabeth?' he pushed her with his words.

'There isn't one!'

He leaned in. 'Oh, so you're not angry then?'

She backed off. 'No!'

He snarled at her then. 'Frustrated, is it then?' he snapped, watching her face and she blushed slightly before replying. Of course she was frustrated. Frustrated with everything, herself, him, everything.

'Fuck you, Michael!' she spat and he shook his head at her, a "tut" on his lips. He hated it when she used foul language. There was no need for it from her. She could come out with far better without swearing and he knew that she was doing it then just to piss him off.

'Of course!' he sounded oddly calm suddenly then. There was a pause, then he announced with a sigh, 'So we're here!' His voice was suddenly low and something in the expression on his face made Beth's heart thunder in her chest. She felt her lips part and her whole stance change, become softer. He was ready then, this was it. This was what both mistakes and fortunes were made of, times like these.

'What?' she said, putting her hands on her hips.

His expression was gentle, his eyes not leaving hers for a second, not even to blink, it seemed.

'Where it happens!' His voice was deep as he went on. 'You want to know what it's all about.'

The more he spoke the more she got flustered.

'What is all about, Michael, what are you talking about?' She was pretending to sound irritated and bored with him then, but they both knew that this one wasn't over. It was far from over. In fact he knew that it was just beginning.

'I'm talking about the way you feel inside right now!' he said confidently, his voice low and very husky. 'Maybe it's time someone enlightened you. Maybe I should enlighten you, isn't that what you really want?' he finished.

Beth's eyes opened to the fullest and she felt her cheeks burning. She certainly hadn't expected him to say anything like that and it threw her mentally off balance.

She didn't notice that she was moving, let alone moving backwards until she touched the wall by the stairs, and she jumped with shock.

'What do you think?' he went on, his soft Irish tones sounding deeper than she had ever heard before. 'Do you think we've ignored this issue for long enough now, or should we just carry on?' His eyes were dark pools.

'I think you're—you're—not even drunk!' She tried to laugh his comment off with a roll of her eyes to the ceiling and move away from him, but his hands snapped to her shoulders and he pinned her to the wall with a light shove.

'Drink is not a factor here tonight, Elizabeth.'

He was so close to her then that she could smell his aftershave as well as feel his breath on her face. 'And I'm waiting,' he added.

'Michael—' she gasped, breathing in his familiar scent. She couldn't look up into his eyes. Her mind was reeling. What to say? He was serious! The words *Oh my God* were all she could hear inside her head. She raised her hands to his chest to push him away and suddenly his grasp left her shoulders and he clamped her wrists in the tight space between them with a strong grip; she was trapped.

'Oh no, you don't!' He drew the words out as he shook his head at her. In her shoeless feet she felt very small. He towered above her and for the first time in her life she felt a strange apprehensiveness in his presence.

'Michael. Let me go.' Her voice was high again. 'You're not funny.' She tried to hide the pitch with another laugh, but was feeling more nervous with every passing second. He tried to steady his breathing as he held her there before him. He hesitated and thought of letting her go and laughing the last few minutes off as a joke, as she was then, but he couldn't. He wanted her more than anything in the world at that moment and he knew deep down inside himself somewhere that she wouldn't push him away; he knew that she wanted him too.

'Not a chance in hell, I've waited too long for this,' he breathed. 'And I'll not be pushed away again now, Elizabeth.'

As he said her name she looked slowly up into his eyes. She recognised naked longing, it was like a memory coming back to her. It was the same expression of lust in his eyes that was always there in her own, when she looked at him. The thought of him excited her but at the same time something was telling her that the situation was wrong.

'I don't know what you're talking about!' she lied, squirming beneath his grasp. She knew exactly what he was talking about, and the clarity of the fact that he was aching inside too was breathtaking.

'You want me!' he breathed, leaning into her. She really laughed then, it was a nervous laugh, but it was a laugh all the same. Was he proposing what she thought he was? The voice was back inside her head again. *Oh my God!*

'Want you?' It was a question, a startled question. 'What makes you say that?' she added, a strange confidence rising suddenly within her.

He smiled down at her then and it lit up his entire face. 'I just know!' he said deeply, and he noted the flush that reappeared on her cheeks.

'How so then, smart arse?' Her voice was suddenly urgent. He was almost touching her, his stance making her feel the heat and pure strength of his body. She went to speak again but nothing would escape her lips and she stood there, almost pouting up at him.

He didn't answer her in words, he just bent slightly and put his lips to hers. There was no rebuff, in fact he felt her relax and mould to him. She could feel his passion as he parted her lips with his own open mouth. His tongue edged into her mouth. She felt her legs quiver beneath her as she felt the moisture of his mouth. She'd been kissed before, yes, but not like this. Not with such warmth, and she prayed that he wouldn't stop. His grip on her wrists released and she was drawn close to his body, his hands running up and down the length of her back and his fingers finding their way through her hair. His arousal was hard against her body then and she faltered as panic registered and took her back over. He felt the change in her and pulled lightly away from her, though not letting go of the grasp he had about her body.

'Sorry!' he breathed. 'I shouldn't have done that, but you did ask.' There was almost humour in his tone. She dropped her head back down, her chin almost on her chest. She didn't know how to reply to him and didn't want to open her eyes, didn't want to meet his gaze. She didn't know what to do. In her dreams she had been so sure of herself and what she would do in this situation but she was completely undone by him and tears of frustration welled up in her eyes, forcing them open. 'Look at me?' he breathed. There was passion evident then.

'You just kissed me!' she managed.

'I did, yes. Now I said, will you look at me,' he said again, not daring to laugh at her sweet little statement. He didn't want to make her feel any more awkward than she obviously already did.

She shook her head at his request. He took her face in his hands and tilted her head up towards his own. She looked everywhere but at him and into his eyes then, blinking away the tears that now threatened to fall down her cheeks. Her mind registered everything around her. It was hot suddenly and the only noise was outside in the street, a car and footsteps but they were distant now. The only light source was from the kitchen below them and then she heard him take a deep breath.

'Elizabeth. Do you trust me?' His voice was nothing but a whisper, and that was when she finally looked into his eyes and he got the answer he hoped he would. She was completely his, as they stood there in the darkness, alone together. He'd waited his whole life for an answer like that, she hadn't said a word but he knew that she did trust him, trusted him with her life.

'Yes,' she said after a long pause.

'Are you ready?' He knew the answer to that better than she did, but had to ask, had to be sure before they went any further, before he went any further. This was to be her biggest step yet and he had to be sure that she was ready for it.

'Yes!' Her voice was light but still full of emotion.

He gazed down into her eyes for a long moment before speaking again.

'Come with me now!' His voice was demanding, even though his accent made it sound like music to her ears.

'Where?' she was weak.

'Upstairs.' There was that low tone again.

'Oh,' she managed. She was completely dumbfounded by the last few minutes. Hadn't they just been having a row?

'Why are you doing this?' It was actually a thought, but she said it out loud.

'Because I want to,' he replied, bringing her back.

She let him lead her by the fingers with one strong hand, slowly up the stairs and into the confines of her bedroom without another word being spoken between them. The door clicked shut behind them and suddenly truly alone with him, him leaning on the door, with nowhere to run to she began to really panic.

'Michael. Please. I can't—We can't—' she began, but he stopped her in mid-sentence with his mouth, his kisses bolder then, showing his confidence.

'It's okay, you're fine,' he said, finally pulling his lips from hers.

'James might come home,' she whispered with laboured breath as he began to undo the buttons on her jacket with large warm fingers. She was panicked. He glanced at her face, his expression suddenly sceptical. That was very unlikely and he knew that that wasn't her concern. She was scared of what was going on.

'Don't be scared, please. Trust me,' he breathed as her jacket slid from her shoulders to the floor behind her. 'Have I ever hurt you before?'

She shook her head. 'Never.'

He skimmed her lips with his own again. 'Then trust me now, Elizabeth!'

Every time he said her name she felt a new warmth run the length of her spine. Her heart was pounding so hard and fast that fleetingly she wondered if he could hear it, and then that thought was gone, replaced with deeper, more wondrous, heady thoughts.

'I want to see you—' He was pulling at the waistband of her skirt. After fiddling with the zip it slid to the floor slowly and he ran his hand down her sides, feeling the difference between her skin and the nylon of her stocking tops.

'Please don't do this!' she whispered, shyness taking her over as he unhooked the clasp of her bra with both hands.

'Ssshh—' he replied. He let his hands slip down her neck, and down across her chest, 'There's nothing to be afraid of.' He looked down her, to her stockings, black lacy items and then his eyes roamed back up her body, taking in her rounded stomach, the curved shape of her hips. He committed every little detail to memory. He had seen her in far less in the past but she was now allowing him to look at her, to feel her and the urge to take her there and then was something that he literally had to stop himself from doing with a long breath held sigh. He reached out again; his touch on her skin was gentle. Her skin was soft and warm and it still held the tan she was so very proud of that summer. 'There, is that so bad?' he whispered and she shook her head at him. Her voice was unavailable for comment at that moment, even though she could feel it somewhere between her throat and her lungs.

He pulled his shirt off over his head and tossed it across the room, listening to her as she breathed him in again, letting out the air with a shaky exhalation. He pulled his belt from his trousers and it, too, landed somewhere on the floor. He kicked off his shoes and bent to remove his socks. All the while he watched Beth, as she watched him in wonder. His chest was broad, she knew it was but now there was no sisterly pretence to hide behind and it was almost daunting. She watched as his muscles flexed and moved beneath his skin and as he undid the button on his trousers her eyes followed the line of soft thick dark downy hair that led from his chest to his stomach and lower. She saw the bulge under the material and tried to pull away from him but he caught her hand in his and guided her to the edge of the zip.

'It's okay,' he whispered. She reached out to touch him through the fabric in wonder. 'It won't bite you.' She put her hand to it. It was solid and the heat, oh the heat. Dropping to his knees, he ran his hands across her stomach, around her hips and slowly down her thighs.

'What are you doing?' she said, her voice urgent as his fingers hooked about her panties and slowly he pulled them down, away from her body.

'Kissing you,' he said gently. He could feel her shaking but nothing was going to stop him now.

'Michael—Please don't—I've never—' She was gabbling her words. She was in turmoil. Petrified of going on but terrified of telling him to stop. His lips on her skin felt so good.

He looked up at her, his eyes flaming in the half-light. 'I know you haven't!' he replied and before she could go on protesting feebly, he slipped his hand up between her thighs.

She was soaking wet, the knowledge making her shut her eyes tight and try to pull away from him.

'Please! Oh God—' he almost groaned, grabbing gently at her, pulling her back towards him as she shook, and then he kissed her. His lips following his expert hands. She ran her hands through his hair and clutched him to her with shaking fingers.

'Oh, Michael,' she groaned as she fought against the urge to cry out. He was enjoying her wetness, wasn't shocked by it and he tugged at her hold-ups with his free hand. Within seconds she was totally naked before him and he stood back up, his mouth still wet from her. She was a work of art, well rounded, perfectly proportioned. He slipped off his trousers. A slight smile crossed his features as he took in her reaction to his naked endowment.

Nothing could have prepared her for it; no strip show, no film, and no steamy novel; not even the chattering and jokes with friends. He was, without a doubt, huge. Was he going to put that inside her? It was never going to fit, even though both logic and her education told her that it would. But she'd struggled with Tampax in the past. *Oh Jesus!* Her eyes widened again and then they met with his. She was almost crying with different emotions then, but his gaze upon her was still gentle.

He could almost hear what she was thinking and fleetingly, he wondered just how far to take her, should he take her all the way or just toy with her? He could taste her on his lips and his mind was set. He was going to have her like he'd never had anyone before.

'Are you okay?' he asked, breaking the sudden silence. She nodded at him, she was unsure of what to say. "Yes" simply seemed a bit lame.

He laid her down on the bed, planting little kisses on her neck and breasts. He toyed with her nipples until they hardened again between his lips, and then slowly he made his way down her body. She groaned quietly as he found her bud again and began to caress it with a steady pace. His fingers slipped in and out of her in rhythm with the pace of his mouth and suddenly she was grasping at him, gasping for breath, unable to decide what to do to make the feeling that now swept over her continue. She wanted to yell out his name, wanted to beg him not to stop but there was no need, his fingers hadn't faltered and the feeling exploded like nothing she had ever encountered before.

Grabbing at his hair she felt him slow to a stop and then he was above her, kissing her, making her taste herself upon his lips. He was hard up against her inner thigh now; she could feel him and all her fears and doubts were gone, flown away by the feeling that still ran through her.

'Are you sure you want to do this?' he asked, silently praying that she wouldn't say no. He wanted her so much at that moment that his body ached but if she said no, he'd—No, no. He wouldn't. For all he was a gentleman, he was first and foremost a man, and the throbbing within him was unbearable. He had to be inside her, had to know how she felt, even if it was just that one time.

She looked into those brown eyes and could feel herself swimming in them. She was aching, almost in pain. Her head was spinning. All she could think of at that time was just how good she felt when he was so near her.

'Yes. Oh, yes,' she breathed, her eyes half closed.

'This'll change everything, you know that, don't you?' he breathed.

'Everything?' Her voice was all but a whisper.

'Absolutely everything,' he replied, his tone the same.

With one deep kiss he entered her, pushing past the torn constriction that made her whimper into his mouth. He eased gently the rest of the way into her until he could go no further. He paused then and pulled his lips from hers. 'I hurt you!' He was breathless, disbelieving that he was inside her then.

'No.' Her own breath was shaky, her chest rising and falling heavily. 'Yes,' she admitted. He smiled gently into her eyes and she smiled back cautiously, almost unsure suddenly of how to do even that as he lay within her. It was such an odd sensation, she thought and almost instinctively she contracted her pelvic muscles around him.

'It won't hurt any more,' he assured her and she believed him, trusted his every word. He moved above her, in and out slowly at first, his elbows resting on the pillows either side of her head and his fingers flitting through the wisps of her hair that framed her face. 'Is that nice?' he whispered between kisses about her face.

'Very.' She sighed deeply, tilting her head back so that he kissed her neck, too. His pace stayed the same for a long while and then she began to move her hips up to meet him and he got faster and faster. He felt her contracting around him and took her head in one large hand, supporting her back with the other as he pulled her up bodily towards him.

'Come!' he begged, enjoying the sensation she inspired around him. 'Don't hold back, don't, please!' He leaned back almost completely on his haunches to a sitting position, pulling her close to him, burying himself within her again and again.

'Oh God!' she gasped. He felt her come for the second time, her wetness increasing and her breathe laboured. He pushed at her harder and harder and she let out a cry. He kissed her hard on the mouth, his tongue exploring hers with incredible fever.

'I'm sorry!' he gasped breathlessly. 'I'm sorry!' He didn't want to hurt her, but neither did he want the sweet feeling to stop, and his arms encircled her like a security blanket, constantly assuring her that everything was perfect. They moved together, their eyes taking in every detail of each other, their lips touching every inch of the other's face and neck. Falling back down on the bedclothes and he hovered above her, supporting his entire body weight on one arm, the hand of his other running up and down the side of her and across her breasts. He was in heaven. He was finally having his way. Finally making love to her. He felt tears in his eyes, the emotion of the moment taking him over and then all he could think of was her, pleasing her, filling her with himself. Then the tears were gone, replaced with the instinct to make her first time the most wonderful that any woman could know. 'Oh God. Please!' he breathed as his pace quickened and he pounded into her as if his very life depended upon it. He wanted the feeling that pulsed through him to last forever but he knew how close to the edge he was and holding her in his arms, he came.

Late the following night Beth sat on a stool at the end of the bar in Baileys. She rubbed her eyes. It had been a steady night, nothing special but she definitely wasn't in the mood for the paperwork that was spread out now before her. The clattering of glass and the constant throb of the washers behind the bar eased and then ceased as the staff finished clearing up for the night. There was something about a bar after closing that always made her feel comfortable and tonight, even though she was tired and it was gone midnight, she felt more at ease than she had ever remembered feeling in her whole life. It felt as if she had said *goodnight* a thousand times but in reality it was more like six. She had a fleeting conversation with Jonathan, their new and overly camp bar manager, and reassured Luke, the doorman, that James would be along shortly to collect her and that she would be quite safe in her own wine bar. She locked up the front doors and was finally alone. She lit a cigarette and helped herself to a double measure of the best single malt whisky from behind the bar; it wasn't something that she would normally have drunk but tonight she felt totally different. In fact, she had felt different since waking up that morning.

She'd woken up in her bed and realised between sleep and wakefulness that she was alone even though she could still smell him there on the bedding, and on her skin. It had been a few minutes before she'd realised what had woken her; her alarm was bleeping at four-minute intervals. She'd risen, throwing the quilt away from her naked body and then she stopped in her tracks, half on the bed and half off. Putting her hand between her thighs to stop the moisture from escaping, she'd grabbed a couple of tissues from her dressing table, thrown on her dressing gown which was still draped on the chair in the corner of her room and had gone dashing into the bathroom. She'd sat on the toilet, waiting a few seconds before daring to look down at the discarded tissue paper. Was it going to be horrific? How embarrassing, because if it was on her—*Oh God*, how could she ever look him in the face again? He'd made her bleed. What had she done, and what had he done! He'd probably never speak to her again. But when she'd dared to look down there was hardly anything there, mainly moisture. It was his, it was him! And that thought bought a strange rush of warmth over her. No one had ever mentioned that that happened before and she'd stifled the urge to laugh at her own innocent ignorance. Of course it was going to come back out again. There wasn't anywhere for it to go, was there!

As she washed herself in the bidet she'd felt the swollen soreness and she'd run her hands across her body, imagining that it was his touch and not her own. Drying, she found herself thinking back to explicit moments from the previous night like snapshots in her mind and she smiled secretly, knowingly. She saw his face, felt the weight of him, a full-bodied, hot-blooded man. She felt the sweat from his back on her fingertips, smelt him on her, and the way she'd tasted on

214

him when they'd kissed. She'd looked in the mirror and noticed that she didn't look any different, and then it occurred to her that she wouldn't and once washed, and dressed in her normal morning attire of cotton trousers and top she'd gone down the two flights of stairs into the kitchen.

James was home and already talking on the phone. He'd nodded at her, a smile on his face as his conversation continued, but he had done nothing else but blow her a kiss. He hadn't seen it on her face the second she'd come down the stairs, and he hadn't begun to yell the house down. He'd simply blown her a kiss, as he always did in the morning and passed her his carton of cigarettes, which she'd taken gratefully. She'd refilled the cup he'd held out to her as he'd continued to talk on the phone. She poured a cup of coffee out of the pot for herself as she'd lit the cigarette; it was exactly the same as the morning before, in fact, it was pretty much the same as every other morning she could recall from the past.

She half listened to him, but was still trying to put the bizarre events of the last night into some sort of order when she'd heard Michael whistling as he'd padded down the stairs. He was unshaven but his hair was dishevelled and wet from the shower. He had on his favourite pale grey tracksuit bottoms, which should have gone in the bin years before, and nothing else. He'd looked incredible to her and she felt her cheeks redden and her heart pound in embarrassment and panic. His eyes had met hers instantly, his lips parting to speak, but then he looked over at James who was just finishing on the telephone. Before he could say anything at all to her or make any kind of gesture James finished his call.

'Oh, get out of bed, did we?' he'd laughed, glancing at his watch for effect and Michael scoffed at his sarcasm. That bastard could go for days on two, maybe three hours sleep and look great on it. Michael, although he could do it, didn't do it as well as James.

'Yes, after about two hours' sleep, thanks to you waking me up coming in at God only knows what time this morning!' Michael's reply was jovial, but he had been grateful to God and indeed James for making such a noise. If he hadn't, Michael would probably still have been in bed with Elizabeth snuggled up asleep in his arms.

As the two men had chatted Beth had poured Michael a cup of steaming coffee and passed it to him with shaking hands. He'd taken it from her and their fingers had touched. His eyes had bored into hers again as they had the night before, just as they had when he had come inside her and she felt her whole body ache to touch his. 'And did you sleep well, Elizabeth?' He'd asked watching the changing expressions on her face.

'Yes, thank you. I slept better than I have in a long time,' she managed as he took the cigarette she had been holding from her fingers with his free hand. He took a couple of lugs of it before placing it between her slightly pouting lips. It was yet another erotic moment for her to store in her mind, along with the four hours of him she had already had. Suddenly she'd felt like crying for no reason at all, but he'd smiled down at her with such tenderness that all the fears of what to do next that had just dashed through her mind seemed to disappear in a second.

A light tap at the bolted glass entrance doors bought her back to the present and she jumped in her seat, her head snapping up to where the sound had come from. There he was! 'Michael!' she mouthed in the dim light, her face lighting up, her heart pounding like a drum in her chest. She jumped up, rushed to the door and flung up the bolt that barred his way. He slipped in, locking the door behind him.

'I told James I'd collect you,' he breathed, instantly putting both hands around her waist and pulling her bodily away from the light and back into the shadows of the bar area. 'I called here earlier, left a message. I tried to call you on the mobile too, it was off. I wanted to see you, to talk to you—' he continued between kisses across her face and neck. 'Today's been so crazy, Elizabeth. God, I wanted to see you!' She savoured the feeling that his lips on her skin set alight within her and followed his lead, caressing his body from over the top of his clothes.

'We were really busy tonight. They're less than useless, they probably forgot. You wanted to talk to me?' she breathed and he groaned, nodding his head, not wanting to let his lips separate from her skin.

'I wanted to make sure that you were okay,' he said finally, looking into her eyes. 'You looked so unsure this morning. I've been thinking about you all day!'

It was true, he had been. In fact he'd thought of nothing else. He'd fallen into his own bed as dawn broke and lain there, a contentment that he had never felt possible washing over him like spring rain. He was tired, but there was no way he was going to be able to sleep. He could smell her on every part of his body and if he closed his eyes he could see her. He could see her face as she came again and again. Feel her body next to his as he buried himself hard inside her. But this was taken from him fleetingly as he thought of the things he could have said to her as they'd lain there. He hadn't told her that he hadn't just acted upon animal instincts and that he had really wanted, with all his heart, to be with her, and to make love to her like he had. He'd wanted to share his soul with her from the moment they'd kissed, something he'd never experienced before, for all his worldly ways. He wanted to ask about James, but something deep inside him knew that she wouldn't be the one to tell him about them and what they had done. He was concerned too that he may have hurt her. All men boasted about their endowments, but Michael was aware that he was truly one of the lucky few, and that in the past he had hurt even the most experienced of women in enthusiasm. She'd bled, but not as much as even he'd thought she would and so he didn't feel the need to tell her about it then. He didn't want to bring her earlier shyness back and besides, what could he expect? After all she was until the night before untouched by anyone other than herself. And he was sure that she had definitely touched herself.

'I feel great!' she almost laughed, tilting her head to the side slightly as she looked up at him. The shyness was gone, swept away by the fact that he was there with her at that moment and he couldn't help but notice how easy she was around him, how sure of herself she was, had always been.

'I know you do, but are you okay?' He asked, his expression sincere. 'I didn't hurt you? Make you bleed too much?' He thought he'd better mention it; make it all a bit more natural.

'Oh,' she blushed. 'Yes. Um, no—I'm fine—It was—' She paused, trying choose her words carefully. 'It was incredible.' There was a blush on her face as she spoke and he clung to her, holding hr tightly.

'I wanted it to be,' he said lightly, not thinking about what he was saying.

'Really?' she questioned, sounding a little taken aback with his response.

'Yes, really.' He pulled her really close then. 'I've wanted to do that with you for a long time.' He was being honest and Beth looked away, embarrassed again suddenly. It was what she wanted to hear from him, but the shock of him saying it to her was something else entirely.

'How long?' she asked.

'If I told you, you wouldn't believe me.' He smiled at her again.

'No, Michael. Tell me,' she almost begged. 'We have no secrets from each other.'

He thought for a while. 'A year, maybe more.' He was vague but knew exactly when it was and he had the feeling that, if she were honest, so did she.

'I knew!' she almost whispered, sounding very far away in thought. 'Yes!' It was a statement. This *was* the time to be honest. 'Was I worth it, worth the wait?' It sounded cheap, even to her ears, but she suddenly needed to know and she watched him in the dimness.

'Every day, every hour and every minute.' He kissed her. 'But now, the waiting is over!' He paused. 'And I want to do it all again, and again and again,' he breathed as he ran his hand down her cleavage.

'You do?' She sounded really pleased. 'When?'

He glanced around them in the silence emptiness. 'Now!' His voice was deep again, and even in her inexperienced state, she was aware that he was aroused. She didn't get to say any more, he was leading, almost pulling her through the bar and with a light shove the office door opened.

It was pitch black in the back office, but he didn't feel on the wall for the light switch. He didn't need eyes tonight. He needed to be inside her again, feel her skin against his. He wanted to hear her and feel her as they joined together, so much that it was almost unbearable. Hard kisses rained down on her as he pulled up her skirt. 'You don't need these!' he whispered as his fingers found the edge of her lace panties, and he ripped them from her body with a swift tug. The action made her gasp and her skin sting but it was far too exciting to make him stop.

'Okay, so they're gone!' she giggled as he half laid, half pushed her back onto the desk, sending papers skidding out of their neat piles everywhere upon it and after fumbling with his trousers, he entered her with one long, purposeful thrust. There was no constriction and she was receptively wet around him.

'God, you're incredible,' he breathed, pushing into her harder and harder until she let out a yelp that made him falter. 'I'm sorry. I don't want to hurt you,' he apologised huskily, his hands running the length of her covered body as she stretched back across the desk.

'You won't. Please don't stop,' she gasped, feeling the warm wave come over her as his fingers explored her. She grabbed at him with her legs, taking him all the way in, begging him with her body not to stop even when she cried out. She said his name over and over, her voice almost gone as she held her breath. She didn't feel like the innocent party in the room then; he did. He was the innocent. He was the one desperate to please, desperate to be pleased. It was the oddest sensation he'd experienced in a long time. It was like making love for the first time again. Everything was new. Everything had the crisp clarity that usually only came with daylight. He understood her and went on, pushing back and forth, his hands on her hips, holding her to him as she moved against the wood of the desk until with a loud groan, he exploded within her. They were still for a long moment, neither of them wanting to move. They could feel each other's breath and heartbeats and Michael kept hold of her, still not quite believing that they were there. He still expected to wake up from a dream, alone in his bed but he didn't. It was the feeling he'd had all day. It was real, she was real and she was all that he had known she would be.

His mobile telephone began to ring on the desk where he had thrown it and they both jumped at the high-pitched bleep it made. Reluctantly pulling slowly out of her, he grabbed it from the desk and looked at the display.

'James,' he said in the darkness, answering the call. Beth listened to him and saw his face in the shadows as her eyes adjusted to the darkness that surrounded them. 'Okay. You? Yes, she's here, hang on—' Michael passed the phone to her, lingering on the touch.

'Hi, sweetie.' She was trying not to sound so breathless. 'No, that's okay. Of course I didn't mind. You have a life too, right? We're just finishing up now. Why, where are you going?'

As she talked, Michael bent and scooped up the scrap of lace that he had ripped from her body only moments before. He tucked it gently between her legs and the realisation that he was aware of what happened to his seed touched her so deeply that the tone of her voice changed as she ended the call to James. 'We'll see you later then. Okay, bye.' She cleared the call and passed the phone back to him as he readjusted himself, tucking his shirt back into his trousers.

'I didn't know that happened,' she blushed as he put his arms around her neck.

'You don't know anything, yet,' he said, sounding suggestive.

'Will you teach me?' she asked, almost politely and he laughed then.

'Do you want me to?' his voice was very, very low.

'Yes,' she nodded.

'Then I will. Now, what did he want?'

'Oh, he said that he was going to take Jenny home.' She had a slight smile in her tone and he could hear the innuendo.

'You think he's keen on her, ey?' he said and she laughed then.

'I reckon so,' she laughed, mimicking James's phrase.

'So he'll not be home any time soon, then?' His tone was suggestive.

'Obviously not.'.

'Good, then let's go home.'

She liked the sound of that, Michael taking her home, to their home and she let him pull her gently to her feet and help straighten her clothes. He was always such a gentleman, and the thought warmed her.

'If you keep looking at me like that we'll never get out of here,' he breathed as Beth gave him a smouldering pout.

He'd been right about those lips. They swelled red and were the sweetest he'd ever tasted. In fact, Beth was the best he'd ever tasted and she wasn't the first innocent he'd encountered in his time. All his womanising seemed to become clear to him and he felt as if every one of them had been a class at school, preparing him for the real thing. Teaching him so that he could teach her and please her the way he wanted to. After he'd planted a few more kisses on her face he led her out of the bar, locked up behind them they walked casually arm in arm across the road and got into his car.

The time that followed seemed to Beth to be filled with questions, and the answers to many that she hadn't even thought to ask. She wanted desperately to please him, to keep him, being only too aware of what she now had in him. She watched with new eyes how he behaved, and how others behaved around him, and instead of the blind rage and jealousy that had filled her before she was left with intrigue. Intrigue calmed only by knowledge. Knowledge and understanding of the feeling she got when she could feel his eyes upon her from across a crowded room. And how, when their eyes met she would know instinctively that no other woman, no matter how beautiful, could make the same deep impression on him as she did. He would be standing near her, his giant presence almost ghost-like and he would smoulder at her with those big brown eyes, almost reach out to her with those strong arms. And she always got the same flip in her stomach that she had got the first time he had kissed her. When she smiled at him and he smiled back there were sparks. Real sparks, sparks that both had trouble at times not acting upon.

He seemed to be with her everywhere, and at every available moment they were together, joined, learning about each other, feeling each other so that even with the slightest glance or touch they knew the other's innermost feelings by heart. It was an incredible feeling to know and to be known in such a way. The relationship they had in the opinion of onlookers seemed to blossom and become richer almost overnight. Beth knew that it was stronger even than hers was with James, because she and Michael shared something special, something deeper even than blood and all the little inconsistencies and hang-ups they had were flown away. Michael had taken something precious from her but in return had given his very soul. The only thorn in their bed of roses was the clear fact that they couldn't share it with anyone. They hadn't spoken of it, it was just something that they both understood. James would go absolutely off the wall if he knew that the only person in the world that he trusted with his life had betrayed him by, in his eyes, seducing his little sister. Beth was also as aware as Michael was that Pat would be of the same opinion. No, they would have to bide their time and wait for the moment to be exactly right before they even suggested that they may have feelings that ran deeper than the façade of brother and sister which everyone was so eager to comment on. So it was agreed without words that that was how it was to be and if they were honest, they both found the thought of being caught almost as exciting as the deed itself.

Michael caught Beth in the hallway as she walked up from the kitchen. He had quite literally just walked through the front door. Throwing his keys onto the bottom stair he smiled. What a sight to come home to, he thought. He slid his hands around her waist and pulled her close to him in the silence. He could hear voices then; people were laughing in the kitchen below them, and the idea that one of them might come walking up the stairs and catch them was almost thrilling.

'You're late. They think you've been having your end away.' Her voice was husky as she enjoyed the feel of him close to her body.

'Good.' He smiled gently into her eyes then, the warmth there showing her that he cared for her more than he'd ever said. He often came in later than they did, talked on the phone as he had before and flirted in the same way as he had. Everything to everyone else looked the same. Nothing had changed. But to them, everything had changed. Everything was different.

'I got talking to young Johnny boy. And what a nice young man he is too!' His voice was camp.

'How was he?' she asked.

He laughed quietly 'Gay!'

'You mean happy?' She laughed too then.

'No, I mean gay. I think he's got a little crush on me,' and he pouted at her.

'I don't blame him one little bit!' she replied.

'Oh, really?' he planted a light kiss on her neck.

'Yes, really!' She liked the feel of it, it was soothing as well as quite sexy.

'So, do you have a crush on me too?' He gave her another nuzzle.

'Might have.' She was enjoying this.

'Don't do that...' he breathed as she pushed into him with her backside. 'Are they all down there?' he asked with a nudge of his head.

'No, just James, Jen and Darren. The others went about an hour ago, but I think they're set in for the night, as there's a bottle of whisky open and James is teaching Jen to skin up. It's not good! In fact, it's scary!' she exclaimed. Michael cringed at the thought of that concoction as he watched her.

She was trying really hard to keep her tone casual but just having him so close made her heart pound, nothing had ever affected her in such a way.

'Well, he'll sleep where he lands tonight!' he smiled. 'Hopefully that'll be down there.' There was a pause and the air around them became heavy. Michael's facial expression changed and Beth bit on her bottom lip. He slowly raised her skirt and moved her panties away from her body with his fingers. He slid into her, touching her bud and making her catch on her breath. 'I'm having that later,' he whispered as he pulled away from her.

She was visibly aroused; her lips had swelled slightly and set in that pout that always got him in the heart. 'I look forward to it,' she breathed. He almost laughed at her tone. She was getting creative. He liked that.

'Come on.' His tone was normal once again and she followed him down the stairs, re-adjusting her attire as she walked.

No more than two hours later Darren surrendered, and he was quite graceful about it for a change and within five minutes of announcing that he was going home, was gone. Jennifer, so pretty and delicate and small, looked dozy and grinned at James, half drunk, half stoned.

'Do you want a hand?' Michael asked James as he got up from the table to help Jen up to bed on unsteady feet.

'No, you're all right, mate,' he slurred and with that he scooped Jennifer up in his arms and carried her towards the stairs. 'Night, people,' he yawned.

'Sleep tight!' Beth replied casually as she watched her brother carry his girlfriend up the stairs to bed.

'You want a coffee?' she asked Michael, aware that he was watching her now that they were alone.

'No,' he breathed.

'Tea?' she suggested instead.

'No.' He rose from the table and followed her into the kitchen area.

'Anything?' Her tone was light.

'Yes!' He pinned her up against the counter.

'What?'

'I want that,' he began, running his hand across the front of her skirt.

'Well, go on then,' she breathed and with no more said, Michael sank to his knees before her and raised her skirt again. He slipped her undies from her body and began to kiss her inner thigh.

Chapter Twenty-One

October 1997

The main doors of Brown's opened and Jason appeared, closely followed by James, Darren and Michael. The cold hit them and their pace quickened as they made their way across the car park towards James's car. 'Brass monkeys, anyone?' Jason laughed as he climbed into the back with Darren, leaving James to drive and Michael to get in next to him. ''Ere, did you see the tits on that bird?' he pointed back towards the bar doors.

'Did I!' James laughed. 'Almost had me eye out!'

'Need papers!' Darren commented casually as he made himself more comfortable. 'And beer!'

They talked in one-liners as the car moved through the streets and none noticed that Michael had said very little, if anything at all. He wasn't concentrating on them, wasn't even interested in them that night, if he was honest. He just wanted to go home. He thought of her there, all warm and soft and so goddamned sexy that he actually caught his breath as he checked his phone for any messages.

'You know what, boys, I think I'll skip out tonight!' he announced, turning slightly in his seat to look at James. 'Can you drop me at the house?'

James glanced at him quizzically. 'You okay, Mike?' James asked. He'd noticed how quiet he'd been all evening, not like Michael at all, but it had been a long day, a very long day.

'Sure, I'm fine, just a bit tired, you know?'

James nodded at him. He did look tired.

'I have to see Pat in the morning. I don't think a smoke or a drink's the best idea.'

James grimaced. 'I hate shitty paperwork,' he said with a shake of his head. 'That's why I get the baby to help with mine!' he added with a grin. 'She's an angel!' There was real love and affection in his tone and Michael smiled then, glad of James's comment.

'Actually, I'm hoping she'll still be up. I could do with a hand myself.' Michael's tone was light, but his thoughts were deep. Paperwork, yeah, okay. He'd be up those stairs and into those arms quick smart.

Propped up on one arm on the bed, Beth lay reading a book in the light of her bedside lamp. She read the same passages over and over again. She loved the romantic books and this one that Jennifer had lent her was fantastic. Her thoughts were interrupted by the sound of her mobile telephone ringing in little bleeps on the dressing table below the window and she put the book down, face down, lightly on the bed and stood up. She looked at the display. It was Michael's number and it showed up on the display as *Answer Me*. Her heart skipped a beat as she pressed the answer button, putting the phone to her ear.

'Hello' she said in a half whisper, trying to disguise the shudder of excitement in her tone. 'Oh nothing much, I was just reading, dreaming of a prince charming,' she continued as she began to walk around in little circles on the carpeted floor, wiggling her toes into the thick depth of it. She listened to his deep tones on the other end of the line for a few minutes and then she heard a light tap at her door. 'Hang on,' she sighed. 'James is home. Where are you, anyway?' She still had the phone to her ear as she opened it and there he was. He held his phone out from his ear, cleared the call and smiled down at her from his position, leaning casually up against the wall by the door frame.

'You're brother just dropped me home,' he said with a smile as he slipped his jacket from his shoulders and threw it towards the banister, leaving him in just a tight white T-shirt and suit trousers. 'He's off to Darren's for a while, with Jason.' He eyed her leisurely. She looked exactly as he thought she would, warm and soft in her large towelling dressing gown. Her hair was up and she smelt gorgeous. 'I told him I had paperwork to do and that you'd help me because I'm so very, very busy and you're so very, very good at that sort of thing!'

She smiled 'Not in that tone, I hope!' She was breathing hard herself.

'No. I said it with far more conviction. Did I miss the bath?' he asked then, a disappointed tone evident in his voice.

She nodded at him slowly, her eyes softly focusing upon his face. 'Yes, Michael. You missed the bath.'

'Damn it!' Before she said anything else he was upon her, pulling at the long cord that was holding the material closed between her skin and his touch. He kicked the door closed behind them, turned her around on her toes and pushed her up against the back of it. His lips were warm and with every touch of them upon her skin she grew more excited.

'Are you sure you didn't you want to go with them?' she breathed between kisses.

'Positive!' There was that deep low tone again. She loved that.

'Why not?' she purred.

'Because what I want's right here.' He was touching her naked body with warm firm hands. 'And what do you want?' Her voice was heavy.

'I want you! Always you! Only you!' He picked her up and she wrapped her legs around his waist as he moved across the room. They landed on the bed, him above her and he stopped, looking deep into her eyes. He wanted to speak then, but couldn't. The words he wanted to say stuck in his throat as he hesitated. She brushed her hand over his cheek, feeling the day's stubble beneath it as she did so. Their eyes locked and thousands of words were spoken in the silence between them. He wanted to tell her how he was feeling, but lying there in the warmth of her room he knew that he didn't have to say a word. He knew that she knew how he felt and that fact alone warmed him to the very soul. He kissed her again then, gently parting her lips with his.

He remembered then their first night, their first kiss and every detail of it as he lay above her now protectively. Warmly, making her feel the safety that he knew his body brought to hers. He rested his elbows either side of her head and with the backs of his hands he touched her forehead and face, letting her plant kisses on his fingers as they brushed over her lips. They were like that for a long while, looking at each other and then he bent his head down again and kissed her full on the mouth. She ran her hands the length of his body, feeling him harden against her from between his trousers and her gaping gown. She pulled at his T-shirt and it slid up and away from his trousers with ease. He pulled himself up onto his knees, his fingers making quick work of his belt. He then kicked the trousers off roughly, along with his shoes.

'Socks' she said with a slight giggle in her tone.

'They're going right now!'

Naked now before her on the bed, Michael pulled her to sitting and she turned her body so that she too was kneeling. Her dressing gown fell from her frame completely and with a tug from Michael, landed on the floor beside the bed. She still gazed at Michael's naked body in wonder every time she saw it. She loved the sheer size of him, he dwarfed her and when he wrapped his thick strong arms around her she felt as if she were finally home. She ran her fingers across the dark hair that covered his chest and belly and then her hand found his penis. He was solid and she toyed with him lightly, enjoying watching the changing expressions on his face as she did it. The way his lips moved in readiness to kiss hers. The way his eyes seemed to smoulder beneath his lashes was in itself enough to set her on fire. Unable to hold back, he pulled her close to him and she settled her palms on his hips as he leaned backwards on the bed, moved his legs towards her until he was lying and she was kneeling in front of him and then he pulled her on to him.

'This is new!' she breathed, feeling him edging towards her mound and she spread her legs a little further apart above him.

'I thought you'd like a change?' he almost laughed. She smiled at him then. He was, in her opinion, which she knew didn't count for much, the perfect lover for someone as inexperienced as she was. He was so gentle with her even though she knew and could feel that he was desperate to just pound into her and control her. His eagerness to share himself with her had been as startling to her as his statement of manhood in making sure that she was ready and satisfied. He was gently and slowly discovering different things with her, and he touched her heart like nothing and no one before.

He tried to ease into her slowly, aware that from his position he could hurt her by going in too far and too fast or too hard. She was tense, he could feel it. He looked up into her eyes, which were now firmly fixed on his. 'Relax,' he whispered. She looked awkward; he was aware that she was too tight. He slid his hands down in between her legs. Her breathing changed as he rubbed gently at her bud. She could feel herself moistening with every move that he made. It was incredible to feel this at ease with someone, to share such things with another person. To think that she had been embarrassed about how wet she'd gotten, when in reality he was ecstatic about it. It was proof that he was touching her in the right way and that she enjoyed him as much as he enjoyed her.

'Oh no, you don't,' he breathed as he watched her face; she was flushed, her eyes almost totally closed and her lips were parted and swollen slightly. She was on the edge of coming and he moved his hand away from her and pulled her back onto him. He slipped into her and let out the familiar satisfying groan. This was somewhere that he loved being, he thought as she moved slowly above him.

'Is this right?' she said, not faltering as she moved back and forth above him.

'Yes, yes it is, very right.' The sensation of her movements excited him more than he could recall from anything in the past. He could feel her muscles around him and he knew that with a couple of swift strokes upon her, she would come. He moved his hand; he was right. After only a minute or two he looked up at her. She was on the edge again, and as the wave took her and she held her breath, her movements quickened. She was on all fours above him, her hips sinking almost onto his. He pulled her down on to him and turned her over, so that she was on her back then and he pushed into her, slowing their pace deliberately.

'What's wrong?' she breathed into his ear.

'Nothing, that's the problem.' he replied. 'You'll make me come too quickly.'

Beth paused for a second or two and then she began to move herself below him.

'What, you mean if I do this, you'll come?' she whispered, her voice mischievous.

'Yes,' he breathed, feeling his orgasm approaching in a hot wave.

November 1997

The first thing either man saw was the leather of her boots, and then of her trousers as she walked down the stairs towards them. She also wore a pale grey V-neck jumper, cardigan and matching scarf. She looked like something straight off the pages of a fashion magazine. She looked magnificent.

'When did you get them?' James asked. He stared at his little sister some more, she was incredible and he was aware that he was actually gawking at her.

'Yesterday, do you like?' She was enjoying the shocked expression on his face.

'Yeah! But it's only Pat and Judy's!' He watched her move. She was so elegant.

'Everyone else is always under dressed. And what do you think?' she said, reaching the bottom.

Michael breathed in; she was wearing his favourite perfume. He stared at her, taking in the sight of her as a smile appeared on his features.

'At the risk of getting a slap,' he began, glancing at James, 'You actually look very sexy, Elizabeth.' The words were odd from Michael in front of James and the two men locked eyes for a long moment. 'Don't you think?' he added with a shrug.

'Actually?' she asked, interrupting.

'Okay. You *do* look sexy,' James added, resigned then to the fact that overnight, well, over the past weeks, his baby sister had become a hotty.

'Good. Let's go,' she beamed.

Michael picked up his keys from the stairs. 'Got the drink already in the car, wallet, brain, coat—

'Where are those little bangers of yours?' Michael asked then.

'Bangers? Trust me, boy, they're fucking touched!' James announced. He sounded really rather pleased with himself. 'They're down stairs. I'll get 'em.' He was excited then, they could tell. It was the time of year that he loved the most. The time of year that he was legally allowed to play with gunpowder and explosives. They watched him make his way down the stairs with a skip in his step.

'If I was to look up *too sexy* in the dictionary, I bet it'd have your name there right next to it!' Michael whispered as he touched her bottom; it was firm beneath the taunt leather. He groaned slightly. 'Nice, very nice.'

She looked into his eyes then, both wrapped up in thoughts of the past, present and future. 'Yep, right next to yours!'

Late November 1997

Seeing Beth around the house in next to nothing was not an uncommon sight. Neither man nor indeed, Mrs. P, really took much notice of her. In fact the usual comment when she appeared at the board in only her underwear was a crack about her ironing one of their shirts while she did an item for herself because Mrs. P didn't do ironing! And today was no different. She stood in the dining area with a rather accentuating black silk and old lace bra on; her jeans were on but the buttons were undone and it just showed the top of the panties that matched the bra. She pressed the little fitted blouse with speed and efficiency, aware that James watched her every move.

'Nice bra!' his tone was suggestive and he rose his eyebrows at her.

'Thank you'. Beth was aware that he was waiting for a stronger retort but she didn't give one. The bra was one that she bought especially with Michael in mind and she wasn't about to tell James that, was she, so she smiled at him instead.

'Where you off to then?' he asked and she stopped and put the iron down on the board.

'I don't know yet. Lucy's got *another* new bloke so I guess we'll go for a drink so I can hear all about him, and all the sordid and disgusting details.' She didn't sound particularly complacent and he looked up into her eyes from his position at the dining table. He thought that she must feel like a spare tart in a brothel whenever anyone spoke about relationships, well, sex anyway. And then fleetingly he thought of laying off on her about it, but something inside him was still so protective of her, and he supposed that he was just taking over where his father had left off. She would never be old enough in his eyes, and no man would ever be good enough for her in his opinion and that was just how it was. But he knew that someone as buxom and beautiful as her, and she was quite beautiful, would one day soon discover what all the fuss was about. And he knew that purely out of spite, and for the sake of saving face, he would have to be the one to make it known that it was unacceptable to whoever she blessed with her innocence.

He stopped in his train of thought then and thought of Michael with a laugh. He was a nightmare lately, worse than even he himself was, when it came to her honour. He fended off the rough and the smooth with such feverish glared warnings that it had been said on more than one occasion that perhaps he was waiting to do the honours himself. That had made him laugh, because it had also been said that Michael was gay and if Michael was gay, so was he! That's how sure he was that Michael was not gay in any way shape or form. About Beth though, sometimes he wondered himself.

'I nearly give her one once,' he said, referring to Lucy, his tone distant. He wondered how long he'd been thinking for, but he noticed that Beth hadn't even unplugged the iron so he knew it couldn't have

232

been that long. His little sister looked at him with perfectly made-up eyes and she smiled a knowing smile at him.

'I know' she said. 'In fact, I've heard this one more times than you've blown your load.' James laughed at her comment. She could make even the filthiest words sound like the songs of angels.

'So she told you then?' he laughed.

'What, about your passionate embrace? The one followed by guilt? Yes!' Beth breathed out with a bored sigh.

She really wasn't up for Lucy at all tonight, she wasn't up for listening to her mindless bollocks about the latest conquest, or that this one was probably the one. She was sick to death of hearing about cock sizes and sexual positions, as if this was all going to either shock or impress her. She was going to have to sit through at least three hours of it, so, she mused, the least she could do was look good.

Michael walked down with a shirt thrown casually over his bare shoulder. Both looked up at him and when he saw the board he smiled.

'Ah-ha, so I'm just in time then.' He stopped and gave her the once over. 'Nice bra!'

Beth looked at him. She didn't bat an eyelid at his comment or the sight of his chest, although she knew that he was taking in every inch of her.

'Well, you know I got it specially with you in mind,' she laughed. 'Sorry, did you want your shirt ironed?'

'Oh, yes please!' Michael gave her a winning smile.

'Well that's a bit unlucky then, isn't it?' She stood away from him and leaned on the counter top behind her, her hand out in a gesture, inviting him to take her place.

'Oh, go on! You do it *so* much better than I do,' he pleaded, waving the shirt at her, the motion of spreading his arms exposing the breadth of his body. She looked into his eyes quickly and then back at James. He was completely uninterested in their conversation. She took the item from him with a look of defeat and he smiled at her again.

'I iron better than you do, I sew better than you do— Tell me, Michael, is there anything I don't do better than you?'

James looked up then, noticing the silence between them. He looked at Michael, raising his eyebrows.

'I can think of one or two things, Babe, yeah!' James answered for him, taking the silence as a stumble with a laugh, and there was laughter then. The innuendo was always there in the house.

'I owe you one!' Michael said, his tone just suggestive enough for her to make eye contact with him again.

'Story of my life!'

As Beth sat opposite Lucy, she put her glass back down on the table between them. She'd listened as Lucy had gone through, in perfect and complete detail, her last date with Steven, the rough and ready car mechanic. Lucy always made Beth laugh despite her irritation. She wanted the money, not to have to work for her living and the best sex that she could handle, but she always thought and picked her men with her throbbing crotch and not her brain. The men she chose were usually piss-poor and from the wrong end of town. Not that that was a problem for Beth; after all, wasn't her own dad like that, wasn't that where she herself had started life, along with Lucy? And she wondered often if that wasn't what Lucy was looking for. The gangster, the one working his way up just outside the law!

'So you're not seeing him again then?' There was a laugh on Beth's lips as she spoke and it wasn't lost on her friend.

Beth confused Lucy. She was rich, good looking, not the slimmest of girls, but she had something; she always turned heads, always caught the smiles, and that was before the fellas were told who she was. After being given that information Beth was usually beating them off with sticks. But still, even with feverish help in that direction from Lucy, Beth was, as far as anyone was aware, a virgin. What was all the friggin' fuss about anyway, Lucy thought often. Christ, it wasn't like hard drugs or something like that! Not that that type of thing seemed to bother that brother of hers. She thought of James then. She wished sometimes that she had shagged him, she could have added him to her line of bedpost notches without too much of a conscience. In fact, she wouldn't have had a conscience about it at all; after all, wasn't he one of the most popular and most powerful men in the area? She sighed and took a sip of her own drink as her thoughts went back to her friend. Sex was completely natural and very, very normal. Beth talked very knowledgably about it all the time and seemed completely unbothered by the fact that she was getting older and not getting any of what Lucy always referred to as *the good stuff.*

'Oh I don't know?' Lucy said with a wave of her cigarette between them. She thought she'd better say something to break the silence. 'He's really nice, but he hasn't got that thing, you know?' She watched Beth raise her eyebrows. 'You know, that—' She stopped again, trying to explain.

'That look, that look that makes your heart jump into your mouth. He's missing that feeling that makes you shiver and your breath come in shakes. That heat when he looks at you and you just know you're gonna get it and get it well,' Beth said absently as she watched two men eye them on their way to the bar.

'Fuck me!' Lucy exclaimed under her breath. She'd never heard the like from Beth and she was more than a little taken aback. That was far too intense for her.

Beth laughed at her shock. 'That's the puppy. That's exactly what you want to say to him. You want him to make you feel like begging for it, and then, when you're getting it, begging him not to stop giving it to you!' Beth looked into her eyes. 'It that it?' she asked then, suddenly sounding really innocent again.

Lucy gawked. 'You've fucking done it!' The excitement was evident in her tone!

'Shut up!' she sounded amused and waved her hand up in protest. 'When would I get the chance, ey? What with James and Michael around!'

Lucy looked disappointed then, and then thought of Michael. 'Ooh, ah, Michael,' she creamed wistfully. 'Now him, God, I bet he fucks like a starved native.' She looked almost sensuous as she went on. 'All the meat and no gravy, oh mate, and the body on it. I bet he's hung like a fucking donkey.' Beth raised an eyebrow. She was trying to hide her irritation.

'He is!' Beth interrupted. Lucy's eyes opened to their fullest, egging her on for more information, so Beth continued. 'Oh, come on! You don't live with someone for that long and not walk into the room at the wrong moment once in a while,' she said sounding rather casual, as if it happened by accident all the time.

'He isn't?' It wasn't really a question but Lucy made the statement sound like one.

'Oh yes, he is!' Beth smiled with a lift of her eyebrows again. She was talking, she could hear her own voice in her head, and the words as they came out of her mouth but she couldn't believe what she was saying. She wasn't committing herself, far from it; she was just fuelling Lucy's imagination, but as she sat there all she could see in her mind was him. She could almost feel his touch upon her and smell his skin, all musky and hot. She went on about how firm he was, and how strong he was, and then she almost blew Lucy's mind when she told her about the voice.

When she got home she went down into the kitchen. There was a note from James on the counter, it read *Hope you had a nice time – you looked nice.* He'd started, for some reason, to mention that type of thing more often, and Beth thought, although she never said it, that it was because Michael did it too, and James was aware that it pleased her to be called pretty and have her looks commented upon. *Don't lock up. Mike'll be home about three, unless he falls asleep, ha, ha! But I'll see you in the morning x x x.* She stuck it back down next to the phone and looked at the clock on the microwave. It wasn't even midnight. She opened a can of Coke from the fridge and lighting a cigarette, sat at the table and flicked through the paper James had been reading before they'd gone out that evening. The phone rang out and within a ring she picked it up off the hook.

'Hello.' Her voice was friendly because she was glad of the interruption.

It was Michael. 'Yes, I'm here alone.' She smiled at his question. 'Yes. I've still got it on.' She bit on her lip, touching her blouse, feeling the lace beneath it. 'Are you coming home?' The question was there but she needn't have bothered asking it. She could hear it in his tone, almost feel his breath on her face as he spoke. 'Okay, I'll see you later then. Drive carefully.'

He walked through the front door and locked it. Punched in the numbers on the alarm pad and made his way up the stairs, undressing as he went. He passed Beth's room and continued up to his own, now only in his trousers. The rest of his clothes were draped over his shoulder, ready to be dumped on the bedroom floor. He'd seen the lamp light in his room through the blind as he'd pulled up and parked the car and now as he opened the door she was standing in the middle of his room wearing nothing but the bra.

'What took you so long?' she asked as he moved towards her, walking her backwards until they fell onto the bed.

'Pat called!' Then there were no more words, only kisses and caresses and the sounds of their breathing.

He touched her, and she touched him. The feel of him so close made her want to come there and then. And she knew that coming was next on his agenda. He loved to watch her as she came. He'd take his time, teasing her until he thought she may just brush him aside and do it herself, and that was when he'd let her. She'd be so wet that he wouldn't even have to push at her. He'd glide in and there inside her he'd be warm. He knelt in front of her on top of the bedclothes, pulling her to him so that he could touch her as he had his way and he was right. She was wet and so close that he could feel her muscles begging him further in. 'Please!' she begged and his pace quickened as he pulled her legs up to his hips and buried himself inside her.

The morning arrived far too quickly and both lay still, watching the light as it made its way through the crack in the curtains and across the floor. Beth held Michael's arm close around her and snuggled right up to him.

'You'd better go down soon,' he breathed finally, and he felt Beth nod at him. 'He'll be back. The day's to begin.' There was a long silence and it was uncomfortable. It was broken with a sigh from Beth, and Michael rolled her over on to her back so that he could see her face. He wasn't surprised to see the tears there in her bright eyes, but still the thought of her hurting inside like that hurt him deeply.

'I hate this,' she whispered. 'It's fun, then it's not! It's exciting, but then it's not!'

He nodded at her, totally understanding. 'I know,' he replied, giving her a kiss on the forehead. 'And I understand. Deceit's not my favourite pastime either, you know.' He thought about telling the world almost every day; why shouldn't he? Then the thoughts of James and Patrick came to mind, then of all those who would see this as an angle, another way to disturb business, so of course he knew they couldn't, that he couldn't.

'I know. I'm sorry,' she sniffed.

'No sorrys,' he smiled, touching her nose with a finger. 'Now, come on. We'll go down together. Make it last just a while longer,' he suggested. His words eased her, he really understood her.

Michael dressed and Beth followed him down the stairs. He waited by her doorway as she too threw on some fresh clothes and then they walked down the stairs and into the kitchen. 'Did you want to go out with me today?' he asked filling the coffee percolator.

'Is that a date?' she giggled.

He nodded. 'Of course, and I want a new suit. We can do lunch and spend far too much money,' He watched her face change from a rather pinched expression to a smile.

'That sounds good,' she beamed.

'Grand, we'll have this and hopefully be out before James comes home.'

It was a light comment but Beth heard an undertone that she never thought she would from Michael and she stared at him for a long moment.

'Is it me that's making you hate him?' she asked, her tone quite innocent.

Michael double took her and let out a deep sigh as he rested his hands on the countertop next to her. 'I don't hate him! You know that. I just—' he paused. 'I'm having a hard time with this too, you know.

I spend more and more time thinking about it, this and—I just want you to be all right. I couldn't bear it if you were unhappy.'

She breathed out. 'I'm fine, when I'm with you.' She smiled then, and he patted her hand with his own. There wasn't any point in having his conversation. It wouldn't solve anything and wouldn't make either of them feel any better. She stared at him. 'Even if you are going grey,' she added then, reaching out and touching his head. There were a few strays growing around the sides of his head.

'Grand, thanks for noticing. You'll be telling me that I'm too old next!' He smiled. 'Go and have a shower, I'll bring your coffee up.'

He watched her disappear up the stairs, and he stared after her for a long while. She'd hit the nail on the head when she'd mentioned James and it startled him that she could know him so well, that well. It was true, he was beginning to hate James. And Pat and Judy and everyone else who interfered, but not hate like he'd felt in the past; it was more like constant irritation. *Keep Beth safe, Michael. Don't let her get hurt, Michael. Keep her pure, Michael. Look but don't touch, Michael.* He wanted to yell at them all that for all their concerns she was now a woman, she was now his responsibility and that he would take that responsibility to the edge if he had to. But he knew that that wasn't the route to go. That would just cause grief for all concerned. He lit a cigarette and got two cups from the cupboard. He'd wait. No, they'd wait. The right time was sure to show itself at some time, and while they waited they would only get stronger, their relationship would only get stronger. He'd waited for her for too long to let more time get the better of him and his mind was then set. He made a mental note not to get so *irritated* with those around them, especially James; if not for his sake, then for hers. He knew and understood his friends' fears. After all, wasn't that why he ended up there in the first place? No! He thought suddenly, he was there because they'd needed him and he had wanted to be there, not because Pat had told him to be there.

Chapter Twenty-Two

December 1997

There was a distinct air of power as James, Beth and Michael walked into the Hothouse. The two men were dressed in black two-piece suits and crisp, clean white shirts. James wore a garish tie, Michael didn't, and his button-down shirt was just open one button. Beth was in a mid-length black pencil skirt, fitted suit jacket and white cotton high-collar blouse, with cuffs that stuck out of her jacket sleeves in a blaze of glowing white. They looked magnificent, a sight to be seen and admired.

Paul and Frank automatically opened the doors for them and nodded a firm greeting. Every one of the seven staff members seemed to take a step backwards. Silence fell all around and no words were spoken between any of them as they watched the three walk through the doors into the bar area. *This should be fun,* Frank thought.

The three saw Pat first. He was standing at the end of the bar talking with a man whom none of them had seen before. Their presence was strong, they could tell by his reaction to them. He seemed to falter in his already rather rigid stance and ill fitting, albeit handmade suit. He looked like a cheap solicitor or at the least, some kind of factor and they knew instinctively exactly whom he was there on behalf of, they could practically smell him.

'Mr. Brown, my business associates!' Pat said, in an introductory tone. He could really lay on the *high and mighty* when he wanted to.

Mr. Brown looked at them each in turn with cold blue eyes, as if committing them to memory. 'The other Mr. Dobson. Mr. Elliott and, of course, Miss Dobson.' He sounded very smug at knowing who they were but they weren't impressed by him at all and it was more than slightly evident in the expressions on their faces.

Back in the reception Paul and Frank had dashed behind the desk to watch the proceedings from one of the cameras. This they had to see. 'Mick'll flip!' Paul said.

'Quit yer whingeing. They looked like the real fucking mob. I ain't missing this for the fucking world,' came Frank's reply.

'You're going too fast!' Paul whispered, as if those in the meeting would hear him if he raised his voice to a normal pitch. They were like a pair of quarrelling children.

'Shut up. I know what I'm doin', boy!' Frank moved the camera round really slowly from the console so as not to attract any attention, but it was no good and as they focused on the scene the first thing they saw was Michael. He was looking right at them and he shook his head discreetly in warning, his eyes hard. Both took a mental step backwards, with every intention of denying touching the camera when quizzed.

'When he does shit like that he really gives me the heeby geebys,' Frank breathed.

'That's nothing mate. I get twitchy when he looks at young Bethy sometimes.' There was a silence between the two men then and they just leaned on the reception desk, staring at each other.

Frank completely understood what Paul had just said. He knew it because he too had seen it too. But this was Michael Elliott and you just didn't say things like that about a man like that, with a reputation and friends like he had unless you were about to back it up with evidence fit for the Old Bailey.

'Do you blame him? Did you see 'er come in just then? Did you see them legs, that hair, those tits? Did you smell that—that—' He waved his hand and Paul nodded. Neither knew quite what to call it, bearing in mind that it emanated from a woman they still, in their minds, classed as a baby. It was perfume and sex, to be exact and only real men could smell it, and every man that worked for Pat Dobson had smelled it on her lately. She'd blossomed that summer. Long gone were the times when she'd look them in the eye without the understanding of what she did to them there for all to see. She'd been woken and broken, that was for sure, but neither Frank nor Paul were about to speculate on who may have done that little deed, though both, if they had guns to their heads, would probably have come up with the same name.

'Mr. Oxley's upped the offer.' Pat's tone was flat and the three of them showed no hint of surprise. 'He also offered me another two tonne in cash to get you to agree to the sale,' he went on. There was silence for a few moments, then Beth spoke.

'Well. I have an offer for Mr.Oxley, Mr. Brown. I'll give it to you for free, no back handers required, and you get to guess what it is!' Her accent was perfect and her articulation exact. She raised an eyebrow at him and the three other men watched him blanch at her unspoken suggestion as he took it in. There was that look in her eye that only appeared every now and then. It was cold and hard and with it came the confirmation that whatever she wanted done to him would be done, and done gladly by those who willingly, and without question, obeyed her. He'd heard about her, knew that she was more than a pretty face, more than a bit of window dressing. But in the flesh, when riled up, she was far more frightening, what with her uncle, brother and Elliott standing with her, not to mention those two lumpy doormen. It crossed his mind that that was the only reason she acted as she did, but then, as he looked harder into those pretty eyes of hers he saw it. She was a fighter. And more to the point, she was a winner.

'Is that the final answer?' his tone was clipped. It was obvious that he didn't want to be there any more than they wanted him there, and fleetingly Beth wondered if that wasn't the reason why he was behaving like he was. Who in their right mind would bother to waste time kicking this fool into touch? Her eyes went to James as that thought entered her head. Both Pat and Michael must have had the same idea, because they were both watching him out of the corner of their eyes too.

'I'm wiv her on that one, mate,' James said, breaking the silence that felt much longer than it actually was.

'You've had my answer already, Mr. Brown!' Pat added and then Mr. Brown looked at Michael. He looked smug as he waited for Michael to speak.

'I'll also have to decline your kind offer,' he said, his tone sarcastic.

Mr. Brown looked smug suddenly. 'Don't you have to liaise with your father about any business matters, Master Elliott?' Mr. Brown said sharply then.

Michael snapped his head up, his body drawn up to his full six feet and more in angry inches.

'My father, for your information, Mr. Brown signed his shares over to me more than a year ago, so no, I think I'm old enough and big enough to make my own choices, thank you! Though I'm happy to ask him his opinion on this issue, and of course his thoughts on how to deal with you.'

James's and Beth's eyes went to him then. They had no idea that Jim had done it. It had been discussed and agreed long before, yes, but nothing more had been said until that moment. Jim had wanted to retire and bow out politely, and it would appear that he actually had. Michael looked at them each in turn. He could see the expressions on their faces and could almost hear the words bouncing around in their minds. He almost grinned then, he saw the look on Beth's face. Yes. He was absolutely loaded. *Get your coat, Elizabeth, you pulled a winner!* He thought. What with the business, the properties, and his cut from the profits from the hotel in Ireland, his dabbling on the stock market and the debt collecting, he still liked to indulge now and then, albeit just for fun. Yes, he was worth a million, in cash alone and more than double that in property, maybe even more.

Mr. Brown made a grunting noise and moved to leave. He was clearly not impressed with the outcome of this meeting, or indeed at having to go back to break this news to his employer.

Pat signed and with a shake of his head walked away and back towards the office. That was easier than he'd thought. And definitely briefer. That fucking Oxley should just give it up. There was no way in hell those three were going to part with their little empire, and in doing so, allow him a controlling hand throughout London and the Home Counties. He'd have to buy more new clubs and bars and get them up and running, Leave them in peace.

'Rich *and* good looking! How refreshing!' she whispered lightly as they stood watching Mr. Brown leave.

'That's *very* rich and *very* good looking!' he corrected her with a sly smile.

'Yes Michael, I saw that look. I'll just get my coat now, shall I?' she replied as James had away walked from them.

Michael looked down at her, into those eyes. The woman before him knew his every move, his every thought and it was then, at that second that he realised what he'd known for some time for sure. She was the one for him. No other had ever even got close. No other had even touched in comparison.

Less than an hour later the three sat in Michael's car, tears of laughter rolling down their cheeks. They were laughing because the situation was funny. There they were dressed to quite literally kill, ready to do the business. Prepared to take it to the edge and all Beth could say was that they should really do some food shopping. Her tone had been quite firm on the matter as they climbed into the car, once sure that Brown had gone, and pulled away from the club. And now, not more than a hundred yards down the road, Michael had had to pull over for fear of crashing the car. There were gasps for air and coughs as they calmed themselves but it was to be short lived; seconds later they were all off again. 'Tesco's or Sainsbury's?' Michael asked, finally composing himself enough to speak. He was unsure of why this had made them all laugh like it did, but for a few seconds he was glad of the respite from the daily grind.

'Tesco's,' James managed. 'I'm collecting points!'

Mid-December 1997

Passing James in the hallway, Beth made her way towards the stairs leading down to the kitchen. She looked really annoyed and he was about to speak to her when Michael appeared on the scene, having followed her down the stairs.

'God damn it, woman!' Michael's barking tone bought both Beth and James to a complete standstill.

'Bollocks!' she said finally, her arm outstretched and her finger pointing directly at him.

'What the fuck?' James's voice was all but a whisper as he leaned up against the wall, watching them. Michael looked at him then but continued as if he wasn't even there, and it was evident to James that he was just as angry as she was.

'Don't you "bollocks" me, woman, I'm trying to talk to you!' he yelled with a point of his own finger back in her direction.

'Just fuck off!' she replied and that was when James finally intervened.

'Hold it!' he bellowed and they both stopped and stared at him. 'What in the fucking hell is going on?'

There was silence. This should be interesting, Beth thought, looking into Michael's eyes through the banisters with a lift of her eyebrows and a pinch of her lips.

'She's a mad woman!' Michael said, waving his hand at her while he looked at James. He was wracking his brains, desperate to think of something to say. He couldn't tell him what they were really rowing about, could he? They'd been at the wine bar. The manager was off sick so Beth was covering. They'd been having a good night. It was busy, but nothing they couldn't handle and then Caroline had to walk in. She'd given Beth the once-over then, after a few moments spent lingering at the bar, had breezed up to Michael, plain as day, a cool expression on her face. Then, what seemed to Beth to be only seconds later, she'd started coming on to him, not just your usual banter. She was full on up for it, and to top it he didn't do anything to stop her. They were at work! In public! He had to keep up the façade, sure, and Caroline was always a bit flirtatious. Beth knew that there was nothing there any more but something inside her had snapped as Michael had laughed at whatever suggestion Caroline had whispered into his ear. She'd stayed for a few drinks. Then, with a bleep of her pager she was gone. For the rest of the night Beth had said maybe four words to him and two of those had been *fuck off*. He was fuming.

All the way home she'd sat tight-lipped as he'd tried to talk to her. He was explaining himself, something he hadn't had to do with Beth for a long time. This was uncharted territory and he knew that it wasn't the act that Beth was worried about, it was always done for show. It was the fact that she knew Caroline and Michael had a history. They'd parked and before he'd even put on the handbrake Beth was out of the car, up the steps, through the front door and up the stairs to her room. He'd followed quickly behind he and caught the bedroom door with a hard shove as she'd gone to slam it. He'd moved towards her. She was going to listen to him if he had to pin her to the wall and that was when James had come home. She'd snatched at the opportunity to escape him and darted past him, down the stairs just as James closed the front door.

There was silence in the hallway still and then Michael spoke. 'I fucked up,' he said softly, his tone apologetic. 'We were at the bar and it was busy. We were two short. Caroline came in!' He locked eyes with James as he spoke. 'She wanted entertaining. I obliged!'

James pulled a face as if to say *so fucking what*.

'And?' James still looked unsure of why that was a problem. What did Caroline have to do with Beth?

Michael sighed. 'I left her to it!' he breathed motioning with his hand towards Beth, 'and we were really busy. It was just a bit of fun, not like I fucked her on the bar or something. I just didn't think, y'know.'

'For fuck's sake, Mike!' James let out a sigh, falling into the conversation. 'She's a fucking whore. No wonder she's pissed at you!' He, too, motioned towards Beth who was now looking rather smug. 'I know, I know. I was trying to apologise and she went off the rails at me. All I've had since closing is verbal abuse!' He smiled inside, James was lapping it up and Beth was then furious.

'But you're sorry, right, mate?' James said it as a question, but it was more of a suggestion to Michael for all their sakes.

246

'Sure I'm sorry. I shouldn't have done it, but!' He left the rest unsaid. He knew that James was aware of what Caroline was. It was a male moment.

'Good. You're sorry. She'll forgive you. Forget it. And you,' he looked at Beth. 'Don't swear, not at Mike, anyway!'

She stood on the stairs, her mouth open. She was speechless.

'Now, can I leave you two alone? Christ, I only came home for me wallet.'

Still in the hallway, Michael nodded at him. The air was cold and he was aware that this was no way over.

'Sure. It's fine,' Michael replied, looking over at Beth, who still hadn't said a word.

Minutes later James was gone and they stood in the hallway, staring at each other. The look on his face was pure lust although to anyone else it would have looked like naked anger. 'Pleased with yourself?' he ground out.

'Well, you will play games with slappers, Michael.'

'Games?' he snorted at her.

'Yeah, and if it's good enough for you it's good enough for me!' she raised her head.

'You think I'd have gone off with—with—that? Is that what you think?' he said and she shrugged.

No, of course it wasn't. It was that she found Caroline threatening. She was, for all that she was a bit of a slapper, and she suspected also a proper paid whore, drop dead gorgeous. He looked into her eyes and almost heard the thoughts in her head.

'You know what it's like, don't you! What do you want me to do?'

There was silence again. He knew that look; it was hurt and confusion. He bet himself money that even she didn't quite know why she'd been so angry with him.

'Was she a good—' Beth began, but she didn't finish the sentence.

He grabbed her bodily and almost dragged her into the lounge and threw her onto the nearest sofa. He landed on his knees before her and dragged her to the edge of the cushion. Her long skirt was up then and her lacy string was ripped from her, exposing her to him completely. 'You—' be breathed. 'God, woman!' He didn't say any more, instead he buried his head between her legs, pulling them apart with strong hands. His tongue found her bud and he caressed it with such fever that Beth was almost beside herself. He let go of her legs as she opened them wider, wanting him to go on and he moved his hands down, sliding his fingers into her. She came then with a shudder that ripped through her entire body and for a brief moment they were still.

'You're the only one,' he breathed, pulling her to the floor. 'I don't want anyone else, d'you hear?' He opened his trousers and seconds later he was inside her on the lounge carpet. She wrapped her legs around him as they moved on the floor. She wanted to feel him there. Wanted him to come inside her. Be hers completely. Her fingers ran through his hair and she pulled his face to hers. They kissed then, tasting each other, drinking until they almost became one.

'Do you understand?' His voice, although nothing but a whisper, was strong. 'No-one else!'

Christmas 1997

Beth woke up and rolled on to her back in the half-light of the street lamps. She turned her head and focused on the doorway, then dozily she smiled. Michael was standing there in his tracksuit bottoms holding a small gift-wrapped box in his hand.

'What time is it?' she asked, sitting up in the bed and giving him a rather nice view of her breasts as the duvet fell away from her body.

'Six,' he breathed as he moved towards her.

'Really? Yuck, it's too early,' she groaned, trying to muster enthusiasm. After all, it was Christmas Day.

He perched on the bed and touched her face with a warm hand. 'I wanted to give you this now,' he said, passing her the small gold wrapped box.

She almost laughed. 'I got you one too!' she said leaning past him and opening her bedside drawer. 'I was going to give it to you last night but—' She paused and looked into his eyes. She was going to say that she'd had too much to drink and had fallen asleep but she knew that he was probably aware of that. He'd been there at Baileys too, and they had definitely had too much to drink. Christmas was their busiest time and it had been nice to all be together at the bar, not working for a change.

'I know! Don't tell me about it,' he whispered with a laugh. 'James is up there snoring his head off. And I've only been out of my pit for a while,' he went on. 'Now, come on. Open it.' With an exchange of glances Beth pulled at the pretty wrapper. She opened the box and took in a sharp breath. Her fingers ran over the white gold and she looked up at him in amazement. She had said that she liked it when they had been out buying James's watch in the East End, and now here it was in a box in front of her.

'Put it on!' he said excitedly and she took the thick bracelet with a small diamond on the clasp from the box and let him fasten it to her right wrist. 'Do you like it?' he asked, already knowing the answer.

'I do, it's great, its beautiful, it's just what I wanted, thank you!' She kissed him and they let their lips linger for a few seconds. 'Now open yours!' she grinned, still fiddling with the gold now around her wrist. Michael pulled at the wrapper and opened the small box. Inside was a gold ring with a single diamond mounted within it. He pulled it from the box and held it close to his face.

'How did you know?' he asked deeply. He, like she had fallen for almost everything in the little Jewish jeweller's shop but the ring had really taken his fancy. It was classy and not too much and he had debated on whether or not to buy it for himself.

'I saw your face when that bloke was looking at it. When we got back I called them up and asked them to hold it for me.'

'It was expensive!' he said, putting it on his little finger, it fitted exactly.

'So what!' she replied, now flinging the duvet from her almost naked body completely and standing up next to the bed. 'I think you're worth it. And besides, I know how much this little number cost you,' she added, waving her arm at him as he pulled her onto his lap.

'I would have paid twice as much,' he said as his hands roamed over her body.

'That makes two of us then, doesn't it, Mr. Elliott. And you can stop that,' she added with a light slap on his hand as he edged towards her panties.

'But it's Christmas!' he breathed with a light laugh in his tone.

'Well you'll have to wait a day or two for that present,' she sighed.

'I don't care, it doesn't bother me!' he protested.

'Well, it bothers me,' she added with a light kiss on his lips, 'so you'll have to wait!'

The doorbell sounded and Michael bounded up the stairs from the kitchen to answer it. He opened it and immediately smiled his biggest smile. 'Merry Christmas!' he cheered in unison with his parents as they stood on the doorstep, laden with presents and bags and other goodies. 'I've missed you' he breathed hugging his mother.

'We've missed you too,' Eve replied.

'Too big to give your dah a cuddle, are you now?' Jim laughed and Michael shook his head before he and his father embraced. It was a warm hug and as they pulled away with light slaps on each other's shoulders.

Jim looked up slightly into his son's eyes. 'You look well, son,' he smiled.

'I am well, Dah,' Michael said, his tone full of emotion. It wasn't lost on either parent and they looked fleetingly at one another. 'Now, come—' he added, leading the way and Eve and Jim followed him down the stairs to the kitchen.

They were greeted just as warmly by Beth, who let out a squeal of delight. She pulled off the apron she had been wearing over her dress and threw it casually onto the counter.

'You're early!' she announced. 'Oh, it's so good to see you,' she added between kisses and hugs alike. 'How was the flight?'

'Just grand,' Jim said, taking the glass of whisky that Michael passed him with a grateful nod. 'But airports are never the place to be at Christmas now, are they?' and he laughed.

Eve let out a sigh as she sat at the table. 'Now, where's that brother of yours, young lady?' she asked with a smile of real affection towards her.

'He's gone to get Pat and Judy,' she replied, taking a sip of wine. It was only eleven o'clock in the morning but it was Christmas Day and she was cooking for eight. If anyone deserved a drink, it was definitely her.

'And of course, young Jennifer!' Michael added, his tone depicting the situation; his tone suggested that this could well be James all wrapped up.

'So. James is finally in love then!' Jim laughed with a shake of his head.

'Something like that, yes,' Beth purred, giving him a wink and he laughed.

'How longs this one been around?' Eve asked lightly.

'Long enough for us to be confident on a bet,' Michael laughed, giving Beth a warm smile.

'Well, I bought a hat!' Beth said, her tone sarcastic, and jovial.

'And what about you, son, is there a lady in your life?' Eve asked. 'There must be by now!'

There was silence and Beth suddenly found the glass she was drinking from really interesting.

'Maybe?' he breathed, aware then that his father was watching him with eyes so much like his own.

'Never one for idle chatter and mindless gossip, ey, son?' Jim laughed.

'Quite true' he replied.

'And what about you, Elizabeth? You look radiant,' Judy observed.

'Me? Oh—' she was floundering.

'Elizabeth's not giving anything away,' Michael interrupted with a smile as he passed his mother a glass of wine. 'If she'll not tell me, what makes you think she'll tell you?'

'Come here, little one,' Jim said softly. 'Come and tell your Uncle Jim all about it!' There was laughter then, real laughter. He used to do that when she was a young child. And as a young child it had worked, she'd tell him all her little childish secrets. But the woman, there was no information coming from the woman.

'Forget it!' she giggled, perching on his knee. 'Who are you, Father Christmas?'

The four elder family members chatted and laughed as they watched the four younger make swift work of laying the table and put the finishing touches to the grand feast that was to be Christmas Day dinner. They worked effortlessly and in harmony with each other. It was a strange sight to take in. None got in the others way or stood on toes as they moved. They were used to being in such close proximity and it seemed to, for the most part, work for all of them.

'Michael, get that out of the oven,' Beth said. Her tone was light and Eve watched with great interest as her son moved around the kitchen. He'd always been helpful, but never like this. Obviously this house share suited him better than he ever made out and she'd ever imagined. Eve watched Michael for a while longer, watched him with Beth and she smiled. Something about them made her feel warm inside.

Dinner was served, and tasted magnificent. Beth sat quietly at one end of the table, watching as the others ate, the relief evident on her face. From across the table Michael caught her eye and she felt her cheeks flush slightly as he nodded slowly at her. He fiddled with the ring on his right little finger casually, as if it had always been there and he smiled secretly to himself as he watched her straighten the bracelet around her wrist.

His earlier thoughts of sex seemed to grow wings and fly away out of his mind as they sat there. Instead of feeling the need to be inside her, he found himself just wanting to be at her side. He wanted to be able to sit with her, walk with her, hold her hand and kiss her whenever and wherever the fancy took him, and he felt a little sad for a moment.

The day had begun and then, within what seemed to be only seconds, was over and they stood on the front steps waving at the taxi that was taking Pat and Judy home, along with Eve and Jim.

'So what time are we there tomorrow?' Jennifer asked as they made their way back inside the warmth of the house.

'About eleven,' James replied, wrapping his arms around her shoulders.

'I'll need to pop home then, in the morning,' she smiled.

'Why?' James looked confused.

'Change of clothes? I wasn't expecting to stay two nights.' Though she was really pleased at being asked back to Pat and Judy's for Boxing Day. She was aware of what a milestone it was and what a milestone it was that James immediately agreed.

'I'd say you could borrow something of mine, but I think I'm just a wee bit bigger than you!' Beth said with a laugh as she stood next to Jennifer in the hallway.

'Only two dress sizes,' Jennifer added gently.

'And about four inches in height,' Michael remarked, looking at the pair.

'We'd better get off to bed,' James purred, 'If you want to get up early!'

'Yeah, if you go up now, you'll get a couple of hour sleep in,' Michael laughed, giving James a light tap on the upper arm.

'You're just jealous,' he grinned. 'Come on, babe,' he added and Jennifer smiled into his eyes. The love there wasn't lost on anyone in the confines of the hallway and Beth looked up at Michael and then at her brother.

'Go on, I'll give you a knock at about nine,' Beth smiled.

'And I'll be down in the spare room!' Michael laughed.

'Yeah, after you've helped me tidy up downstairs!' Beth announced. There, that would definitely keep James up in his room with Jennifer for the rest of the night: the thought of housework.

Just before New Year 1997/1998

The warmth from the amount of alcohol she had consumed, along with the beat of the music around her, made her heart race as she moved on the dance floor. She closed her eyes and let the music take her over. She loved the nights when she wasn't working. She loved being there at the club, surrounded by people she knew, able to really let her hair down because those times were actually few and far between lately. It had been work, work, work over the festive season. She opened her eyes again and saw Lucy gyrating beside her. Here she goes, she thought, Lucy's on a mission. God help all of the male population.

Michael leaned on the balcony rail above them, his eyes not leaving her for a second. She was aware of him, he knew it; he could tell it by the expression of self-satisfaction that she now had on her face. He listened to the din of the chatter around him ,not registering anything in particular until he heard someone say, "No, the one with all the hair!" He looked beside him to where a crowd of young men had gathered. They were watching the dance floor with great interest, comments passing between them quite heatedly.

'Oh. Mate!' one of them exclaimed just as Lucy began to slide up and down another dancer's backside. 'Look at that move, Christ!'

Another joined in. 'No, sorry, lads, looks far too easy. It's got to be the other one, she's what I call fit!' he said, pointing at Beth. Michael turned completely around to face them, his expression was almost amused as he watched and listened to them. 'She's got that innocent filthy look!' There was laughter.

'Fifty quid says I can get her number,' one exploded, the drink inside him making him confident in his statement.

''Ere, mate,' the tallest said then, looking over at Michael. He'd been aware of him throughout their conversation. 'Which do you reckon? The blonde or the hair?'

Michael looked over the balcony again and smiled then. It was just harmless fun, what could he expect? They were, after all, making quite a scene down there. 'Oh, I think her, definitely,' he called, tilting his head towards Lucy. 'Because, you see, lads, the other one's with me!' he continued, his eyes settling for a few seconds on Beth and then back on the crowd before him. His voice was light but they all caught the underlying tone.

'Oops! Sorry!' one of them laughed, tilting his beer bottle up in a toast to him. 'You lucky bastard!' another added.

'She's definitely got that something a little bit special,' another said and Michael laughed with them then. Oh yes. Elizabeth was definitely a little bit special.

She looked up from the dance floor and saw him looking down at her, both his hands gripping the rail. He motioned for her to go to the bar with a subtle flick of his head and she nodded at him as she began to make her way off the dance floor. 'You and young Lucy are causing quite a stir!' he whispered into her ear as they pushed up against each other in the noisy bar area.

'Oh, really?' she replied with a laugh.

'Yes,' he said, his eyes taking in every detail of her. He took in a deep breath; she smelled great. 'You have admirers,' he went on with a gesture of his head towards the balcony and Beth looked up. She saw the group of men above them and looked at them each in turn as they nudged each other, aware of the fact that Michael was obviously telling her about them. She smiled then and waved up at them.

'All very nice,' she said, leaning right into him, 'but they don't do anything for me at all, I'm afraid. As you know, I'm a very selective young lady and I've made my selection, thank you very much!' She paused then, then smiled. 'Oh yeah, and Lucy's coming right up behind you!' She saw him physically cringe before putting on a large friendly smile, his business smile.

Lucy was starting to get right on his nerves. She was like a dog on heat, she never let up with the innuendos and the suggestions. He was amused at what Beth told her she had recently said about him, aware that Beth wasn't worried, but all the same, she was another one that irritated him, another one who they hid from, and for a long moment his mind reeled at all the scenarios. He had to admit that he regretted not just saying something at the start. Now there would be more issues, issues of deceit and that was going to be yet another mountain.

Chapter Twenty-Three

January 1998

Michael strolled across the landing and knocked on James's bedroom door. He waited for a response before entering even though he was aware that James was alone. 'Morning,' he smiled as he leaned up against the doorframe and watched as James finished dressing. 'Wet the bed?' He glanced at his watch.

'Oh, ha, fucking ha!' James replied. 'It's not *that* early!'

'True,' Michael added with a shrug. 'James, I'm on the ponce!'

'Shoot!' came the reply as he talked to Michael's reflection in the mirror.

'Are you free tomorrow?' he asked and James looked across the room at him with a shake of his head.

'No, mate, I'm out, ain't I? I'm interviewing all day then seeing that new place up town. Why?'

Michael pulled an irritated expression. 'Oh shit, yes!' He clicked his fingers. 'It's just that I've a job and I need another driver,' Michael said, the sigh evident.

James looked at him. Michael was always chasing the green. When was enough gonna be enough for him to just relax? He thought for a second or two. 'Where is it?'

Michael breathed. 'Manchester!'

'Manchester? Does it have to be tomorrow?'

'Aye, yes, it does, we don't want to lose the car to another gig,' he nodded.

'Take the baby, she can drive a car, can't she?' he suggested.

Michael stared at him as if James had just slapped him. 'On a collection?' Michael lowered his head and uncrossed his arms, settling his hand low on his hips.

'Yeah, she'll be wiv you!' James replied, shaking his head at Michael's obvious shock at the suggestion. He paused then, looking a bit worried. 'Why, is there gonna be trouble?' Should he regret this suggestion?

'Ah, no! No way, it's just that I didn't think you'd have that!' Michael replied honestly.

James tucked his shirt in and went over to the mirror again and then went on talking. 'I ain't got no problem with it! If I can't trust you with her, who can I trust, ey?'

There was a silence as Michael watched James check his appearance in the mirror on the wall. Okay! That made him feel more guilty than ever before! *If I can't trust you with her, who can I trust?* The words bounced around inside his head, hitting every nerve he had in there. He composed himself as James turned to face him again.

'It's not like she'll be doing anything. She just has to drive my car back again. I'll ask her then, see what she says. She might already be busy?' Michael was busting to sound casual and wondered if he wasn't overdoing it. 'Thanks, James. That's a nice tie, by the way,' he managed and with a nod of his head he left the room again and closed the door behind him. He was grinning as he went down the stairs to Beth's room. She was *not* going to be too busy, if he had to cancel whatever she would be doing and drag her there himself!

Beth sat in Michael's car and watched him walk up the pathway towards the house in what was left of the late afternoon light. She saw him check the car over casually and then knock on the door. She could just imagine the panic inside at that moment, bearing in mind that it was Michael Elliott at the front door. It opened and there was a conversation between the two men. Beth tried to see what he looked like, other than almost bald, because the mental picture she had of what the area would be like was quite wrong, but Michael seemed to block the entire doorway.

Whenever she thought of debt collecting, she thought of squalor, but nothing could have been further from the truth. The rich, Michael had said, were worse than the poor when it came to not giving up their possessions, paid for or not. The finer things in life, like the thirty thousand pound BMW that was on the driveway, with only four payments made in eight months, were important to them. Poor people had fuck all and expected to have fuck all for the rest of their lives. They took the good times as they came along and the bad as an everyday occurrence. And the rich were proving Michael right yet again, because she was sat outside a rather nice-looking detached house with a well-kept garden and clean net curtains at the windows.

Only moments later, Michael turned and led the man out to where the car was parked so nicely on the driveway. She saw him then. He was middle aged, nothing special. Nothing out of the ordinary and Beth found herself not wanting to stare at him, she felt ashamed for him. How awful must that be? He opened the car door and systematically they emptied it of his possessions, then they did the same with the boot. That took next to no time; it was almost as if he'd been expecting them. He signed a form confirming that he was aware that it was being taken and why and that nothing of his was left in it and then Michael got into the car, started the engine and pulled it off the driveway.

Beth followed in Michael's car and they pulled up on the forecourt of a petrol station not five miles down the road. They got out, wrapped in thick overcoats to guard against the cold wind and there was a silence between them that even the passing traffic couldn't interrupt. They were miles from home, alone together, the collection had gone more than well and it felt good.

'It's getting late,' he called as they walked towards each other. 'Did you want to stay?'

She waited until they were close and face to face to answer his question.

'Well, we did say that we probably would, didn't we?' She smiled and he nodded at her. 'But I forgot my pyjamas,' she added with a drop in her tone.

'If you think that you'll be needing those tonight, you are so wrong, woman,' Michael breathed. 'So, is that a yes?' he asked with a tilt of his head. She nodded at him and their eyes met.

Michael parked the burgundy BMW next to his own car. He opened the driver's door for Beth and she took his offered hand in hers as she got out. 'Well this is nice!' she smiled taking in the sight of the hotel that loomed before them. It was the Manchester Airport Hilton, a modern building, a conference centre combined with what was supposed to be a five star hotel.

'It'll do' he replied taking her hips in his hands and pulling her to him so that he could kiss her. 'We'll book in, then give James a call.' He let go of her and made his way to the back of the car and opened the boot.

'Then eat?' she suggested. He looked over at her as he took their bags from it.

'Are you hungry?' he asked, realising they hadn't yet stopped properly today.

'Aren't I always?' she replied honestly.

'True!' he laughed, closing the boot with a solid sounding thud.

'Why a suite?' Beth asked as they made their way up in the lift to the seventh floor. 'Isn't it more expensive?'

He looked sideways her. 'Money?' he said, looking at her. 'Bedroom for you, bedroom for me,' he added as the doors opened and they got out. 'It'll show up on the bill.'

Beth nodded at his logic. They really did have to be one step ahead all of the time. It was quite mind boggling, as well as tiring, and boring sometimes.

'I'm paying, but it's in case anyone asks, you know?'

She nodded again as they reached the door for 704. She walked into the darkness of the suite. Michael turned on the lights and put the bags down in the centre of the living room. It was nice, but not quite home to either of them. Suddenly Beth felt awkward as she stood there. This was another of those firsts for her and Michael looked down at her.

'The first time I really get you all to myself!' he breathed, slipping his hands around her waist. 'What shall I do with you?' He pulled her close.

'We'll come up with something,' she replied and then they kissed, it was a gentle moment and a warmth that could only be described as home rushed through her.

'Of course he got it!' Beth announced, quite shocked at James's question of whether Michael had been successful. 'He's here. Do you want to talk to him? Okay, hang on.' She held the phone away from her ear and waved it at him. 'James wants a word. He's on the mobile. Says that yuppie pub seems okay, here!'

He took the receiver from her. 'James! Oh grand. She was great,' he said with a smile. 'What about you?' He listened as James half talked, half yelled on the other end of the line. 'No, no trouble at all, I'm showing her the high life. We're at the Hilton, room 704.' He was giving this information, but knew that James wouldn't call them. 'We'll be home midday, maybe a bit after. I've to drop the car off. Okay. And you. Bye.' He replaced the receiver, seeming a bit calmer than he had in an hour or two. 'Now, dinner!' he said brightly, glancing at his watch. It was almost ten. 'We've not eaten this early for a long while. Do you want to go down?' There was a pause and their eyes met. 'Or shall we order in?'

'Order in!' she breathed, pulling the band from her hair and letting it cascade down her back. He watched her every move then. He loved to watch her and wondered then if he would ever tire of her. He hoped not, he really did.

Beth sank into the bath just as Michael walked in, dressed in only his trousers. He was holding a bottle of red wine in one hand and two glasses in the other. He looked at her and then the size of the bath.

'They obviously didn't have you in mind when they designed this little thing, did they?' she laughed.

'What, you think I'll not fit in that with you?' he questioned and she shook her head, her hair all covered in bubbles and with that, he stepped in, standing between her legs. He knelt down as she sat up and in that position they both fitted, just.

'You still have your trousers on,' she mentioned, trying not to laugh.

'I thought it'd make a change, you know,' he laughed, splashing her. 'Here.' He offered her a glass and poured.

Michael lay on his back on the bed, savouring the feeling of Beth's lips upon his skin as she kissed his body. She toyed with his erection, stroking and caressing, making him groan as she got ever closer to it with her mouth.

'You want to—' he said quietly. She looked up into his eyes and was suddenly embarrassed. 'But you don't know how!' he finished as he reached out and brushed her face with his fingers. 'Give me your hand,' he breathed. He took her fingers and pulled them slowly up to his mouth where he began to kiss them, licking slowly up and down. 'Like that,' he breathed. 'Slowly.' She crouched above him, feeling her own excitement mounting as she began to kiss him. It was a very strange sensation. It felt nothing to her lips, like it did to her hands. She held him with one hand and stroked, not needing guidance then; something else was guiding her, making her want to do it, want to taste him, as he did her so often. She let her mouth explore him with fever she didn't know existed, listening to him as he breathed in and out, groaning quietly as she discovered what he liked and didn't like. He put his hands to her head and went to pull her away.

'That's something that maybe should wait.' His voice was husky and she looked up at him, seeing him with different eyes. She knew what he was trying to say. But she wanted to taste him, wanted him to do it. She wanted to share everything with him and her pace quickened and her tongue flitted until she could feel his pulse throbbing, feel him swell in her mouth. His hands were in her hair then, he wanted to clutch her and push into her but couldn't because he wanted to hold back too, and let the feeling continue. But those that rushed through him were too much and so instead he lay back and let it happen. He came hard for all his trying and Beth faltered for a split second. It got her in the back of the throat and she tasted it, felt its sticky warmth. It was him and the thought of what she should do with it was gone from her mind as she swallowed. She didn't care. All she knew then was that he loved it and she was responsible for it. She slowed then as his breath turned to quiet pants and then pulled gently away from him. He was staring at her, wide-eyed and open-mouthed.

'Was that right?' she asked and he pulled her up to him, making her feel the warmth of his body.

'Incredible!' he whispered. He was actually at a loss for words. He thought it would have been at best *average*, what with it being her first time, but it wasn't. In fact it was like their very first encounter, and very far from it. He'd felt her want to do it, her need to do it and it had done nothing but intensify the moment. He was quiet for a long while then and with her in his arms he put the day's events into order in his head. He was at peace with the world at that moment, and it was then that sleep would normally have come, but it didn't, it was replaced with more longing, more wanting and without him saying a word, she looked up into his eyes.

The next evening Beth sat at the bar in Baileys watching William, the new barman. He was a funny-looking man, with cropped grey hair and wrinkled features from years of smoking, but his eyes, bright blue, were attentive. He'd been on for about an hour, and she had to admit that she was impressed. She added in her head, for an older bloke, and then sat chastising herself for being so nasty. He wasn't that old. Maybe fifty-five? Possibly sixty. She'd started to read his application form, but had to be honest, she preferred to hear him talk. He had a soft but rough East London accent and everything he'd said so far sounded like the beginning of a great story. He was a very interesting man. Apparently he'd owned a own pub for years, but after his wife had died, he'd given it up. It wasn't the same without her, he'd said. He looked into her eyes then, obviously knowing about her parents and he smiled warmly at her, his understanding obvious.

'You want another?' he asked as she finished her Coke and she nodded at him. She was about to speak when she saw Michael at the glass entrance doors.

'Is that Mick Elliott?' he asked Beth, his tone impressed as Michael breezed in.

'The one and only!' Beth laughed.

'Christ, I ain't seen him in years! I seen him fight once, oh five, six years back. That boy's got some moves.' He sounded wistful.

'Fight?' She was all ears then.

'Yeah! Proper fighting, not that boxing bollocks. Never lost his temper though, just stood up and knocked that poor bastard flat to the floor.' He almost smiled as he spoke. It was obviously something that had impressed him.

'Really?' Beth looked surprised.

'Yeah. Middle of my bleedin' pub it was too. Blood everywhere—' He paused. 'Offered to have the carpet cleaned.' He shook his head in amusement. 'What's he having?' he said then, changing the subject and his tone. 'Bud, tall glass. Clean tall glass!' She looked into those blue eyes. 'He gets upset if you give him a dirty glass.'

Will poured just as Michael joined them at the bar. He stood really close to Beth and planted a very casual and friendly kiss on her cheek. She smiled at him. 'Missed you!' he whispered to her, his eyes settling on Will. Beth smiled, aware that Will had probably heard him. He had, and it was instant, the feeling he got from those two. There were sparks flying in the busy bar and no one but him seemed to notice.

'I've been hearing about some more of your fighting talents!' she smiled. He looked at her in confusion.

'Michael, Will. Will, Michael!' It was strange, but she was really happy to be introducing them to one another. The two shook hands and then Michael's expression changed to one of concentration and thought.

'I know you!' he said bluntly.

'You do! The Cherry Tree,' Will smiled.

'That's right. How's your carpet?' he laughed. Will waved his hand in a light-hearted brush-off gesture.

'Phah, it was worth it just to see one of those lads go down—' he said, stopping there.

He saw the look in Michael's eyes. It was clear to see that Elizabeth wasn't let in on quite everything.

'Can I leave you two here for a while?' she asked.

'Where you going?

I just got here!' he was a little crest fallen.

'Just the office. I've got a couple of calls to make.'

'Don't be long. Did you eat yet?'

She shook her head. 'No, you?'

'Not yet, no,' was the reply, and they stared at each other for a few seconds. She slid from the stool and walked through the door at the back of the bar. Michael watched her leave, and Will watched Michael watching her leave. He was right. No man looked at a woman like that unless he was close, very close.

'Nice young lady,' Will said, drawing Michael's attention.

'Correct,' Michael replied softly.

Will paused. 'Um, At the risk of having me head kicked in, does everyone know about you two, or is it just me?' Will asked then, as he stood behind the safety of the bar, polishing each glass as he pulled them from the washer.

Michael looked him up and down, and then settled a steady stare on his face. What a perceptive man he was, Michael thought then. He hadn't done or said anything out of the ordinary, had he? 'I'm sure I don't know what you're talking about,' he said, sounding remarkably cool.

'That's what I thought, so that's the way it'll stay, son,' Will replied. 'And while we're on the subject of the little lady, do you wanna give me the rub on the rules?'

Michael laughed then and it was a real laugh. He liked him, he was a funny man, a real man.

Late January 1998

Beth wandered through the crowds clad in a mid-length black dress with thin shoulder straps and very low neckline. She settled against the gallery rail overlooking the dance floor in the Hothouse. She noticed with smiles, the men that passed behind her as they eyed her. But she paid them no more attention than that, she was far too busy scanning the sea of bodies below her. She hadn't seen much of him all evening and she was feeling a little lost, despite the fact that she hadn't stopped since arriving four hours before. She closed her eyes for a second or two and when she opened them again, she saw him. He was one level below her, making his way through the crowds, and then he stopped and looked up as if he was looking for her too. Her heart jumped into her mouth and he smiled then, noticing the expression on her face. He motioned for her not to move with a point of his finger. She tightened her grip on the rail, watching him as he made his way towards the stairs.

Within seconds it seemed that he was beside her and his closeness in such a public place made her stomach flutter.

'Are you ready to go home?' he asked, leaning as close to her as was publicly acceptable. 'James is busy down stairs, I don't think he'll be joining us,' he continued and she caught the tone in his voice.

'Who with?' Beth smiled up at him.

'That nasty Lisa woman. She's a slag if ever I saw one! Thinks she's caught herself a big fish and she's just reeling him in. Wait till Jennifer finds out!' Michael said slowly.

Beth laughed at his expression and tone of voice and then gave him a look from head to toe. 'I thought I saw her all over you earlier,' she breathed into his ear.

'Oh, you saw that, did you?' he chuckled. 'You don't miss a trick, do you?' and she shook her head at him as their eyes met again. 'Were you jealous?' he laughed.

'Should I be?' She pulled him close to her by his sleeve, under the pretence of talking into his ear again and in doing so she pushed her entire right side up against him.

'Do you want me to behave like a mad woman?'

His heart quickened. 'Not here, no!' he said, his voice then deep. He could feel himself getting aroused and casually he took a step back from her. 'You've no idea what you do to me, have you, woman?' She gave him a sly but quizzical look and he went on. 'You'd have me on my knees, wouldn't you?' he finished.

She brushed past him, feeling his groin against her back. 'Absolutely!' she purred.

James was otherwise engaged, and for a second or two Beth was really quite annoyed. Lisa was spread, literally, all over him at the bar, her slim frame reminded Beth of a spider's web. There was no need for this, she thought. He had Jennifer now and she was really nice. She stopped in her train of thought. James was play-acting, doing his job. Like Michael did his job, and when she was allowed, like she did her job too – keep those credit cards flowing. It was a popularity contest.

As she and Michael neared them she donned one of her winning smiles. Locking eyes with James, her suggestion to him was clear that she wasn't impressed. He understood her as plainly as if she had said it aloud and he nodded at her with a light shrug of his broad shoulders.

'We're starved!' Michael said lightly. 'I think we'll grab a takeaway and head home. If we go now we'll catch the Chinese.' He looked at his watch to confirm that he was right; he was.

'I shouldn't wait up for me tonight,' James said casually and both Michael and Beth nodded at him.

'I'll lock up then, shall I?' Beth said, leaning past Lisa to plant a kiss on her brother's cheek.

'Nah, just don't wait up!' He sounded firm on the matter. He may play, sure. But he wasn't about to spend the night with that haddock.

'I'll cover for you,' Beth said casually and she and James locked eyes again. He knew that she wouldn't say a word to Jennifer about his little added extras, his fun. But the threat was there and he accepted the challenge.

'You do that,' he smiled, showing his teeth.

'See you later,' Michael laughed. Then, taking Beth's hand in his own, he made his way through the crowds.

'Stop winding him up!' Michael said in a half whisper as they walked through the club and into reception where Paul passed Beth her overcoat.

'What did I do?' she laughed, her features mischievous.

'You know what you did!' Michael replied as he watched Paul help her slip it on and she smiled at him. 'He's not shagging it, you know.'

'Michael!' she exclaimed. 'Thanks Paul,' she added, her tone lighter and he reddened slightly. Michael saw him and smiled.

He knew that Paul wasn't the only man in the club who thought she was amazing. In fact he knew that he had been right all along about how she would affect people, men in particular, as she grew in to the woman she now was. She had a way with them. She had them all falling over themselves to help her and instead of being like maniacs, he and James actually found it amusing; she was amusing.

He wondered fleetingly then if James would find their situation as funny. After all, wasn't it partly his fault that they had fallen together so easily? He was never in lately; he was always off in search of adventure. No, it wasn't James's fault at all. James trusted Michael with Elizabeth's honour, as well as her life, and the familiar shameful feeling crept over him like a dark cloud across a blue sky. How in the hell was this one going to come out all right in the end? James would go absolutely crazy and he also knew from recent conversations with Pat and Judy that they had noticed a change in Elizabeth. She emanated a sexual aura that none of them could explain. She had indeed become a real woman. But he had denied noticing it when quizzed; he had simply passed it off by suggesting that it may have a lot to do with the fact that she had so much put in her lap with the business. Pat had agreed with his logic and he remembered then the feeling of relief that had rushed through him. Then he thought of all the comments about himself that people were making more frequently lately. Was he gay? Was there someone serious on the scene that was keeping the formidable Michael Elliott right in check or was he just getting old? He laughed at that one. If only they all knew just what was going on in his life, in his mind. They'd see a side of Michael Elliott that even he hadn't realised existed. The completely satisfied Michael Elliott, the warmed through Michael Elliott.

In the quiet of the car Michael started the engine silently, the interior light went off and he leaned across the cool leather to kiss her. She was receptive and her fingers flitted through his thick hair and then down his cheek, where stubble was just starting to appear from the long day.

'Are you really hungry?' he asked.

'Yes, if you are,' she smiled. He looked deeply at her then.

Everything they did lately was for each other only. They were one. No one else seemed to be there, even when they were in a crowd. No one else mattered. Nothing else mattered. It was just the two of them and it was beginning to show, show a lot. They'd have to be more careful, or come out in the open. So, he mused, enjoying the feel of her hands upon him, they'd have to be more careful!

'Chinese?' he suggested then, breaking away from his thoughts and picking up his mobile phone from on the dashboard. She nodded. He flicked through the menu on the display of saved numbers. 'Charlie.' His voice was loud in the silence of the car. 'It's Michael. Oh yes, grand, thanks. Can I put in an order? About ten minutes,' he said, looking at his watch. 'Egg rice, lemon chicken?' He looked at her for confirmation. She nodded. 'A chilli beef and a chow mein. Thanks.'

Michael followed Beth down into the kitchen, white bag of take-out in hand, and he placed it down on the counter top next to where she was now perched. He took two forks from the drawer and held one out to her. She tried to take it from his hand but he had a firm grip on it and he nudged into between her legs.

'I prefer cold Chinese!' he whispered.

'Now there's a bit of luck!' She was watching him as he slid off his jacket, threw it on the stool beside them and undid another button of his shirt.

'Did you say luck?' he asked then, slowly pulling his shirt from his trousers.

Beth leaned forward, pulling it roughly over his head. 'I did!' She wanted to see his body, feel his skin under the touch of her fingertips. His fingers toyed with her inner thigh, slipping dangerously close to her warm moist mound. She let out a small groan of expectation with every movement he made and when he finally slid his fingers into the silky material of her underwear she lay back, her dress then hitched up to her hips. He continued to explore her with one hand, enjoying her wetness while he made quick work of his belt, button and zip with the other. With both hands on her hips he pulled her towards him. No guidance was needed and he slid into her, sinking to the fullest he could without hurting her.

'Slow down!' he breathed as her pace quickened.

'Why?' she replied, not slowing until he physically stopped her with his hands on her hips again.

'I'll come. And I don't want to yet,' he whispered.

She wrapped her legs around his waist and pulled him back into her again. She wanted the sex, needed to feel this close to him whenever she could. She wanted to be his completely, have him be hers completely.

'I don't care,' she said, her voice heavy with excitement and then he was undone. He pushed into her, knowing that she wanted to feel him inside her, wanted him to come.

As they sat at the table a while later, pushing food around warm tins, she could feel his seed and her own moisture between her legs. It made her feel at peace with the world. His tone was low as he almost whispered the little insignificant comments and conversation. Secret things, things they alone in their little world shared.

'I got you insured on the car today.'

She beamed at him. 'Did you? You're so good to me,' and she sounded really pleased.

'Yes, so you can drive it legally now,' he smiled back at her. Seeing her happy in itself made him feel happy.

'James'll be pissed,' she smiled then.

'I don't much care!' His tone was blunt. 'It's for work anyway,' he added a little more softly.

'Me neither. Shall we just not tell him?' Beth added then, aware that this had darkened his mood a little.

'Good idea,' he breathed.

They were quiet for a while then, both lost in thoughts as they debated on whether or not they could eat any more.

'Judy was talking about you this afternoon,' Beth said, looking up at him.

'Oh yes, your shopping trip. What did you get?' he'd finished eating.

'Um, shoes, shoes and—oh yeah, shoes,' she laughed.

'Anything else?' he was quizzical in his tone.

'A suit!'

He looked away. 'Not the black one with the roses on the lapel?' he asked softly.

'No, the short brown one. Why?' she looked confused.

'Because I got you that one yesterday, it's upstairs.' As he spoke he gave her hand a gentle squeeze.

'You're spoiling me.' Sshe was pleased.

'I certainly hope so.' There was a pause.

'Did you say Judy was talking about me?' he changed the subject back again.

'Yeah. She was asking if there's a woman on the scene at the moment.' Beth's tone was flat.

'Why?' he laughed then.

'Michael, you're losing your touch. You haven't had the appearance of a casual fuck in ages. People talk, you know.' She was laughing too then and then he was quiet for a long while. He just clung to her hand. He hated being Michael Elliott at times like these. Everyone noticed everything about him. He sighed.

'Did she ask if I was gay again?' There was a laugh in his tone. Now that had been funny.

'No. I think you made your point the last time she asked.'

He sat up slightly in his seat. 'So, what did you tell her?'

'I said yes, and that I was the woman in question and that although our sex life was none of her business, it was all going very well and I thanked her for the enquiry.' She almost made it through the whole sentence without laughing, but failed.

'Now, what did you really say?' He liked her smart mouth at times like these; these times were hard, hard for them both and he knew it.

'I told her it was nothing to do with me, and that I'm neither here nor there on what you do.'

He let out a sigh as she finished speaking. If Judy was asking, then Pat would have noticed and that couldn't happen. And if they noticed, others would too, and he wouldn't risk Beth becoming a chip on which to bargain their livelihoods, especially with Oxley still on the scene. He face blackened as the name entered his mind. That man really was a fucking shite, along with that minder of his, King. True scum.

'Well, I suppose I'm going to have to have a shag then, aren't I? Something quite public at any rate, Elizabeth.' He sounded really unenthusiastic until her name tumbled from his lips, that sounded softer. 'Do you mind?' he asked then. It sounded ridiculous as he said it and they both laughed then, lightening the moment.

Chapter Twenty-Four

February 1998

The postman made his daily delivery bang on the dot of nine o'clock and all three dashed down the stairs barely dressed. James was the first to the mat and he scooped up a large wad of envelopes of all different colours and sizes. Beth went to grab them from him but Michael tapped her hand. 'You know the rules!' he warned. 'Come on.'

They went down into the kitchen and while James sorted the envelopes into three piles on the counter Michael filled and switched on the coffee percolator.

'Fuck me, Babe! You're popular this year!' He sounded surprised and Beth grabbed the pile from his grasp. She stood with a cigarette hanging from her lips, her make-up smudged all over her face and her hair a little more erratic than usual, pulled off her face with a scrunchie.

'I wonder if all these blokes'd find you so attractive now?' he added, giving her the once over with a shake of his head.

'Oh, and you look better on three hours' sleep, do you?' she retorted.

'Ah! Ah! Ah!' Michael intervened leaning between them at the counter. He sniffed at Beth then at James and then Beth again. 'Well, she smells better than you do, my friend. You stink!'

James looked right into his eyes and without so much as a blink let out a loud fart.

'Get it?' James laughed.

'You fucking animal'. Michael waved his hands about, disbursing the air around them.

'I only count seven!' Beth said, changing the subject.

'Shut up, there's nine there!'

'Yes, one from you, one from Michael. That's seven real ones!' she smiled. The two looked over her head at each other with a shrug.

'Charming. You hearing this, James?' Michael said.

'Yeah, init. I told you she was too old for all this crap now,' James laughed.

'Did you want to take the chance that she wouldn't get any?' Michael replied, pretending to ignore her. He was talking to James as if she wasn't even there then, and he was doing it deliberately.

'Okay, mate, I know me place. I'll go and get back under me rock, shall I?' James laughed too.

'You do that.' Michael was still laughing and then he stopped. 'Seven!' he said suddenly, pretending to sound shocked.

'That's more than I got,' James added with a shrug.

They watched her open them one by one. Each was different; different types, different writing and different postal marks although they were all posted in and around London. She read one of them over twice as she stood there. It was handcrafted cream watered silk with a velvet heart on the front of it. Inside it read *For You*. Other than that it was completely blank.

'Now, that's a bit special!' James remarked.

'It's lovely,' Beth said, glancing quickly at Michael. He smiled at her, aware of the emotion in her tone. It was from him. He'd had it made specially and it had cost more than he'd ever spent on a card before in his whole life.

'It's like Christmas!' James giggled, rather nonplussed by her cards then. There were all sorts sent to James and Michael. Most were vulgar, some smelled quite nice and some were just plain amusing. Michael opened his last one. He'd done that deliberately. He knew it was from her. Even the envelope screamed "expensive". He looked at the front. Gold leaf on fine white card read, *Once in a lifetime—* and casually he read the words printed inside.

Once in a lifetime someone touches you so deep

You can still feel them even when they've gone.
I just wanted to tell you, let you know awake or asleep
that that person is you, that you are that one.

'Made an impression then, mate!' James laughed, reading it over his shoulder.

'Obviously' he replied slipping the card back into the envelope. He was saved from saying anything else by the doorbell ringing out above them and in unison, pointing at one another, both men said 'Flowers!'

Beth was the first up the stairs. She opened the door and sure enough, there was a young woman standing holding a rather nice bouquet of red roses. 'Miss Dobson?' she smiled.

'That would be me!' She looked very pleased and took the roses from her and was about to close the door when another delivery van pulled up. An older man got out and walked around the back of his Interflora van. He opened the door and pulled out a large bouquet, again red roses.

'Miss Dobson?' he asked and Beth nodded, a laugh on her lips.

'I've got two more in here for you, too. You're a popular lady today,' he added just as Michael and James appeared at the door behind her. He looked past her and at them.

'Morning,' he smiled with a tilt of his head.

'Morning,' both men replied.

'Take those,' Beth said as the man handed one bouquet to James. Minutes later Michael took the other two, white roses this time, without having to be asked.

'They all from the same person?' James asked signing for the flowers. He was suddenly asking himself a lot of questions.

'No, mate, I don't think they were even booked out from the same shop,' he replied with a cheerful grin.

'Downstairs?' James asked Beth and she nodded.

'Yes please, baby,' she replied and he turned around. She looked up at Michael and mouthed, "Thank you", before following James along the hallway. Once downstairs again Beth busied herself taking the cards from the wrappings. She found all this rather amusing. Both James and Michael had said nothing. They both just stood there watching her.

'Four bouquets!' James said finally. "To my Baby, with all my love, Happy Valentine's, James", Beth read out. 'Thank you.' She leaned over and kissed his cheek. She looked at the other bouquet of reds.

'Michael's is bigger!' she laughed.

'Just open the card,' James smiled, his tone depicting slight sarcasm. He'd forgotten Michael would probably send some too. That left two more.

'To the only woman I've seen, and still loved in the morning. Happy Valentine's, Michael,' she read.

He smiled as James nudged him. 'It's supposed to be all sloppy and romantic, you sick, sick man!'

'Thank you, Michael. They're bigger than James's,' she said lightly, again for effect, still winding her brother up.

'Size isn't everything,' James said, finally taking the bait.

'I beg to differ.' Michael coughed.

'That's enough from you! Who's the others off?' James said with a wave of his hand. Beth opened both envelopes. She laughed and James immediately snatched one of the cards from her fingers. It read *Is James pissed yet?* He looked at Michael just as the laugh escaped his lips. 'You bastard!'

'I'm sorry!' he managed.

'I couldn't resist it,' Michael replied giving Beth a wink.

'And these from you, too?' James asked, pointing at the other bouquet.

'No! No way! Two's enough. It was only a joke, Christ.' James took the other card from Beth then. He stared at it and then the envelope. Even the writing on that was different. 'To Elizabeth. You are my Valentine!' he read out, then he looked across at her as she lit herself a cigarette. 'Is there something you wanna tell me?' he asked.

'No.' Her reply was casual, almost honest to the untrained ear and he stared at her for a long while before giving her a smile. 'Just asking?'

'Leave her be!' Michael interrupted brother and sister. 'She's a big girl now.' He looked at James with a smile and the two nodded at one another. Michael was right, again and as usual.

Late February 1998

'Michael! Can I borrow your car?' Beth called loudly up the stairs. 'Mine's not back from the garage. I said I'd pick Lucy up from work. I don't wanna leave her standing on a street corner in this weather.' By the time she'd finished speaking Michael was on his way down the stairs, the keys for his car swinging on his forefinger.

'Isn't that where we'd usually find her?' he smiled.

'Bitch!' she smiled sarcastically at him.

'Where you going anyway?' he added.

'Out!' she replied casually as he pulled her close to his body.

'Okay. But don't forget to fill it up before you come back,' he said keeping his voice normal as his hands slid over her body.

'I will.'

'Actually—' he began as his hand found the top of her stocking. 'James!' he called up the stairwell.

'Hello,' Came the reply, seconds after the bedroom door opened. He was leaning over the banister but still couldn't see them from his position.

'You home tonight?' Michael asked, now pinning Beth to the far wall.

'No. Why?'

'Beth's car's not back from the garage so she's taking mine. Can you drop me off at the club? I can't be arsed with a cab.'

'Oh, I see. She gets to borrow it, but I don't.'

'That's because I don't use it as a shaggin' wagon when I get to use it!' Beth piped up, desperately trying to keep her voice at a normal pitch as Michael rubbed at her.

276

'Yeah right, sure you don't,' he laughed. 'Yeah, go on then,' he agreed before disappearing back into his room.

'Will you pick me up?' Michael asked, his tone lower now that they were alone again. 'It would appear that we have unfinished business.'

'Yes, it would appear that way, wouldn't it' she breathed as he pulled his hand from her reluctantly.

'About one o'clock?'

'Maybe earlier, we're only going for a drink.'

'I'll see you later then.'

'Okay,' she breathed. He turned.

'Oh and Elizabeth. Drive carefully.'

'I'm always careful,' she smiled.

Michael was in reception waiting for her when she arrived to collect him. It was just gone eleven and the evening was just getting started. She made her way through the crowds of people queuing to get in and there was a wave of displeasure and complaint about queue jumping and the like. One young girl was shoved bodily by another, and she landed against Beth with a nasty thud, making both unsteady on their feet for a second or two. Beth spun around on her heel and focused on a group of sniggering teenagers just as Leon appeared at her side at the scene. They were like vultures and Beth disliked this little group, had done for a while.

'I'm sorry!' the other poor girl blurted, and another gust of laughter surrounded her rising embarrassment.

'Oy!' Leon's deep black voice was sharp, but Beth shook her head at him, then she looked back at her; she could have been no more than eighteen. The expression on her face was fear. She knew who Beth was, and fleetingly Beth tried to place her face in her past but she couldn't, she'd met too many people to be able to remember everyone.

'It's okay. They with you?' she asked her then.

She shook her head at Beth's question. 'No, they don't like me much,' she added.

'Let her in, Leon,' Beth said, sizing her up. It was like something out of a western as the two eyed each other some more. He motioned for her to go through and past the rope, and she passed another three doormen.

'Dawn, you got a drinks pass?' Beth added as they crossed the threshold of the club. The receptionist slid a pass across to her and she took it. 'Free till closing. That should make them laugh even louder!' she laughed with a tilt of her head. 'On top of them being barred!' and she looked at Leon again, who gave her the nod. He'd seen who it was and even with an army, they weren't getting in.

'Thank you,' she beamed. She was thrilled. Elizabeth Dobson had just stood up for her and she was pleased as punch.

'Can we go now, please?' Michael said, pretending to sound impatient. He wasn't, he was watching her, and how she handled herself, and the situation. She didn't get the hump or swear or throw all of her toys from her pram. She'd gone with the, *This is my manor, and you're all barred,* approach. He liked that. He led her outside just as the group were being given the bad news and there was a ripple of whispers as they passed by.

'Wanker!' one young man directed at Michael. Beth leaned into him, really close. She could smell cheap aftershave and cigarettes on him.

'Does he look like the kind of man that has to do that himself?' she asked. Her tone was really friendly but he got the message, and his gaze flitted to where Leon now stood with Paul. He was speechless and obviously embarrassed.

'Good girl!' Paul laughed after them. Michael turned and gave him a wave and then they were off into the darkness of the car park.

'Why does he always get to take her home?' Paul asked Leon once they were out of sight.

'Don't beat yourself up mate, at least that all he's doing with her, ay?' The innuendo was there.

'Leon, mate, sometimes I wonder. I really do,' Paul breathed, still staring after them. He'd seen something in Michael's eyes when he looked at her lately, even that night as he'd watched her outside the

278

doors. He was ready to protect her, even from a bunch of silly and drunk teenagers. That wasn't a job, that was infatuation, he was sure of it.

Then he thought back through the past months in his mind. Images came to him. He could see the way they looked at each other, the way they were around each other. Maybe he was reading too much into it? he thought with a shrug and then the thought was gone from his mind and he was back on the job, watching as the crowd that had started tonight's little ripple walked away.

March 1998

Elizabeth sat quietly at the counter in the kitchen, listening to James as he talked with Michael. Drink inspired conversations between those two were always funny, and tonight was no different.

'She's perfect,' James gushed and Michael shook his head. James was always a bit over-emotional when he'd had a drink. All Michael had asked was how things were going and he'd had chapter and verse on just about everything.

'Poor Jennifer!' Beth said, pouring out another glass of red wine. 'You make it sound like she's got wings and a halo!'

'She has to me, Babe!' James replied with a wink. 'She's great.'

Michael looked across to where Beth sat. She kept eye contact with James but was aware of him. She could feel his eyes upon her. She crossed her legs slowly, deliberately. She was wearing one of her many little black dresses. She knew that he liked them on her, and it was her secret way of letting him know that she wanted to please him all the time and not just when they had stolen moments together, and he thanked her for it. It was hard to try and show that it wasn't just sex that was between them without being overly obvious and it was getting harder.

'What about you, mate?' James said, looking over at Michael, who had been staring intently at Elizabeth and hadn't actually heard a word he'd said.

'Me what?' he asked, suddenly extremely attentive.

'Women?' James said laughing.

'Oh, yeah, sure,' he began but James butted in before he could continue.

'He's a shirt lifter!' he laughed. 'Not a bird in months.'

Beth saw Michael's expression change from amusement to panic and she swallowed the mouth full of wine she had just taken.

'James! Don't wind him up,' she laughed. 'You know he's not. He's had that Kelly calling him for months, not to mention Lisa the web and God alone knows how any others we haven't seen,' she finished and James smiled.

'And Caroline!' Michael added, pointing his finger in Beth's direction. She nodded at him.

'Thank you, Michael! Yes, and Caroline!' Her tone was almost venomous as she said the name.

'I was just kidding, Babe! Bloody 'ell,' James laughed. He looked back at Michael who was now on the verge of grinning at Beth's wonderful defence; she should be famous! What an actress!

''Ere, Mike, I really don't think she likes Caroline,' he added with a smile. Michael was saved from saying anything at all on that subject as James's mobile telephone began to ring with an almost unrecognisable classical tune. He turned away from them as he answered it and spoke.

Beth watched him for a second or two and was confident that he wasn't about to turn back around. She had Michael's attention again then and uncrossed her legs slowly, her hem rising as she did so and he saw the stocking top, then her bare leg and then he faltered as he noticed that apart from the stockings she had nothing on underneath the dress at all. She re-crossed her legs as if nothing out of the ordinary had happened.

'We know!' she laughed. 'Don't wait up, you'll not be home till after breakfast!'

'She wants me,' James laughed. 'What can I say?'

'No?' Beth suggested jokingly.

'Elizabeth is right about you, young James, you really can be a slag!' Michael smiled and he laughed at his friend as he pulled his jacket back on and took a step towards Beth, giving her a kiss on the cheek.

'No I'm not, I'm just getting her share, that's all,' he giggled, jerking his head at Beth.

'Leave her!' Michael joked. Then James was gone and Michael looked at her.

'Do that leg crossing thing again.' He stood up from his seat at the dining table and moving towards her. Beth lowered her head, tilting it to one side slightly. She looked at him from beneath long mascaraed lashes. His eyes moved focus from hers down to her parted legs. 'Now, have you been walking around like that all night?' he asked and she nodded at him.

They heard the front door bang shut above them and James's distinctive footsteps as he descended the stone steps to the street outside.

'And why would you want to be walking around with no panties on in the middle of March?' He was right in front of her now. 'Don't you know what can happen to a young lady like yourself? Flashing the likes of me your—' He paused, leaning over to the switch and flicking off the main light. 'Stocking tops,' he finished, whispering the last two words.

'No. No I don't,' she said, her voice low and husky. 'Are you going to enlighten me?'

'Put your life on it!' he said leaning into her. He kissed her for a long moment. 'I didn't think he was ever going to leave,' he breathed.

She pulled at his trousers then, practically ripping them down his legs and his erect penis sprang free. He grabbed her roughly and half carried, half dragged her to the floor, with him kissing her full on the mouth as he entered her on the carpet.

'What, no foreplay?' she laughed and he shook his head at her.

'No, not tonight.' His movements above her continued, he was bold and powerful and she savoured the feeling of his arousal as he pulled almost out of her and then pushed back in. His breathing quickened with his pace and with a shudder he came.

For a long minute he didn't move, he was just propped up on his elbows above her. She was quiet and he looked into her eyes. She hadn't come, but all the same a strange, satisfied expression appeared on her face. The knowledge that she could do that to him, make him want her so badly that he stopped being the gentleman that he usually was, surprised her. She could look at him sometimes and almost read his thoughts word for word, and sometimes his looks weren't just lustful, there was something else there in his eyes too and she would feel a rush of real warmth go through her.

He pulled out of her with such care then that it was hard to believe that he had just been so harsh and ravenous.

'Thank you,' he said finally.

'For what?' she asked.

'For letting me be a selfish bastard!' he croaked and she wrapped her arms around his neck, pulling him back down onto her.

Chapter Twenty-Five

April 1998

Their flight was delayed by an hour at Stanstead and by the time they'd collected their luggage it was late on Thursday evening when Michael and Beth finally pulled up outside the main entrance of the hotel in the taxi, but both Jim and Evelyn were standing on the stone steps waiting for them.

'There she is! Looking lovelier than ever,' Jim smiled, kissing Beth on the cheek and giving her a squeeze as he wrapped his big arms around her.

'Come here!' Eve beamed, taking Beth's arm when he'd finished, pulling her close to her. 'We missed you. How are you?' She was all questions and hugs and smiles. She was always that way. Beth loved her for it, especially after the long journey.

Michael paid the taxi driver, helped pull the suit carrier and two large bags from the boot and then was immediately embraced by his mother, who still had hold of Beth with her other arm.

'Nice flight?' Jim laughed, aware of the delays.

'Oh, ay, grand,' Michael replied sarcastically.

'Here, give me those,' Jim said then, taking the case from his son's grasp.

'Come away in,' Eve said, her voice full of excitement and love for the pair before her. 'Your rooms are ready. Go on in!' she urged.

Inside the reception hall Michael caught Beth's eye. He smiled at her, then he rested his gaze on his father who was smiling as Evelyn's chatter continued. It wasn't an unpleasant noise at all, far from it. But both were tired, and if Beth was honest, for the first time in her life she felt a little apprehensive about being there. Eve and Jim were both very perceptive people. They always seemed to look past the obvious and she had a feeling that she and Michael were going to have to be very careful this weekend if not to be found out. She knew that James was blind to what wasn't directly in front of him when it came to her these days; she never gave him reason to question her and Pat and Judy were, she knew, still totally unaware. She sighed inwardly, but it would be tough to hide anything from Eve and Jim and she wondered how they would react if they knew about her and Michael. She stopped in her train of thought then: what were they doing? Shagging? Bonking? Having an affair? They were both single adults, weren't they? Yes, to the outside world they were, but she knew that in their world she would always be the over-protected one and he, if Pat and James ever opened their eyes, would be the dead man who had taken advantage of her.

'You okay?' Michael said, looking down at her and she came back to the present.

'Yes, just a bit tired.' It sounded lame even to her own ears and by the look in his eyes she knew that he didn't believe her. She didn't lie to Michael well, it wasn't something she'd had much practice at doing. She even thought fleetingly that maybe the same thought had crossed his mind. They were, after all so very similar and so in touch with each other in more than a physical way.

'We'll go and put the bags up, then have a drink, ey?' he suggested and she nodded at him. It sounded like a great idea.

She really had needed this weekend, a lot more than she cared to admit actually. She needed to think and to get her thoughts in order, and then carry on, and she was glad that James had insisted that she come with Michael for the break, and she hadn't needed persuasion, she thought, a slight smile crossing her lips. She knew that Michael had some business to attend to while they were there. It had also occurred to her that James had ulterior motives for ushering her off to Ireland for the weekend. It was clear to both Michael and her that he was hooked, for the want of a better word, on the rather lovely Jennifer. Both were well aware that he had planned a long, romantic weekend in the house with her, although he had tried his level best to hide it and that with Beth and Michael away, he'd have the place to himself.

Beth left her neatly packed bag on the bed after pulling out a black woollen dress and matching cardigan. She'd washed and dressed again, touched up her make-up and slipping on her shoes. She eyed herself in the full-length mirror on the wall adjacent to the double glass doors that led out on to the small balcony. She looked good, she knew, and she was more appealing to men nowadays, though she wasn't sure of exactly why, but she was definitely aware of it. She looked older in her own eyes, she thought, maybe even wiser too.

She came out of the lift on the ground floor. The young, smartly dressed receptionist gave her a friendly smile and pointed towards the main bar with the tip of her pen without saying a word. It wasn't as busy as she thought it would be, but then it was a Thursday night and the hotel was mainly a weekend venue for weddings and parties; the weekdays were usually filled with businessmen. She found Michael and his parents in the residents' lounge. They were sitting on a leather suite talking and laughing, the men sipping whisky and Eve drinking gin and tonic from a tall glass. And as she neared them, she couldn't help noticing how much like Jim Michael looked. Michael watched her walk across the carpet. She looked so beautiful when she was relaxed and when she smiled at him he felt proud that she was his, even if he couldn't show it to the world.

'What would you like, my lovely?' Jim asked her, standing up and putting his own drink down on the table beside him.

'Oh, um—A glass of red, please,' she smiled, sitting down next to Eve, who gave her arm a friendly squeeze.

Jim walked up to the bar and spoke softly to the young man serving behind it. 'Michael was just telling us about your plans for the garden,' Eve said, placing her own drink on the table. Beth looked at him. He took notice of everything in her life. He was interested in her ideas, for all that some of them were a little wacky and wild.

'Oh, yeah. It'll be like a building site for a few weeks, but it looks a bit regimented as it is. It needs bringing into the nineties,' she smiled. 'Not nearly as grand as yours, but infinitely better than it was.'

'Rubbish! Your design's brilliant,' Michael added quite firmly, but with a smile. Eve heard the tone in her son's voice and looked over at him. He was looking at Beth.

'Steven will bring it over in a minute!' Jim interrupted, referring to Beth's drink, resuming his position on the chesterfield by the windows that over looked the sweeping drive. He looked at her with the same eyes as his son and she smiled at him. Was that what Michael would look like in his fifties? she found herself thinking as she studied him some more. He had fine lines on his face, but they seemed to suit him and the inevitable grey of someone so dark haired was quite distinguished.

'Did you want something to eat?' he asked then, breaking into her thoughts. He was smiling and she wondered what he was thinking then. He looked through her. Saw something behind those pretty green eyes that make a bell go off in his head. She looked—what was it? Different? Older? He couldn't decide, but there was something there.

'No, thanks, I'm fine. Michael, do you?'

He shook his head, taking a sip of his drink. Her asking him before either of them got the words out wasn't lost on them and that was it. It was clear on Jim's face as Michael glanced at him.

'I'll get something later, Dah.' His tone was completely casual but still Beth felt her cheeks burn.

They sat talking about everything and nothing until they noticed that the bar had emptied around them and the exceedingly quiet night-time housework had begun.

'You're out early in the morning, Michael?' It was a question, Eve was planning ahead again.

'Yes, I'm into town for a bit, but it won't take too long.' Michael smiled and both women noticed how father and son looked at each other then. This was business.

'Well, I'll wake you at eight then, shall I?'

'Please,' he replied as Eve stood up. She kissed both Michael and Beth goodnight and after giving them both a lingering look, left them sitting in the lamp light. 'I'm off too. Have a nice night. I'll see you in the morning,' Jim smiled as he finished his drink in one gulp. He got the urge to say something else, but didn't, so instead he said, 'Sleep tight.'

Once alone they sat looking at each other and there was absolute silence.

'Who you collecting for?' Beth asked lightly as she exhaled cigarette smoke.

He looked into her eyes, there was no way of getting anything past her. 'Collecting? What for?'

'Michael!' Her tone was slightly clipped.

'Derek' he replied, and before she could ask any more of him he jumped from his seat, pulling her from hers with a firm grip.

'Come on,' he said, a mischievous tone to his voice.

'Where are we going?' she laughed, letting him lead her back into the main hall, through double doors and down the stairs that led to the gym and pool.

'For a swim!' he said firmly.

'But I haven't got my—' she began to reply. He stopped dead in the stairwell and looked into her eyes. 'Michael! Really!' she gasped, pretending to be shocked by his inferred suggestion.

'There's no one about. I promise,' he continued and before she had time to protest further they were at the doors leading to the indoor pool.

It was surprisingly dark inside and Michael locked the large doors behind them. 'Get your kit off, woman!' he laughed, pulling off his own clothes, and Beth followed suit, leaving her dress and cardigan on a chair by the poolside. Naked, they slid down into the warm water. Their laughter echoed in the room and the only other sound was the water lapping over the sides of the pool as they swam towards one another.

From the window in the study Eve watched with interest as her son took Beth's arm in his. They wandered leisurely across the lawn back towards the house, pausing every few steps as they obviously chatted between themselves. Michael had been out all morning, working. Then after lunch he'd announced that he was taking Beth out for a walk around the grounds. They'd been gone for hours. Eve found herself looking some more; they looked so easy as they chatted and although she couldn't hear them or see their faces clearly in the late afternoon light, she could see something in their body language. She looked away for a second or two and then down at them again. How could she have been so blind! she thought suddenly, realising what had been staring her in the face. When had she first noticed the difference, Christmas? Yes, it was Christmas. A smile crossed her face then and as they neared the house she moved away from the window.

Beth woke up in the large wood-framed bed, aware that she was not alone, but she didn't move in panic. She could smell him and she recognised the steady pace of his breathing. He was awake and she could feel his weight next to her on top of the covers.

'Did I wake you?' he said softly, brushing the hair from her cheek, peering over at her now-open eyes. She sighed, turning her head to face him in the moonlight. He was propped up, bare-chested on one arm. His eyes were gentle on her and she smiled at him.

'Have you been here long?' she asked, her voice still a little croaky from sleep.

'No, not long,' he lied. He had actually been there for about an hour. He still found watching her sleep soothing, and he wrapped his strong arms around her, pulling her close to breathe in the sweet smell of her. 'Go back to sleep,' he whispered softly.

'No. You woke me up, now entertain me!' she giggled quietly, struggling with the covers that were now tangled around her legs as she tried to rise. Free now, she swung her leg over his body and straddled him.

'My pleasure.' He wiggled out of his tracksuit bottoms beneath her and kicked them off the bed.

The loud knock at the door spurred Michael into action and he leaped from beneath the covers, grabbing up his tracksuit bottoms from the carpet by the bed. Beth sat bolt upright and looked around the room like a trapped wild animal.

'The bathroom!' she half whispered, pulling on her own discarded nightclothes. She rushed to the door and unlocked it just as Michael closed the bathroom door behind him.

'Eve!' she said, sounding surprised. She was actually telling Michael who it was and she imagined him cringing behind the locked door.

'I was going into town in a while,' she said, stepping into the room, her gaze roaming the expanse as if she was looking for something. It was awfully tidy, everything but the bed was exactly as she had left it two days before. 'I thought you might like to come. We can do a little shopping,' she continued.

'Great, I'd love to!' Beth replied, trying not to sound desperate to get her out of the room before she noticed anything odd that they may have missed in their rush to get him hidden in the bathroom.

'Good. We'll go after breakfast. In about an hour?' she smiled in a gentle tone. She turned to leave the room and then paused and Beth's heart pounded in her chest like a drum. 'Oh, I don't suppose you've seen Michael this morning, have you? He's not in his room.' Her eyes settled on Beth's.

'No. No, I haven't!' she lied and Eve gave her a little nod.

'I'm sure he'll turn up.' With that she left the room, having caught the distinct scent of her only son's aftershave, and Beth closed and locked the door, leaning on it for support for a second or two.

The bathroom door opened and Michael appeared at it, a strange expression on his face. Beth looked up at him as he moved across the room towards her, his body proud and strong. He slipped his arms around her and held her close to his naked chest so that she could smell the morning upon his skin.

'She knows!' he said simply, nuzzling his face into her ear. Beth didn't need telling; she was well aware of that fact herself. The thing that she found strange was that she wasn't, or rather, didn't seem that bothered.

Jim waved and watched as Beth and Eve left the grounds in the car and then he turned to walk back through the reception hall. He didn't look shocked to see Michael standing behind him, although he had to admit that he hadn't heard or noticed him arrive. They walked through the lounge and up to the bar without saying a word. Michael sat on a stool beside his father and the two men were silent for a while longer.

'Did Mum say anything to you this morning?' he asked finally and Jim nodded slowly, knowingly at him.

'She did!' his reply was blunt, but not hard.

'What did she say?' Michael had been expecting this.

'She thinks you're having some with Elizabeth, son.' Jim spoke softly but in his usual blunt manner. 'And, I take it she's right?' He was aware of the thoughts that were no doubt in his son's head at that point. There was no use in riling Michael up, none at all. He also knew that if Michael had bought Beth there with him, it was for some good reason, and he wondered if it wasn't to get it out into the open with him and Eve. Jim knew his son better than anyone and Michael didn't like deceit.

'I'm not—' he began; he was struggling with his words. 'I love her, Dah!' Michael said suddenly. Jim nodded at his statement, trying not to show his surprise at his son's outburst, although, if he were honest, that much was plain to see in Michael's eyes if you bothered to look closely enough.

'So what are you going to do? Your mother's right, you can't keep creeping about. And what when Pat finds out?'

'Oh, Dah, I don't know!' He paused with a sigh and lit himself a cigarette. He didn't know what to say next. He wasn't having to explain himself to his father, but he felt the need to tell someone, anyone, that he wasn't just using Elizabeth to his own end. That he really did care for her, love her and that he needed help and guidance. Jim knew what he was trying to say and patted him lightly on the arm.

'It can't go on like this,' Jim said, his tone still light but factual. 'Pat'll go mad and James—' He paused for a few seconds before going on. 'James'll—' He paused again and thought for a moment. 'He'll look at it as if you've let him down, betrayed him, son. You know the deal with Elizabeth, always have. Christ, you were given the task yourself and now what've you done. You're risking everything. Including her!'

'I know. You're right. I just have to find the right time, you know?'

'I know' Jim nodded sagely.

'What do you think?' Michael asked then. He sounded like a little boy again, asking for his dad's opinion on trainers or something of the like.

'I think you two were made for each other, always have, always will!' There! He'd said it. It shocked Michael and he smiled to himself before going on. 'You can handle her, son. And all the crap that's going to come with it.'

'I don't handle her! She does as she likes!' Michael replied and there was silence again as Michael thought of his mother.

'She's not giving her a hard time—' Michael began but Jim was already shaking his head at the unfinished question about Eve.

'Good God, no, you should know your mother better than that, son. But we both know, she'll be hard pushed not to say anything at all!'

'God, I hope you're right,' Michael sighed, making himself more comfortable on the stool. 'I don't want her hurt, not by anyone!' His tone was firm and even his own father shuddered inwardly at the thought of anyone hurting something that his son loved as much as he knew he loved that girl.

The word "girl" seemed to echo in his mind and his eyes settled on Michael. What was he, eight, no, nine years her senior. Thousands of thoughts went through his mind at that moment. He tried not to think of his son having sex, it wasn't something that men did, but he knew, as a father did, what kind of a man his son was. He nodded absently at himself. This situation was almost amusing. Michael had been given the task of protecting Beth from the world and what had happened? He'd gone and taken her and done it himself.

'I know I shouldn't ask—' Jim said, his voice low in secrecy. 'It's none of my business, but did you make me proud, son?' There was a laugh on his lips as he asked and Michael looked into his eyes, a smile evident there on his face too.

'Dah!' Michael exclaimed. He lowered his head, a smile appearing on his face. 'Okay, yes, I did!'

Jim warmed then, seeing the sincerity in his son's face.

Beth held the dress up against herself and Eve nodded in approval at the choice. It was calf length and fitted, in chocolate brown. 'Go and try it on,' she suggested. 'And the jacket.' She flicked through the rail for a matching jacket in a sixteen. 'There.' Beth came out of the fitting room and Eve looked her up and down. She looked beautiful and she smiled approvingly. 'Grand. Just grand.'

'You like it?' Beth was smiling at her.

'I love it. Very sophisticated.' She paused. 'And Michael likes brown.'

There was a long pause as the two locked eyes.

'But I get the impression that he'd like you in anything, so what you wear is really of no consequence.' Her tone was light and its usual sing-song and Beth knew that her own face was burning.

'Ah!' she managed, as a slight smile appeared on her lips. She looked away for a few seconds as she thought of something to say. Her mind was blank.

Eve held up her hand as a casual gesture. 'You don't have to explain yourself, Elizabeth. I'm not one to judge, you're a big girl now.' That was true. 'And to be honest, I'm not surprised. It's always been Elizabeth this and Elizabeth that with him. I should have guessed months ago. I did, but didn't realise until yesterday for sure.' She reached out and brushed Beth's flushed cheek with a warm hand. 'And as I don't care for gossip, no one'll hear anything from me.' She answered Beth's next question without her having to ask it and Beth felt tears of love well up in her eyes and then fade just as quickly.

'Is my son treating you well? Of course he is,' she added in almost a whisper, her expression knowledgeable. 'Now.' Her voice was back again. 'Buy that dress. He'll love it. It's so pretty.'

Michael closed the door behind them and flicked the lock with a click. He looked over at where Beth now stood in the light of the windows and watched as she slipped the jacket from her frame and laid it on the chair beside where she stood.

'This feels weird,' she said, sounding remarkably coy all of a sudden.

'Weird?' Michael approached her.

'Yeah, not sneaking about after dark,' she said.

'Nice weird or nasty weird?' He lingered on the last two words, making her laugh with the tone in his voice.

'Nice weird,' she said as he pulled her to him. 'Very nice weird. Extremely nice weird.'

He held her close for a long time.

He could hear her heart beating against his own and something deeper than the sex they shared stirred within him. He wanted to hold her that close for ever and never let her go; wanted to wake up every morning and go to bed every night knowing that if he turned his head on the pillow she would be there right next to him. It was something that he, as a grown man, had never experienced before. She woke something within him that could never be explained in words.

She could feel him, so close. So close that she wanted to cry, wanted to squeeze, make him feel how much he meant to her. She could never find the words to express herself with him, when it came to him. He was her world, more than James was even, and more than the clubs were and the money was. She knew in her heart that if it came to it, she'd choose Michael over her very soul and that knowledge alone made her ache from the inside out.

'Michael,' she breathed, feeling the warmth of his hands as they ran the length of her back and lingered on the zip. He nodded into her neck, kissing and nuzzling at her until she tipped her head backwards to face him. 'Michael. I—I love you.' She felt him falter and her heart leaped into her mouth. Was that the wrong thing to say to him? She cringed, waiting for the second when their eyes would meet in the darkness and suddenly she wanted to cry. Had she just blown it? It wasn't what he wanted to hear, even though she was sure that he knew it to be true.

His stance changed, his arms slipping from her body, his strong fingers searching for her hands. He stood upright and then and as she predicted, their eyes met. It was the tears that had welled in his eyes that made her gasp on her breath.

'Say it again!' he managed, his right hand rising to stroke her cheek.

'I love you!' She repeated herself, her tone strong in the silence of the room.

A single tear fell from his cheek then and instinctively she raised her free hand to wipe it away. 'I love you too, Elizabeth.' He paused. His words seemed to echo in her head. 'I love you more than I love life itself. Have done since you were born. I'd stop the world from spinning if you said you wanted off.' His voice was low and she felt like she was melting into him then. Their lips met and they lingered on the kiss, tasting each other on hot lips.

Snuggled up against the warmth of his naked body Beth watched the sun begin to light the sky. It was going to be a beautiful day. She was no weather expert, she could just tell from the haze and the pitch of the bird song outside the window. She felt Michael stir behind her and she smiled as his arms pulled her just a little bit closer. There was something about him in the mornings, she wasn't quite sure of what it was but it always made the day seem to start well, very well. Maybe it was the smell of him, all manly and comforting to her; maybe the fact that they had just spent the night together, the whole night. Truthfully, she didn't know and she didn't much care. All she did know was that it got her every time. He was hard up against her back then and she thought fleetingly that maybe that was what she liked about their mornings.

'Can't we pretend that it's night time again?' He smiled into her back, his tone suggestive.

'Oh, no. I need a shower. I smell!' she almost whispered.

'Yes, you do. You smell lovely' he breathed into her ear as his hand cupped her breast.

'And I'm all sticky,' she continued her protest, although it was a feeble effort.

'I don't care!' He continued his exploration with one hand and then without warning, almost completely flipped her around and onto her back.

Late April 1998

From the window in the office Pat watched Beth closely. She moved through the crowds of heaving bodies, reminding him of a sleek cat, turning or lingering occasionally as someone caught her eye. His focus was drawn from her to another. He followed her line of sight and settled his gaze on Michael. He watched as a conversation took place, a silent conversation. Those two were too close sometimes, he thought. There was something between them that made him cautious. There were looks sometimes and half spoken sentences. *If he's gone and done it, I'll fucking kill 'im,* a voice said inside his head.

He didn't get to think any more. His attention was bought back to the present with a bit of a crash. It was like the parting of the Red Sea down there suddenly. There was one man at one side, holding a bottle and another man at the other and neither looked like they were about to back down. He watched as bouncers appeared on the scene. This was a fight over a woman, he could tell. It was like a cockfight. Peacock feathers were up and someone was going to get hurt. He saw Michael then. He was standing back a little and there, right behind him, nice and protected, was Beth. He looked around at her and she nodded at whatever he'd said to her and then he was off. He took two steps, maybe three and the larger man was on the floor, reeling on the carpet. Pat didn't even see Michael's arm move. He then turned to face the other, his expression hard, his stance firm. He spoke above the music, which hadn't faltered and with a nervous nod of his head, he backed down, lowering the bottle he was wielding, when it was then taken from him by Paul who was a step behind Michael. Michael looked up at the mirror then, aware that Pat was in the office, and aware that he was probably watching. He gave him a little wave, making Pat want to step back into the dimness of the room. He hated it when he did that!

Chapter Twenty-Six

May 1998

Beth watched from her favourite perch on the counter top as Michael made one of his legendary cooked breakfasts. He took pride in the preparation as much as the finished product and for the amount of time and effort involved, the kitchen was decidedly tidy.

'You'd better get him out of his bed,' he said, looking across as her and she nodded, sliding to the floor. She disappeared up the stairs and then up another flight and returning moments later. 'He's on his way now. And, surprisingly he's got a hangover!' She moved up behind him, slipping her arms around his waist. He patted her hands lightly with one of his own. She moved her hand down, feeling him beneath the material of his trousers.

'Stop that now, woman,' he half whispered. 'You'll get me all worked up!'

She purred at him. 'Will I?' she asked, tilting her head round so that they were looking at each other.

'Yes, you know you will. Wait till he's been and gone, then you can play all you like,' he breathed. He was going to continue but they heard James's footfalls in the hallway above them and Beth moved back a couple of paces, then turned and busied herself getting cups out of the cupboard.

'Morning,' James managed.

'Ah, good morning. The walking whisky bottle wakes!' Michael laughed loudly, turning around and waving the spatula in his hand like a sword. 'Did you find your way out of the said bottle?' he added, just as loudly.

'I did!' James was very quiet.

'Well, congratulations,' Beth remarked.

'You really smell' Michael said, placing a full plate in front of James on the table.

'Mate, you have no idea. And I still managed to—' He was going to go on, but he looked up at Beth who, for the first time ever, was very interested in what he had to say for himself on the sexual antics score. 'I can't say any more, sorry.' He ended his words with a mouthful of food and a wave of his fork in their direction.

'You don't have to. We had to help her put you to bed. Shagging, my arse!' Beth laughed.

'What time are we off?' Michael asked Beth, changing the subject as they too sat down at the table with their plates.

'Where?' James asked, interrupting.

'The club? We're interviewing, remember?' Beth breathed.

'Anything young, fresh, innocent?' he asked lightly.

'Shut up your filth!' she laughed, sounding remarkably like Michael. 'We're not employing anything for your entertainment. We're having quality, and besides, I was under the impression you were off the market.'

Beth watched with flinty eyes as the young woman they'd just interviewed sauntered from the office. The door clicked closed behind her and she then looked across at where Michael sat, perched on the edge of the sofa. He shook his head, a laugh on his lips, a smile on his features.

'What d'you think?' he asked.

'Slut!' she replied, moving from behind the desk, to leaning on the front of it.

'So you don't want to take her on then?'

'Sure, I'll take her on. But I'll not employ her! There's enough tits and arse here as it is! We sell beer here!' she spat out the words, and he laughed at her. James was right, she was picking up his tone, and his terminology.

'Are you sure now?' he asked, his tone amused. He sounded very fresh off the boat and she laughed then.

'Oy! Stop taking the piss!' That was better, very English. 'You pick one. If I see one more pair of legs today, I'll scream.' She was agitated, he could tell.

'Okay, what's really up?' he asked then, looking into her eyes.

'Do they all *have* to want to bed you?' she breathed. He almost smiled then, but then wasn't the time. This was something that came up from time to time. It wasn't jealousy, it was frustration.

'I love you. I want you.'

'I know, I just, well—' she faltered.

'Do you want to tell them?' he asked then. She looked into his eyes, saw the sincerity there again. She wanted to say yes. Wanted it to be over. Wanted to be like a normal couple, with a normal relationship, like the ones that were started on the dance floors and at the bars of their places, but she knew that it would finish them. She knew that Pat'd bounce off walls and that James'd never forgive him, so instead she shook her head.

'No, Michael. I won't risk losing you!' Her words sounded old, wise. He stared at that pretty face and saw the pain upon it, but he knew as well as she did that that was not the time for this one to come out into the open.

June 1998

In one swift movement James tipped Beth onto his shoulder and mounted the stairs with Michael close behind him, her shoes and clutch bag in his hand. She was out for the count and both men could see the funny side of it, her state, because both could remember being in the same state once or twice themselves in the past.

'If she chucks on this suit I'll kill 'er!' James laughed quietly. 'She was fine until she got outside,' he was whining then.

'Reminds me of someone else I know!' Michael replied, and he grunted as the memories came flooding back to him. He'd been in an awful state on his birthday, and to top it Beth had arranged for yet another stripper for him. In she'd walked, her boobs wobbling around inside the flimsy top she'd worn. If it hadn't been so funny, it would have been nasty.

'Should we undress 'er?' he asked as they entered her room.

'I think so, yes.' Michael flicked on the bedside lamp and pulled back the quilt before James laid his sister down gently on the bed. She didn't make a sound or stir even though the two men chattered as they pulled her, about to take the dress from her body. Michael noticed the necklace he'd given her that morning around her neck. Fine, fine white gold with a small square-cut diamond on it. It was just something silly, something personal, he'd said, but it had cost him quite a bit. Not that that bothered him.

'She looked good tonight,' James said, a proud tone in his voice. 'You got 'er this, didn't you?' He held the little pale grey satin dress in his hand. Michael looked at it and his mind went back to the previous week. He'd been aware that she had been debating on what to wear on her birthday and had gone out shopping with that his sole objective. He knew her shape exactly and also that if he got size sixteens from certain shops, they would fit exactly. The boutique he'd been in was one of them; it was somewhere Beth shopped often.

'I did! It spoke to me! I got in that little place down by the King's Arms. It said, "Buy me, she'll look great in me!" He chatted on casually, aware that James was now watching how expertly he pulled the clips from her hair. He even gave it a little brush though with his fingers, like she did whenever she took clips and bands from it. He then stood over her, pretending not to notice the white lace bra and panties she was wearing. He wondered what James would have to say if he knew that he had also bought her that rather sexy little number and that on more than one occasion he'd taken those panties down with his teeth. 'She'll regret tonight in the morning,' he added, his tone amused.

'Beth with a hangover. I can't wait!' James let out a long sigh. 'She grew up so fast.' His tone was wistful suddenly and he touched her hair.

'Ay, yes, she did! And you've done a grand job!' Michael smiled.

'You think so?' he asked, his voice was wistful.

'Yes, I do,' Michael replied. He looked down at her. She looked so peaceful even in a drunken state. 'She's loved and does love, and now she's all grown up. You couldn't keep her a baby for ever.' He pulled the quilt up a bit further over her shoulder as he spoke.

Michael's words were not lost on James. 'I don't want to, Mike. I just don't want anyone to take the piss! She's had enough grief. I just want her to be happy.' His words touched Michael deep inside. 'You know?'

Michael nodded. 'Yes. I do know, and somewhere there's a man who'll love her for everything she is. He'll love everything she was and what she will be.' His tone changed pitch very slightly but James noticed it and the two stared at each other for a long moment.

'You love her too, don't you!' he remarked.

'Ay, yes, yes, I do.' Michael spoke honestly. 'She's my family, like you're my family. And I, like you will *never* let anything bad happen to her, not ever. She is always safe with me, James.' Nothing else was said and the two walked quietly from the room, closing the door behind them.

July 1998

The sun was on its way down as James and Beth got into the car to go to the Hothouse. She lit two cigarettes and passed one to him as they pulled out onto the busy high street. She sat silently in the passenger seat and James glanced at her. She looked so lovely with a tan. The little pale blue dress she wore complemented it, but he couldn't help but notice the slightly sad feeling that emanated from her, and had all day.

'You okay, Babe?' he asked.

She nodded absently at his question as she watched the street whiz by the window. He blew out the smoke through his nostrils thoughtfully. 'Painters in?' he asked taking a long shot and she turned to look at the left side of his face.

'Yes!' she snapped and he scoffed at her. 'Okay. So you'll need a drink then.' He smiled then, with her.

They didn't speak for the rest of the journey. It wasn't a difficult silence, but it was definitely a silence. Paul greeted them at the door with a cheery smile and took her cardigan from her shoulders.

'I'll put it in the office for you,' he said, being overly helpful for her, as he always was. Beth noticed the way that the receptionist looked at James as he stood chatting briefly to Frank and she rolled her eyes at him as their eyes met.

'Number four hundred and what?' she asked jokingly as they walked through the double doors. They weren't here to work tonight and they headed straight for the bar.

'She can try, but she won't get anywhere. And besides, you're only jealous,' he laughed, putting his cigarettes down and waving over one of the four bar men serving.

'James, how old am I?' she asked suddenly and he looked at her.

'Twenny,' he replied and she nodded at his answer, raising her eyebrow slightly as she did so. 'So what is it makes you think I haven't already done it?' she said, her tone matter-of-fact.

His expression changed and she raised her eyebrow at him again in question as she waited for a response.

'Yeah, right!' he laughed finally and Beth laughed with him then.

Let him think what he liked. He'd only hound her for a name or give everyone else the nod that she wasn't to be left alone again and that was something that she couldn't deal with again; she'd go crazy.

A while later she stood alone at the bar. There were a couple of slower songs on and she suddenly hadn't wanted company and she was glad that James had gone off to phone Jennifer. As she stood there watching people go by she wanted Michael, but he wasn't there. He was in Ireland and there had been no excuse for her to go with him. She hated it when he was away and the past few days had dragged on like none she had experienced since the week before her parents' funeral. From the moment he'd left the house he was all that she could think about, which wasn't unusual in itself, but it was getting worse. She ached for his touch and kept telling herself that it was just another few days before he was home again, but it didn't help much. She still found herself sitting in his room when James was out, taking in the smell of him and wishing he were there.

She felt someone in front of her on the opposite side of the bar and she looked up from her empty glass. Will looked at her and gave her an understanding smile.

'You on your own tonight then, little lady?' She nodded at his question. 'Well that can be your last for about an hour, then,' he laughed, placing another vodka and orange before her. 'Can't have you falling over drunk, can we?' he laughed.

She smiled at him and his concern for her well-being. 'What you doing here?' she asked then, just noticing suddenly that he was not in his usual place.

'I took a couple more shifts to try and keep the old grey ones active!' he looked at her with a smile. ''Ere, you all right?' he looked old and wise.

'Yeah, I'm okay.' She let out a huff-like sigh.

'Yeah! Looks like it. Go have yourself a dance, aye?' he suggested. He knew what was wrong with her. It was written all over her face. She was missing the Irishman.

'I'll see you in a while,' she smiled, then she was off. She made her way across the bar area, up the stairs and over to the balcony. She liked watching all the bodies below her, dancing and loving so openly. She often wished that she and Michael could be like that and she wondered if their relationship would be as strong if they were a couple in the true sense of the meaning, but she could never answer herself. She really didn't know and that fact alone bothered her more than anything else. She wandered back down stairs with an empty glass in her hand; she needed another drink. She met James on her way down.

'I was just looking for you, Babe,' he said, the familiar look of coyness in his eye. 'I'm gonna scoot. Paul said he'd drop you home whenever you're ready.' He paused and looked into her eyes. 'And you are to let him take you right to the door, okay?' he said firmly.

'Okay,' she smiled, giving his arm a little squeeze, and he kissed her lightly on the cheek before disappearing back into the crowds below her.

She continued back down to the bar where Will put a fresh drink in front of her and watched as she lit a cigarette. He scanned the sea of bodies around her in the bar and then turned towards the fridge. He retrieved a single bottle of Budweiser, popped off the cap and poured the contents into a tall glass. ''Ere, this'll put a smile on yer face!' he said, putting the full glass down next to hers on the bar and she gave him a questioning look, then she looked past him and into the mirrored wall behind the bar.

He pressed up behind her and nuzzled his face close to her ear, brushing her hair away from her neck as he did so. Just the glance had been enough and the touch sent her over the edge. She was hot suddenly, and then he spoke. 'I couldn't take another day!' he breathed and she turned to face him, desperate to wrap her arms around him and hold him close to her. Thousands of words were spoken between them in the crowded, smoky room and then they smiled at each other. He took in every feature of her; her hair, her eyes, happier now then when he'd seen her on walking in. The blue outfit that she wore was so pretty and he felt his heart aching in his chest.

'Will,' he nodded the greeting and the older man smiled at him.

'That's better!' Will replied with a smile. 'She's so pretty when she smiles.'

'No, Will, she's pretty all the time!' Michael corrected him.

It was still warm out from the day's heat and coolly they walked through the car park towards where he had parked. It was a darkened corner and she watched him move to open her door for her.

'God I missed you!' he breathed before he bent and kissed her feverishly on the lips, pulling her so close that she could hardly breathe.

'I missed you too!' she said slipping her hands around his waist and feeling the familiar warmth of his body beneath her fingertips. 'I hate it when you're not here.'

'I know, but I'm here now.' She noticed the change in his tone. 'Michael,' she whispered, 'James is at home with Jennifer and besides I have my—'

He stopped her in mid-sentence. 'I know. I can count, you know.' His voice was light but it brooked no argument and she warmed. 'I just want to hold you close,' he finished and she understood him completely. Her bed always seemed too big when she was alone in it, too, and when she woke up alone she always felt like crying out loud so that he would come rushing down the stairs to her.

'So the lovely young Jennifer's there, is she?' he said and he smiled then. That would give him an excuse to sleep in the spare room next to Beth's. James wasn't exactly the quietest of men and on many a night since Jennifer's arrival on the scene he had used it as justification for not being in his own bed.

They were still up when Beth and Michael got through the front door and they could hear them down in the kitchen. Beth led the way down stairs and on seeing Michael behind her, James got up from his seat, embracing his friend warmly.

'When did you get back, you old bastard!' he asked brightly.

'About two hours ago,' Michael said, giving Jennifer a smile over James's shoulder. 'Hello, Jennifer.'

'Hello, Michael,' she replied. She had sat quietly watching the pair of them while Beth had stood at the counter watching her. She was a nice one, Jennifer, Beth thought.

'Did we disturb you?' Beth said lightly. Jennifer had the decency to blush slightly and give off her coy look, the one that made her look more innocent even than Beth.

She liked Beth; she would even go as far as to say that she was growing to love her. But there was something in Beth's eyes that she couldn't pinpoint, something that told her that this young woman had a secret that she was just busting to tell someone. She sometimes thought she was laughing at her and other times she got the impression that Beth understood from a first-hand perspective much, much more about what was going on around her than she ever let on.

That thought made Jennifer smile to herself. She found James's over-protectiveness a little too overbearing, even though it had nothing whatsoever to do with her, if she was honest. He was always giving men in the clubs the evil eye when he saw them get a bit too fresh with her, even more so than when they did it to her. She mused that it was because Beth was one of the world's untouched that he did so; then her eyes went back to Michael.

He was another one, but he fended off the rough in a different way. He didn't even have to raise his voice. Just the lift of an eyebrow could have the same effect as a thousand words when done by Michael. Yes, he was a total contrast to the other two and somehow they all fitted together and lived together in an almost unnatural harmony.

'No, not at all,' she smiled after a long pause, pouring Beth a glass of the white wine that James had just opened and put on the table in front of her. 'Mike, do you want one?' she asked, holding up a glass.

'Sure, go on then!' He settled down at the end of the table nearest to where Beth sat then. James sat back down practically on top of Jennifer and she let him pull her close and hug her. She returned the gesture, and as she did, she noticed Beth look in their direction and then at Michael, the oddest look on her face. He looked up at her from under those thick lashes and a conversation took place although neither said a spoken word.

'How was your mum and dad?' James asked, lighting two cigarettes and handing one to Jennifer.

'Grand, aye. They're coming over soon. Going to stay with Pat and Jude for a few days, but they've invited us all over there later in the year. When we've time. Coming?' he said, looking at Jennifer then, aware that she had been studying both him and Beth since they had come down into the kitchen.

'Really? That'd be right nice!' she said enthusiastically, prodding James with her elbow but he didn't need prompting.

'Oh yes, mate!' he replied, then looking at his sister. 'She needs a rest, Mike. Bin a bit moody last couple of days, know what I mean?'

'You okay?' Michael asked her, then looking concerned. He was aware that there was nothing wrong with her that he couldn't put right, but in front of James and Jennifer, he thought it best to ask.

Chapter Twenty-Seven

September 1998

Clutching a slip file of papers that Pat needed for the Baileys audit that was due to start in the morning, Beth walked slowly across the car park. She was tired and she sighed to herself. She saw James's shiny new BMW parked a couple of cars away and she wondered fleetingly if Michael was with him. She hadn't seen either of them all day and she missed them when they weren't there.

Looking up at the office window she saw the light was on, even though with the club now closed for the night all others were off. She heard light footfalls behind her as she neared the edge of the car park. The steps quickened and whoever it was got closer and then her heart began to race; she could feel that something was desperately wrong. She was about to turn around but didn't have time. In fact she didn't have time to do anything.

She was suddenly face down on the ground between two cars and had landed with a heavy bump. There was something very, very heavy on her back, pinning her there. She realised that it was a human body, a heavy body, a heavy male body. She tried to scream but nothing happened. She'd winded herself with her own arm, hitting herself in the chest when she'd fallen, and all that came out was a deep gasping sound. She could feel hot breath on her neck, the smell of cigarettes was strong and she felt aggressive fingers digging into her shoulder muscles.

'Not a fucking sound, you bitch!' he commanded in a half whisper. Her mind reeled then as his hand roughly found her thigh. 'Oh, I'm gonna enjoy this little job.'

'No! Get off me!' she managed, and he gave her a shove that made her crack her head on the gravel beneath them.

Something snapped deep within her suddenly, and she threw back her head, catching him in the face with a thud. She had to get away. This wasn't going to happen to her, but he was so much stronger than she was.

'Bitch!' he barked roughly.

She squirmed beneath him, spinning her head around to see his face, but she could see nothing in the shadows that now surrounded them. She felt bile in her throat as his hand found her panties. The reality of what was about to happen to her hit her like a physical blow and she seemed to lose all her fight and she lay still in horrific anticipation, her own breath coming in short painful gasps. Feeling the fabric of her underclothes rip beneath his tug, she closed her eyes tight, awaiting the inevitable touch. His fingers pushed at her and she could feel him against her exposed skin. She felt strange then; she had always imagined that women in this situation would put up a real good fight. Scratching and clawing and screaming to keep what was theirs sacred; she'd always imagined herself doing so, anyway. But there in the darkness, on the gravel, on her stomach, she felt nothing at all.

'They say you never forget your first!' he said into her ear with a snigger. She shuddered. This man knew her, and she tried to put his voice to a face that she recognised but she couldn't. All she could see was darkness and a sickening, shameful feeling washed over her.

'Get the fuck off her!' a voice demanded loudly from above, and suddenly she felt the weight of him leave her. She was free and she spun around on the ground just as he landed with a painful-sounding thud, face down on the bonnet of one of the cars they had been on the ground between, denting it. Michael held him down, a terrifying expression on his rugged dark features, his breathing hard.

'You. Fucking. Piece. Of. Scum!' He spat out every word with a bang of his head against the car and he struggled desperately to rise from his unfair, pinned-down position. 'What? Can't you handle playing with the big boys, ey?' His tone was so angry that he sounded as if he were almost laughing.

'Get off me, Elliott!' he yelled, throwing his arms around, aimlessly trying to catch Michael with a lucky blow.

'Not. A. Fucking. Chance!' Michael yelled, suddenly exploding. 'You are a dead man, I'm looking at a dead man. How dare you! How dare you touch her!' He got a firmer grip on the back of his clothes and lifted him off his feet, cracking his head once more on the car's side panel, denting it as he knocked him unconscious.

From out of nowhere Paul appeared. He'd heard the commotion from the doorway and had looked out of reception just as Michael had lifted someone into the air and thrown them down onto the bonnet of a car. He had seen Michael fight many times, but never had he seen anything like that before. Michael never lost his temper. In the few seconds it took him to run across the car park Michael had scooped Beth up in his arms, and on seeing them between the cars Paul faltered.

'He didn't!' Beth began, her voice urgent.

Planting kisses on her hair and face he hushed her. 'Hush now, I know he didn't, my darling!' Michael said, his voice now soft despite his breathing, and as he looked back at him he thought, *Yes—That's the only reason he's still alive.*

'Oh, no!' Paul breathed.

Michael looked up at him, one arm supporting Beth's head, the other now stroking the side of her face.

'No!' Michael said firmly and Paul's features flickered with relief at the answer to the unspoken question.

Paul looked a little closer at the man spreadeagled on the bonnet, blood running from somewhere on his head, presumably his nose.

'Fuck me! It's King!' he exclaimed, sounding very shocked.

'I know it's King,' Michael barked, and then he turned his attention back to Beth, who was clinging to him with her fingers so tight that his flesh ached. 'You're okay now, my darling,' he breathed into her ear. 'I'm here. It's all okay now.'

He lifted her to her feet and pulled his jacket off his broad frame in one swift movement. 'Let's get you inside, come on now.' He looked up at Paul who was feeling a little bit out on a limb. It was obvious to Michael that he had never been in this kind of situation before and that he was unsure of what to do.

'Is everyone gone?' Michael asked, referring to the club patrons and Paul nodded at him.

'Yeah. I was just gonna lock the main doors when I—' He stopped in mid-sentence and took a deep breath. 'Yeah,' he said again, but this time he didn't go on in detail. Michael didn't look as if he needed chapter and verse right at that moment in time.

'Go and get someone to help you inside with that!' he said, nodding his head towards the car behind them and Paul nodded again before setting off towards the club doors.

Once inside the club Beth was seated on one of the sofas in the bar, Michael's jackets still tight around her shoulders.

'Pat's on his way,' Frank said, putting the glass of brandy that Michael had asked for down on the low table. 'And Dawn's found Jimmy for you, mate!' he finished and the two men looked at one another thoughtfully. 'What else?' He awaited more instructions from Michael. This was a very, very weird place to be right now.

'Nothing, yet. Thanks.' Michael locked eyes with him and the anger in them was evident. He shook his head and then turned his attention back to Beth. 'Drink this,' he said, holding the glass to her lips and she sipped the liquid, coughing as it reached her throat.

A few minutes later Paul walked up to them, his face was pale. 'Mike. You got a sec?' he asked, his tone neutral but his face far from it.

He gave Beth the once over. She'd been a lucky, lucky girl.

'Sure,' Michael breathed, standing up from his crouched position in front of Beth, and turning to face him. He stared at him for a long moment and then in hushed voices the two men spoke.

'He's in the cellar,' Paul said.

'Who's with him?' Michael was clipped.

'Steve, and he's not impressed, Mike. Says if he moves, he'll kill him,' Paul stated flatly.

'Good.' Michael liked his choice. Steve really wouldn't be impressed with this little get-up at all. He really liked Beth. They all did and tonight's warmth proved it.

'Not that I care, but he's in a bad way, mate,' Paul added.

'Good.'

Michael's tone was cold enough to send a shiver up Paul's spine and fleetingly he did feel sorry for Nick King. 'I think we should dump him in case he croaks,' he said bluntly.

'We'll wait for Pat!' Michael's tone brooked no argument and Paul nodded before disappearing out of the bar again.

Everyone heard James arrive with Pat. James was yelling the place down without actually saying a word. He slammed doors and his footfalls on the floor were hard. With anxious features the two entered the bar.

'Where is she!' he exclaimed, looking wildly around the empty bar. 'Babe! Oh, Babe!' he breathed, landing next to Beth on the sofa and taking her in his arms.

'I'm all right,' she said, sounding stronger than she was really feeling at that moment.

'What was you fucking doing?' he asked, he sounded relieved and angry and pent-up all at once.

'I was dropping off the papers for the audit,' she breathed.

Pat let out a groan and all eyes went to him.

'I'm okay!' she said then, looking at him.

'Oh, Bethy,' he sighed. He made eye contact with Michael, who still stood silently beside her like a dark angel. Pat got the urge to hug him at that moment. He'd been there. He'd saved her. There was an unspoken conversation between them and then, only after a long pause, were a few words spoken out loud.

'Where?' Pat said flatly.

'Outside,' Michael replied.

'Did he—' it was unfinished.

'No!' and Michael's tone had a grateful edge to it.

'Is he still—' Pat started.

'Yes. For now,' and boom, there it was, the Michael he knew and loved.

'Good. Where?' Pat asked.

'In the cellar with Steve,' came Michael's reply.

'Who knows?' it was numbers time.

'All in here, no one else!' Michael was flat.

'Good. Keep it that way,' Pat said firmly and Michael nodded in agreement.

James looked up at them. There was naked hate in his eyes then. He'd been so wrapped up in Beth that he hadn't bothered to ask if her attacker was still there, or if he'd got away. 'He's still 'ere! I'll fuckin' kill him! The dirty stinkin' bastard!' He rose from his position and went to speak again.

Pat held up his hand to silence him. 'Take Bethy home, James! Judy'll meet you there. We'll follow you in a while—' He looked briefly at Michael and then back at James; he saw the protest on James's face.

'Don't argue, son, we'll deal with it!' He had spoken and it was final. He pulled his mobile phone from his coat pocket to call his wife and get her to go to their house. He knew that Beth didn't need her, but he wanted someone to look her over and thought it had best be a woman. She'd had enough male attention for one night.

Beth looked up then and her eyes met Michael's. She looked sad but not as shaken as she had before and he smiled gently down at her.

'You ready to go?' Michael asked in a low tone of voice, and she nodded at him, unaware that Pat was watching every move and gesture as he spoke to his wife in brief hushed tones. He saw the expression on Michael's face and something inside him tingled inside like someone had run their fingers up his neck.

'Come on, Babe,' James said in a more controlled tone, taking her hand in his. She let him help her to her feet and she slipped Michael's suit jacket on properly, taking in the smell of him upon it. A faint smile crossed her lips when she looked up at him.

'I'll come back!' James said then and he stared deeply at his uncle.

'We'll deal with it!' Pat said firmly to James's unspoken question of what would be happening to the scum that had attacked his baby sister.

'You do that!' he said sounding aggressive.

'Don't you go worrying about that now. You just get Elizabeth home' Michael added, and he and James looked thoughtfully at each other for a long moment.

'Thank you, Michael,' Beth said softly, brushing close to him. He took a deep breath and nodded slowly at her. He didn't know what to say to her in front of all these people. He wanted desperately to hold her in his arms and comfort her but he couldn't and as clearly as it was on her face, it was on his. They couldn't go on like this and the reality of the fact hurt them both more than anything else anyone could say or do.

'We'll see you in a while!' Pat said, breaking into their thoughts.

Once they were gone Michael followed Pat silently down into the cellar. It was starkly lit with strip lighting and Nick King was slumped in a corner, bleeding. He opened an eye as the door opened but neither Pat nor Michael thought he could have seen much through it.

'I didn't tell anyone to touch him!' Pat said loudly and Steve looked at Paul and then at Michael. They were panicked. Pat at the best of times was bad, but Pat pissed off was something else entirely.

'We ain't!' Steve said abruptly, standing up from his perch on one of the metal barrels.

'Don't be daft, man. Look at it, for fuck's sake!' Pat snapped, pointing a finger at the mess on the floor before them as Paul closed the door.

'They haven't touched him,' Michael said quietly from just behind Pat's shoulder and he turned to look at him.

'You did that?' Pat said sounding a little more surprised than he actually was. 'God, Mike, he's—he's a fucking mess!'

Michael's face didn't change. 'He is!' was all that Michael said. He felt nothing except pure hate for the man before them.

Pat looked into his face. His mind was reeling. In all his years he'd never seen anything like this mess, and he went over what Paul had said had happened in his mind in case he'd missed the bit where Michael had actually hit him. If what Paul had said, was what had actually happened. No, it couldn't be, he must have missed something. It literally looked as if someone had stamped on King's face a few times. His eyes were both split and the rest of his face was swelling at a rapid pace, with his jaw fractured, at the least, along with one eye socket. No one could have done all that damage without any punches. They would have had to have been in a blind rage and that wasn't Michael's style at all.

He looked at Michael again then. 'And you reckon you didn't actually hit 'im?' he asked finally.

'No, I didn't actually hit him.' Michael sounded very controlled and cool, and that alone sent another shiver up Pat's spine. Pat stood there and desperately wanted to make an example of King. How dare Oxley do this! She was nothing but a baby. And he was willing to do that to her for what? Some bricks, some mortar. It was sick. He got the urge to kick him then, as he lay slumped on the floor, and then the idea entered his head to have him raped. He knew some really lovely people across the bridge that would just love a bit of fresh white meat. But he couldn't decide—

'What to do?' Michael said coldly, bringing Pat back to the present.

'Is there much more you could do to it?' he asked. He saw Michael's expression change then and his previous thoughts shot to the forefront of his mind.

'Steve. Paul. Get rid of it, play with it if you like. Don't kill it, for fuck's sake, but get rid of it. Come on Mike,' Pat said, calmly turning and walking from the cellar.

Once outside, Pat leaned on the roof of James's car and waited for Michael to unlock it, but he didn't. Instead he walked further into the car park. Pat stared after him and then followed. The first thing he saw was the bonnet of the car, lit now by the lights, which would be on all night every night from now on. Their club wasn't going to get the reputation for being unsafe and he was even more angry. He watched Michael bend down and pick up the file, and something else. He put the something else into his pocket, then he turned.

'This was for you,' he said, handing Pat the file.

'And what was that?' Pat replied, looking down Michael's body to his pocket.

There was a long pause and then Michael let out a long sigh. 'Her underwear,' he said bluntly. 'I don't think it's something to have lying around, do you?'

Pat nodded at him; what could he say to that? Michael was just protecting her dignity.

Judy helped Beth off with the remainder of her clothes and examined her from top to toe. She sat on the bath edge with Beth standing before her. She had some gravel grazes and bruises on both her knees. A red bump was coming out on the side of her head and a cut from her own tooth was on the inside of her lip, but other than that, there was nothing physically wrong with her and Judy felt the relief rush through her like her blood itself.

'My poor baby!' she soothed after turning the shower on and Beth looked into her eyes.

'I'm okay, really,' Beth said bravely.

'I know you are. You were lucky Michael was there.' She smiled and Beth stepped under the hot water without saying another word.

Not long after that Beth snuggled down into her bed and Judy pulled the duvet up to her chin.

'That's it,' Judy soothed. 'Now, you get some sleep. We'll be downstairs if you need anything. Unless you want me to stay here?'

'No, thanks. I'm gonna get some sleep.'

When Beth had settled into the big bed Judy walked back down the stairs and down into the kitchen. The three men looked quizzically at her.

'Is she okay?' James asked.

'Yeah, she'll be okay,' she breathed. 'Just keep an eye on her ,ey boys?'

'Should we maybe call a doctor?' Michael suggested, knowing full well that in their circles you had to be dying before you called out a doctor.

'No, no. She's okay, really! Just a few cuts and bruises is all.' Judy kept her voice light although it was evident that they were all concerned for Beth's general wellbeing; there were sessions for this sort of thing. Pat leaned back in the chair and watched Michael light himself a cigarette. He couldn't help getting the feeling that he was waiting for something.

Michael looked at him, his entire face still hard, but his eyes sparkling with some unspoken secret. Pat went to speak, but couldn't think of anything worthwhile to say and he found that it was he who averted his gaze first.

'I'd better call Jen,' James said with a sigh as Michael followed him back down to the kitchen after seeing Pat and Judy out. 'She was well worried. Wanted to come over and everything!' He sounded gratified.

'It's still early,' Michael commented, glancing at his watch.

'What is the time?'

'Almost five.'

'I'll go check on her, ay?' James was like a cat on a hot tin roof.

'Leave her be.' Michael almost smiled at James's concern. 'Judy said she was asleep. Call your Jennifer, tell her that Elizabeth's okay,' he suggested.

'Yeah!' James sighed, he was feeling a little bit lost now that everything seemed a little more normal, although he was still a bit pissed at the fact that King had been let go. He'd have killed him, he thought, made it hurt real bad. *Touch my baby sister, Fucking tosser.* Then he stopped. No, no, he wouldn't have. That would just cause even more aggro, and aggro was something they'd had enough of for one day.

'I'll just let her know what's going on!' he breathed.

Michael listened as James gave Jennifer a brief rundown on the night's events. He could almost see her in his mind, being genuinely worried for her young friend. 'No, I'll see ya later. I'm fine. Yeah, I know, go on. Get back to bed.' He cleared the call and looked across at Michael.

'You can tell her you love her in front of me, you know. I'll not laugh at you!' Michael said then.

'Shut up, fool!' James said. Michael could have sworn he saw him redden. He'd been rumbled.

'Is she okay?'

'Yeah. She offered to come over but—' He stopped and looked at Michael.

'Will you just go!' Michael laughed then. 'I'll call if Elizabeth needs you.'

'I should stay!'

'Why? So you can drive me crazy! She'll be fine. I'll stay up. Just go on, will you!' He was smiling then. James walked towards the stairs and stopped in his tracks, turning back around to face him.

'Thanks, Mike,' he said softly, and the two men looked warmly into each other's eyes. 'Not just for tonight, but for everything. I couldn't have done any of this without you! You know that, don't you?' and he motioned with his hand around the room.

Michael understood him well and he smiled at his friend.

'Go on,' he laughed. The emotion emanating from James was strange and Michael thought that if they continued to talk one, if not both, would cry. And so, without anything else being said, James disappeared up the stairs.

Michael stood in the dining area and lit himself a cigarette. He was letting the emotions from the past hours clear from his system. He wanted calmness and clarity, just for a while.

Taking a few seconds to steady his breath after dashing up the stairs, he opened Elizabeth's bedroom door silently and stepped inside, closing it behind him. The curtains were closed and it was quite dark so he made his way carefully across the room to the edge of the bed.

He settled his gaze upon her, letting his eyes adjust to the light. Her eyes were open and for a few seconds they just stared at each other. He took in a long breath as if breathing again after the longest time, tears threatening to well up in his dark eyes.

'You okay?' he managed to whisper, and she nodded at him. Then suddenly he was kneeling on the bed, the duvet was off her and she was in his arms. He was kissing her skin with soft lips and running his hands over and under her pyjama-covered body as if he was brushing Nicolas King off of her skin for good.

'Oh, my God, I love you!' he whispered breathlessly as he took her face in his strong hands. 'My Elizabeth! I love you so much! I wanted to hold you so much!' He paused and looked down into her eyes, his expression full of longing.

'I love you too, I wanted you to hold me. Michael, I was so scared!' she whispered.

'She said you were okay? I've been out of my mind down there!'

'I'm fine now you're here!'

'I am that! And I'm not going anywhere.' He kissed her again 'God, I was so angry! He hurt you!'

'My pride more than anything!'

He laughed at her tone. She was such a strong-willed little thing.

'I never thought they'd do it!' she breathed.

'Neither did I—' he replied honestly.

'How's your head?' he said, running his fingers lightly across her forehead and the bump upon it. 'Filthy scum' he continued, and although his voice was light Beth could hear the underlying tone of hate there.

'It hurts—' she paused. 'It's not the end, is it?' she sighed, settling almost on top of him on the bed and he wrapped his arms around her, pulling her close to him.

'No, it's not!'

'Is he dead?' she asked, keeping her tone neutral.

'No, not dead! Not comfortable, but not dead.'

'What happened? I gather he was a bit of a mess!'

'They dumped him outside the Royal. He'll think twice before ever touching something—' he stopped himself in mid-sentence, his features softening again. 'I mean, something so precious.'

Beth touched his hand with her own; she felt him wince slightly. How much damage had he done, she wondered? She was trying to remember every little detail but couldn't, it was in little snip bits.

'I couldn't get him off me!' she whispered as Michael ran his fingers through her hair. 'He was so heavy. He was laughing at me, Michael. He was laughing at me. Maybe I should surrender and become a fucking secretary or something. Judy's right, this is a man's game—' She breathed back the tears that were welling up in her eyes.

'No!' he breathed. 'No surrendering, we're not quitters, do you hear!' He gave her a gentle squeeze and she nodded. 'And as for this being a man's game, not many could have got a full-grown lump like him off their backs. Women aren't designed that way. No one expected you to be able to fight him off. You should never have been in that position in the first place and we all know it!' He sounded earnest and she eased as he spoke.

She knew he was right, knew that she was good at her job, the PR queen. It had just never occurred to her before just how vulnerable she really was and how much she relied upon, and hid behind, the others. Well that was something that was going to change. If Oxley, the skinny little prick, wanted to fight, then so be it.

Michael felt her stance change in his arms and knew almost word for word what it was that she was thinking and he had to admit to himself that he had the same plans as she did. This was far from over. If anything, a whole new game was now about to be played and they had every intention of winning it.

Chapter Twenty-Eight

October 1998

There was a spot under two large oak trees that was perfect for a picnic despite the threatening winter chill in the air. The four of them sat on the ground, wrapped up in winter woollies like pale-faced Eskimos. James opened a bottle of red wine with a purposeful pop and poured it out into four large plastic beakers with stems just like real wineglasses.

''Ere, d'you remember the first time we did this?' he asked, looking at Beth and Michael in turn. He squeezed Jennifer's hand, a sign of affection and that even though they spoke of the past and days gone by, she was still at the forefront of his mind. He waited a second or two and then she squeezed her warm reply to him.

'Yes, I do,' Michael smiled warmly.

Warm old memories came to the fore and there was a moment of comfortable silence as they were all wrapped up in their thoughts of years gone by. It had been a warm summer day; that memory was sure in their minds. The sky had been clear and blue and the only sounds around had been wildlife and the sounds of their laughter. They had all been there. Eve, Jim and Michael, Andy and Louise with Beth and James, along with Pat and Judy too. It had been their first trip to the hotel so it must have been the summer of eighty-seven. Eve and Jim had bought the house in the spring, and the summer was the first time all of them had been able to get away together. They'd packed two old-fashioned hampers with food and drink and had walked the half a mile to the spot where the four sat now, years later and all grown up. They'd eaten and drunk and laughed into the early evening.

'What was your mum like?' Jennifer asked James as she lay with her head in his lap. There was silence and she wished then that she hadn't asked. He didn't know quite what to say, and he looked across at his sister.

'Beautiful.' Beth whispered a reply. She smiled at her brother and then at Jennifer. 'She was a beautiful person, inside and outside. She had a way with people. Everybody loved her,' Beth smiled.

'Like you!' Jennifer smiled too then. Beth let out a tinkling laugh and that sound inspired both men. Jennifer was right. Elizabeth was just like her mother.

'No, my mum was really beautiful!' Beth said, sounding embarrassed suddenly.

'Oh, and you're not?' Michael said without thinking and all eyes went to him. 'Well, she is!' he exclaimed.

'She is,' James breathed. 'Another day, Jen. Another day I'll tell you about me mum, and me dad. Not today, ay?' and he kissed her on the forehead.

'Okay,' she whispered.

After a rather large dinner that evening, the four sat in the lounge, crammed around the fireplace. There were plenty of chairs about, but that evening was one of warmth and comfort and one of being with the people you cared for the most. They talked quietly so as not to disturb the guests that milled around. Their whispered tones didn't stay that way for long and it was only minutes before a loud outburst of laughter. James stood up from his seat and settled his gaze on the flames. They licked and curled at the logs in the hearth and for a long moment he was silent. Michael felt his stomach turn over beneath his jumper and for a second or two his eyes met with Beth's. He knew what was coming and the reality of it startled him. He never thought he'd hear or see James do what he was about to do, even though after their earlier conversation he was aware of the intention.

'I remember the way me dad used to look at me mum.' James paused and looked at Beth for a second or two, a smile on his lips. 'He'd eat her up in a glance and I never understood it, what they had.

Not like I do now. I understand it now, more than I did yesterday.'He took in a deep breath as he turned and looked down into Jennifer's large blue eyes. He could feel himself drifting away in her gaze. 'Oh yeah, I understand it now all right!'

He bent down before her on the carpet and she squirmed in her seat, aware that tears were welling in her eyes and that both Beth and Michael were almost on the edges of their own seats in anticipation.

'Jen, I love you and I know you love me. What do you say? Will you marry me? Be my wife!'

As he spoke, he opened his right hand and enclosed within his grasp was an engagement ring. It was a knot of gold and diamonds. It was lovely.

'Be your wife?' Jennifer's voice broke through the silence and James nodded at her, his features sincere.

'Wife. No muckin' about! Just you and me!' He sounded odd, like someone else other than James. He was being quite romantic and it sounded really weird. No wonder he was so popular with the ladies, if he could swoon like that. It was something Beth had never paid too much mind to, how he managed it; all she knew was that he did it.

'Yes, James. Yes, I will,' she managed as the tears came.

He scooped her up then and held her in his arms, ring on finger.

The weekend after their return from Ireland the doorbell rang and Beth pulled the lock on the solid wood panel from its stay. Jennifer stood on the step, her cheek flushed from the cold, her petite frame wrapped in a warm, rich-looking overcoat. The two stared at each other for a long while just smiling.

'Welcome!' Beth said. Her tone was light, and she saw Jennifer visibly relax before her.

'Is this okay with you?' Her tone was tight as she waited nervously for Beth to reply. With all of the excitement and the merry congratulations, Jennifer hadn't had time to speak to Beth about the events of the last week, although she was aware that James had; probably before he'd even asked her, if she was honest with herself and it was decided.

'Okay?' Beth laughed. 'It's more than okay. I've got myself a new sister! Someone to shop with! Someone to hang with! I'm thrilled!' Beth smiled widely, and before Jennifer could say any more she was being dragged over the threshold and down into the kitchen.

The two sat at the dining table. The idea of coffee was gone and now a wine bottle sat open on the table.

'Michael's going to move downstairs, next to me, permanently so you two'll have some privacy,' Beth said casually as they chatted, and Jennifer smiled at her.

'I don't want to turf him out,' Jennifer said, suddenly sounding awkward. 'I don't want to be any trouble!'

'Rubbish! It's no trouble. This is your home too, now, and I for one hope that you're very happy here with us.' Beth smiled at her and Jennifer could feel her warmth. She was really and truly a brilliant little pal to have and on top of that, they'd be more that pals, they'd be family. 'Is your stuff in the car?'

'Yeah. There's lots of it too. Mostly clothes and shoes though!' She laughed and Beth laughed with her. If there was one thing they did have in common it was their capacity for shopping until they dropped.

'We'll leave that for the boys to deal with though, ey!' Beth smiled. She looked at Jennifer. She looked awkward again.

'What? Am I talking too much? I'm sorry, it's just that I'm excited. I want you to know, that's all!'

'I'm fine if you're fine. It's just, well—There is one thing Beth. I wanted to ask you!'

'Anything,' Beth beamed. 'I've been thinking, and before you say it, no, it wasn't James's idea. I want you to be my bridesmaid, my maid of honour.'

November 1998

After maybe an hour of watching from the sidelines, stairwells and balcony Michael finally wandered down, then up to the D.J. stand. He spoke briefly, and then after another few minutes he walked up behind Beth on the dance floor and let his fingers slide up and down her sides. *G Spot* came through the speakers the second he was close to her and she could feel him moving with the beat of the music. She wiggled her body close to his with a lambada type motion in her hips and they rocked together in time with the music.

'They're watching,' she breathed as his hand settled on her hip.

'I don't care. You can't keep dancing like that without me,' he replied, his voice low, his lips close to her ear. To the trained eye it was clear to see that these two were intimate, very intimate indeed.

She turned around and leaned back, letting her hair almost touch the floor behind her. He pulled her back up and pushed right into her, feeling the warmth of her body against his own.

'So, what you doing later?' she asked lightly.

'Making mad passionate, hot and steamy love to the most amazing woman I've ever met in my entire life,' he replied.

'Who's that then?' she laughed and he gazed into her eyes.

'What? You need reminding?' he caught her as she spun.

'Absolutely.' She was laughing again. It was a sound he loved, and it made him want to kiss her then, right in the middle of the dance floor, with her big brother and the rest of the world watching. She saw the expression on his face and squeezed his arm. 'We'll show them one day,' she breathed.

From the balcony James and Jennifer watched, fascinated as the pair moved together. 'You know they practise this in the house?' James laughed with a shake of his head.

'Yeah, I know. I've seen it.' She smiled and linked her arm in his. 'How did it start?' She was intrigued. She'd watched them together and saw something. She couldn't pinpoint it. She didn't think it wasn't sexual. But it was a bond, something that ran deep.

'Michael was teaching her to dance, coz as you know, I have two left feet.' They both laughed then, knowing that to be true of James when it came to dancing slowly. 'I dunno exactly, but it went from there. There's something about this tune—' he pointed casually around them and she nodded.

'She was teaching me, but I ain't no way as good as that!' Jennifer laughed then, imagining James and Michael at home, alone and dancing to this song.

'Come on, come and show me your moves. Dance with me!' she purred and only seconds later they too took to the floor. James took Beth from Michael's grasp and they back-to-backed, crouching almost to the floor and then back up again. Michael grabbed Jennifer by the waist and they too began to move slowly in time with the music.

'You two dance well together,' she said into his ear. He turned his head and looked into her eyes, he saw the suggestion there.

'Well, she was an attentive student,' he replied, deliberately giving her food for thought.

She looked into those big brown eyes of his and almost blushed. He was hot, a hot-blooded man, and his power emanated like sweat. The song ended and another began, they didn't falter. This was a night to really let their hair down, and they certainly did. It was rare that two songs by the same artist were played together but Matthew could hardly believe his eyes and he let the Wayne Marshall CD play on. When the next song ended and the four left the floor there was a round of applause and cheering from the staff and club goers alike. They revelled in the limelight, bowed and then went up to the top bar and sat at a free table.

'Beer. I need beer!' James called, banging his hands on the table 'What you having?' he asked loudly.

'G and T?' This from Jennifer.

'Bud!' Michael replied with a nod of his head.

'Elizabeth?' and she thought.

'Coke!' came her response.

'Bullshit! She'll have a vodka!' Michael said with a wave of his hand. 'We'll get a cab home!'

Chapter Twenty-Nine

Late November 1998

'Wait here. We won't be long,' James said as he opened the door and got out of the back of Michael's car. Beth looked at him through the window and then at across at Michael. He paused in his seat, half in, half out of the car.

'We'll be no more than quarter of an hour, I promise. Beep the horn if you need us, okay?' he added. He smiled then, but it didn't quite reach his eyes.

'We shouldn't 'ave bought 'er,' James commented as they walked across the car park. 'Pat'll have a fit.'

'She knows what's going on, James. I'm wondering whether or not we should actually bring her in.' He paused in mid-step, flicking his cigarette away. 'They mean business, but if we show that we're not scared—' He didn't finish his sentence and instead opened the entrance door.

Beth watched them go inside and then glanced at the clock on the dashboard. It was eighteen minutes past twelve.

Almost half an hour after James and Michael had gone in, the main entrance door of the Fox opened again and Beth walked in, her long-legged stride purposeful. She almost barged though the overweight man who was passing as a doorman, standing by the cigarette vending machine. He was obviously there to stop just anybody going in when the pub was only open by invitation, purely by looking at them. There was no way that this man was a fighter and she counted on it as they made eye contact.

'I'm with them!' she said sharply, pointing to the table in the centre of the smoke-filled room. As she continued to walk towards them she scanned the pub. She counted four men, which was about right for the three cars in the car park out the back. The man at the door, who was neither use nor ornament; one at the far end of the bar, one propping up the bar and King. He was close to where Oxley was now seated. That man really was like the grim reaper, always lurking in the background looking nondescript.

She was within a few feet of the table where James, Michael and Sean Oxley sat when the man she had seen standing by the far door began to move towards her. Oxley raised his hand to him and he stopped in mid-step.

'Elizabeth,' he said, standing up and motioning for her to take a seat. She disliked him quite intensely, and this really wasn't lost on him at all.

'I'll stand!' she replied, her voice like ice as she made eye contact with him and then with James and Michael in turn.

'What are you doing? I told you to wait in the car!' James said, his irritation evident, but Michael locked eyes with him, shaking his head for him not to go on.

She couldn't just walk into this kind of meeting unannounced, James thought. But for all that, he was grateful for the intervention at that moment. Badly and heatedly were understatements as to how the meeting was going.

'Get cold in the car, did you?' Michael asked her, his voice was light and it made the men near them look at him. 'My coat was in the back!'

She looked at him, her eyes sparkling as he spoke. 'Yeah, I saw that' she replied.

James listened to her tone and turned his head upwards slightly so that they were then face to face. Two pairs of green eyes met and there was a mischievous sparkle in both.

'We were talking business, Miss Dobson,' Oxley said interrupting them.

'For God sake! Haven't we had this conversation?' she snapped at him. 'Don't you get it yet? Nothing can be done without all four of us agreeing on a sale and no matter what you do, that isn't going to happen. You know, I'm surprised you've done so well for yourself, Mr. Oxley.'

Always polite, Michael thought listening to her.

'Because for a business man, you just a fucking childish idiot.'

Maybe not, he corrected himself with a lift of an eyebrow.

'You're very sure of yourself, little lady,' he said, his tone patronising. 'Let me rephrase, we were talking big boy business. Are you a big boy?' The air became very cold as the two stood eyeing each other.

'Are you?' she replied. It wasn't a retort, it was an honest question. 'Starting fires, screwing suppliers—' she paused. 'Having women attacked and nearly raped!' Her eyes went to King then and he at least had the decency to look away, giving her a side view of his twisted nose and the still-to-heal damage to the side of his face.

'You don't know what you're talking about, Miss Dobson,' Oxley breathed. He was unsure of her then. She was hiding something, something big.

'I grow tired of this same old, same old,' she said, her tone sounding bored and Oxley almost laughed at her front.

'Get rid of her! But gently!' he said suddenly, with a flick of his hand.

James went to move, but Michael caught him, sitting him down again, and before any of Oxley's men had moved, from nowhere Beth pulled out a dull black handgun and pointed it at him. All eyes went to her. The room fell silent.

'Fuck me!' James exclaimed. His features were shocked but his tone, almost amused.

'Good girl!' Michael said in a half whisper as he gave James a knowing nod of his head.

'They touch me and I kill you! How do you like *that* offer?' She looked into Oxley's eyes and for a moment she could have sworn that she saw his lips moving in prayer for his life. He honestly thought that she was about to shoot him dead in the middle of his flagship public house. There she was, surrounded by some of the toughest men in England and she had the balls of brass to walk into the pub and start waving a gun around. It was priceless.

'Where in the fuck?' Oxley began in question as to where she would have gotten access to a gun from, and then he looked into Michael's eyes; he was almost smiling.

Out of the corner of her eye, Beth saw King move slightly and a strange look crossed her features, it was almost pleasure and then that look was gone, replaced by a blank, almost featureless cold face. King edged from foot to foot and Beth settled her eyes back on his.

'Oh, please do! Give me an excuse!'

He looked into her eyes. There was no hate there, in fact she looked as cold and calculated as any villain he had seen before. Fleetingly, he looked across at his employer, the expression on his face making it quite clear that he was taking the young woman in front of them very seriously indeed.

'This is going to stop now, Mr. Oxley,' she said, lowering the gun. 'We're not going to sell and you're *going* to quit.' It wasn't a suggestion. 'You're going to quit because someone's going to get hurt soon and this won't be the game you all think it is now!'

She didn't just look at him and his men as she spoke, as she was aware that both James and Michael were enjoying this feud in their own ways too. It was a test of manhood and she was going to put a stop to it before someone was actually killed.

'Be honest, you don't even want the house now, do you? It's just a case of winning, saving face now, isn't it?' There was silence as they all took in her words. 'I'm aware of what this meeting is about. Not everyone treats me like china, Mr. Oxley.' All eyes then went to Michael. 'We're quite a suspicious family. We've learned the hard way about trust. So you can talk to these two till you're blue in the face. They won't budge, they know who to trust. And you are not on that short and distinguished list. Oh, and if you think that having me raped, attacked or just fucking me is going to make them sway, then please step into the back, we'll get it over with and then you'll know for sure!' She looked around the room. 'Or maybe you'd like to trash another car. Start more fights in the clubs. Break into our house again, it was a personal favourite of mine, you know!' She raised an eyebrow as she heard her brother's intake of breath.

That was years ago. How in the hell did she know about that? He looked at Michael and he shook his head at James. He hadn't told her.

Both men stood up then. It was time to leave. They'd made their statement of unity in front of him and if Oxley pushed Beth any further, she'd probably shoot him and then they'd have to explain it all to Pat. If he even knew that she'd gone with them to the meet he'd have someone's bollocks off and James had the sneaking suspicion that it would be his.

'I think what she's trying to say is that no means no, Mr. Oxley,' Michael said as he took the gun from her grasp and tucked it into his trouser waistband. 'We came here today in good faith. You had no intention of letting us leave until you'd won. Well, you lost and we're leaving.'

He watched as James led Beth towards the door. They weren't stopped and within seconds were outside and out of earshot.

'Oh, and one more thing. If so much as one hair on her head is ever, ever and I mean ever, touched by any of yours again, I'll kill you myself.' His tone was as hard as his features and Oxley looked into his eyes. He knew that moving on Beth had been a mistake. In fact, he hadn't slept well in months. He was waiting for revenge, but none had come. He'd hoped they would have buckled, but instead, they'd grown stronger and it had come to this. He was the hunted. He could have given the order to have them killed where they stood, but he wasn't confident enough that the job would be finished. He was confident, however, that Michael would keep his word and he nodded at him before he watched him leave the pub.

Pat stared at James as if he had grown another head right there before his eyes. His mouth was set open and he took in a couple of deep breaths through his nose.

'What in God's name made you take 'er in the first place? Christ, Jimmy. You're a fucking wonder to me sometimes. Are you mad, boy? Putting her in harm's way like that. Your dad'd turn in his grave!'

James stood still; he couldn't think of anything to say to him that wouldn't drop Michael right in it. They'd agreed to take her along together. Well, it wasn't one or the other really and if he were honest with himself, he knew that Beth was going to go regardless of what he or Michael said.

'I know it might cause some grief!' James managed.

Pat was off again and he got up from his seat.

'Some grief! Some fucking grief! She's their one way in and you two practically give her to them!'

Beth stood up then. 'Don't you start, I'm here too. You can talk to me!' Beth interrupted, but Pat carried on as if he hadn't heard her.

'And I ain't even started about the fucking gun yet!'

His voice rose and he was about to go on when Michael walked into the office and close the door behind him. The latch clicked and Pat was verbally upon him.

'And you! You're supposed to be looking out for her, not letting her wave fucking guns around. You know, I heard about this over an hour ago! Where in the hell have you lot been?'

'Pat, will you just calm down,' Michael said, his voice soothing in the frosty air within the office. He settled himself down on the edge of the sofa as if he didn't have a care in the world.

'Calm down?' Pat bellowed and Michael nodded at him, a smile toying with his lips.

'It was beautiful. She was brilliant!' he said finally.

'She wasn't supposed to be there!' Pat replied.

'You said—your exact words were, "I don't care what it takes, just get it sorted" Michael remarked and he felt James's eyes on him. He turned slightly and looked directly at him. 'Sorry,' he shrugged, 'But it wouldn't have been the same, had you known it was going to happen.'

'What?' James was almost laughing, he was so surprised. 'You knew she was going to do that?' He was almost gabbling his words as he looked at Michael, then Beth, then back at Michael.

'Can I talk now, has the testosterone level dropped enough?' Beth asked, walking across the office to where Michael sat. 'Yes James! Michael knew. Michael planned it. Not all of it, obviously, but most of it.' She paused and looked at Pat then.

'And the gun?' he asked.

She nodded and he closed his eyes and opened them again with a shake of his head. 'So please don't be angry with them.' She smiled and Pat was undone. Even he hadn't seen this one coming. Those two were too close for comfort sometimes.

'Oh come on now, Pat, you'd have been so very proud of her! She was magnificent!' Michael said, giving Beth a light tap on the back. 'In she walked, head high. I swear, butter wouldn't have melted.'

'She *was* good,' James added then, finding his voice again after staring at them for the longest time.

'And what was the outcome of this little outing, Mister Elliott?' Pat sounded more at ease then, as well as totally intrigued.

'Well, I think they just realised that Elizabeth plays a rough game,' he breathed. 'I also think he'll not quit. We'll have to finish this one ourselves.' His tone was flat then as he spoke. 'We saw the land lie, true, but we also ruffled his tail feathers. I think we're in for some rough weather, but it'll end it, one way or another.'

Oxley sat in the armchair in the corner of his office and stared out of the window at the rain as it fell in large noisy drops. All he could hear in his mind was his own voice saying the same thing over and over again. *The fucking balls on her.* These words continued until he was almost dizzy inside. Each well-played-out plan had thus far failed. And he shuddered as he thought of the last idea King had had at unsettling their little empire. That had been a poor move, a very bad and extremely poor move. Plus it had totally backfired. He was still smarting over it too. He'd had no idea that King would actually do the deed himself. The last time they'd had to send such a message out across the smoke, they'd had a couple of Yardies from the south deal with it, so as to have been a safe distance away despite getting the point of power across. When he'd seen King in the hospital, he'd thought about actually putting a pillow over his sedated face himself. Who in their right mind did that? Who actually raped, themselves? *A rapist, that's who*, a voice inside said, and he nodded at himself in silent reply. He didn't actually like King, but he got the job done, usually. They'd divided and conquered across England to build up their stock of the best clubs and bars and businesses, but the Dobson Elliott empire was still a sticking point, and the more they dug their heels in, the more he wanted what they had. Theirs were the best venues in the North London area and they were making a fortune. He paused and thought for a moment more. Imagine what he could make if he added his usual mix of drugs and sex to the mix. He rubbed sore temples. She was right. This was a stalemate if ever there was one, and unless he could come up with something hard and fast, he'd actually consider leaving well alone for a while.

February 1999

Even the bitter wind that blew down the centre of the market stalls and the greyness of the day couldn't quieten the sounds of the traders calling. The sound of different radio stations playing on blown speakers was almost relaxing and the low din of people bustling to and fro between bargains was easy. Beth held one bag; it contained a pair of black leather boots that she had been unable to resist as she wandered slowly up the lane, looking at every stall. If there was something that Beth liked, it was a bargain. She heard the unmistakable sound of her mobile telephone ringing and she pulled it from her three quarter length leather coat pocket. She stopped in the middle of the hustle and bustle and put her bag down between her ankles.

'Yes?' she said, placing her free hand on her other ear as she spoke. 'Where are you?' Her tone was light even though her voice was loud. The background noise wherever he was at that time was loud too and she strained to hear him. 'You're where?' she asked. Her eyes widened. 'Standing where!' she exclaimed loudly, spinning around on her heels, searching the crowds, and then she saw him. He was watching her from the corner of one of the side roads. Still with the phone to her ear, she began to walk towards him. 'Are you following me again?' she asked and she saw him shake his head, a sensual smile on his dark features as he watched her approach.

'You look really sexy in wool, have I ever told you that?' he said into his phone, 'Do you have underwear on under that dress?' he asked, as if asking for the time or something.

She returned the look that he was giving her. 'You look rather tasty yourself,' she continued. 'And no, I haven't,' she smiled.

'Walk quicker,' he urged as she moved towards him.

In truth, Michael had followed her. He'd listened and heard her plan and he didn't much like it. There was no way she should be going off on her own around London, so he'd had one of the lads follow her for a while and keep an eye on her, then he'd leisurely made his own way there.

Right up until they were almost touching they kept their phones to their ears and their eyes locked. There was a long moment of sexual energy between them in the crowded street and they felt as if they were completely alone. They could hear nothing, and see nothing else except for each other. It was always the same when they saw each other in public places like these. They could stare at one another for long periods and sometimes they touched as only lovers touch without being special in other people's eyes and today was one of those days and Michael reached out, touching her cheek with large fingers.

Their little interlude was interrupted by a group of young women with buggies and they had to move apart, then the moment was gone.

'What did you buy?' he asked finally, taking the bag from her hand and opening it. 'Oh, now they're nice,' he said peering into the plastic bag.

'What are you doing here?' she said, he shrugged his shoulders as he gave her a sideways look. 'Were you following me?' her tone was sceptical.

'No. I promise. I heard you say that you were coming here this morning when you were on the phone to one of your pals, and I was in the area so I thought I'd see if you wanted lunch.'

'In the area?' she said, tilting her head and looking up at him from under thick lashes.

'Okay. Not in the area. Not even close, but hopeful!' He laughed.

'Well, I'll let you buy me lunch because I'm starving and then, we'll have to see how good you are and how much you spend on me,' she laughed.

'Oh, so you want me for my money, do you?'

'Why, yes,' she laughed, sounding almost aristocratic.

'Liar.' He was smiling as he spoke. She heard the sincerity in his tone and reached out, touching his arm with gentle fingers. 'I can think of at least one other thing you want me for!'

'And what would that be?' she asked, already knowing the answer.

'I'll show you later. Now, where did you park?'

'Oh, I didn't, I got the tube. Quicker!'

'So you'll be needing a lift home then?'

'After more shopping, yes,' she laughed.

'Come on then. Where next?'

Chapter Thirty

April 1999

Michael kept his promise to Jennifer and Beth, and kept James well away from the Hothouse that night, but he was so intrigued by all the secrecy and all the phone calls, that he left him with Jason and Darren in Brown's and made his way there alone.

'I've got instructions not to let you in tonight!' Paul sounded strained as he looked up at Michael.

'Are you serious?' Michael's tone was amused. He was aware of Beth's instruction but presumed that it didn't apply to him. 'Do you want to stop me now then?' he added lightly and Paul sighed.

'For fuck's sake Mike, she'll have me bollocks off!' he protested.

'You'll enjoy it though, my friend!' Michael smiled, aware of Paul's little crush.

'Oh, go on. But I wasn't 'ere, right!'

'Sure, you're a pal!' Michael laughed, giving him a gentle tap on the arm as he passed.

The entire balcony area was roped off, and full to overflowing with women. Wall to wall women! No wonder she didn't want James there. He'd have had a field day, his future wife's hen night or not. He spied Beth from the stairs; she was laughing and chatting, a full glass in her hand. He watched her every move for a while and then as he was about to continue up the steps she looked across at him, her eyes settling on his instantly. She smiled. She wasn't surprised or annoyed that he was there. With a wave of her hand and a few words to the small crowd she was standing with, she made her way across to him.

'You're later than I thought you'd be,' she smiled.

'So, you were expecting me!' he replied, a little relieved.

'No, just hopeful,' she replied.

He looked her up and down. She had on the grey dress he'd got her for her birthday and she looked fantastic.

'How was your fitting?' he asked, trying not to think of her in the way that was now making his body ache.

'Quite good, actually,' she managed. She could feel his arousal and see it in his eyes as he looked at her then. 'I had an underwear fitting too.' She was toying with him again.

'You'll be wearing some? That'll be nice and refreshing for you, won't it, I bet?' He wasn't going to rise to this one. It wasn't fair. There was no way she was going to be able to get out of here for hours, and even when she did, the house would be full of men in different states of drunkenness. They'd have no privacy for at least another day, maybe two, so they stood staring at each other for a while longer and then Beth glanced at her watch.

'Can you spare me ten minutes in the office?' she asked. 'I need you to look at something for me.'

There it was, what an invitation. How could he refuse? And without a word, he followed her through the crowds, towards the locked door.

At the altar James stood next to Michael, his heart pounding in his chest like a kettledrum. They looked very different in top hat and tails as they both scanned the sea of familiar faces that now packed the church to the rafters. Pat and Judy sat with Eve and Jim in the front row and Jennifer's mum sat on the opposite side of the aisle wearing a large navy blue hat. She kept smiling at James through tear-filled eyes. She was so happy.

'You okay, young James?' Michael asked, looking at James. He was flushed and Michael was genuinely concerned. This was to be the single most important day of his life and Michael was aware of just how seriously James was taking all of this. He'd never actually had James down as a religious person, far from it, but something had made him want to do it right by Jennifer, and that touched Michael deeply.

He could understand completely the love he had for her, the urge he got to make her life as perfect as possible.

'No mate, I'm sober as a judge and I feel as sick as a bastard dog!' James whispered through a smile.

Michael tapped him light=heartedly on the back and smiled back. This was very bizarre. They were on show up there at the alter until the bride arrived.

'You're a brave man. And I think you're doing the right thing. In fact, I'm sure of it!'

'I know. I'm sure too, I'm just nervous,' James replied.

'Just remember, when the music starts, turn around. I'll tell you when to turn back to see her, okay?'

'Okay! Christ!' he paused for breath. ''Ere, d'you ever think I'll do this for you?' James asked then and Michael looked away from him.

'Maybe, one day?' was all he had time to say. The organ music sounded and both men then stood rigid, facing the altar. The doors opened at the opposite end of the church.

'You can turn around now,' Michael breathed as Jennifer appeared at the doors on her father's arm.

'I can't look,' James whispered, facing Michael. But Michael wasn't looking at him. He was staring down the aisle.

'Holy Mary, Mother of God!' Michael said in practically a whisper, and upon seeing the strangest look on his face, James couldn't hold back and he too turned slowly around to see his future wife.

Jennifer walked down the aisle still holding her father's arm. In the other hand she held a trailing bouquet of red roses. She looked absolutely beautiful in a cream, fitted bustier dress that fanned out like an evening gown. The neckline was low, trimmed with tiny burgundy silk rose buds and she seemed to heave out of it despite her small frame. Her face was perfectly made up, although obscured by a short lace veil; the silk flowers on the headdress attached to it were shaking just as much as she was.

Michael looked past her and his eyes settled on Elizabeth as she followed Jennifer and her father. She was dressed in a burgundy version of the dress that Jennifer wore and her skin seemed to glow beneath it. Her hair was pinned up softly with clips attached to small rosebuds. She held her bouquet and he couldn't help but notice the flowers shaking. She looked up the aisle towards him and smiled, then she turned her attention to James. He looked so nervous. They both did, but they looked fantastic in the morning suits they wore, except for the fidgeting with the top hats they were holding. Michael checked his burgundy silk cravat and instinctively ran his fingers through his hair.

'Do you, James, take Jennifer to be your lawful wedded wife, to have and to hold, for richer for poorer, in sickness and in health and forsaking all others, from this day forth until death do you part?'

James looked into Jennifer's eyes. 'I do!' he said firmly.

'And do you, Jennifer, take James to be your lawful wedded husband, to have and to hold, for richer for poorer, in sickness and in health and forsaking all others, from this day forth until death do you part?'

She gazed at him.

'I do!' Her voice was croaky with emotion but as bold as James's was and he gripped her hand in his.

'I love you,' he whispered as they exchanged rings.

'I love you too,' she replied.

Michael stood up from his seat to a round of applause and cheers of appreciation. There was an outburst of table drum rolling and then as his eyes crossed the room, silence fell.

'Ladies and gentlemen, friends.' He paused 'I know that you only came today to see if he'd really do it! I'll collect winnings from all of you after consummation!' There was an outburst of laughter.

'I suppose that this is where I'm supposed to tell all of James's darkest secrets, his most embarrassing moments, but time is short, so it's not going to happen. I think we all know him well enough! However, I have taken the liberty of setting up a website with full details, including photos, for you to visit at your leisure. It's www.maleslag.com.' There was more laughter and a few called comments from the surrounding tables.

'What I am going to tell you is that my friend, James Dobson, has found a soul mate in Jennifer. She's a very special person and I know that James loves her very, very much.' He paused again. 'I wish that James's mum and dah were here to see him wed today. They'd be very proud, and more than impressed at how many friends are gathered here today for such a grand occasion. They are missed, but remembered every day as a couple who loved and were loved, and I only hope that James and Jennifer are as happy together in their lifetime.' There was a ripple of appreciation for those words and Michael looked briefly down at James, who had tears of joy and love in his eyes. 'But, you are all here, friends, relatives and loved ones and on behalf of the bride and groom, I would like to thank you for coming here today to share in this special day, so, it only leaves me to ask you to please be upstanding for the bride and groom, Jennifer and James!'

The entire room stood up and in unison they called out, 'Jennifer and James.'

The first few notes of the first dance song began and James took Jennifer by the hand and led her onto the floor to more applause.

'Is this where you stamp on my feet?' she laughed softly.

'Oh no, Beth's wedding present to you was to teach me how to do this properly!' James replied and he led her across the floor without so much as a toe being damaged.

'And what a present it is,' she purred, the smile not leaving her face for a second as they moved. 'How long did she have you doing this, then?' she asked.

'Weeks!' he replied with a slight shake of his head.

'I think we can join them now,' Michael whispered into Beth's ear as they stood on the sidelines, watching. 'It's part of my duty today to dance with the maid of honour, you know,' he added, extending a hand.

'Well then, we'd better dance,' she breathed as she felt his hand on her hips.

'You look beautiful today,' he said, keeping his tone casual, but Beth could see the look in his eyes and she blushed. 'You look beautiful every day, but today—Today you look just grand, stunning.' He was hungry for her, and had been since she'd entered the church. 'That's quite a cleavage you've got there!' He let his eyes roam casually as they moved in time to the music.

'It's killing me,' she admitted.

'It's killing me, too!' he laughed.

'No! I mean, I can't breathe and the bones are digging in places I didn't know I had places.'

He laughed at her comment, making those around them look at them. Then he composed himself. 'So you'll be needing help out of that dress tonight, then?' he was hopeful.

'Definitely!' she purred.

'Then it's a date. Your room, whenever we get there!'

She really smiled then, just thinking.

'Yes! We have the house to ourselves for two whole weeks,' she breathed out, feeling his fingers dig into her waist with a squeeze.

She wanted to continue with a comment about them being a real couple in the real sense of the word, but she knew that it wasn't him holding back from telling the world. It was their stupid situation and it was getting out of hand, and so they danced slowly to two songs and then Michael was pulled away by one of Jennifer's friends, Nicola. He went willingly but gave Beth a backward glance as she too was immediately swept away by James.

'What you two laughing at?' he asked her.

'This dress,' Beth replied honestly.

'Yeah, I saw the chest. Nice,' he smiled. 'You having a nice time?' He was genuine in his question.

'Me? Yes, what about you? How's your big day?' she replied.

'Brilliant. I've just married a wonderful woman, I'm surrounded by my best friends, and I'm dancing with one of the two prettiest women in the room.'

He left the rest unsaid. It wasn't necessary. Michael had said all that had needed saying about their mum and dad. And he'd said it perfectly.

In the morning Beth rolled over, her head spinning like a top, her mouth like well-used sandpaper. Michael lay beside her on his stomach, one arm off the bed, the other under his head. She took in a deep breath and inhaled the scent of him. Even when he stank of drink and stale cigarettes, he smelt great to her.

'I'm awake!' he said as she reached out and touched his shoulder. 'What time is it? His voice was muffled from the pillow he now had his face buried in.

'Ten,' she said, lying back down next to him after observing the array of discarded clothes around the room.

'Yuck! Too early!' he sighed. 'They'll be in Jamaica soon.' He spoke slowly, almost checking each word as it left his mind to come out of his mouth.

'Good!' she breathed.

'Go back to sleep!'

She rolled on to her back again.

'No! It's no good. I'm up now!' he announced, rolling over. He pushed back the quilt and kicked it off the bed completely.

'I can see that!' she breathed, taking in the sight of him. He looked down at himself, giving a little laugh at her comment as he put his arms above his head. 'Why does he do that?'

'He likes you!' he replied in a whisper.

'I like him, too.' She slid her hand across his belly, the sensation making him shudder.

'None of that! I need a shower,' he decided, turning his head to face her on the pillows. 'Would you like to join me?'

They stood under the water, letting it penetrate their senses. He was still hard and she pushed up against him in the large cubicle as they washed.

'You've panda eyes!' he smiled as she pulled her hands away from her face.

She added more soap and scrubbed again. 'Better?' she asked.

'Better. Here, let me do that,' he said as she reached for the shampoo. He took some in his hands and ran them through her hair. The lather was almost immediate.

'That feels nice,' she sighed as he took the shower head off the hook and began to rinse.

'It sure does!' he replied almost wistfully. 'Turn around.' He rinsed her off and she ran her hands across her face, then and turned back to look at him. He looked back at her, observing the expression on her face. She was smiling only with her eyes.

'What?' he asked with a laugh.

'You!' Her voice was soft.

'Me what?'

'Why do you love me?' she asked.

He turned off the shower, still gazing at her. 'Now there's a question! Why do you love me?' he answered the question with a question as he pulled a towel from the rail and wrapped it around her.

'Because of things like this!' she said as he tucked the towel firmly around her. 'Y'know, stuff,' she added.

'Stuff!' he laughed, wrapping another towel around himself as she got out of the cubicle. He watched her wrap one around her head, scooping up all that hair and he knew exactly what she meant.

True love was made up of all of the tiny little things. The way they'd smile or look at each other from across a room, the way no-one else really mattered. The stupid text messages they sent on the mobiles when in their rooms late at night. The way they cared for each other. They didn't argue about who'd make the coffee in the morning, they'd go down and make it together. There were never any tuts or huffs and puffs about the trivial things, and it wasn't just because the trivial things didn't matter because they had money, and other people to do things for them. They were just the perfect match for one another and both knew it. Their love wasn't a competitive sport. It was a team sport.

'If I put it into words, we'll be here all day,' he said finally. 'Just know that I do and that I do because of everything, every little thing.'

Calmly Michael paid the cab driver. He turned and watched Beth walk up the steps towards the front door. Her back moved before his eyes and within seconds they were behind the closed door. He was upon her against the hallway wall, pulling at her clothes. She'd been playing with him all evening, her eyes as suggestive as her movements had been. She'd been aware of his arousal. He'd made it clear to her with those big brown eyes, devouring her in the middle of the club office as they'd sat with Pat and gone through piles upon piles of paper.

His hand found her panties and he pulled them aside with a purposeful tug. She was wet and as his fingers slid into her she let out a satisfied groan. Her breathing was hard on his neck and she tugged at his shirt, practically ripping the buttons from it in her haste to touch his body. 'God woman, I love you!' he breathed as she ran her hands across the bulge against his trousers and pulled at the hook and zip. He was free then and she took him in her hand, her actions slow and deliberate. 'Go on!' His tone was husky as he felt her come beneath the pace of his fingers. She was always so demure about the act and sometimes he just wanted her to let go completely. She waited for him to slow, but he didn't; his pace actually quickened and she felt another wave come over her.

'Jesus,' she managed between gasps. 'Don't stop, please—' Her hand had left him and she was almost clawing at the wall behind her and then at his head, running her fingers roughly through his hair. He nudged towards her, pinning her completely to the wall and with a slight bend, he was inside her, buried so far that he could go no further. He took all of her weight on himself and lifted her off the floor. She wrapped her legs about him and clung to his body, feeling him inside her. They slid down the wall to the floor, her on top of him. She knelt above him, pulling at the remainder of her clothes.

Like every other Monday morning, Mrs. P let herself into the house and slammed the door behind her. The noise bought Beth to a sitting position in the bed and she spun suddenly, looking over at Michael who was already out of the bed, pulling his trousers onto his body with

344

much haste. He looked up at her and put his finger to his lip to silence her. 'She's going downstairs,' she mouthed. There was no need to whisper though, they both knew that you could hear nothing from room to room, let alone floor to floor in the house. It was the fear of being caught that kept them close to silence.

'You go on!' he said, now dressed. She gave him a slight smile then left the bed. She made her way down into the kitchen where she found Mrs. P boiling the kettle for the first of several cups of tea that day.

'Morning,' she smiled. 'You slept late.' She didn't look at Beth, she was too busy with her own thoughts and that pleased Beth in a way. Mrs. P was always there on hand, but never too much in her face.

'Yeah, Michael and I had a bit of a late one last night.' The two women were silent for a long moment, getting their heads around the morning and preparing for the day ahead.

She turned around, watching Beth's back view. What a beautiful young thing she was, she thought. She seemed to breeze everywhere, never angry, never uptight and she felt the familiar odd pride that she got whenever she thought of James and Beth. They had taken on the world and had succeeded. Good bloody luck to 'em. She was bought back to themoment as Michael walked down the stairs towards them. She studied him. He was a big lad, tall and strong.

'Good morning, ladies,' he said firmly but warmly, aware that she, like so many others, loved to hear the sound of his voice, his Irish tones, God only knew why.

'Mornin', Michael. Did you sleep well?' She kept the stream of chatter up.

'Aye. Yes, I did, thanks,' he replied to her question but his eyes followed Beth's every move. That small gesture got Mrs. P's attention and she looked a bit deeper, harder, at the pair now before her, past the smiles and the jokes, past the brother-sister thing they had, and then she saw it, clear as day. She noticed suddenly an unspoken conversation as they busied themselves in her presence, making coffee and lighting cigarettes. The simple, easy way they moved around each other, touching, but not touching. Talking but not talking. It was like a dance or play-acting maybe. She pushed the thought from her mind but it was there now, the seed was sown.

'I'll start with the washing,' she said, her tone its usual sing-song light. 'Are you two up now, then?' She asked that question deliberately and two pairs of eyes met each other and there was another conversation, it lasted seconds, no more but there was definitely a conversation.

'Um,' Beth was being indecisive and she looked at her watch for effect, but in reality she was wracking her brains. Was it okay for her to go upstairs?

'Yes, we're up!' Michael said firmly.

Beth looked at him and he tilted his head at her. He'd done it. Cleared his stuff from her room and ruffled his own duvet.

'You said you wanted to go shopping this morning, didn't you? This is no day to be lying in that pit of yours.' Beth looked away from him. Nice save she thought, very nice indeed.

'Good, we'll just have this, then I'll get started. Can't dawdle. There's a messy house to clean.'

Beth looked around the immaculate kitchen and then over at the dining area. Messy, she thought? Yeah, right, it was a right pig-sty. There must have been at least one used newspaper on the table and, oh no, three butts in the ashtray. Messy indeed!

The conversation, such as it was, was light for the time it took Beth and Michael to drink one cup of black coffee each and smoke two cigarettes. All the while Mrs. P watched them like a hawk. Her mind reeled at all little alarm bells that had rung in her head in the past. All the times she'd wondered about the two of them, all the—She stopped and looked up again from her cup. Michael was looking directly at her and by the expression on his face, she wondered if she had said something out loud. The two stood silently, it was as if they were both waiting for Beth to leave the room but even when she did announce that she was going up for a shower nothing happened, nothing was said.

'Out with it, Mrs. P' Michael said finally.

Mrs. P had the decency to look away, a flush on her cheeks, but not for long and her eyes then returned his steady gaze.

'Michael, Michael, Michael,' she breathed slowly. 'Tell me I'm wrong and I'll say nothin' more about it.'

He looked in deep thought for a few seconds, a smile tracing his open lips.

'What do you think's going on here, then?' he asked.

She looked into his eyes again as she answered. 'You've had her!'

He hesitated, not really expecting her to have been so blunt.

'I have!' His pride and his honesty got the better of him.

There was a long silence. She looked into him, seeing the man before her with new eyes. Gone was the banter about his male ways. She saw then the real man, the man that was usually hidden. She saw the man in love.

'Better you than some little guttersnipe,' she said bluntly after another long pause. She looked away for a few seconds. 'But you'll hurt that child.'

'You are more than wrong!' he replied finally. 'And she's no child. She, for your information, is a woman, a real woman!' His words touched her, she understood him. 'I love her!'

She reached out then and touched his naked arm with wrinkled, washed hands. 'I think you do,' she smiled. 'I think you always have, love, and I hope you always will.' She stopped again. 'I hope the luck of the Irish thing's true too. You'll need it with them lot.'

He almost smiled down at her.

'Now go on. Go and see to your missus.'

Chapter Thirty-One

May 1999

With attentive eyes, Jennifer watched Beth as she flicked through rows of clothes on the rails. Beth could feel her staring; it was something Jennifer did a lot, she studied her much and was still sizing her up. It didn't bother Beth but she thought she should ask why, now that they were family.

'What do you see?' she said finally.

'A secret.' Jennifer was instantly aware of what Beth was asking her.

'What secret?' There was that defensive laugh again.

'A woman's secret. Is it a man?'

Beth pulled a face. 'What makes you say that?' She kept her voice light, with a laugh, but she was aware of how red she was getting.

'It is a man!' Jennifer was correcting herself. She hadn't needed to ask, she just knew.

Beth was silent for a while. She pulled the dress from the rail and held it up against herself, casually looking at her reflection in the mirror. 'Would you tell anyone if it was?' Beth was cagey now and Jennifer smiled at her.

'Not even your brother.' She made it plain that she was aware that that was what Beth was implying, and Beth also noticed that she didn't mention Michael in the statement.

'Do I deny all or bare my soul?' Beth said, her tone reflective.

'Bare all, please Beth, bare all!' Jennifer replied, her own tone now low, ready to receive the secrets Beth held so close to her chest. She looked away and then directly back into Beth's eyes. 'I have an idea already! That is, I think I have an idea,' she confessed watching Beth's body language change from casual to pensive as she continued to talk. 'You see, there's this man. And he is a man, in fact he's the original tall, dark and far too sexy for his own good—' She sounded suggestive, and both laughed then. 'He's stinking rich and completely approachable and I get the distinct impression that he's got a bit of a crush on a certain young lady. Any ideas on who he might be and who he might have a bit of a crush on?'

'Who indeed?' Beth smiled.

'So are you going to speculate on this one?' Jennifer suggested.

'Okay—' Beth paused for a moment or two. She had to be completely honest with herself. She knew that Jennifer knew about her and Michael. You couldn't walk into that house, live in that house, halfway through their little affair and not notice it. She also knew that Jennifer would stick to her word, and that she wouldn't tell a soul so she re-hung the jacket she had been clutching. 'You got me!'

They didn't speak about it any more in the shop. There wasn't time. Jennifer announced that they should go for lunch and it seemed like only moments before Beth was sat at a table with Jennifer opposite her, and a bottle of white wine between them. All Jennifer kept saying as the waiter took their order was, 'I knew it. I just knew it!' And she was thrilled.

June 1999

'I'm not taking them! They make me sicker!' Beth said chucking the box of tablets into the kitchen cupboard with the rest of the medicines that no one in the house ever took.

'You've got tonsillitis!' Michael reached in and took it out again.

'Can't drink on them! Not taking them!' She held up her hand to him.

'Oh, sure you can, just don't go mad, woman.' He was getting annoyed with her. He would have raised his voice, but he didn't want to have this conversation with an audience.

'No!'

'Elizabeth! This isn't a discussion—' his tone was warning and she turned to look at him.

'Baby tactics?' she was getting annoyed.

'No! I'm worried. You wait till the last minute to say you're sick, then when you get stuff to make you well, you won't take it!'

'Fine! I'll take them!' she said finally, snatching the box from his hand.

'Elizabeth.' His voice was so gentle, so suddenly after their last words that she turned and looked up into his eyes. 'Please don't be like that with me. I'm just worried, y'know. I want you to be well, that's all.'

'I know. I know you care, and it's not the drinking. It's just shit that it's happened now! If it wasn't for bad luck—' she began.

He kissed her lips before she finished. 'You'd have no luck at all,' he added. 'Now, woman. Take your pills, get some rest and be on top form for your birthday!'

July 1999

Beth sat on the edge of the bath, silent tears streaming down her face. She willed it to come every day, but it didn't. All that came was the sickness and the heavy feeling of foreboding. She was going to have to do something, but what exactly, she didn't know. She sat, almost praying to her mum and dad. She wished they were there then. She sniffed and wiped her eyes again. She sat for a long time and heard Jennifer come down the stairs. She held her breath. She didn't want her to wait for her to come out. She didn't want to see or talk to anybody. Thousands of thought bounced around inside her head. What would he say? What would he do? She didn't know the answers to those questions, all she knew was that she didn't want to get rid of it. Didn't want him to ask her to. It was her baby, their baby. A special thing made of a special thing.

She cleared her thoughts as she stood in the shower cubicle. The sickness faded away for another day and she calmed inside. Today was to be the day to tell him about it. To have it out in the open. She had to tell him, keeping this from him was making her feel worse than anything else. She'd never lied to him about anything.

'You okay?' Michael breathed as he passed her in the hallway on his way up from the kitchen. She had been in the lounge, reading yet another book. She looked tired and he wondered if maybe she wasn't working too hard, too many hours. He couldn't help but notice that her body clock was out by more than just a few hours. She was sleeping later and later, and he knew that she stayed up well into the dawn hours. He also noticed the amount she had been doing over the last few weeks; they'd hardly seen each other since James and Jennifer had returned. And then he wondered if it was that, their return, that was bothering her. They had had such an excellent time alone together. They'd been just like a real couple, in a real home, with a real and normal relationship, and as they stood there looking at each other she let her face fall into a false smile.

'I am,' she said sounding bright but her eyes were dark, a sure sign that she wasn't.

'What's wrong with you, Elizabeth?' he asked. 'Are you not well again?' He was at a loss with her and he sighed out loud. He wanted to raise his voice but both were aware that James and Jennifer would be home at any time and that a scene in front of them would just start them thinking.

'I'm fine, really, just a bit tired,' she said weakly.

'Are you sure now? You've not been yourself for—' They locked eyes and there was a long silent pause. He stared into her and she felt as if he was searching inside her mind. She would have answered a few seconds later with a cheerful smile that she was just fine, but the look that crossed his face told her that she didn't have to and that the penny had dropped.

She could almost hear him counting backwards in his head and then he turned white, the colour returning to his cheeks within a second or two.

'Oh, God!' He was almost panting with the reality of it. 'How long have you known?' His voice was calmer than he felt, not giving away anything that he was feeling.

Her fear must have shown on her face like words on the page of a book. She didn't answer him; couldn't answer him.

'How long!' he said again, his tone demanding and she looked grave.

'A week, for sure,' she got out finally with a choke and then the tears came.

He pulled her to him and brushed her hair with his palm. His mind was reeling at the thought. This young woman before him was carrying his child within her. In all the time they had been together this had never actually crossed his mind. Then it twigged as to why she had been working so hard, staying up so late. She was exhausting herself and he knew why. God help them. This was the beginning of the end. He'd be dead and she'd—He stopped himself almost before the words registered in his mind and something else filled the vacant space. No! nothing was going to stop him from being with her and no way was he going to let anyone persuade her to kill his child. He pulled her a little closer to him and he felt her clinging to his body.

'I love you!' he breathed. He could feel that she needed to feel that he wasn't angry with her, didn't hate her and he could feel it in every move she made as they stood there. 'Why didn't you tell me before?' he asked softly into her ear and he felt her shrug.

'I couldn't. I didn't want you to be angry with me,' she managed after a long moment between them.

He shook his head, burying his face in the sweet scent of her hair. 'My darling, never,' he breathed. 'I couldn't even if I tried. Oh my darling Elizabeth.'

They walked up into her bedroom and she flicked on the radio for background noise and then settled herself on the bed opposite where Michael now half lay, half perched. They were silent for a long while and listened as James and Jennifer came into the house and down into the kitchen.

Beth looked at the clock. It was almost five o'clock. They would have to start getting ready soon. They were both due at the Hothouse for a meeting at seven and neither of them had even showered.

'What are we going to do?' she asked looking up into his eyes. They were warm upon her and his lips were set in almost a smile.

'Do you want to keep it?' he said sounding awkward. He knew the answer but had to ask her anyway. She was still so young in so many ways, but he knew how she felt about him for sure, and he hoped that she would feel the same way about having his child, despite the trouble it would undoubtedly cause.

She looked away from him for a couple of seconds and then returned her gaze to his.

'Yes, Michael. Yes, I do! I could no more kill your baby than I could kill myself.' Her words were simple and honest and they reached into his soul and soothed him.

'Then we'll keep it!' he said, a smile almost showing on his lips, 'and we'll do this together.'

Late July 1999

Jim had been at the airport for a while and he sat patiently waiting for Michael's flight to get in. He settled into a chair opposite the arrivals board and sipped cheap reheated coffee from a polystyrene cup until he saw that Michael's flight from Stanstead had landed. Michael walked through the arrivals area and Jim saw him immediately; he always seemed to be head and shoulders above everyone around him and even with his shoulders visibly sagged, he still looked big.

'Dah!' he managed and for the first time in years, Michael clung to his father like a child, desperate for security.

'Come on, son. Let's get out of here, ey?' he said, taking one of the two bags Michael was holding.

They were pretty much silent on the way back to the house, just the occasional word or two was said and even when they got there and were inside, Michael was having difficulty in beginning what he had to say. Jim looked at Eve, who, too, sat patiently waiting for Michael to speak. They had a sneaking suspicion of what was going on but neither of them had voiced their opinions, even to each other really. Speculation wasn't something that was done in their home. It was either black or it was white.

'Elizabeth's having my child,' he said finally, standing up from his chair in their private lounge. He looked out of the window and out across the green fields instead of at either of them. He was expecting an intake of breath from one, if not both of them, but it didn't come. He waited for the reprimand, the parental advice but none came. Instead he heard his mother move from her seat and cross the room towards him.

'Is our grandchild well?' she said slipping her hand on to her son's arm.

He turned and looked at her, tears in his eyes and he nodded.

'So far everything's grand. But it's a wee bit early to tell yet.'

'And Elizabeth?' Jim asked, joining them. He looked at his son. He saw the look in his eyes and was so proud, so proud.

'She's fine too. But we've not—' he began.

'They'll get over it!' Eve interrupted. 'And if they don't, well, you'll have to come here for a while.'

'Did you want me to talk with Pat?' Jim suggested, for the sake of something useful to say.

'No, Dah, this, this we have to do on our own!' Michael said then.

'You do it together, won, but no matter what, and I mean, no matter what, we'll back you,' Jim managed.

His words touched Michael so deeply that he felt the sting of tears in his eyes. He was going to be this kind of parent one day. He'd back his child, no matter what occurred.

'I love you two so very, very much, y'know,' he whispered. Eve went to him and he wrapped his arms about her, pulling her to him.

Jim strode to them, his one arm settling on Michael's back, the other on his wife's. 'We know you do, son.'

Chapter Thirty-Two

August 1999

'Michael!' Beth screeched at the top of her voice as the edge of a broken bottle swept before her eyes. There seemed to be a long time lapse before she felt anything and then there was a stinging sensation and moisture. Michael lunged out, pulling Beth from harm's way. She landed a couple of feet from him, and up against the empty bar. As he moved in front of her, he felt the clean coolness across his arm that only came just before blood and pain. More male bodies suddenly appeared before him and the pain left him. All he could feel was the rush of adrenalin. Self-preservation kicked in like the first wave of a drug-rush through his veins, and he was off. He caught the one of the four that was making his way to Beth with a powerful blow of his fist, followed by an elbow to the back of the head. The young man fell to the ground, hitting both the handrail and the foot rail with his jaw on the way down. The man who brandished the bottle had recovered from the heavy shove he had received from Michael and was making his way back towards him. Michael stood tall and firm on the ground, and as he got to within a foot, Michael thrust out his palm and caught him in the throat. The motion, along with winding him, obviously did some damage and he reeled backwards, clutching his neck as his face reddened.

Paul and James arrived on the scene in the upper bar area seconds later and then all hell broke loose. There was a low din of violent voices as the few remaining onlookers from a relatively busy night began to take steps backwards. Two more of the bouncers appeared as if by magic and pulled one man from James just as he reached for a broken glass and then he was off bodily down a flight of stairs. Paul hit one man in the face with a heavy crack of his head and the blood spurted out across his head and over his shoulders before the man fell to his knees behind him like a sack of potatoes. Michael looked around him, his eyes like that of a wild animal. All the while his body was in the stance of protector in front of Beth as she stood up against the bar, nursing a bleeding head, a disgruntled expression on her face.

Within only a few moments it was almost silent in the bar; only the hard sound of male breath and the odd sniff and groan could be heard above it. '

She's bleeding!' James said, making his way across to where his sister stood.

'I'm okay!' she said, pulling her free hand away from her head and looking at the blood on it. It was tacky, not red and liquid like the blood now coming from Michael's left upper arm.

'Oh my God, Michael, you're gushing!' she exclaimed, and he looked down at the liquid seeping from his upper arm. It ached, it didn't hurt and he looked back up at her, his eyes filling with tears of frustration and fear of the reality of the past minutes events. She could have been killed. This was no place for a woman in her condition. She was going to have to stop at some time, but then they would have to tell people. It was then that his mind was set. He was going to tell them. He'd rather be sliced and diced than see her put in any more danger.

'Where do you want 'em?' someone asked, backing up to the stairs, ready to drag one of the three remaining men down them.

'Don't much care,' James said, his breathing still hard. 'Just get 'em out of our club.' He perched on a stool and watched as Michael observed Beth's head. She was right, it was just a knickknack, just above her hairline.

'You're a lucky bitch, do you know that!' he smiled down at her, looking into her eyes. 'That could have been your eye out.'

She smiled wanly at him. 'No, not with you here!' she replied lightly. There was love there, along with pure trust and faith. She glanced at his arm. 'You'll need that seen to!' she continued and he really smiled then.

'Know any good nurses?' he asked and she shook her head at him. 'No, but I know a grand turkey stuffer!'

'Should I get Frank?' Paul said as he saw the extent of Michael's injury. That would definitely need stitches and he shuddered at the thought of someone other than a qualified nurse giving them to him.

'No. no, I'm sorted!' Michael replied.

'You okay, baby?' Beth said, looking up at James, aware of the fact that he had been watching them for quite some time.

'Yeah I was just thinking about the turkey crack,' he said lightly, prodding Michael's good arm with his finger. 'It's easy. Just like the Christmas turkey, you fucking wankers.' He was laughing then.

'You know me, I do like having my stitches,' Michael replied coolly. 'She has a grand bedside manner!'

'That's enough of that from you!' James's laugh was calculated and Beth caught the expression in Michael's eye.

Up in the office a small crowd had gathered to watch Beth sew up the gash on Michael's arm. It was legend that she was a bit of a whiz with a needle and there was almost complete silence except for the odd sarcastic comment or effort to make her laugh as she prepared to sew. Michael sat on the edge of the desk with Beth now standing between his legs, her head down and one hand holding onto a blood-soaked swab.

'Don't you wanna wear gloves?' someone said from behind her. She shook her head at the question.

'But you don't know where he's bin!' Frank added with a laugh.

She took a breath and stood up, turning as she did so. 'Will you lot shut up, I'm trying to concentrate. It's not me he's going to slap if the bloody things are pissed now, is it?'

'Fifty quid says it's ten uneven stitches!' Frank laughed again.

'If you give me half your winnings I'll give him ten, but for unevens you'll have to pay me a lot more than twenty-five quid,' Beth said, her tone cool, and she looked fleetingly up in to Michaels eyes.

He smiled into hers, giving her the look he reserved for their times alone and for a second or two she felt her cheeks flush.

'Oh, 'ello, he's getting nervous,' James laughed from the other side of the desk. He blew cigarette smoke from the side of his mouth.

'You ready?' she asked and he looked into her eyes. Of course he was ready. This woman could amputate his arm and he wouldn't mind and she knew it, he thought, seeing the expression on her face.

She pulled the swab away from the wound and looked at it in the harsh light of the shade-less desk lamp. It gaped open, showing off the raw pink flesh below his skin. It was about two, two and a half inches long and quite deep but the bleeding had slowed.

'Six,' she mouthed to him and he nodded.

'A ton says it's six!' James exploded on seeing her mouth move and she shot him a look to silence him.

'What? I've gotta try, ain't I?' he laughed.

Beth slipped the bent needle into Michael's arm and he didn't flinch. She tied each stitch off with the same skill and speed as a surgeon. She had been right and there was a row of six neat black knots. She patted her work lightly with some TCP on gauze before drying it off and placing a giant sticky plaster-like bandage over the top of the whole lot.

'Now don't you go doing anything strenuous for a few days,' she said with a laugh, even though she tried in vain to sound serious, and he nodded at her suggestion, his eyebrows raising slightly.

'He'll not be having a wank then!' James laughed over his shoulder.

September 1999

Now seated on opposite sides at the dining table, James and Beth spent a long moment looking at each other. She watched him light a cigarette and offered her the packet. She refused it with a wave of her hand and he looked deep into her eyes.

'You wanted to chat?' he said, sounding casual.

'Yes I did, didn't I?' She breathed deeply.

She wondered what Michael was doing at that moment, and how James was going to react to what she was about to tell him. Better than Pat had, she hoped. Still, she was grateful that Pat hadn't been straight on the phone. He had respected her wish to tell James herself. She supposed that James, too, would demand to know who the father was, and quite rightly so, she thought. She would always be his baby sister no matter how old they got and how life changed. And it was about to change now.

'I'm pregnant!' she said in a flat tone, not giving away any emotion for the time being.

She watched James's face, he almost shuddered as her words sunk in and then he was up off his chair.

'Please, tell me you're fuckin' joking!' he bellowed, almost laughing, hoping that she was. But something inside him was saying no, she's not joking, mate. She's up the duff and you know it's true.

He lit another cigarette, throwing the pack and his lighter onto the table with a clatter. His eyes bored into hers and he saw the caution there. There wasn't fear, only caution.

'Oh my fucking life! How far gone are you?'

Beth looked into his eyes. She almost heard the thought that went through his head at that moment and with a glare she stood up.

'Too far!'

James gave her a sarcastic look with a shrug attached before speaking again.

This was never something that he thought he would have to deal with with *his* sister. He prided himself on the fact that she was still a virgin even though common sense told him that at her age and with those looks there was no way that she was.

'Do I know 'im?' he asked.

She'd been waiting for this question and there was a long pause between them.

'Yes.'

'Well? Who the fuck is it then?' he yelled banging his free hand down on the table. 'I'll fucking kill 'im.'

'No, you won't!' she replied, her tone surprisingly gentle and calm.

He stared at her. She was no longer pure in his eyes and still he loved her more than anything, more than his own wife.

'I suppose Jen knows,' he added, for the want of something to say to her at that point. If she said yes to this one he'd have a few words to say to her, too.

'No, she doesn't,' Beth lied. Of course Jennifer knew, Beth had confided in her a few weeks before, but it had been agreed that when it all came out, that Jennifer shouldn't know, and at that moment, Beth was glad of the decision. James wasn't going to lose it with her, but Jennifer? She wasn't sure. 'But Pat does. I saw him this morning.'

'For fuck's sake, Beth! Who is it? Did you tell Pat?'

She shook her head as she stared back at him, watching him as he calmed down from almost exploding.

'You really don't know, do you?' She almost laughed. He really didn't have a clue, even after two years. He looked away from her for a couple of seconds as if something had just occurred to him.

'Why don't you tell me who it is?' His tone had changed, it was lower, suspicious and she knew that the penny had just dropped for her brother. 'And tell me why I'll not kill 'im?'

Michael walked into the silent office and took one slow look at Pat's face. He knew then that his little secret was definitely not a little secret any more. Pat's eyes almost burned through Michael's skin as he sat there at his desk, deciding how to play the situation.

'I've had Beth in 'ere this morning!' he said, grinding out his cigar with such force that he looked as if he could have smashed the ashtray beneath his thumb and forefinger.

Michael didn't say a word, he simply moved into the centre of the room and stood with his hands clenched together at his front.

'She's got a bit of news. Any ideas on what bit of news she might have?' His voice was still light but even his jaw muscles seemed to be sticking out of his face by inches.

'Yes!' was all that Michael said at that point. He wasn't sure of what to say next because he wasn't sure if Beth had said anything about him. He had said that he would do the deed, and tell the family, but she had insisted that it would be better coming from her. In his mind he'd planned this moment to the letter but now, with just the two of them in the room he didn't want to make a big thing of it.

'It's funny,' Pat said as the two men made eye contact. 'I thought you might—'

'Why?' He was interested to hear this one. Did he know? Had she told him? Had he guessed or had he known all along?

Pat slammed his hand down flat on the desk and fleetingly Michael thought that it must have stung like hell. 'Don't treat me like a fucking idiot, Elliott, and don't you stand there and fucking lie to me!' He was bellowing now and Michael could just imagine the cleaning staff standing stock-still in the hallways behind the door, listening to every word.

Pat watched with cautious eyes as Michael stood bolt upright. Six feet and a few inches, more than fifteen stone of well-built thirty-year-old Irishman looked across the desk at him and he felt a prickle of fear, something that he hadn't felt so much in a long time.

'What do you want to hear, Pat?' he asked, his tone low and menacing.

'The truth!' Pat bellowed.

'What truth?' Michael almost spat back at him.

'Is it you?' Pat demanded and there was a long silence between the two men. Michael stood proudly before him as he answered.

'Yes. It's me. Its mine and she's keeping it, so don't you go sticking your nose in where it's not wanted, Pat, do you hear!'

Pat shot him a look but Michael was unmoved by it. He wasn't scared of Patrick Dobson, or any of the things he knew he could have done to him.

'She's my niece and she's up the goddamned fucking duff—' Pat added with a growl.

'And?' Michael was almost goading him. Let's have this all out right here, right now he thought.

'And I promised her father, my brother, that I'd look after her if anything ever happened to him and yet, here she is, up the fucking bastard duff, Michael!' He was still yelling.

'She's an adult!' Michael replied.

'So it would seem!' Pat said, slightly less loudly, his tone sarcastic.

'And she's not your responsibility any more!' Michael said then.

'Oh, really. And whose is it then? Yours?' Pat laughed loudly then.

'Aye. Yes!' Michael said flatly, leaning over the desk so that the two men were almost nose to nose.

'Phah—' Pat retorted with a wave of his hand. He could have slapped him, he was so close.

'Don't you laugh down your nose at me. She is my responsibility now Pat, she has been for a long time now.'

There was a deathly silence in the air then.

'She's not your fucking responsibility, sunshine. You, my boy are out of here. I need you in Ireland.' Pat was standing up straight again then.

'Bollocks!' Michael exploded without thinking.

'I need you in Ireland and you're to leave as soon as possible, Mister Elliott.' There was another deathly silence between them and then Pat went on. 'I've spoken to your dad. Perhaps a cooling off period is in order.' He was being sarcastic, his tone suggestive about the relationship between Michael and Elizabeth. Michael had expected many things from Pat but not this. He was sending him packing, although in hindsight he knew that it had crossed his own mind on more than a couple of occasions.

'Are you handling me?' Michael asked suddenly, his tone clipped.

Pat looked deep into his eyes and saw in them the heart-wrenching confusion of a grown man suddenly a child again.

'Yes. I am!' he said with a point of his finger.

'Fine. Then she goes too!' Michael replied, see how he liked that one.

'Oh, no! She stays here. If you're so fucking sure, it'll be fine, won't it!' Pat was getting angry again now.

'And who'll be there?' Michael was stalling. He knew that Pat was deadly serious, he'd known him an age. It was his way of being in control.

'I will. Trust me! She'll not leave my sight!'

Lucy sat in the lounge, staring at Beth, waiting for her to laugh, willing her to laugh, but she didn't. She couldn't believe it! The first thing she felt was hurt; she was hurt that Beth hadn't confided in her, but seconds later she knew that Beth hadn't confided in anyone. They were interrupted by Beth's phone. It was Jenny.

'It's me. Where are you?' she asked.

'Lucy's,' Beth replied with a sigh.

'You okay?'

'I'm fine. Where are you?' She could hear Jen's clipped tone.

'At my mum's, I thought I'd let the boys get on with it for a while,' she said.

'Oh God! I hope he's okay,' Beth breathed down the phone.

'He's a big lad, he'll be fine. Look, call me before you go home. I'll follow in about half an hour,' she suggested and Beth nodded as if Jennifer could see her down the line.

'Will do. And Jen?'

'Yeah?'

'Thanks.'

'Shush. I haven't done anything yet!'

Judy opened the front door as Beth pulled up on the driveway. She stood in the doorway and waited for Beth to get out of the car. She looked a bit pensive, but Judy's instant squeal and hug soon put any thoughts that she was angry too out of her mind.

'Why didn't you tell me!' she gasped, ushering Beth into the house. 'Patsy called me and said—I don't know what to say to him. But love, I'm really happy for you!'

'You are?' Beth sounded more than a little surprised. She followed Judy into the kitchen.

'Bethy… I may be a bit of a *dolly*, but you'd have to get up just a little bit earlier than that to get one past me!' she smiled, filling the kettle. 'I knew you'd been welcomed into the world of women, as it were, a long time ago, and I had my suspicions as to who it was who did the welcoming—' she smiled again and Beth felt herself blush. 'So I watched and watched and there it was, plain as day. Michael Elliot in love with Elizabeth Dobson!'

'In love? You knew that?'

'Course I did? Why else do you think I took such an interest in it all? I was hoping you'd have told me, but you didn't, so I thought I'd just let you get on with it. You two seemed happy enough!'

Beth stared at her aunt and listened to every word she said. There were some serious revelations going on that day, that was for sure.

'Did Uncle Pat know before I said?' she asked then.

'He thought he did, then he didn't, then he did. But you know what he's like!'

Beth looked sad suddenly. 'I thought I did!' Beth replied.

Judy turned then and looked straight into her eyes. 'There's going to be an awful lot of peacock feathers stretched to their limit today, love. He's pissed all right, but he'll get over it, they always do.' she paused and turned, leaning against the counter. 'Bethy, he promised your mum and dad, we all did, that if anything ever happened, we'd take care of you. His pride is the thing damaged today. And of course if I'm honest, lovely, he's more pissed off that you never said anything. He loves Michael, always has, but he's seen this as a betrayal and that's not to start on what everyone else is gonna have to say about it all, either to his face or behind his back. Give him some time to calm down, get his head around it all and it'll be okay.' She smiled then, a heartfelt smile, and Beth mirrored her.

'Are you really happy?' she asked then and Judy nodded.

'For you? Yes, lovely, I am!'

When Michael opened the front door and walked into the house, he was aware that it was James who was waiting for him down in the kitchen and not Beth. She had talked to him briefly on the telephone from Lucy's house. He'd suggested that she stay there that night while he and James talked but she'd opted to just linger, go and see Judy for a bit instead. He had said talked to James, but they both knew that James was furious and that words would probably be quite thin on the ground.

He was resigned and ready and he walked down the stairs with a bold step and looked across the room as James stood up from his seat at the table.

He'd been there for about two hours, just sitting, smoking cigarettes and thinking. He'd thought about what Beth had said. She'd been right, he had been blind because he didn't want to see what was going on around him, not because he didn't see it. He knew it was Michael before she had said it and he admitted to himself that he'd known about them for a long time, if not for the two years that she said it had been going on. As he'd sat there his anger towards his friend had faded. He didn't want to fight with him. He actually wanted to hold him close, just as Michael had done to him after his parents' funeral.

'Get it over with,' Michael said. His tone was low. He was prepared for a beating, or at the least a good slap, but James didn't move towards him even an inch.

'You fuckin' wanker!' James breathed as tears appeared in his eyes. 'I don't know what to say, Mike. I trusted you! You're my friend, my best friend,' and he poked himself in the chest as he spoke.

'I am your friend!' Michael bellowed at him.

'Then how could you do it to me?' His tone rose a couple of pitches and for a second Michael thought he may well actually cry. 'Why didn't you tell me?' There was real hurt there.

'Me? Do what to you, James?' Michael paused as he stepped further into the room. 'I've done nothing to you except not tell you something, something private and special. We told no-one, no-one. It was safer that way.'

James was getting cross again. He could almost understand the logic. 'Don't you talk to me about special, Mike.' He stopped. He was about to say that Michael knew nothing of special, but he knew that that was a lie. Michael probably knew more about special than anyone else James knew. He looked into Michael's eyes then, desperate to find nothing there so that he could be angry again. But there was something there. There was love there and James saw that look with new eyes, as if for the first time. Michael loved his sister. He loved Elizabeth. Had made love with Elizabeth and now she was carrying his child and James wasn't sure how to feel about that.

There had always been something there between them, a bond that without this revelation, looked almost sibling-like. But James now knew better and he could have kicked himself for all the times he'd pushed those thoughts from his mind in the past.

'I have never hurt you. But if you make me choose, James—' There was a silence as the two locked eyes. 'She'll win. She'll always win, not just with you and Pat. Everyone. She is my life, like Jenny's yours. Don't make me choose.' Michael's tone was almost begging, a plea to his friend as he stood there.

'Just go, Mike!' James said. There were tears in his eyes. He was gutted, absolutely gutted.

Chapter Thirty-Three

September 1999

Michael put his bags into the car. He didn't dare look back up at the house because he knew that if he did he would see her and then he would never be able to leave. He sighed deeply. He had lost a friend. He'd betrayed a true friend, but still that was nothing in comparison to the hurt he felt when he thought of when he would see her again, feel her again. The early morning was warm and the sun threatened to appear at any moment. He looked up at the sky and hoped that it wouldn't. It wasn't fitting for the mood of the day to have sunshine and for a second or two clouds appeared overhead. He opened the driver's side door and was about to get in when Beth's voice called after him.

'Michael, wait!' she gasped, taking the steps down to the roadside two at a time. He spun on his heel, ever cautious that she would slip or fall and damage herself or their precious package. They stood face to face then, close as close could get and that was when the tears came. She tried to speak but nothing came out of her mouth but the gasps and shudders only associated with the act of crying. He pulled her closer, wrapping strong arms around her as he soothed in whispers into her ear.

'Please don't go!' she managed.

'I have to go. Please don't make this harder than it is,' he breathed.

'I'll never see you again!' she breathed and he let go of her and took her hands in his.

'This is very temporary, my darling!' he said, his tone firm and thick with emotion. 'I love you Elizabeth, nothing's going to take me away for long. Let them cool off for a week or two, see our side of it.

It'll be fine, you'll see.' He still sounded tough, but inside he was cowering. This was going to be a long hard slog.

'I'll come over!' she sobbed.

'You bet you will,' he smiled.

As she watched his car pull away she was joined in the street by Jennifer. She put her arm around Beth's waist and squeezed lightly. The two looked at each other, two separate people joined together more deeply than ever before under the most strange of circumstances. If they weren't close before this, they were then.

'Is he up?' Beth asked.

'Yeah. He was up since five,' Jennifer replied.

'Did he say anything?' Beth asked quietly.

'He didn't have to!' she sighed. She was torn. She was livid with him for what was going on, but she understood it too. He'd cried for the first time in front of her last night. He was gutted and scared and confused and angry. She understood the face saving, the feelings and talk of the bonds being broken, the betrayal, but it was Michael! If it had been some little shite, she could have understood it better, but it was Michael!

'The sick thing is, We knew they'd do this. He wanted to tell them so many times, even before the baby, but I always said no, let's wait, and now he's gone, Jen.'

'I can't see him being away for long,' she tried to smile into Beth's eyes, but as she looked at her she saw the pain there. Hadn't these people had enough pain? Wasn't there trouble enough without all of this mess too?

'Did it begin with love?' she asked quietly as they stared off to the end of the street.

Beth looked at her again, her stare deep. 'Even before we knew it' she whispered.

'Then that's how it'll end. Just you wait and see.'

October 1999

Oxley sat in the bar, sipping coffee through smiling lips. What a catch! What a thing to have in his grasp. He almost laughed at himself then, thinking back through the past months, years. The dirty little bitch. All that time, butter wouldn't melt and all the time she was banging Michael Elliott. No wonder he was so upset before. She was his.

'Are you sure he's gone?' he asked again and Nick King nodded, lighting himself a cigarette beside him at the bar.

'Yeah. But it ain't a permanent thing. The word is—' he paused and exhaled, 'The old man went off the wall at Elliott. Suggested he go home for a while.' He said *suggested* but his facial expression told Oxley that there was more to it than that.

'What about James?' he asked.

'He's not said a word to anyone about it, any of it.' Oxley digested this news. Added it to the rest of today's news and smiled again. They were divided, so now all he had to do was conquer.

Pat looked across the desk at Beth. The second their eyes met, hers turned to flint and then she looked away with a slight lift of her head. She hadn't said more than twenty words to him since the day Michael had left.

'Is it going to be this way for long?' he asked suddenly.

She looked back at him, her eyes showing the hate that was there inside her along with her unborn baby. 'Sorry, were you talking to me?' she said, her tone cold. 'Only, I wasn't listening.'

That was it. Pat lost his temper and he practically jumped from his seat. 'God damn it, Bethy! What did you think I'd do, shake his fucking hand? His job was specific. There wasn't a clause telling him that it was okay to jump you! Fuck you all across the smoke and certainly not get you up the fucking duff,'

His words sank in and Beth was getting crosser and crosser with every word that fell from his lips. 'His job? Protect me, yes. Be close to me, yes. But he did not jump me. I was just as willing as he was.

I'm interested, what made you lot think that he was above being human? He's a man, I'm a woman. Yes, a woman. A hot blooded woman, inspired by a hot blooded man! What did you think would happen if we were left to our own devices?'

'Don't you blame me!' Pat yelled.

'I'm not fucking well blaming anyone. I can't see the problem!'

There was silence as Pat thought. What was the problem? They were both adults—He stopped himself. Michael was the problem. He'd humiliated him in public. Let him down, and let James down. He'd lied to them all and got Beth pregnant. He faltered. Had he lied? He wracked his brains, flicking through past conversations with Michael. He couldn't come up with one instance when he'd asked or Michael had lied. He pushed that thought away with a wave of his hand.

'I knew better, and now we're weak, Beth! Weak, all we need now is to be fucking weak!'

If the truth was known, Pat was surprised that Michael had gone on his word. He'd never in his lifetime known him to back down so easily. It occurred to his that he did it for Beth's sake. She didn't need the three men in her life fighting over her, and certainly not in her condition, and the more he thought the more he understood why Michael had gone and besides, it wasn't like he'd gone for good.

'What did you want, anyway?' he added.

'I'm taking a break. I'm going to Ireland for the weekend,' she practically spat at him.

'Fine!'

'Good!' Beth stood up, her small bump showing under her top, and without another word she left the office with a satisfying slam of the door.

He sat back in his seat. Bollocks, he thought. Now he'd have to go home and explain himself to Judy. He wasn't in the wrong, he hadn't done anything wrong, but fucking hell, she was as annoyed with him, as Jennifer appeared to be with James, and if he was really honest he knew that even James was pining. Michael had always been there for him and despite this fucking mess he knew that James still loved that man, loved him like a brother.

Beth walked through the arrival gate and scanned the sea of bodies for him. She noticed as she paused in the gangway that no-one barged her as they would normally have done. They excused her indecisiveness because of her bump and she smiled to herself, touching her belly lightly with her fingertips. Everything about having a child was incredible to her, from the sickness, to the changes in her body, to the way other people behaved towards her. It was, she imagined, almost like being famous. She looked back up and there he was. He was no more than ten feet away from her and moving with a firm stride. He seemed to be the only person in the airport then as she looked at him. Her heart jumped into her mouth, as it always did and the next minute she was in his arms and they were kissing and holding each other close. He took in the smell of her, the warmth of her, the feel of her and held back from squeezing. He'd missed her like air and sunlight. Relief washed over him at seeing her safe, seeing her well, seeing her there.

'God, I love you!' he breathed into her ear.

'I love you too! Did you miss us?'

'Did I!' he laughed, taking her hand in his, and taking her bag from her.

They pulled up outside the hotel and Michael got out to rush around and open her door for her. 'I warn you, they've spoken of nothing else,' he smiled in reply to Beth's question as to whether Eve and Jim were waiting. 'She'll be all questions and kisses,' he added as Beth stepped out.

Inside reception just about every member of staff they had, and Eve, appeared. She squealed with excitement at seeing Beth and hugged her really close for what seemed like ages.

'We missed you!' she announced. 'Did you have a good trip over. Are you all right now. Hungry?' she flapped. Beth laughed then.

'I'm fine, the baby's fine and they fed me on the plane.'

'There she is!' Jim exclaimed, making his way through the bodies towards her. He took her in his arms and she got another warming hug. 'You look so well!' he smiled. 'It suits you.' He took in the sight of her. 'He's missed you!' he added in a whisper.

'I've missed him too,' she replied.

Completely naked, Beth stood by the bed and Michael examined her, his features showing intrigue. 'It's bigger than I thought it would be,' he said, his hands on the bump. 'It feels so strange. That's our child,' he breathed, taken over with emotion.

'Yes, it is. Made with love,' she replied.

'Speaking of which—' he said, his tone suddenly suggestive.

'Yes we can, but gently! We can do that right up to the last minute!' she smiled.

'Really?' he was pleased, though this was not the be all and end all.

'Really!'

'Good!' he breathed. 'What else did they say?' He wanted to hear all of it, every last word from the doctors.

'They'll know more after the next scan. Baby was at a funny angle apparently,' she said. The talked for a while, quiet and calm. This was how they were and this was what both needed, just to be together.

He laid her down on the bed, kissing her belly with warm lips, touching the swell of her breasts with warm hands. He wanted to be inside her then and he slipped in between her legs, supporting his weight off her with strong arms. *My God,* he thought. Nothing and no one was going to keep them apart. Nothing and no one was ever going to be able to keep him from being with her, feeling her like he did then. She was the other part of him. She was the part of him that was good and pure, the part of him that was strong. She was him!

She watched him, his eyes, and could almost hear what he was thinking inside. He was aching for her as she was him, and the sensations inspired were always the same. It was like being home, like wearing her favourite jumper on a cold day, eating her favourite food when she was hungry. She was home and safe whenever and wherever she was with him.

She pushed the past weeks thoughts from her mind then. He was hers, and she was his, and they were together. He was as faithful as she was to their love and just feeling him there inside her was proof enough for her, not that she needed any. He had hold of her heart with a glance, a breath, a word and it was amazing. This was real love. The real thing.

'Is that okay?' he asked gently.

'This is more than okay. This is us,' she breathed. He was undone, and he pushed at her slowly, making her groan, feeling her wetness, making her feel him. They moved slowly like that for a long time. Keeping their eyes on each other, kissing each other, seeing each other and it was heaven. She wanted him there, needed him there just like he needed and wanted to be there. And when they came, it wasn't hard, it was gentle; it was a fulfilment, not a statement.

November 1999

James knew that an all-out slanging match with Oxley and his men in the middle of the Cooler wasn't the best idea he'd ever come up with but at that moment, he didn't care! Not with the adrenalin pumping through his veins as it was. He was hurting and he wanted the world to hurt with him. Not even Will had been able to dissuade him from going. So in he'd marched and off he'd gone and then, standing outside in the car park without a scratch he realised that he didn't feel any better for the rant, and fleetingly he wished that Michael had been there, he'd have changed his mind. Michael was his conscience.

By the time he got back to the club the word was out and Pat bowled in. 'Don't you think we've got enough fucking problems?' he yelled, completely oblivious to everyone else around them. 'For fuck's sake, what were you thinking?' He looked into James's eyes and saw the tears of frustration there. 'Get up into the office!' he demanded, to save James's face.

Inside, the two men were silent. Pat watched James sitting on the sofa, his face set. He looked so depressed and with a twinge of guilt he knew full well why.

'Any word?' he asked finally, knowing full well that there wasn't and hadn't been.

James answered straight off, glad to finally be talking to someone about it all. 'She talks to him every day, but never says he's said anything. They're gonna move into his place next month.' He paused. Pat didn't look surprised. Michael was never going to stay in Ireland, that was for sure. He made good money in London and both knew that Michael would make even more so that Beth and their child would want for nothing. She'd never have to work a day again; not that she had to now. But Michael would always make sure she had the best of everything and he'd work hard for those things.

Pat stared away from James then. Michael would provide for her, he loved her, he wanted her and he would move heaven and earth for her, and what had Pat done? He suddenly realised what a complete tosser he'd been about all of this and he realised then, too, that James was just following his lead. They should have been absolutely ecstatic about it being Michael. They would truly be one big happy family. A family full of love, but Pat had had to play the hard man, had had to save face, had to follow through what he'd always said about the first of Beth's encounters. He'd just never banked on it being Michael. He'd never let what was staring him in the face enter into the equation. He could hear Judy's words inside his head then, but they registered with his own dead brother's voice. *I knew,* she'd said. *I knew as well as you did. You just didn't want to see it, that's all. None of us wanted to admit that she was an adult. A woman, a real woman.*

'Jen fucking hates me, she's got the hump with me. She says talk to her, but Beth won't talk to me any more. My baby won't talk to me—' Tears welled up in his eyes and then the dam burst. 'I don't want to lose anyone else, Uncle Pat! I miss 'im. I wanna ring 'im, but I can't!'

Pat was undone by his words and landed on the sofa next to him, pulling him to him and the two embraced for the first time in years.

'I know, son. I know!' And as James's tears fell on to Pat's neck, his mind was set. He could change this, he could make this pain go away, and that was what he was going to do.

Chapter Thirty-Four

December 1999

James saw the gun rise and went to move, but missed his step. A single shot rang out, bringing the expanse of vaulted room to a silent and total standstill for a few seconds. As he dropped to the floor, blood ran like water from his chest and then Jennifer let out a scream. A high-pitched squealing noise that ended only when a hand swiped across her face and then all hell broke loose. As someone in the background screeched for someone to call an ambulance, Jennifer landed on her knees next to where James lay and pushed her hands on the hole in his chest. He tried to speak but she hushed him, pulling off her T-shirt to try and stem the blood. 'Don't talk, darling,' she sobbed. 'You'll be okay, just don't try to talk.' She was covered in his blood. He was pale, and he was quiet, very, very quiet. Frank was on his knees, too, covered in blood as he took the pressure from a now very subdued and clearly shock-ridden Jennifer. Someone slipped a jacket over her naked shoulders, and she was pulled to her feet, and away from him as the paramedics arrived out of nowhere on the scene.

Suddenly the club was very loud again, as if someone had turned up the volume. There were police everywhere and door-staff and bar-staff were crawling all over the place. Had anyone seen the shooter? was the question asked again and again and again, but no-one had. All anyone had seen was James slump to the floor, still trying to protect his wife.

Outside the hospital, Beth waited with bated breath as the telephone began to ring at the other end of the line. Her face was ashen, she could hear her heart beating in her chest and suddenly, as the receiver was picked up at the other end, the tears came. 'Michael! They shot James,' she wailed out the words, desperately fighting with her emotions. 'They tried to kill him. Come home, Michael! Please come home!'

With a pounding heart Michael walked into the club. It was raining out and he was soaked from having stood by his car, debating his next move. He knew that Beth was at the club and not at the hospital; he'd called there. Jennifer was there with James, still in intensive care. He walked up to the table and looked at the three people seated at it in turn. First Pat, who looked a little more than surprised to see him, but all the same he was already on his way out of his seat, his stance relieved. Michael's expression changed and something made Pat land back down on the chair with a bump; he hadn't realised that it was actually Beth pulling him back down. Then at Frank, who obviously wanted no part in this and what was going to happen.

'Good to see you, Mike!' he said with a tilt of his head, and then he rose from his seat and left the empty bar.

Michael's gaze then settled on Beth and his features changed, became so much gentler than seconds before that it was quite startling.

'You came!' she breathed, the relief evident. There was love in his eyes as he looked at her, then he turned and looked back at Pat.

'I'll ask you not to get in the way!' he said generally in his direction. He took Beth by the hand and helped her to her feet, taking in every detail of her as if seeing her for the first time. She was almost radiant. Her hair was down and softened her face, which glowed with health despite her current anguish; then his eye took in the size of her belly. The bump began at just under her breasts and swelled downwards and outwards. He decided at that moment that being pregnant suited her and he pulled her close to him and put strong arms around her.

'Well it's about fucking time you came back!' Pat said finally from below where they stood, staring at each other. His eyes were warm on the two and Michael found himself smiling. 'I thought you'd 've been back for her last month. In fact, I'm surprised you even left!'

There was a pause as Michael and Pat studied one another.

'Oh I'm back all right, Pat. Back for her, back for my child and I'm back for my friend.'

'Friend?' He rose an eyebrow at Michael, his expression warm.

'Aye, my friend! I gather there's been some issues. I'm home to deal with them.'

Michael stood at the door for what felt to Beth to be a long time. He was staring intensely at his friend, lying asleep on the white linen bed in the centre of the room. He looked pale, even with the sun-bed tan, and so small. He looked to Michael almost childlike. After a long pause he moved into the room, with Beth's hand firmly in his. From beside the bed Jennifer reached out and touched Michael's arm, the movement making him look down into her eyes, and it was then that she saw the pain of the past months within him. She also saw the love that was there and when she looked away from him and at Beth who stood close by she saw the same in her.

'How is he doing today?' he asked finally, his voice full of emotions that he couldn't have put into words for love or money.

'Okay. They moved him down here yesterday.' Her voice broke and Beth went to hold her, but Michael took her up in his arms instead and held her close for a moment or two.

'Michael, they tried to kill my husband. The dirty rotten bastards, they tried to kill my James!' She was crying again now and the venom within her was right to the fore.

Beth put her hand on her shoulder and patted it lightly. When was the grief going to stop? she thought. Michael looked at her and it was only when he answered her that she realised she must have said it out loud.

'Now, Elizabeth! The grief will stop now. Today!' His tone was firm and both women recognised the look in those dark eyes. It was revenge and Beth felt her stomach kick out.

'Ooh—' She put her hand to the bump protectively. 'Just a kick!' she said with a wave of her hand before either could enquire. 'It's getting crowded in there!'

Michael looked down at her and she smiled at him.

'You all right?' he began but before he could go on James stirred. He opened his eyes and looked directly at Michael.

'Thought I heard your dodgy Irish trap,' he croaked and Michael laughed back the tears that welled suddenly in his eyes. There was an odd silence then, as Michael and James eyed each other.

'She's missed you like mad!' he croaked with a laugh as he looked up at Beth. 'We all did!' He breathed hard. ''Ere, did you tell him yet?' he asked then and she shook her head at him.

'No, not—' Beth began, she looked a little annoyed. Now was not the place or time.

'Tell me what?' Michael asked.

'I'll tell you later on!' she smiled.

'No, Elizabeth, you'll tell me now.'

'Michael!' James croaked.

'What?' He looked back down at James for an answer and without having to be pushed James replied.

'All in working order, ey boy!' James croaked.

Michael looked at him, then at Beth, then at Jennifer, then back at Beth again. His expression was one of recognition. 'Is it?' he asked her. There was no one else then, just the two of them, or rather, the four of them. She blushed, something that in itself made his heart thunder within the confined of his chest. And then she nodded at him, tilting her head to the side slightly.

'Yes Michael. It is!' she half laughed, half sobbed and he took her in his arms then, feeling her warmth against his. His emotions and feeling towards her were clear, more than clear to see. This man loved this young woman and this man loved his unborn, both of them.

Chapter Thirty-Five

December 1999

Oxley saw Michael on the camera just outside the office door and felt his heart sink into his stomach with a painful growl. He was completely alone in the little club, having sent the others off on the rounds, and Michael had now made in this far undetected. The door burst open with a crash against the wall, and before he could reach into the drawer of his desk Michael had made his way across the room in one stride and slammed it shut, trapping Oxley's fingers between the wood panels of the oak. He yelped like a kicked dog but Michael was unmoved. Michael perched then, on the edge of the desk, one foot on the floor and settled his hands in his lap as Oxley fell back, nursing his bloody open injury. The heavy door behind them creaked shut. They were totally alone and Oxley felt his bowels churn some more.

'You're not supposed to be here, Elliot!' Oxley almost spat. 'I thought you were still licking your wounds in Ireland, with your tail stuck between your legs, in place of your dick!' Even in this position he was being vile and trying to rile Michael up.

'Thought wrong then, didn't you, you limey fucking prick!' Michael glared, and he took a deep breath, sighed and then without any warning at all, he punched Oxley squarely in the face. He felt Oxley's nose crumple beneath his knuckles and as he pulled away he took in the sight. Filing it away in his memory for prosperity; in fact, it felt so good, that he did it once more to really drive the memory for himself home.

'For fuck's sake, Michael!' he exclaimed, his voice muffled from clutching his face in his already damaged hands.

'For fuck's sake nothing! You, you pathetic English wanker. You cause us nothing but aggravation. You cost us thousands upon thousands of pounds with your petty bollocks and your hare-brained ideas. Then you go and try to have my Elizabeth raped.' He paused, taking in a deep breath. That was bad enough on its own in his eyes, but there was more. 'You waltz around London with a gun like you're some kind of proper hard man, and you go and shoot my best friend—' there was another pause, 'And you honestly, really think that I'm not going to come home and deal with you? Are you that fucking mad, as well as obviously fucking stupid?' Michael's tone was menacing and yet, almost held a hint of humour. He took Oxley by the hair and banged his head on the desk, again, covering the papers upon it with more blood. 'You've threatened, bribed, beaten and cheated almost everyone in the country and you're still here! I don't understand it, because you're obviously human! I can see that from the shit coming out of your face now.' His tone was completely calm. 'I wonder, will you die? Should we try and find out perhaps?'

Oxley reeled backwards on his chair and Michael gave him a swift kick in the bollocks for the sake of it, the force of the action sending him backwards on the desk a few inches. 'Yes. You are over!' He stood again, and was about to finish Oxley off when the door burst open again, and King, along with another man entered the room, filling it. Oxley's relief was such that he slumped back into his chair, his head back, a groaning coming from somewhere in his busted face.

King launched himself at Michael from the doorway and caught him in the side of the head, sending him off balance. They took hold of Michael, each grabbing an arm, holding him in a downward facing position, his arms behind his back in arm locks. Oxley leaned forward and standing up from the chair, gave Michael a bloody smile then.

'You're the one that's over, you fucking pikey bastard!' he spat. 'And before you go, Elliott, as a passing shot, and in answer to that age old question of what exactly happened to the fucking super duoper Mr. and Mrs. Andrew Dobson. It was me! They died by my hand. I had the fucking car run off the road!' Michael's mind was reeling. He could hear the words and understand them but he didn't believe them.

He looked up at Oxley then at King, who was still grinning, his face twisted from their last violent encounter.

'We finished them, and we'll finish the rest. James was lucky, once. Patrick'll spend a long time waiting, and guess how your young bit of skirt's going to get hers?' He bared his broken teeth as he spoke and Michael struggled against the grip they had on him.

'Is she as juicy as she looks?' King laughed then. 'I suppose I'll find out, won't I, you fucking Irish tosser.'

That was it, Michael snapped then and suddenly had the strength of a hundred men.

'No!' Michael pulled at the men still then holding his arms with a burst of strength that came from out of nowhere. They both stumbled, grabbing at furniture to steady themselves but he was too fast for either of them. A shot rang out and the blond fell to the floor with a thud. Focusing, after a second or two all that could be seen behind where he had been standing was blood and what looked like lumpy mucus, but what was in reality brains. Michael aimed again, this time at Oxley and as the shot went off a sharp pain rushed through his side. He knew the sensation and looked quickly down at himself. There was a knife sticking out of his ribs and already blood was seeping from the wound. With the gun still in his hand he pulled the handle of the blade and wrenched it free, a strange painful groan escaping his lips as he did so, and with the blink of an eye the knife landed with a crunch in King's chest. He let out a screech, sinking to his knees on the carpet, clutching at the handle as it protruded from his shirt.

'You cunt!' he managed as blood ran from his mouth.

Oxley was frozen to the spot. He couldn't believe his eyes. Michael wouldn't go down. He just kept coming.

'Now you're fucked,' Michael breathed. 'Before *you* go, know this. It was me that killed you, Mr. Oxley, me who ended your life!' The menace was back in Michael's tone and on the last word he pulled the trigger.

The force caught Oxley, and the movement was as if someone had punched him. He doubled up, clutching his chest and then without another word or breath escaping his lips he fell, hitting his head on the desk on the way to the floor.

The room seemed to go black. All Beth could hear or see was the newscaster. She watched the lips on the screen move, almost disbelieving what she was hearing. *The fire that swept through one of London's most popular clubs earlier tonight is thought to have claimed the lives of three men. One of these is thought to have been the owner, Mr. Sean Oxley, seen here at the opening of the Cooler back in 1998—*

Suddenly she was up and off her seat. Her eyes were wild and she clung to her belly protectively, before grabbing at the phone, practically clawing at the keypad. She mis-dialled, despite it being pre-installed. 'God damn it! Son of a bitch!' She cleared the call and re-dialled with more care, yet with still shaking fingers. 'Come on, Michael! Answer the bloody phone.'

There was a long pause as the call was connected, then another as it rang into her ear. 'Oh Jesus!' she gasped as the call was answered. She could hear his voice on the other end of the line. It was like music, sweet music to her ears.

'Are you okay? Where in the fucking hell are you?'

Less than half an hour later Beth rushed into the casualty unit of the Royal and up to the desk. 'Elliott! Michael J.,' she said before the duty nurse had even opened her mouth.

'Are you a relative?' she asked taking in the sight of Beth's bump.

'I'm his mother!' she replied sarcastically.

'I'll get someone to take you round.' Her tone was now clipped, she was obviously as unimpressed as Beth was. Relative! Was she fucking blind?

Surrounded by green curtains, Michael sat upright on the bed, his right arm raised with his hand on the back of his head. A short nurse peered at the wound and then up at him. What a body, she thought. Didn't smell too bad, either.

'I'll clean it, then we'll get you stitched up,' she said finally, looking up into his eyes. 'I'll get you some pain killers.'

'No, thanks. Just sew. I can't stay long,' he said firmly. She looked up into his eyes. There was no pain there, just the obvious need to be elsewhere. The nature of the wound was her first choice, but as she stared at him she saw something else. He needed to be somewhere, with someone and she felt no malice there.

'Not your first time?' she questioned, noticing the neat white scar on his arm. 'I bet that hurt. Stitches were nice and tight, though.' Michael didn't get to answer her. Beth pulled the curtain open slightly and was shown in by one of the porters.

'Thank you,' she said over her shoulder, the relief that he was upright evident in her tone. She was already on her way across the cubicle to where Michael sat. 'You silly bastard!' she breathed, almost crying. He took her by the hand and pulled her to his left side. He kissed her full on the mouth, his fingers slipping through her hair.

'Let me see' she breathed, pulling away from him slightly after a long moment. She looked at the hole in his side. It was deep. 'I think I've seem more of the inside of you than the outside,' she laughed, making light of the situation.

'It's fine!' he breathed, more relaxed then. 'Hazard of having nice things,' he added, for effect only. He's already stated that he'd been set upon for what he presumed was his car, or maybe his wallet, or maybe both. Right then he didn't actually care. She was there with him. Safe with him and he could deal with anything as long as she was there. He looked at the nurse and then the scar on his arm. 'Do you want to do it or can she?' he said looking quickly at Beth.

'Did you do that?' she asked, taking a closer look.

Beth nodded. 'There's more of her handiwork upstairs in Wallace,' he added, his tone proud.

'Wallace Ward? What, not the rather dishy Mr. Dobson?' She sounded surprised.

'My brother, for my sins!' Beth said with a smile. James had obviously made an impression in the hospital.

'Oh God. Are you Michael Elliott?' she said, her face flushing red before looking back at his notes.

'That would be me, yes,' he said, his tone light.

As Beth and Michael made their way back through the accident and emergency reception, two policemen appeared. They looked directly at them and Beth felt Michael's grip tighten.

'Let me deal with it?' she asked quietly. He looked down into her eyes and nodded at her; he trusted her.

'Mister Elliott?' one of the two asked and he nodded, his movements hard, his thick jaw set. 'Can you come with us, please? Just a couple of questions for you, then you can be on your way.' They'd been briefed not to piss him off. That much was clear.

Making life simple, they were led into the relatives' room. Beth perched on the table next to where Michael now stood and waited for the questions to begin.

'Can you please confirm your whereabouts this evening?' the taller asked, pen poised and ready to write with.

'He was almost mugged, and being stabbed outside our home!' Beth interrupted, none too politely, and both officers turned to stare at her. Up to that point she hadn't said a word, and her soft tones stating something so abrupt, so flatly, was startling. There was nothing either man could say to something like that, was there, and the expression on Michael's face asked that exact question. They weren't going to get anywhere with this and both were resigned then.

'Perhaps at a later date you'd come and make a statement at the station?' the taller suggested. He no more wanted to be there quizzing Michael Elliott, than Michael Elliott wanted to be there. There was no way that was a mugging gone wrong; there would have been more bodies to deal with, he mused. Michael caught the expression on his face, as if his thoughts were written on it, and nodded politely.

'Of course, when I've time,' was all he said and with a nod, both were gone.

Four days later, Pat sat in the Hothouse office. He looked up from his desk as the door opened silently and Michael, as he walked through. Pat was about to rise from his seat when he was waved to stay put.

'You should be resting.' His tone was filled with genuine fatherly concern.

'I can't do that Pat, we have a thriving business to run now!' Michael said, his voice low, but there was humour there too.

Pat studied him some more. He looked serious. He knew that look very well. Both men had things to discuss and if Michael was feeling up to it, why not get it out of the way now?

'At least sit, then?' Pat suggested, offering Michael a seat opposite the desk. He poured them both a drink and Michael took the glass with a grateful nod of his head. 'I've been meaning to talk to you'.

'Yes?' Michael looked away, out of the window, allowing Pat to go on.

'About—' he stopped. 'Everything. I meant what I said. I didn't think you'd go, I really didn't, and then it was too late! I didn't call you and I should have, I just didn't want to back down.' This was Pat's starter for an apology and it sounded very strange to Michael.

'There's a lot of that going around!' he joked softly.

'Tell me about it,' Pat replied and he looked into Michael's eyes. 'I'm proud of you, Mike. You remind me of your dad when he was your age.' Pat was wistful for a moment.

'I need to ask you something, Pat. All joking aside. I've spoken to James and—' Michael began.

'Please Mike. Don't even ask. Just do it! Do it before she drives me mad with guilt at sending you packing in the first place!' Pat said, his face animated.

Chapter Thirty-Six

January 2000

In the large hotel suite, a kick woke Beth from what had actually been a relatively good night's sleep. As she pushed the duvet back she suddenly realised that Michael wasn't beside her.

She was on her way out of the bed when the door opened and he walked back in holding a large tray, and whatever was on it smelled great.

'You hungry?' he asked.

'We're starving.'

'You slept well!' It was a statement, not a question.

'Yeah.' She looked warmly into his eyes and her mind drifted back to the previous night. He was so gentle, so tender because she was so delicate, and the gift so precious, and he touched her with a feeling that she could never put into words. 'Did you?' she breathed lightly.

'I did,' he smiled. They both knew that Michael had probably spent two or more hours of the night just staring at her, holding her, touching her face and hair.

She often woke to his touch or the feel of his eyes upon her. He'd always do the same thing, too; he'd lean and kiss her on the lips, brush her hair with warm fingers and pull her really close until she fell asleep again.

Michael put the tray on the bedside table and knelt in front of her on the carpet. He laid a hand on her tummy and felt it move under the touch of his fingers.

'Be gentle with your mummy, d'ya hear now,' he said putting his face up to her belly button and planting a light kiss upon it.

After breakfast, she was dressing, and she looked out of the window. It was a crisp day with the sun forcing itself through the pale scattered clouds. Her attention turned to the commotion on the driveway below. There were cars and delivery trucks arriving and leaving in short intervals, on and off for about an hour.

'What's going on?' she asked casually.

'Wedding!' Michael said casually, looking out over her shoulder. 'It's going to be a big one by the looks of it, maybe we should go out for the day. How do you feel?'

Beth looked back out of the window. 'Great. I feel great. Where shall we go?' Her eyes were bright and he couldn't help pulling her close and holding her.

'Well, you look great too!' he smiled. Just how much he loved her was the thought that bounced through his mind every time he saw her, thought of her. He loved everything, even the pale silvery stretch marks that had appeared on her belly and the curve of her hips that he knew was now there to stay. She was all woman!

'Beth, Michael—' Eve called down the hallway after them. 'I need you!' She looked flustered.

'Oh, are you busy then?' she asked, stopping and Eve nodded. 'I'm short staffed. Can you stay and help me?' She looked at Michael then added, 'Nothing strenuous!'

Michael looked slightly irritated, then smiled at his mother.

'Sure! We were only going so we weren't in the way, anyway,' Beth smiled before Michael could protest. He was worse than ever before about where she went, what she did and how she did it, and she supposed it was with good reason.

'Grand. Michael, can you go and find you father, please? He's in the banqueting suite somewhere, they're having the ceremony in the library.' She waved her hand in the air with a deep sigh as if weddings were everyday, and Beth supposed they were for Eve and Jim. 'It's all good clean fun!'

'See you in a while,' Michael breathed, kissing her on the lips.

'Where do you want me?' Beth asked then, eager to assist in her swollen state.

'Oh, um. Can you give me a hand upstairs? I wouldn't ask, it's just—'

Beth rubbed her hands together, suggesting that she really was ready to assist. 'Eve, it's no problem, really,' Beth smiled and the older woman reached out and touched her face.

Beth followed Eve to the lifts and they got in. She pushed the button and with a bell sounding, the door closed.

'You're a real life saver,' she smiled. 'I just need it to be a two o'clock and not a twelve o'clock wedding!' She laughed and Beth nodded knowing, exactly what she meant. There were never enough hours in the day when you were busy.

Outside the room, Eve called, 'Be with you in a tick.' She flustered, ushering Beth into her own bedroom suite. The door closed behind her, and Beth looked around the room for the sake of something to do. She presumed that it was Michael who was needed, not her and she found herself wondering how long all this help was actually going to take. Then she felt bad for the thought and focused on being useful. Her thoughts were distracted. Laid out on the bed was a full-length cream shift dress. It was beautiful. Beth moved closer, studying the detail. There were tiny pearls on the neckline, and the stole was long, with pretty tassels. Eve reappeared in the room carrying a hat box. She saw Beth staring at the dress and smiled.

'This is gorgeous!' Beth said, touching the fabric lightly with her fingertips. It just screamed to be touched by delicate hands.

'Now that's good!' she replied, looking red-faced and very relieved.

Beth looked into her eyes, the question evident in her mind at that moment.

'Because the wedding today, Elizabeth—it's yours!' Eve announced, and before Beth could even think, or register the words she heard, the door opened behind them and Judy walked in, followed closely by Jennifer, Lucy and two other women Beth had never seen before. Beth felt her stomach move again and for a second or two she thought her waters would break with the shock.

'He never does anything at half cock, does he?' Judy laughed, seeing the absolute shock and joyous surprise on Beth's face.

'Oh! My! God!' Beth managed. 'I can't believe it. I don't believe it'.

They were all grinning at her, trying not to well up in case of ruining their perfect make-up.

'Well, do. Because you've an hour,' Eve said, now a little more composed.

As they did her hair and make-up and slipped her into the dress, the whole incredible story was revealed to her. Piece by piece, and snippet by snippet, from each of them, starting with Jennifer. After his meetings with James and then Pat, Michael had been pondering about how he would ask her to marry him. James had said, *Well, you know how she loves surprises* and that was it, he was inspired. He simply wouldn't ask her, he'd just tell her that that was what they were doing. They'd spent the past weeks planning and scheming, even caught up with Beth's midwife to confirm her growth so that a dress could be made. The invitations were sent out and everyone was sworn to secrecy, quite literally on pain of death. More than two hundred people had flown from London that morning and were, as they stood there in Eve's bedroom, preparing for the afternoon's events.

They left the room and James stood outside the door, nervously waiting for them. He was dressed in a rather expensive-looking suit and on seeing his sister, his eyes welled up. This was it, this was that day, and here he was now giving her to his best friend. She looked magnificent and she glowed, Michael made her glow, he was the one, James thought firmly.

'You look so—Oh!' he began. He was speechless. 'And it fitted.' He laughed back the tears then, taking Beth's hand and looking at Eve, referring to the dress.

'You're giving me away!' Beth breathed.

'I am! Are you ready?'

'Definitely!'

The double doors of the library opened to the gentle sound of traditional Irish music and Beth caught her breath. The giant room was full to overflowing with familiar faces. Everyone was smiling at her and she took them in, committing them to memory. And then she saw him. He was staring straight at her and she saw nothing else, heard nothing else, but him. He was dressed in a new black suit and white shirt, with no tie. He looked completely calm and then his expression changed and he gazed at her. It wasn't a stare; it was a gaze. He watched her every move; even with the bump she was graceful. She reached him on James's arm and instinctively she took his outstretched hand in hers. He leaned and kissed her and there was an outburst of laughter.

'That comes later!' the registrar smiled, leaning forwards slightly.

'Sorry,' Michael breathed. 'I was just checking that she was real.'

'I'm real, Michael,' she whispered, giving his hand a squeeze.

'Friends, we are gathered here today to bear witness to the marriage of Elizabeth and Michael.'

Beth couldn't take it all in, and the next few minutes were spent floating in her thoughts and in Michael's eyes.

'Who is giving Elizabeth away?' the registrar asked, looking at James.

'I am.' His tone was strong and full of love. He glanced over at where his own wife stood. If Michael felt anything like he had, he was truly touching heaven.

'Elizabeth, please repeat after me—'

'I, Elizabeth, take you, Michael, to be my lawfully wedded husband, to have and to hold, to love and honour in sickness and in health, for richer, for poorer and forsaking all others from this day forward until parted in death.'

'Michael?'

'I, Michael, take you, Elizabeth, to be my wedded wife, to have and to hold, to love, honour and protect in sickness and in health, for richer for poorer and forsaking all others from this day forwards until parted by death. I love you, Elizabeth!'

Chapter Thirty-Seven

March 2000

'That's it, good girl!' a deep black female voice urged as Beth half lay, half sat, straining against the pillows, her face red and covered in sweat.

'I can't,' she said breathlessly, her eyes flitting to the door between gasps and pants to steady her breathing.

'Slow it down, girl! And for heaven's sake, will you please breathe?' She laughed as Beth's face reddened even more.

The midwife was about to urge her some more when the doors opened and Michael rushed in, followed by a young man dressed in a green cotton jumpsuit.

'See, I told you he'd get here!' she said loudly as she watched him cradle Elizabeth's head against his broad chest and speak soothingly into her ear.

'I think I've probably lost my licence,' he laughed, making light of the fact that he had run every red light in the area to get there from the club as he went to kiss Beth on the forehead. 'What did I miss?'

'My waters breaking. Told you it'd happen if you left me on my own!' she laughed with a pant. She was better now that he was there with her.

'Contractions?' he asked, looking up at the midwife knowledgeably. Michael had read every book he could lay his hands on and had been a religious parenting class participant.

'We're nearly there. But I think she was waiting for you.' She smiled broadly showing a large set of whiter than white, perfectly square teeth. 'And now that you are, do you think you could help?'

she laughed and Michael pulled off his jacket and began to roll up his shirtsleeves. No-one in the room was about to ask him to pause to change into sterile pyjamas, that was for sure.

The midwife watched the pair before her in the large white delivery room. Oh yes this was love, it was so refreshing to see it in people so young. Well, not that he looked that young. She thought that he was maybe thirty and she knew from her notes that Beth was not even twenty-two, still she couldn't help but notice how Beth eased now that this giant of a man was with her.

'Okay, ready?' she asked again and this time Beth had hold of Michael's hand as she pushed.

'You're doing so well,' he soothed, stroking her forehead with his free hand. The other was at that moment being crushed, she had quite a grip.

'Never again, Michael Elliott!' she almost screamed 'You are never coming near me ever again!' and he was more than a little taken aback by her outburst of swearing as another contraction took her over.

'Only panic if she doesn't slag you down!' the black woman laughed, and Michael let Beth grip at his hand a little tighter.

'It's coming,' she exclaimed, looking up from between Beth's legs. 'Do you want to see?' she asked Michael, waving her hand at him to move down and look. He was unsure for a second or two, and then something took him over and he had to look. He had to see his child born into the world. He leaned over with Maryanne and saw a dark crown, covered in filmy blood and what looked like a chalky substance. There was a strange slurping noise and then it appeared before them and Michael took in a long breath. Never in his life had he felt such a feeling of absolute bewilderment.

'Congratulations. It's a very healthy boy!' she said, snipping the deep purple-coloured cord and passing the tiny, white and bloodstained, now screaming bundle to the nurse who had been holding Beth's other hand until that point.

'Let me see him,' Beth breathed, struggling to sit up further and Michael moved back up to her and held her from beneath her arms as she gazed, glazed eyed at their son.

'He's beautiful!' she breathed, more tears welling up as she reached out and touched the tiny bundle that the nurse had a firm hold on.

'Don't you stop yet, girlie!' Maryanne said with a light laugh in her Jamaican tone, and Michael looked on in absolute wonder for a few seconds. 'Once more, girl,' she said reassuringly.

'Come on now, my beautiful darling—Push!' Michael breathed with her, now even though his eyes were on his son, who was screaming at being out in the cold world.

'I know how he feels. I like it in there, too!' he laughed into Beth's ear and she strained out a humorous retort.

'I'm glad your memories are so clear, because I was not kidding, Michael Elliott.'

Michael caught Maryanne's eye and she smiled widely at him, shaking her head slightly as she did so. Beth strained some more, until she thought her eyes would explode and then she felt calm. Another chalky bloody crown appeared from inside her, and Michael was, for the first time in almost his whole life, lost for words.

'That's it, honey!' she soothed. 'I can see the head. Michael, do you want to cut this one?' she asked, easing out the head and shoulders.

'A girl. I knew it would be one of each! Thank you, God!' he exclaimed, looking up at her face from between her knees. 'Elizabeth. You are just fantastic!' he laughed as tears of pure joy welled up in his eyes and rolled down his reddened face. 'I love you, you clever girl—look what you did!'

Michael put his head out of the door and looked up the corridor. Maryanne had suggested that he give Beth a few minutes to get cleaned up, and the other nurse time to properly weigh his children. He had protested at first; he'd never seen so much blood from a labour and it was only when Maryanne asked how many labours he'd actually witnessed in his life that he had to admit to none. Nevertheless, he was concerned regardless of whether they said it was quite normal or not.

He saw the back of James and almost ran up to him, his entire face alight with life. He felt fantastic!

'I'm a dah!' he exclaimed as James spun around and the two men embraced. 'She gave me a boy, and a girl! And they're perfect!' he beamed.

'Where? Can we see 'em?' James asked. 'How's Beth, is she okay?'

'Aye, she'd grand. They're grand. They're cleaning her up, we can see them in a wee while.'

'Mr. Elliott,' someone called from behind him a few minutes later. 'Can you please sign this on your wife's behalf?' He smiled then. He liked the sound of that. Mrs. Elizabeth Elliott and their children, Andrew and Louise.

Chapter Thirty-Eight

August 2005

The large garden was filled with the sound of laughter, childish giggles and joyous pure laughter. It was a comfortable warming sound, and Michael sat, quite relaxed in a deep chair on the patio staring out, as Andrew chased Louise and James and Jenny's boys, Richard and Pete, across the expanse of lawn of their new house, with the hose in his hand. They were growing up so fast and now they were almost five and his nephews four and three.

His mind filled with the memories of the last years. His first nappy change; now that had been nasty. Their first steps, cutting teeth, haircuts, tummy bugs; he hadn't missed a thing. It had been him with Beth, always. Then he thought of Beth, her smile, the glow that hadn't faded after the birth of their children. She'd taken every day in her stride and hadn't faltered in her love for him. If ever there was a woman for him, it was her, and if ever there was a mother for his children, well, that was her also, and he had not once faltered in these thoughts.

He loved their new home, too, and was glad now that Beth had been so forthright about buying it, despite the hefty price tag. Never in his life had he thought that good schools, large open plan kitchens, huge safe gardens and more toilets would be his priorities, and he smiled at how life had changed them all. He smiled too as he recalled how James had sulked and growled, because Jenny had happened to see that the house next door but one was also available for sale, just after Beth had mentioned it to her, upon completion day. Oh, happy memories, he smiled to himself.

Beth appeared at the French doors with a couple of drinks, and he looked up at her. She was stunning and those buxom curves were like home to him, every inch of her was like home to him. The gentle breeze through the house whirled around the skirt of her long dress and the dark brown of her legs blazed through cream cotton.

'He's going to fall,' she smiled with a shake of her head.

'Andy, be careful there now!' Michael called as his son stumbled across the grass, the green hose wrapped around and around him like a watery snake. 'They'll be worn out soon, then they'll all sleep!' he continued, now looking at Elizabeth and accepting the drink she offered him.

'It's quiet without your brother around too, ey?' He stretched out long tanned legs and pushed his sunglasses back up his nose. 'I thought it was the children that were supposed to make all the noise anyway?'

'What, James is the child, you know that! All those toys he bought them, upstairs—' she pointed lightly with a perfectly manicured finger above her, 'Aren't for the kids, they're for him!' Beth laughed. It was such a pleasant sound that Michael wished it would go on for ever.

'Another four days,' he sighed. 'I wonder if they're having as much fun as we did?' His tone was suggestive and he watched his wife. She was so easy around him, more so than he would ever have dared to hope.

'I do hope so,' she replied in almost a whisper. 'It's been a busy year. But business is good, and all is well in the world,' she added. There was a long pause between them and they watched the children. Michael nodded. She was right, of course.

Things were good for them all now. They'd settled all differences within the business community a long time ago, and there was relative peace. There were still those who tried their luck, but they rode on the wave of what had happened to Oxley and his crew, though they now kept their end clean and above board, but still bought the odd new place, just to keep their hand in. They managed business well, but the iron fist was gone, replaced with good solicitors, excellent managers and great door teams. Yes, life was simpler now. No-one was looking over their shoulder; none of them worried about saving or keeping face these days. It was simple and Michael actually liked it. He'd even gone back into the markets, though only on a consultancy basis. A little something for their retirement, he'd mused.

'Do you love me?' she asked, sitting down opposite him, resting her elbows on the table.

He looked at her for a long moment through the tint of his glasses, and then over the top of his glasses. 'You know I do!' he almost breathed it out. She was his world. It didn't spin without her and she knew it. 'Why do you ask?' The last time she'd asked that she'd slipped the particulars of the house they now lived in, in front of him.

'Do I look different?' she asked, not answering his question. He shook his head slowly at her.

'Okay, do you remember our little holiday?' she went on. He nodded. 'Do you remember the hot sex?' He nodded again, more forcefully then, as she gave him a smouldering stare. 'I do!' And he thought back. They'd gone to Corfu for a week the month before, leaving the children with James and Jenny—well, James, Jenny, Pat, Judy, Jim and Eve, really. They took a shortish break from everyone, every year, because life was still as hectic and busy as it had ever been and now it was James's and Jenny's turn for a time out.

'Do you love them?' she asked, motioning with her head towards the rabble of toddlers still charging about, soaking wet and screaming with joy on the grass. He looked back at them and smiled, a real hearty smile. Of course he did. He worshipped his children, and the others too. They could do no wrong and he spoilt them all to distraction. Nothing was ever too much trouble, and he always had time for them, always.

He looked at her again then, at the gleam in her eye, the purity on her tanned, fresh features. 'Out with it, woman!' He was leaning on the table directly opposite her now. He had the feeling that he knew what she was going to tell him, but didn't dare hope. They'd discussed it months before, but what with the twins and the business and life in general, nothing more had been said.

'Well—we did it again!' she smiled.